"OUT!" MY GRANDFATHER'S VOICE CUT US OFF. "Get out of here. Out of my granddaughter's life. How dare you expose Kate to mortal danger. How dare you bring these monsters through our door. Get out and stay out."

"No!" I cried, and running to Papy, grabbed his arms. "Papy, no. Vincent's . . ." All my arguments flashed through my mind and fell away as I realized that they were useless. *Vincent was protecting me,* or *It's already too late, the numa know who I am.* Nothing I could say would convince Papy. Because he was right: I *was* in danger because of Vincent. I settled for one true statement—the only one that my grandfather couldn't refute. "I love him."

Papy freed his captive arms and wrapped them around me, hugging me as if he had lost me for years and then found me again. After a second, he held me away and said, tenderly but seriously, "Kate, you may think you love him. But he's not even human."

Also by Amy Plum

Die for Me
If I Should Die
Die for Her: A Die for Me Digital Novella

UNTIL I DIE

AMY PLUM

HARPER TEEN

An Imprint of HarperCollinsPublishers

HarperTeen is an imprint of HarperCollins Publishers.

Until I Die

Copyright © 2012 by Amy Plum

All rights reserved. Printed in the United States of America.

No part of this book may be used or reproduced in any manner whatsoever

without written permission except in the case of brief quotations

embodied in critical articles and reviews. For information address

HarperCollins Children's Books, a division of HarperCollins Publishers,

10 East 53rd Street, New York, NY 10022.

www.epicreads.com

Library of Congress Cataloging-in-Publication Data
Plum, Amy.
    Until I die / Amy Plum. — 1st ed.
        p.   cm.
    Sequel to: Die for me.
    Second book in the revenants trilogy.
    Summary: "The sequel to *Die for Me*, set in Paris, where a girl and
a boy with a terrifying paranormal destiny fight dangerous forces to be
together"— Provided by publisher.
    ISBN 978-0-06-200405-5 (pbk.)
    [1. Supernatural—Fiction.   2. Love—Fiction.   3. Paris (France)—
Fiction. 4. France—Fiction.]   I. Title.
PZ7.P7287Unt   2012   2011052407
[Fic]—dc23   CIP
                                                             AC

Typography by Ray Shappell

13 14 15 16 17 CG/RRDH 10 9 8 7 6 5 4 3 2 1

First paperback edition, 2013

For Laurent.

O my soul, do not aspire to immortal life,
but exhaust the limits of the possible.
—Pindar, Ode, Pythian 3, circa 474 BCE

ONE

I LEAPT, DRAWING MY FEET UP BENEATH ME, AS the seven-foot quarterstaff smashed into the flagstones where I had been standing a half second before. Landing in a crouch, I sprang back up, groaning with the effort, and swung my own weapon over my head. Sweat dripped into my eye, blinding me for one stinging second before my reflexes took over and forced me into motion.

A shaft of light from a window far overhead illuminated the oaken staff as I arced it down toward my enemy's legs. He swept sideways, sending my weapon flying through the air. It crashed with a wooden clang against the stone wall behind me.

Defenseless, I scrambled for a sword that lay a few feet away. But before I could grab it, I was snatched off my feet in a powerful grasp and crushed against my assailant's chest. He held me a few inches off the ground as I kicked and flailed, adrenaline pumping like quicksilver through my body.

"Don't be such a sore loser, Kate," chided Vincent. Leaning forward, he gave me a firm kiss on the lips.

The fact that he was shirtless was quickly eroding my hard-won concentration. And the warmth from his bare chest and arms was turning my fight-tensed muscles to buttery goo. Struggling to maintain my resolve, I growled, "That is totally cheating," and managed to work my hand free enough to punch him in the arm. "Now let me go."

"If you promise not to kick or bite." He laughed and set me on the ground. Sea blue eyes flashed with humor from under the waves of black hair that fell around his face.

He grinned and touched my cheek, with an expression like he was seeing me for the first time. Like he couldn't believe that I was standing there with him in all my 3-D humanness. An expression that said he thought *he* was the lucky one.

I rearranged my smile into the best glare I could muster. "I'm making no promises," I said, wiping the hair that had escaped my ponytail out of my eyes. "You would deserve a bite for beating me again."

"That was much better, Kate," came a voice from behind me. Gaspard handed me my fallen staff. "But you need to be a bit more flexible with your hold. When Vincent's staff hits yours, roll with the movement." He demonstrated, using Vincent's weapon. "If you're stiff, the staff will go flying." We walked through the steps in slow motion.

When he saw that I had mastered the sequence, my teacher straightened. "Well, that's good enough for sword and quarterstaff today. Do you want to move on to something less strenuous? Throwing stars, perhaps?"

I held my hands up in surrender, still panting from the exercise. "That's enough fight training for today. Thanks, Gaspard."

"As you wish, my dear." He pulled a rubber band from behind his head, releasing his porcupine hair, which sprang back into its normal state of disarray. "You definitely have natural talent," he continued, as he returned the weapons to their hooks on the walls of the underground gym-slash-armory, "since you're doing this well after just a few lessons. But you do need to work on your stamina."

"Um, yeah. I guess lying around reading books all day doesn't do much for physical endurance," I said, leaning forward to catch my breath, my hands on my knees.

"Natural talent," crowed Vincent, sweeping my sweaty self up into his arms and pacing across the room, holding me like a trophy. "Of course my girlfriend's got it. In truckloads! How else could she have slain a giant evil zombie, single-handedly saving my undead body?"

I laughed as he set me down in front of the freestanding shower and adjoining sauna. "I don't mind taking all the glory, but I think the fact that your volant spirit was possessing me had just a tiny bit to do with it."

"Here you go." Vincent handed me a towel and kissed the top of my head. "Not that I don't think you're totally hot when you're dripping with sweat," he whispered, giving me a flirty wink. Those butterflies that suddenly sprang into action in my chest? I

3

was beginning to consider them permanent residents.

"In the meantime, I'll finish your job and take out that pesky nineteenth-century weapons master. *En garde!*" he yelled, as he flicked a sword from off the wall and turned.

Gaspard was already waiting for him with a giant spiked mace. "You'll have to do better than that measly steel blade to make a dent in me," he quipped, waving Vincent forward with two fingertips.

I closed the shower door behind me, turned the lever to start the water, and watched as the powerful streams spat forth from the showerhead, sending a cloud of steam up around me. My aches and pains flew away under the steady pressure of the hot water.

Incredible, I thought for the thousandth time, as I considered this parallel world I was moving in. A few Paris blocks away I led a completely normal life with my sister and grandparents. And here I was sword fighting with dead guys—okay, "revenants," so not really dead. Since I'd moved to Paris, this was the only place I felt I fit in.

I listened to the noises of the fight coming from outside my pinewood haven and thought of the reason I was here. Vincent.

I had met him last summer. And fallen hard. But after discovering what he was, and that being a revenant meant dying over and over again, I had turned my back on him. After my own parents' death the year before, being alone seemed safer than having a constant reminder of that pain.

But Vincent made me an offer I couldn't refuse. He promised

not to die. At least, not on purpose. Which goes against every fiber of his un-being. Revenants' compulsion to die when saving their precious human "rescues" is more enticing and powerful than a drug addiction. But Vincent thinks he can hold out. For me.

And I, for one, hope he can. I don't want to cause him pain, but I know my own limitations. Rather than grieve his loss over and over again, I would leave. Walk away. We both know it. And, though Vincent is technically dead, I'll venture to say that this is the only solution we can both live with.

TWO

"I'M HEADING UP," I SHOUTED.

"Be right there," answered Vincent, glancing briefly to where I stood on the stairs. Gaspard took the opportunity to smash the sword from his hands, and it went clattering across the floor as Vincent raised his hands in defeat.

"Never . . ."

". . . take your eye from the fight." Vincent finished Gaspard's sentence for him. "I know, I know. But you've got to admit, Kate is more than a bit distracting."

Gaspard smiled wryly.

"To me," Vincent clarified.

"Just don't let her distract you from saving her life," Gaspard responded, placing his toe under the hilt of the fallen sword and, with a quick movement, flicking it up in the air toward Vincent.

"This is the twenty-first century, Gaspard," Vincent chuckled, catching the grip of the flying sword in his right hand. "Under your tutelage, Kate will be just as capable of saving mine." He grinned at me, lifting an eyebrow suggestively. I laughed.

"I agree," Gaspard admitted, "but only if she can catch up with your half century of fighting experience."

"I'm working on it," I called as I closed the door behind me, blocking out the earsplitting clash of metal that resonated from the resumption of their fight.

I pushed through a swinging door into a large, airy kitchen and breathed in the bready aroma of freshly baked pastry. Jeanne was bent over one of the slate gray granite counters. Nominally the cook and housekeeper, she was more like a house mom. Following the example of her own mother and grandmother, she had cared for the revenants for decades. Her shoulders shook slightly as she put the finishing flourishes on a chocolate cake. I touched her arm and she turned to face me, revealing tears that she tried unsuccessfully to blink back.

"Jeanne, are you okay?" I breathed, knowing that she wasn't.

"Charlotte and Charles are like my own children." Her voice cracked.

"I know," I said, putting an arm around her ample waist and leaning my head on her shoulder. "But they're not leaving forever. Jean-Baptiste said it was just until Charles gets his head sorted out. How long could that take?"

Jeanne straightened and we looked at each other, a silent message passing between us. *A long time, if ever.* The boy was seriously messed up.

My own feelings about him were mixed. He had always acted

antagonistically toward me, but after Charlotte had explained why, I couldn't help but pity him.

As if reading my thoughts, Jeanne jumped to his defense. "It's not really his fault. He didn't mean to endanger everyone, you know."

"I know."

"He's just more sensitive than the others," she said, bending back over her cake and concentrating on the placement of a sugar-spun flower. "It's their lifestyle. Dying over and over again for us humans and then having to leave us to our fate takes its toll. He's only fifteen, for goodness' sake."

I smiled sadly. "Jeanne, he's eighty."

"*Peu importe,*" she said, making a motion like she was swatting a ball backward over her shoulder. "I think the ones who die younger take it harder. My grandmother told me that one of their Spanish kindred did the same thing. He was fifteen too. He asked the numa to destroy him, like Charles did. But that time the poor thing succeeded."

Jeanne noticed me shudder at this mention of the revenants' ancient enemies, and though no one else was in the kitchen, she lowered her voice. "I say it's better than the other extreme. Some—very few, mind you—get so jaded by their role in human life and death that their rescues become only a means of survival. They don't care about the humans they save, only about relieving their compulsion. I would prefer that Charles be overly sensitive than coldhearted."

"That's why I think that getting away will be good for him,"

I reassured her. "It will give him some distance from Paris, and the people he has saved." *Or not saved*, I remembered, thinking of the fatal boat accident that had set off Charles's downward spiral. After failing to save a little girl's life, he had begun acting strangely. He ended up trying to commit revenant suicide, unwittingly allowing an attack on his kindred. "Jean-Baptiste said they could visit. I'm sure we'll see them soon."

Jeanne nodded, hesitantly acknowledging my words.

"It's a beautiful cake," I said, changing the subject. I scraped a bit of icing off the platter and popped it into my mouth. "Mmm, and yummy, too!"

Jeanne batted me away with her spatula, grateful to reassume her mother-hen role. "And you're going to ruin it if you keep taking scoops out of the side," she laughed. "Now go see if Charlotte needs some help."

"This isn't a funeral, people. It's New Year's Eve. And the twins' moving party. So let's celebrate!" Ambrose's baritone voice reverberated through the pearl gray wood-paneled ballroom, drawing amused chuckles from the crowd of elegantly dressed revelers. A hundred candles glistened off the chandeliers' crystal prisms, casting flecks of reflected light around the room better than any disco ball could.

Tables along the edges of the room were heaped with delicacies, tiny chocolate- and coffee-flavored éclairs, melt-on-your-tongue *macarons* in a half-dozen pastel colors, mountains of chocolate truffles. After the enormous feast that we had just devoured,

I didn't have an inch of space inside for these masterpieces of French pastry. Which sucked. Because if I had known these were still to come, I would have skimped on the bread and skipped the cheese course.

Across the room from me, Ambrose tapped an iPod nestled inside a large speaker system. I grinned as Jazz Age music trumpeted from the sound system. Though the native Mississippian listened to contemporary music on his headphones, he had a soft spot for the music of his youth. As the gravelly voice of Louis Armstrong electrified the dancers, Ambrose grabbed Charlotte and began shimmying her around the room, her creamy complexion and short blond hair the mirror opposite of his brown skin and cropped black hair.

They made a striking couple. If only they *were* a couple. Which—Charlotte had recently confided in me—was something that she longed for. And which Ambrose for some reason unbeknownst to me (and maybe to himself) did not. But his brotherly affection for her was as obvious as the doting smile on his face as he swung her around and dipped her low.

"Looks like fun. Let's have a go," whispered a voice inches from my ear. I turned to see Jules standing behind me. "How's your dance card look?"

"Double-check your century, Jules," I reminded him. "No dance cards."

Jules shrugged and gave me his most flirtatious smile.

"But if there were, shouldn't my boyfriend have the first dance?" I teased him.

"Not if I fought him for the honor," he joked, throwing a glance across the room at Vincent, who was watching us with a half smile. He winked at me and returned to his conversation with Geneviève, a strikingly beautiful revenant who I had once been jealous of before finding out that she was happily married.

Counting her, there were a few dozen revenants attending tonight's party who were not members of La Maison. (No one referred to it by its official name, the Hôtel Grimod de la Reynière, *hôtel* in this case meaning ridiculously huge, extravagant mansion.) Jean-Baptiste's residence was home to our venerable host, Gaspard, Jules, Ambrose, Vincent, and, until tomorrow, Charles and Charlotte. After their move to Jean-Baptiste's house near Cannes, two newcomers would arrive to take their place.

"Okay. To avoid World War Three, I guess I can give the first dance to you. But if Vincent tries to cut in, you better be ready to draw your sword."

Jules patted the imaginary hilt at his waist, then took me in his arms and swept me to the middle of the floor near Ambrose and Charlotte. "Kate, my dear, the candlelight does suit you so," he murmured.

I blushed in spite of myself, both from the bold way he touched his cheek to mine as he whispered, and from his flattery, which—though I was unquestionably into Vincent—still managed to warm me with delight. Jules was the ultimate safe flirtation, because I knew not to take it personally. Every time I saw him out at night, he had a different gorgeous woman with him.

He pulled me close until we were practically plastered to each other. Laughing, I pushed him away. "Jules, you incorrigible rake," I scolded in my best Jane Austen lingo.

"At your service," he said, and bowed low before grabbing me again and whirling me around. "You know, Vincent's not the jealous type." Jules smiled slyly as he held me tight. "He has no reason to be. Not only is he the most handsome of our kindred, or so I'm told by every woman around, but he's Jean-Baptiste's second"—he paused to dip me before scooping me back into his arms—"*and* he's won the heart of the most lovely Kate. There's no fighting the Champion."

Although I couldn't help smiling at the "lovely Kate" bit, I latched onto the new information he had given me. "Vincent is Jean-Baptiste's second? What's that mean?"

"It means that if anything ever happens to Jean-Baptiste"—Jules paused, looking uncomfortable, and I filled in the blank for him: *if he is ever destroyed*—"or if he decides to step down as the head of France's revenants, Vincent will take his place."

I was shocked. "Why hasn't he told me this before?"

"Probably because of one of his other fine points: modesty."

I took a couple of seconds to absorb the whole "second" situation before looking back into Jules's eyes. "And what did you mean by 'Champion'?"

"He hasn't told you about that, either?" This time Jules looked surprised.

"No."

"Well, I'm not going to spill all his secrets in one night, then. You'll have to ask him."

I mentally tucked that in my to-ask-Vincent file.

"So if Jean-Baptiste steps down, Vincent will be your boss?" I said it to teasingly bait him, but paused as his expression changed from his usual lighthearted nothing-affects-me flippancy to one of fierce loyalty.

"Vincent was born for this, Kate. Or reborn, rather. I wouldn't want the responsibility he's going to have one day. But when the time comes, I will do anything he asks. In fact, I already feel like that, and he's not even my 'boss.'"

"I know that," I said truthfully. "I can tell. Vincent's lucky to have you."

"No, Kate. He's lucky to have you." He gave me one final spin, and I realized that he had danced me across the room to where Vincent was standing. As he released my hands, he winked ruefully at me and deposited me gallantly into the arms of my waiting boyfriend.

"Still in one piece?" Vincent teased, pulling me close and planting a soft kiss on my lips.

"After dirty-dancing with Jules? I'm not sure," I said.

"He's harmless," offered Geneviève.

"I take offense at that," Jules called from the other side of the table, where he was serving himself a flute of champagne. "I consider myself very dangerous indeed." He saluted the three of us with his glass before sauntering off toward a pretty revenant across the room.

"Have I told you how gorgeous you look tonight?" Vincent whispered, handing me my glass.

"Only about twelve times," I said coyly, flouncing out the skirt of the floor-length pewter-colored gown Georgia had helped me find.

"Perfect, then, because thirteen's my lucky number," he said, and gave me an appreciative once-over. "But gorgeous doesn't quite do you justice. Maybe . . . dazzling? Stunning? Ravishing? Yes, I think that's better. You look ravishing, Kate."

"Stop it!" I laughed. "You are totally doing this on purpose to see if you can make me blush! It's not going to happen!"

Vincent smiled victoriously and brushed my cheek with his finger. "Too late."

I rolled my eyes as the bell-like sound of a spoon being tapped against a wineglass quieted the room. Ambrose switched the music off, and everyone turned to Jean-Baptiste, who stood before the crowd in all his noble stuffiness. From the portraits decorating the room, his clothing and hairstyle could be seen to evolve over the last 240 years, but his aristocratic demeanor hadn't changed a bit.

"Welcome, dear kindred, revenants of Paris," he announced to the forty-odd guests. "Thank you for joining us this evening in my humble abode." There was a stir of movement and a swell of bemused laughter.

He smiled subtly and continued. "I would like to make a toast to our beloved departing kindred, Charles and Charlotte. You will be sorely missed, and we all hope for your expeditious return." Everyone followed Jean-Baptiste in raising his glass, and as one chimed, "*Santé!*"

"Well, that's a diplomatic way to put it, when *he's* the one who sent them into exile!" I whispered to Vincent, and then glanced over at Charles, who was perched uncomfortably on an ancient upholstered settee on one side of the room. Since the day he had put his kindred at risk by handing himself over to the numa, his perpetual sour, sulking expression had been replaced by one of despair and depression. Gaspard sat beside him, lending emotional support.

Jean-Baptiste continued, "I'm sure we would all like to join the twins in the sunny south, but our work is cut out for us here in Paris. As you all know, ever since our human friend Kate"—he waved his glass in my direction and nodded politely at me—"dispatched so handily our enemies' leader, Lucien, just over a month ago, the numa have maintained complete silence. Although we have remained at the ready, there has been no attempt at vengeance. No counterattack.

"And more worryingly there have also been absolutely no numa sightings by our kindred. They haven't abandoned Paris. But the fact that they are avoiding us on such a thorough basis is so egregiously out of character for our old foes that we can only surmise that they have a plan. Which also means that they must have a leader."

This was a revelation to the group in the room: Their patient expressions suddenly changed to looks of consternation. Whispering began among a few, but Vincent's steady gaze toward the speaker told me that he was already privy to this information. *Jean-Baptiste's second*, I thought with a mix of wonder and uneasiness. I couldn't wait to get Vincent on his own so I could quiz him about it.

Jean-Baptiste silenced the discussions with more spoon clinking on his glass. "Kindred, please." Once again, the room fell silent. "We all know that Nicolas was Lucien's second. But surely, considering his short temper and love of ostentatious gestures, if he had taken over we would have heard something by now. Silence is our clue that someone else has assumed control. And if we don't know who we are up against, or when and where their eventual attack will come from, how can we prepare our defense?"

The murmuring started back up. This time Jean-Baptiste's raised voice quieted the crowd. "AND SO . . . in the face of a *potential* critical situation, we are honored to have the assistance of the person who knows more about our history and that of the numa than anyone else in this room. The person regarded as the most knowledgeable among our kindred in France, and an influential figure in our worldwide Consortium. She has offered to help us investigate the problem at hand and plan our strategy for self-defense, or—if necessary—a preemptive strike.

"Without further ado, I introduce to those of you who haven't had the opportunity to make her acquaintance, Violette de Montauban and her companion, Arthur Poincaré. We are honored to have them join our house during the absence of Charlotte and Charles."

From behind Jean-Baptiste stepped a couple I had never seen before. The girl's snow-white complexion was set off by black hair that was pulled back from her face with a bunch of vivid purple flowers. She was tiny and fragile-looking, like a sparrow. And though she looked younger than me, I knew that for a revenant that didn't mean a thing.

The boy moved in a distinctly old-fashioned style, stepping up to her side and holding his arm out for her to take it with the tips of her fingers. He was probably around twenty, and if his streaky blond hair hadn't been tied back into a tight ponytail and his face so clean-shaven, he would have looked exactly like Kurt Cobain. With a major case of blue-blood.

They bowed formally to Jean-Baptiste and turned toward the room, solemnly nodding their acceptance of the enthusiastic welcome. The girl's eyes paused on me and continued to Vincent, who was standing behind me with his hand resting on my hip. Her eyes narrowed slightly before moving on to scan the crowd, and then, seeing someone she knew, she stepped forward to chat. Jean-Baptiste followed her cue and began talking to a woman standing next to him.

The speech seemingly over, I searched for Charlotte to gauge her reaction to her replacements' presentation. Their introduction during the twins' party must have been a last-minute decision.

Charlotte stood at the back of the room with Ambrose, who had his arm draped securely around her shoulders. I guessed that the support he was giving was both physical and moral. Although she didn't look surprised, it looked like her smile was costing her a lot of effort.

"I'm going to go talk to Charlotte," I murmured to Vincent.

"Good idea," he said, casting a worried glance at her. "I'll make sure Charles is holding up." He leaned over to kiss my temple and then, straightening, walked away.

I set off toward Charlotte. "Just wondering if you wanted to go outside for a breath of fresh air," I said.

"I would love that," she said, and reaching for my hand, she transferred herself from Ambrose's custodianship to mine. Not for the first time, I wondered how she was going to hold out in the south of France—a whole nine-hour drive away from her support system. I didn't doubt Charlotte's strength. She had certainly been a solid shoulder for me to lean on. But now that she needed her friends the most, she was being forcibly separated from them.

We grabbed our coats on the way out and stepped into the bracing December air. The moon lit up the courtyard, illuminating its large marble fountain, which contained a life-size statue of an angel holding a woman in his arms. It was an image I never failed to compare to Vincent and me. In my eyes, the personal symbolism it held was as weighty as the stone it was carved from.

Charlotte and I sat down on the edge of its empty basin and huddled against each other for warmth. I looped my arm through hers and pulled her close. Getting close to Charlotte had helped me ignore the guilt of cutting off my friends back in New York. During the very worst period of my grieving for my parents, I had deleted my email address and hadn't contacted them since.

"Did you know that your"—I hesitated, searching for a word less offensive than "replacements"—"that Violette and Arthur were coming today?"

Charlotte nodded. "Jean-Baptiste told me yesterday. He said he didn't want me to feel like he was in a rush to replace us. But Violette offered to come, and he needs her. I can't help but feel bad about it anyway. You know . . . unwanted. Like I'm being punished."

"Even if it feels like a punishment, which Jean-Baptiste has assured everyone it *isn't*, you're not the one who's being sent away. It's Charles who messed up, no matter how unintentionally." I squeezed her arm in support. "Jean-Baptiste's rationale does make sense. If something big is going on with the numa, this would be a dangerous time for Charles to be here in the middle of it, indecisive and confused. Plus, he said *you* could stay if you wanted."

"I can't live without Charles," she said mournfully. "He's my twin. We've been through everything together."

I nodded. I understood. We had a lot in common, Charlotte and I . . . if you didn't take our mortality into account. Both of us had experienced the death of our parents. We were both left with only a sibling to link us to our former lives. I had my grandparents, of course, but my sister felt like the last remaining thread that connected me to reality. Although the meaning of the word "reality" had radically changed for me in the last few months.

"So do you know the new guys?" I asked.

"Yeah. I mean, I've never met them, but everyone's heard of them. They're part of the 'old guard.' If you think Jean-Baptiste's old, they're ancient. Although they're just as aristocratic as him."

"Yeah, that's pretty obvious," I laughed. "Violette looks like she died really young."

Charlotte smiled. "Fourteen. Her father was a marquis or something, and she was a lady-in-waiting to Anne of Brittany. She died saving the young queen's life during a kidnapping attempt."

"Queen Anne? That makes her practically medieval!" I racked my brain for names and dates from my French history classes, but Charlotte beat me to the punch.

"She died right around 1500."

"Holy cow. She's more than half a millennium old!"

Charlotte nodded thoughtfully.

"How about Arthur?"

"He's from the same era. They actually knew each other in life. He was one of her father's counselors, I think. In any case, they both reek of courtliness. She and Arthur live in a medieval castle in the Loire Valley, where I'm sure they feel right at home." There was a bitter tone in Charlotte's voice. It sounded like she wished they would go back to their château and leave us all alone.

"Their coming here is like a dream come true for JB. They've been around so long they're like living encyclopedias. Kind of like Gaspard times ten. And Violette's known all over the world for being the expert on revenant history. She knows more about the numa than anyone. Which makes her the perfect candidate for helping JB strategize." She shrugged as if that conclusion were obvious.

The creaking sound of the front door opening interrupted us. We turned our heads to see the topic of our conversation, her nobility so tangible it was like a cloud of expensive perfume suspended in the cold winter air.

"Hello," Violette said. Her voice mixed the high pitch of a little girl's with an older woman's self-assurance. This creepy discrepancy quickly disappeared as her rosebud lips curved up into a friendly smile that was so infectious, I couldn't help but smile back.

Bending over, she gave us the regulation kiss on the cheeks, and then stood. "I would like to present myself. Violette de Montauban."

"Yeah, we know," said Charlotte, studying her shoes as if the silver strappy heels held the answer to the universe, and might just reveal it if she stared hard enough.

"You must be Charlotte," Violette said, acting as if she hadn't noticed the brush-off, "and you"—she turned to me—"you must be Vincent's human."

The sound that burst from my mouth was a half sputter, half laugh. "Um, I actually have a name. I'm Kate."

"Of course, how silly of me. Kate." She turned her attention back to Charlotte, who still refused to meet her gaze. "I'm sorry if our sudden arrival has caused you distress," Violette said, accurately reading Charlotte's body language. "I was afraid it might come across as unduly insensitive myself, but once I offered our services, Jean-Baptiste insisted that Arthur and I come with the greatest of haste."

"'Greatest of haste'? You don't get out much, do you?" said Charlotte rudely.

"Charlotte!" I reproached, nudging her with my elbow.

"That's okay," Violette laughed. "No, Arthur and I keep to

ourselves. I spend most of my time with my nose in old books. And as guardians-in-residence of the Château de Langeais, we don't, as you say, 'get out very much.' I'm afraid that is apparent in my mode of speech."

"If you're never around humans, how do you integrate enough to save them?" Charlotte said, visibly trying to temper her bitterness.

"As I'm sure you're aware, the longer we are revenants, the less compulsion we have to die. I was nearing sixty when I spoke with Jean-Baptiste a couple of weeks ago. Since then, I managed to save a few gypsy children playing on the train tracks, and Arthur rescued a hunter from an attack by a pack of wild boar. So we're refreshed and ready for the job ahead of us. But that's the most animation"—she paused to smile at her pun—"we've seen for decades."

I shivered, not from the cold but from the thought that this young girl had recently looked the age of her own grandmother—that is, if her grandmother weren't already lying around mummified somewhere. And now here she was, younger than me. Although I should be used to it, the whole revenant concept of reanimating at the age you first died was still hard for me to wrap my head around.

Violette studied Charlotte's face for another second, and then touched her arm with an elegant finger. "I don't have to stay in your room if you don't wish me to. Jean-Baptiste offered me the guest room if I preferred. Your taste in decorating is, of course, much more appealing to me than his penchant for dark leather upholstery and antler chandeliers."

Charlotte couldn't keep herself from laughing. Reaching out toward Violette, she took her hand and stood to face the ancient adolescent. "I'm sorry. This is just a really hard time for me and Charles. I consider these kindred my family, and the fact that we have to leave them during a crisis is literally killing me."

I stifled a smile. Charlotte noticed and grinned. "Okay, not literally. You know what I mean."

Violette leaned toward Charlotte and, opening her arms, gracefully wrapped them around her. "Everything will be okay. Arthur and I will look after your kindred for you, and the present difficulties will be over before you know it."

Charlotte returned her hug, a bit stiffly since the younger girl was standing as if she was wearing a corset. But it seemed like peace had been made between the two. I couldn't help but wonder if Charles was faring as well.

THREE

ONE OF THE BALLROOM WINDOWS SWUNG OPEN, and Vincent leaned out looking like an old-fashioned movie star in his vintage tuxedo. "Ladies, it's almost midnight. And I, for one, hoped not to have to resort to kissing Gaspard when the clock strikes twelve." He grinned and looked over his shoulder at the older man, who rolled his eyes and shook his head in despair.

Violette, Charlotte, and I made our way back to the room just as the guests began the New Year's countdown. The air practically crackled with excitement. Considering how many times some of these people had celebrated New Year's Eve, I found it intriguing that they hadn't tired of it long ago. Humans saw it as the beginning of a fresh new year: one of only several dozen that fate would allot them. But with revenants' unlimited number of fresh new beginnings, it was curious that they would treat this as a special day.

Vincent was waiting for me by the door and swept me into his arms as the counting continued. "So what do you think of our first New Year's Eve together?" he asked, looking at me like I was his own personal miracle. Which, funnily, was exactly how I felt about him.

"I've had so many firsts lately, it feels like I swapped my old life for a brand-new one," I said.

"Is that a good thing?"

In response, as the counting reached "one," I pulled his head to mine and he wrapped me tightly in his arms. Our lips met, and as we kissed something inside me pulled and tugged until I felt my heart was going to burst. With a drowsy, eyes-half-closed smile, Vincent whispered, "Kate. You are the best thing that has ever happened to me."

"Well, I'm here because of you," I whispered.

He looked at me quizzically.

"You saved me from my darkest place."

I wondered, not for the first time, what would have happened if I hadn't met Vincent and emerged from the prison of crippling grief that I'd been locked inside after my parents' fatal car crash. I would probably still be curled up in a fetal position on my bed at my grandparents' house if he hadn't been there to show me that there was a very good reason to go on living. That life could be beautiful again.

"You saved yourself," he murmured. "I was just there to lend a hand."

He swooped me up into an eternal hug. I closed my eyes and let his affection soak through me like honey.

Finally releasing him, I held his hand and leaned my head on his shoulder as we took in the scene around us. In the flickering candlelight, Jean-Baptiste and Gaspard stood proudly side by side at the front of the room, their elbows practically touching in their yes-we're-the-hosts-of-this-grand-event pose. Gaspard leaned over to whisper something conspiratorially, and Jean-Baptiste responded with a loud guffaw. The tenseness created by his speech had all but disappeared in the romance of the enchanted evening.

Ambrose was hugging a delighted Charlotte, holding her like a rag doll about a foot off the ground in his tree-trunk arms. Jules stood near the bar, watching me and Vincent. When my eyes caught his, he puckered his lips and gave me a sarcastic air-kiss, before turning to the sultry young revenant talking to him. Violette was standing next to Arthur, her head leaned affectionately against his upper arm as they surveyed the crowd. And I noticed several other couples among the revenants who were hugging or kissing.

Some do find love, I thought.

Charlotte had told me that Ambrose and Jules were players, dating human girls but never getting serious with anyone. Jean-Baptiste didn't exactly encourage revenant/human relationships—he banned all human "lovers," as he put it, from the house. Besides a few police officers and ambulance drivers the revenants had in their pocket—and a few other human employees like Jeanne, whose families had worked for Jean-Baptiste for generations—I was the only outsider who had been taken into their confidence *and* allowed into their home.

Since the enforced secrecy of their existence pretty much ruled out the possibility of their dating a human, finding someone among their own kind was the only possibility for love. And, as Charlotte had said, there weren't a lot of revenants around to choose from.

An hour later the crowd began thinning, and I told Vincent I was ready to go home. "We have to wait for Ambrose," he said, draping my coat around my shoulders. My heart fell a little. I had been dying to ask him about being Jean-Baptiste's second and the whole "Champion" thing. But it looked like that would have to wait, since I doubted he would want to discuss it in front of Ambrose. Jules was right about Vincent's modesty. Bragging wasn't his style.

"Do I need two bodyguards?" I joked as we headed out the front door toward the gate.

"Three," Ambrose responded. "We've got Henri, an old friend of Gaspard's, along playing guard-ghost."

"Oh, right. *Bonjour*, Henri," I said out loud, thinking, *Okay, that felt weird.*

As I had learned a few months ago, for three days each month the revenants returned to a dead state, which they called being "dormant." The first of those days they might as well be stone-cold dead. But for the next forty-eight hours their minds were awake and could travel. This was being "volant." When they were out looking for humans to save, revenants walked in pairs accompanied by a volant spirit who, seeing a few minutes into the future, could tell them what was about to happen nearby.

"All this security for me?" I said, smiling as I took the arms of my two embodied escorts. "I thought Gaspard said I was getting better at fighting."

"Ambrose and Henri are here for my safety as much as for yours," Vincent reassured me. "Tonight might be the moment the numa finally decide to attack. It would make tactical sense, with most of Paris's revenants grouped together in one building. But even if they don't, there are enough drunk weirdos wandering around on New Year's Eve to make things interesting." Vincent smiled his crooked smile and pressed a button next to the gate.

The automatic lights flicked on, and I looked up and waved at the security camera. If anyone ever bothered to look at the video, they would see me wearing an evening dress worthy of a red carpet, accompanied by two handsome men in tuxedos. *Not bad*, I thought, *for a girl who never had a real date until a few months ago!*

The moon was like a spotlight, casting molten silver onto the ancient trees lining Paris's streets. Couples in formal dresses and suits made their way home from their own celebrations, giving the town a festive, holiday feel. The mouth-watering smell of baking pastry dough wafted from a *boulangerie* whose pastry chef was conscientious enough to stick to his early-morning baking hours on a holiday. Danger was the very last thing on my mind as I squeezed Vincent's arm.

But a couple of blocks from my house, the casual manner of my companions suddenly changed. I glanced around, failing to notice anything dubious, but both were on the alert. "What is it?" I asked, watching Vincent's features harden.

"Henri's not sure. Numa would be heading straight for us, but these guys are acting weird," he said, exchanging a glance with Ambrose. They immediately picked up the pace. We jogged across the avenue, my high heels making me decisively more wobbly than my usual Converses would have. As we headed down a side street toward my grandparents' building, I wondered what would happen if we were set upon by the revenants' enemies.

"Numa wouldn't do anything in public, would they?" I asked breathlessly, yet remembering how a couple of them had stabbed Ambrose outside a restaurant a few months earlier.

"We never fight in front of humans . . . if we can help it," said Ambrose. "Neither do the numa. Our secret status would be a bit compromised if we started pulling out battle-axes left and right in front of mortal witnesses."

"But why? It's not like people are going to hunt you down and destroy you."

"The human radar isn't the only one we want to stay off," he continued, one of his long strides matching two of my own. "Like I said, there are others—and no, I'm not going into a discussion of which supernaturals actually exist outside of fantasy novels. We all have our own code of honor, you know."

"Henri says that whatever they are, they're headed this way," Vincent said, his grave tone erasing all further questions from my mind.

We sprinted the last few yards to my front door, and I

speed-typed my digicode as if all our lives depended on how fast my fingers could fly. Vincent and Ambrose stood behind me like overdressed bodyguards, their hands on the hilts of whatever weapons they wore beneath their coats.

As the security lock released and I pushed the front door open, the noise of a speeding car came from the direction of the avenue. Headlights lit up the dark street, as the three of us turned to face the oncoming vehicle.

With radio blasting, an Audi full of teenagers pulled up in front of us. The door opened to allow a guy and a girl to spill from the passenger seat. The four partygoers sitting in the back let out a whoop as my sister picked herself up from the sidewalk and made a dramatic bow. "Good night, y'all," she drawled in her best Southern belle impression.

The boy on whose lap she had been balancing stood, brushed himself off, and gave her a peck on the lips. "Door-to-door service. Only the best for Georgia," he said, and leapt back into the car. "*Bonne année!* Happy New Year!" rang a chorus of voices as they sped out of sight.

Ambrose and Vincent let their coats drop back down over their weapons, so Georgia didn't even notice our heightened state of alert.

"Hi, Vincent! And hello, Ambrose, you handsome thing," she cooed, striding over to us in her short, lacy dress. Her pixie-cut strawberry blond hair was gelled into a dramatic style, feathering down around her freckle-dusted skin. "Just get a look at you boys in black tie. If only the Chippendale dancers we ordered for the party had been as handsome as you, then it might not have been a complete disaster."

She glanced at her watch and gasped in horror. "It's not even one thirty in the morning and I'm already home! How humiliating! Why the police think they have the right to close down a party for being too noisy on *New Year's Eve*, I will never understand. This was the lamest night ever!"

She looked at where I was half-hidden behind the door. "Kate, what in the world are you doing?" Without waiting for an answer, she smiled her most dazzling smile at the boys, and then, giving my arm an affectionate squeeze, brushed past me into the building's foyer.

"Is it just me, or is she in Georgia Overdrive?" chuckled Vincent.

"She's making up for lost time after taking a five-week break," I responded, remembering how Georgia had sworn off men after almost getting us killed by her then-boyfriend, numa leader Lucien.

"Well, we could definitely hire her as extra security. She and her entourage could scare off every shady character in the neighborhood," Ambrose said with a smirk.

Which reminded me . . . "What happened to whatever was following us?"

"The mobile New Year's party scared them off," Ambrose responded.

"Listen, Kate," Vincent said, peering warily down the darkened street. "Jean-Baptiste was right in saying that we don't know when the numa will strike. And with whatever it was back there following us around, I'm wondering if maybe you could use a chaperone once in a while. I have some projects that JB has asked me to take care of"—he exchanged a look with Ambrose—"so I can't be around all the time."

"A *chaperone*?" I said with a different kind of alarm.

"What's wrong with a guardian angel? Or two?" Ambrose asked. "You date a revenant, Katie-Lou, you better count on being followed around."

"Well, if I'm not hanging out with you moving targets, I'm not of much interest to the baddies, am I?" I retorted. Walking around with my boyfriend was one thing. The idea of being trailed around Paris by other revenants was something completely different. I shook my head. "Do I get a good-night kiss or would that interfere with your *chaperoning*?"

I lifted my face to Vincent and he obliged with a slow, tender kiss that made my body turn to marshmallow.

"Bye, Katie-Lou." Ambrose gave me a little salute and turned to leave.

"Good-bye," I called as the two revenants walked away from me into the dappled moonlit shadows. When they were out of sight, I turned to follow my sister up to our grandparents' apartment.

Georgia had already stripped off her party dress and replaced it with an oversize T-shirt by the time I got to her room. "What's the deal with the two-man escort?" she asked.

"Three," I responded. "Some guy named Henri was floating

around above us. Vincent's paranoid about me being leapt upon by bad zombies. With their leader gone, the numa are in hunker-down mode, and the revenants are waiting for a surprise attack."

"Disappearing numa sounds like a good thing to me." She leaned in toward her mirror and wiped her lipstick off with a tissue. "Personally, I'm happy I haven't run into a murderous killer since, well . . . since you chopped my ex's head off with a sword." Although my sister was playing lighthearted, a shadow of fear still lurked behind her practiced carefree demeanor.

"Vincent's talking about giving me a bodyguard when he's not around."

"Cool!" Georgia said, eyes wide with expectation.

"*Nyet* to the coolness," I responded. "I don't want someone following me everywhere I go. That's so . . . weird."

"Don't think 'following.' Think 'accompanying.' And what difference would it make? You're already with Vincent or one of his friends on a pretty consistent basis."

I studied her face. She wasn't saying it as a criticism. For my super-social sister, it was normal—even preferable—to have people surrounding you 24-7.

"Remember who you're talking to, Georgia? It's me. Your one and only sibling. Who is not queen of the Paris nightlife and actually likes to spend some of her waking hours alone."

"Well then, just tell Vincent you don't want a babysitter. He worships you as is. Your word should be his command."

I rolled my eyes. If only. "He actually used the word *chaperone*."

"Vincent's so hot when he talks like a grandpa," she joked. "Next thing you know, he'll ask Papy if he can start courting you, then everything will be downhill after that. False teeth. Saggy Y-fronts."

"Eww!" I laughed, fake-punching my sister on the arm.

From somewhere inside her purse, Georgia's phone started buzzing. She pulled it out and began texting. Then she looked up at me and said, "By the way, Katie-Bean, you look gorgeous in that dress."

I leaned over and hugged my glamorous, social butterfly of a sister and left her to continue her New Year's Eve socializing.

FOUR

BEING NEW YEAR'S DAY, THE GARE DE LYON TRAIN station was practically abandoned. Kamikaze pigeons soared in eccentric looping flight patterns under the massive glass-and-steel ceiling. Our small group of six stood dwarfed in the colossal space, watching Charlotte and Charles board the ultramodern high-speed TGV train that would take them from Paris to Nice in just under six hours. Ambrose loaded a small mountain of suitcases onto the luggage compartment of their carriage as the twins leaned in for hugs from Jules, Vincent, and me and more formal cheek-kisses from Gaspard and Jean-Baptiste.

As a digitized woman's voice announced the train's imminent departure, Charles broke away from Ambrose's crushing bear hug and climbed onto the train without looking back. Charlotte brushed away tears as she turned. "You'll return before long," stated Jean-Baptiste, a rare trace of emotion tingeing his voice. She nodded mutely, looking like she was struggling not to burst into full-fledged sobbing.

"Email . . . and phone!" I reminded her. "We'll keep in touch—I promise!" I threw her a kiss with both hands as she stepped onto the train and disappeared behind the darkened windows. Vincent draped his arm supportively around my shoulders. I turned so that the twins wouldn't see me cry.

Charlotte was the only girl I had gotten close to since we moved to Paris almost a year ago. It was my fault: I hadn't actively been looking for friends. For half of that time I had been a hermit. Then along came Vincent, and it was like he brought a prepackaged group of friends with him. It hadn't escaped my attention that I preferred to spend time with the undead rather than the living. I tried not to think about what that said about me.

The sound of the conductor's whistle pierced the frigid air. The train shuddered once and then pulled away. Our mismatched group waved at the darkened windows before wordlessly ambling back toward the station entrance. Everyone seemed lost in thought as Vincent's phone started to ring. He checked the display and answered, "*Bonjour*, Geneviève." After listening for a moment, he stopped in his tracks, his face ashen. "Oh, no. No."

Hearing his mournful tone, everyone froze and watched him, waiting. "Just stay there. We'll be right over." He switched the phone off and said, "Geneviève's husband died this morning. He went to bed last night and never woke up."

The group inhaled as one and stood there, stunned. "Oh, my poor Geneviève," said Gaspard finally, breaking the silence.

"Has she notified—" Jean-Baptiste began.

"The doctor already certified Philippe as dead, and his body was picked up by the coroner. She would have called earlier, but was afraid that if Charlotte knew, she wouldn't have gotten on the train."

Jean-Baptiste nodded.

Although Geneviève lived halfway across town and wasn't often at La Maison, she and Charlotte had been friends for decades. Charlotte had once told me that it was hard hanging out with guys all the time. Before I had arrived, Geneviève was the only girlfriend she had, and Charlotte would run off to her house every time she and Charles had a brother-sister spat.

"She hoped that a couple of us could come over to help with the funeral plans. Kate, do you want to come with me?" Vincent asked. I nodded.

"I'll come," Jules and Ambrose said as one.

"Ambrose, I had hoped to have your services moving Violette and Arthur into their rooms," Gaspard said. "But of course . . ." He held up a quivering finger, as if he was unsure of the fairness of his request.

Ambrose hesitated, torn, and then relented. "No, you're right, Gaspard. I'll follow you back to the house. Give Geneviève my love, and tell her I'll stop by later," he said to us, and then, shifting his motorcycle helmet to his other hand, clapped Vincent on the shoulder and strode out, with Gaspard and Jean-Baptiste following close behind.

Jules, Vincent, and I hopped into one of the taxis parked outside the station and within fifteen minutes were at Geneviève's house on a tiny street in the Mouzaia neighborhood of Belleville.

As we climbed out of the car, I looked around in amazement. Although we were still within the Paris city limits, the streets were lined with little two-story brick houses complete with tiny front yards—instead of the typical multi-floor Paris apartment blocks. We walked through a white picket fence and across a tree-shaded yard to the front porch, where Geneviève waited, leaning on the door frame as if she couldn't stand without its support.

As Jules and Vincent approached, she fell into their arms. "He died in his sleep. I was reading when he went, and didn't even notice," she confessed in a dazed voice. Her pale blue eyes were shiny with tears and fatigue.

"It's going to be okay," Vincent soothed, handing Geneviève over to Jules. We followed them down the hall and into a bright, spacious living room. Jules seated her on a white couch as carefully as if she were made of spun glass and then settled in next to her. She cuddled up to him and dabbed at her swollen eyes with a tissue as Vincent and I sat on the floor at their feet.

"What needs doing?" Vincent asked softly.

"Legally? Nothing. Philippe and I have been preparing for this for a while. The house and money is mine—you took care of that paperwork for me a while ago," she said, nodding tearfully to Vincent.

"A law degree does come in handy when you have to register property and a bank account in a dead woman's name." He smiled grimly.

"Philippe had already decided on his own funeral arrangements. No church service, no announcement, just a small ceremony among our own at Père Lachaise."

Only the most famous cemetery in Paris, I thought with awe, remembering a tour my mother and I had gone on that included the graves of Victor Hugo, Oscar Wilde, Gertrude Stein, and Jim Morrison, among others. Philippe—or more likely Geneviève—must have some powerful contacts to have secured a gravesite for him there.

"I would love a cup of tea," Geneviève said to no one in particular.

"I'll get it!" I popped to my feet, grateful to be given a task. "Just point me to the kitchen."

Once there, I lit the gas burner under a kettle and rummaged through the cupboards until I found a teapot, some cups, and a box of tea bags. Framed photos hung on the kitchen wall, and I wandered from one to the next as I waited for the water to boil.

The first was an old black-and-white photo of Geneviève in a wedding dress, being carried in the arms of a tuxedoed man through the front gate of this house. Geneviève's dress and crimped hairstyle dated the picture from around World War II. They were both laughing in the photo, and looked like any other blissful couple on their wedding day.

The next picture showed the same man outside a garage, wearing a light-colored jumpsuit with grease stains on it. He leaned over a car and gave a thumbs-up, holding a wrench in one hand. His face didn't look any different than in the wedding photo—still 1940s or '50s, I was guessing.

I moved to the next photo, which must have been taken in the 1960s—I could tell from Geneviève's Jackie O hairdo. She looked exactly the same, but her husband was graying and his face was that of a man in his forties. Still . . . they could pass for a middle-aged man and his much younger wife.

But not in the following images. The color photographs made their difference in age increasingly obvious. I leaned in to see an inscription written across the bottom of the most recent portrait: "60 years on the millennium. My love for you will last forever. Philippe." In the photo the man was sitting in a club chair with one of those metal walkers standing beside it. Geneviève was perched on the arm, leaning over and kissing his cheek as he grinned directly into the camera lens. He looked ancient. She looked twenty. And they looked as in love as they had on their wedding day.

I jumped as the kettle began whistling on the stove behind me. I had forgotten where I was as I became gradually sucked into their history—a history full of love and happiness, certainly, but one that had ended as a tragedy worthy of Homer.

When I returned to the living room, carrying the tray with teapot and cups, Jules was pacing around on his cell phone, spreading the news to their friends. Geneviève sat on the couch with her head on Vincent's shoulder, staring off into space.

My boyfriend's eyes were dark as he watched me cross the room and set the tray on a coffee table in front of them. An expression of pain flashed across his face, and I knew we were thinking the same thing. The story of Geneviève and her human husband could one day be ours.

FIVE

WE STOOD IN THE GRAVEYARD, AMONG THE TOMB-stones, forty-some dead people and me. A couple of my fellow funeral-goers had even been in their own coffins, deep under several feet of French soil, before they had been dug out by Jean-Baptiste or another like him who had "the sight."

As Vincent had explained to me, a revenant-in-the-making sends off a light like a beacon shooting straight up into the sky, visible only to those few revenants who have the gift of seeing auras. And if the "seer" gets to the corpse before it wakes up three transformational days later—if they provide food, water, and shelter for the awakening revenant—a new immortal is born. If not . . . ashes to ashes, dust to dust.

Although Philippe hadn't met the revenant prerequisite of dying in another human's stead, Geneviève didn't take any chances and waited until the fourth day after his death to bury him. And now she knelt by the graveside, swathed in black crepe and throwing bunches of tiny white flowers down onto the casket.

"Thee only do I love," came a girl's hushed voice from just behind me. Vincent had left my side to stand next to Geneviève, picking up a handful of dirt and throwing it down among the flowers before giving another mourner his place. I turned to see Violette standing next to me.

"What did you say?" I asked.

"The tiny white flowers Geneviève is throwing—they're arbutus." She saw my confusion and corrected herself. "I forgot that they do not teach the language of flowers nowadays. That was a staple of a lady's education. Every flower has its own meaning. And arbutus flowers mean 'Thee only do I love.' Geneviève would be aware of that—that is why she chose them for her one and only love."

I nodded blankly.

"It is tragic," she continued in her strange old-fashioned speech. I had a hard time following some of it—at times her words came out like she was quoting Shakespeare, but in Old French. "Why anyone would put themselves through such misery is quite simply beyond me. How could she expect anything other than grief, remaining attached to a human?"

The words came out almost flippantly, and then Violette turned to me with her mouth in an O and eyes wide. "Kate. I am so sorry! You blend in so well with all the revenants here, I completely forgot you were not one of us. And with you and Vincent being . . ." She grasped for words.

"Together," I said bluntly.

"Yes, of course. Together. Well, it is so very, very . . . *pleasant*. Please forget that I said anything."

Violette looked like she was on the verge of tears, she was so embarrassed. I touched my hand to her shoulder and said, "Don't worry. Really. Sometimes it's hard for me to remember there's any difference between me and Vincent." Which was kind of a lie, since that difference was almost always on my mind. But she seemed mollified and, after nodding gratefully at me, stepped forward and bent down to scoop up her own handful of grave dirt.

There was a stir as Vincent held his hand up to quiet the crowd, who had begun conversing softly among themselves. "Excuse me, friends," he called out. "There is something that Geneviève wanted to read you herself, but she has asked me to take her place. It was a favorite passage of hers and Philippe's from the book *The Life and Opinions of Tristram Shandy*. She said it helped to keep them 'in the day.'"

He cleared his voice and began reading.

"'Time wastes too fast . . . . the days and hours of it . . . are flying over our heads like light clouds of a windy day, never to return more—every thing presses on—whilst thou art twisting that lock,—see! it grows grey . . .'"

Vincent looked up and caught my eye and then, looking troubled, returned to the page and continued.

"'And every time I kiss thy hand to bid adieu, and every absence which follows it, are preludes to that eternal separation which we are shortly to make!'"

My heart lurched in my chest. Not just symbolically—it caused actual physical pain. The passage seemed to have been written for me and Vincent. My worst fear about our future had been spelled out in the poetic lines that he was reading like a dirge.

This could be us, I thought once again. Whatever happened, we seemed damned by fate. Even if Vincent suffered through the agony it would cause him to resist dying and grow old with me, someday he'd be like Geneviève, a beautiful teenager standing by his elderly lover's grave.

And why am I even thinking about growing old with someone? my internal voice of reason protested indignantly, making me feel like a sappy idiot. *I'm just a teenager! How do I even know what I will want five years from now, much less sixty?* I couldn't help it, though. The tragedy felt real and immediate, and I couldn't throw it off with rational explanations.

Irrational and premature grief raked my heart, forcing stinging tears to my eyes. I had to get out of there. I had to escape from this crushing reminder of mortality's final result. I backed slowly out of the assembly, hoping no one would notice my flight.

Once I was clear of the group, I strode quickly away, pausing briefly to look over my shoulder. No one had seen me leave. Everyone faced Vincent, who was now hidden by a sea of black suits. I myself was lost for a minute in a mob of passing tourists, holding up maps that pointed out the celebrity graves. "Edith Piaf, two aisles over and one up," called a guide leading a group of American teenagers. *Just a year ago, that could have been me*, I thought, looking at a smiling, carefree girl my age. I let myself be swept along with them until I was a safe distance away from the funeral.

Not caring what direction I was heading, I plunged deeper into the acres of graves. A cold rain began to pelt down like frozen darts, stinging my skin, and I ducked into a little Gothic-style structure carved in stone.

The roof was supported only by pillars, giving me shelter from the rain, but leaving me exposed to the cold wind. I hunched down next to an aboveground tomb topped by two statues lying side by side, their hands pressed together in eternal prayer on their marble bed. After a moment of casting around in my memory, I remembered where I was—I had stopped here on the walking tour with my mother. It was the tomb of Abelard and Héloïse. *How fitting*, I thought, *that on today, of all days, I end up at the grave site of France's most famous tragic lovers.*

At the base of the monument, I sat with my knees up pressed against me, pulling my coat around my legs to shield me from the elements. I felt more alone than I had in months. Drying my face with the edge of my sleeve, I took a couple of deep breaths and tried to think things through in a rational manner.

I had to concentrate on the here and now. Why was I so afraid?

I picked up a shiny black stone from the base of the tomb and rolled it around in my palm until it was warm. Then I set it on the ground next to my foot to mark Point One of my List of Fears: Even *if* Vincent was able to resist dying, it would mean decades of emotional and physical pain for him. It was cruel and selfish of me to expect him to endure that, and all because of my own weakness.

I picked up another stone and placed it next to the first. If Vincent *couldn't* hold out, I would have to deal with the constant specter of his ravaged corpse every time he died for someone.

I felt my brow wrinkle and placed shiny black stone number three by the pair on the ground: *If*—even after that—I was able to stay with him and learned to live with the trauma of his deaths, he would be the one watching me age. And then die.

The three black stones looked like ellipses, waiting for something else to follow. Well, I could add to my List of Fears the revenants' one occupational hazard: Another vengeful numa like Lucien could come after Vincent to destroy him—and succeed this time. Then *I* would be the one left alone.

Stop it, Kate, I ordered myself. Aging and death were still far away, and I would deal with that when the time came. That's *if* we stayed together. Which, being realistic, wasn't certain no matter how much I wanted it to be. Mortal couples have a hard enough time making things work.

As for the rest, it was no use trying to second-guess what would happen. If I didn't try to project into an unknown future, I could handle the here and now. I *had been* handling it . . . just not for the last hour or so.

Stay in the present, I thought. In the present, Vincent and I were fine. And right here and now, all I wanted to do was go home. Making that simple decision made me suddenly feel more in control. I pushed myself up against the cold stone into a standing position, and began texting Vincent to tell him I had left before he started searching for me.

I had just keyed in his name when I heard the sound of crackling leaves. Tensing, I glanced around, but saw only gray headstones and monuments stretching out for miles.

A sudden movement caught my eye. As I saw a cloaked figure step out from behind a tomb a few yards away, an irrational panic gripped me. I couldn't see his face, but his hair was a wavy salt-and-pepper—dark brown mixed with gray—and he was as tall as me. I absorbed this in a second, as I went into automatic fight mode, calculating how to best defend myself against his height and weight.

But without looking my way, he turned and walked off among the gravestones. I exhaled, relieved, as my brain registered the fact that it was just a man. A man in a long fur coat who was walking away from me. Not toward me. *A man. Not a monster*, I thought, chiding myself for freaking out about nothing.

As I watched his form disappear among the graves, I rose out of the defensive stance I had subconsciously taken. Just as I lifted the cell phone back to finish my text, a strong hand gripped my shoulder.

I let out a yelp as I turned to see a pair of dark blue eyes staring angrily into my own. "Kate, what do you think you're doing?" Vincent said, his voice sounding all strangled in his throat.

"What am *I* doing? You almost gave me a heart attack sneaking up on me like that!" I pressed my chest with my hand as if that could still its frantic beating.

"I wasn't sneaking up on you," he said frostily. "I wouldn't have even known where you were if Gaspard weren't volant. He returned to get me after following you here. You could have been in serious danger."

Even though Vincent couldn't have known how unnerved I'd been by the man in the fur coat just moments ago, my fear transformed to anger in a split second. "Danger? Here? In broad daylight? From what? Psycho Jim Morrison fans? Falling tombstones?"

"From numa."

"Oh, please, Vincent. We're in the middle of a major tourist site. Père Lachaise is practically Disneyland for the Dead. It's not some Buffy soundstage with vampires rising out of the ground every time someone turns around."

"Kate, we are on high alert right now. No one knows where the numa are or what they're up to. This would be exactly the type of event that they would jump at to attack us. Dozens of revenants in one place at one time? It would be their dream situation. That's why we all came armed." He held aside his coat to show me a sword at his waist and knives strapped to his thighs.

That shut me up.

"Why did you go wandering off by yourself?" The fear having left his voice, his expression now showed unsettled confusion.

I stared at him for a moment, and then glanced at the statues next to us—the tragic lovers lying side by side. Vincent turned to see what I was looking at, and comprehension dawned on his face. He closed his eyes as if to block out the image.

"I had to leave the funeral, Vincent. I couldn't take it," I began to explain. But the sorrow and the rain and cold and fright all seemed to gang up on me at once, and my words stuck in my throat.

"I understand," he said, putting his arm around me and pulling me away from the tomb. He turned me to face him. "It's freezing and you're drenched. Let's get out of here."

I couldn't help but peer over my shoulder as we left. There was no trace of the cloaked man—he was long gone—but now that Vincent had mentioned numa, it made me wonder why I had had such a strong reaction to the man's appearance. Could a numa have been following me through the graveyard?

It didn't matter now, I decided, and would only freak Vincent out if I said something about it. I put it out of my mind, and pulled my boyfriend closer.

SIX

BEFORE MEETING VINCENT, MY DAYS ALL SEEMED to speed by like one of those passage-of-time visual metaphors in movies that show pages falling off a calendar. But lately, every day seemed significant: The first time Vincent met my grandparents. The first movie date (*Holy Grail*, where Vincent earned major points by quoting the best bits in English right along with me). Our first New Year's together.

Today was my last day of freedom before school resumed post-holidays, marking exactly one year and one semester to go before my high school education was officially over. Which made it another significant day. So of course I planned on spending it doing the thing I loved most.

I flitted down our building's creaky wooden staircase with a feeling of elation buoying my footsteps. The whole day stretched out in front of me like a new country to explore. With my favorite person.

I caught sight of him as soon as I stepped out the door. Shaking my head in disbelief, I jogged to the park across the street and pushed through the metal gate.

"What are you doing? I thought we were going out for breakfast," I laughed, pointing at the picnic blanket he was lying on, with wicker basket and thermos by his side.

"You can't get much more 'out' than this," Vincent responded, his eyes hidden by mirrored sunglasses.

His languid smile did its regular job on me: It was as if an invisible hand took my insides and squeezed. Hard. It happened every time. And it made me wish that I could freeze-frame the moment and stand there feeling that delicious, squeezy feeling for the rest of my life.

Inhale and then exhale, I reminded myself. I tore my gaze away from his face and noticed that he was cocooned in a warm coat, wool scarf, and knitted cap, with his dark hair waving out from underneath. He lay back on his elbows, propped on the blanket that was spread across the frozen grass.

"Let me get this right. We're having a picnic in January in the freezing cold?" My breath came out in a warm puff of mist as I stood above him, hands on my hips.

He pulled off his glasses, and the amusement in his eyes warmed me more efficiently than a bonfire. "I thought we could have a day of doing things we've never done before. I've never had a picnic in January. Have you?"

I shook my head and, bemused, sank down onto the blanket next to him.

"Perfect," he concluded. "Since it has to be something that neither of us has ever done, this totally counts."

I glanced up at the people walking by: mainly businesspeople carrying briefcases and backpack-wearing tourists out for an early start. They all stared at us as if the park was a circus and we were its freak-show headliners, and a few laughed out loud. Vincent said, "I hope you don't mind spectators," and then leaned forward and took my face in his hands, kissing me.

"I think I can deal." I grinned, and then shivered as he let me go.

"We'll make it a speed-picnic," he promised, unwinding his scarf and double-wrapping it above my own.

We munched on croissants that were baked exactly how I love them: crunchy on the outside, light as air inside, with an inner core of doughiness. The café au lait was hot enough to warm my insides, and I sipped the supersweet freshly squeezed orange juice while Vincent caught me up on the news of how Charles and Charlotte were settling in the south. "We were talking about a road trip to take them more boxes, but JB claims he needs me here," Vincent complained, popping the end of his croissant into his mouth.

"Sucks being JB's second."

"Oh, so you know about that?" he asked, amused. "Have my kindred been talking about me behind my back?"

"Yeah, Jules said something about it the other day. Right before he told me you were some sort of champion. Which I've actually been dying to ask you about." I eagerly leaned forward on my elbows, watching as Vincent's expression turned to one of dismay.

He covered his eyes with his hand. "Here we go again," he moaned.

"What's that mean?" I asked, intrigued by his reaction.

He leaned back until he was lying down on the blanket and addressed the winter gray sky above us. "There's this ancient prophecy written by a revenant back in the Roman era. It said that one of us would arise to lead our kind against the numa and conquer them."

"And what does that have to do with you?" I asked.

Vincent stared at the sky for another second, and then rolled onto his side to face me. "Jean-Baptiste has gotten it into his head that I'm the Champion."

"Why?"

"Who knows? Probably because I was able to hold out for so long without dying. In that way, I apparently am stronger than others my 'age.' But it's all so vague. Although everyone's heard of the prophecy, no one knows exactly what it means."

"You sound pretty sure it's not you," I said, feeling a twinge of relief. Dating a revenant was a big enough step without having to wonder if he was the supreme commander of the revenants.

"I think that it's all a load of crap, and that it doesn't matter anyway. What's going to happen will happen, whether or not anyone knows about it ahead of time. What bugs me is that Jean-Baptiste has actually told people his opinion. And there's nothing more intimidating than everyone watching you like a hawk, waiting for the moment you transform into the undead Messiah."

I laughed, and Vincent reached for me, wearing that slow smile I couldn't refuse. I kissed him—a long, warm meeting of our cold lips—and then, leaning back, I asked with as much seriousness as I could muster, "So if you're the revenants' Champion, and I saved you from Lucien, does that make me the Champion's Champion?"

Vincent shook his head in despair.

"No, really," I continued, unable to suppress a teasing grin, "I want a cool name too. Maybe you could start calling me the Vanquisher. Although I think I'd need a luchador mask to go with it."

Vincent let out an exasperated growl and pushed me down on the blanket, pinning my shoulders to the ground and forcing me to give him another kiss. He placed a warm hand against my cold cheek, and the corners of his eyes crinkled as he smiled. "Well, at the moment calling you the Ice Queen would be more accurate." He rose and, taking me by the hand, pulled me to my feet.

I rubbed my gloved hands up and down my arms to get my circulation going. "Okay! Picnic in January . . . check!" I said with chattering teeth.

Vincent stuffed the thermos and blanket inside the basket. "And how's it feel to do something you've never done before?"

"It feels like I'm freezing my butt off!" I said, squealing as he dropped the basket and picked me up in his arms.

"Okay, that's a little warmer," I conceded as he held me off the ground in a bear hug.

"Let's drop this basket off at my place, and then we'll be on our way to destination number two," he said, setting me back down and swooping the picnic basket up on one arm.

"Which is?" I asked, wrapping my hands around his free arm and drawing him closer as we left the park and headed toward La Maison.

"Well, that depends. Have you been to the war museum at Les Invalides?"

I scrunched my nose in distaste. "I know where it is. But since it doesn't have many paintings, I never bothered. Are we talking tanks and guns and, um, *war* stuff?"

Vincent glanced down at me and laughed. "Yeah, they have tanks and guns *and* a fascinating World War Two collection, but to tell you the truth, it's a bit of a downer. Especially for those of us who lived through it. No, I was planning on skipping those parts and taking you directly to the ancient weaponry section. The pieces in that room are as much art as a painting by John Singer Sargent."

"Hmm. I have a feeling that's going to be a matter of opinion."

"Seriously, there's this thirteenth-century dagger worked with silver and enamel inlay that deserves a room to itself at the Louvre."

"Do they have crossbows?"

"Do they have crossbows! Only a whole roomful. Including Catherine de Médicis's gold-encrusted one. Why?"

"I love crossbows. They're so . . . I don't know . . . badass."

Vincent's surprised laugh was between a sputter and a cough. "Note to self: Add crossbow lessons to Kate's regularly scheduled training sessions!" He pushed his front gate open, placed the basket on top of the mailbox, and pulled the gate shut behind us. "Do you think you could arrange for that, Gaspard?" he added.

"Oh, hi, Gaspard!" I said to the air.

"Gaspard asked me to reassure you that he's not crashing our date," Vincent said.

"I don't mind if you want to come along," I said. "Knowing you, I doubt it'll be your first time at the war museum."

Vincent offered me his arm and began leading me back in the direction we had come from. "Gaspard actually contributed the research done on the oldest pieces in their collection. He knows the place better than most of the museum's curators." He was silent for a few seconds, listening. "He says he'll pass on the museum, but will accompany us for a few blocks since we're going in the same direction he was heading."

We started toward the museum, a good twenty-minute walk away, carrying on our bizarre three-way chat for a couple of blocks before Vincent stopped abruptly. "What is it?" I asked, watching his face as he listened to words I couldn't hear.

"Gaspard sees something. We just have a couple of minutes. Come on," Vincent said, and, taking my hand, began running down a small street toward one of the larger avenues.

"Where are we going?" I asked as we ran, but Vincent was too busy listening to Gaspard and shooting questions like, "How many people?" and "Where's the driver?" My alarm mounted when we reached the boulevard Raspail and Vincent said, "Kate, stay back, and watch out—there's a truck . . ."

And then we saw it cresting the top of the hill: a large white delivery truck careening down the middle of the four lanes. It weaved dangerously as it straddled the center line, obviously out of control. I gasped when I realized that there was no driver behind the wheel.

Turning to the crosswalk, I spotted several pedestrians crossing the intersection, completely unaware of the danger heading toward them. Although it was still two blocks away, the truck wasn't slowing. And at the speed it was coming, the people in the middle of the crosswalk had no chance of escaping its trajectory. "Oh my God. Do something!" I urged Vincent, horror coursing like ice water through my veins.

Vincent was already looking from the pedestrians to the truck and back as he gauged the situation. He hesitated for a split second and glanced quickly my way, furrowing his eyebrows as if weighing something. Something that had to do with me.

"What?" I asked, my voice panicky.

Something clicked in his eyes. His decision made, he shuffled off his coat, dropped it to the ground, and took off toward the oncoming truck.

My heart pounding, I screamed in French in the direction of the pedestrians, "*Attention!*" A middle-aged woman glanced back at me, and then followed my gesture up the boulevard.

"*Oh, mon Dieu!*" she shrieked, and turning, she threw her arms out wide to push the man and child flanking her back toward the safety of the sidewalk. They would never make it in time. Nor would the college-age girl wearing headphones who hadn't even heard me yell.

Running faster than seemed humanly possible, Vincent reached the truck, leapt, and landed on the running board. The impact threw him backward, threatening to jettison him off into the road. He scrabbled to hang on to the door handle, steadying himself, and then wrenched it open, grabbing the steering wheel and jerking it to the right. In a screech of skidding tires, the truck jumped off the road and flipped onto its passenger side. It careened a few feet across the sidewalk before smashing with a sickening crunch into a stone wall, only a couple of yards short of the crosswalk.

A split second of shocked silence followed, before a cacophony of shouts and cries began. The couple and their child were on the ground, just short of the sidewalk, having attempted to throw themselves off the road. Passersby rushed over and helped them to their feet. Someone else ran up to the girl with the headphones, who stood in shock in the middle of the road, mouth open and bags spilled on the ground around her feet.

A police siren split the air, as a couple of cop cars pulled off the boulevard Saint Germain into the middle of the intersection, blocking vehicles from both directions. One policeman leapt out to divert traffic, while the others rushed for the accident site.

Vincent pushed himself off the driver's door, which was now on the top of the flipped truck, and dropped to the ground. Lying on his back on the sidewalk, he folded an arm cautiously across his rib cage, dropping the keys he had pulled from the ignition.

As I reached him, he squeezed his eyes closed in pain, and a small stream of blood oozed from a cut on his forehead. I crouched down beside him, feeling like I was the one who had been thrown to the pavement, the breath knocked out of me. "Vincent, are you okay?" I asked, blindly sticking my arm into my bag and coming back with some Kleenex. I dabbed at the blood before it could run into his eye.

"Hurt rib, but I'm fine," he said, gasping for breath. "But the driver's in the truck."

I cupped his face in my hand and breathed a sigh of relief. "Oh, thank God, Vincent." I turned to the approaching policemen. "The driver's still in there," I yelled, coughing and blinking as I inhaled the acrid smell of burned rubber.

One climbed up onto the truck and, after taking a look inside, pulled out a walkie-talkie and called for emergency assistance. Another knelt down next to us and began asking Vincent questions. Was he okay? Could he move his fingers? His toes? Was he having trouble breathing? Only after Vincent sat up (against the policeman's advice) and reassured him that he had only had his breath knocked out and cut his head in the impact did the policeman turn to ask me what had happened.

By then a crowd had gathered around us, and an elderly man spoke up before I could respond. "I saw the whole thing, officer. That truck was out of control, with no driver behind the wheel, rolling steadily down the boulevard. And that boy there," he said, pointing to Vincent, "commandeered it, steering it off the road. If he hadn't, it would have plowed right into the people crossing the road." He pointed to the headphones girl, who had been led to the sidewalk and was sitting with her head between her knees as someone rubbed her back.

The bystanders began buzzing excitedly with the news—the word "hero" being voiced more than once—and cell phones were pulled out as people began typing messages and making calls. Vincent closed his eyes tiredly and then, as someone tried to take a picture, pulled his sweater's hood up over his head and asked me to help him up, wincing as he stood.

"Are you going to need me, Officer?" he asked the policeman who was mapping the truck's path with another witness.

He saw Vincent and said, "You really shouldn't move, sir, until the paramedics arrive."

"I told you, I'm fine," Vincent insisted politely. The way he held his arm carefully across his torso suggested that he was anything but.

The policeman looked conflicted. "We'll need your testimony," he said finally.

"Then can we wait in your car?"

"Yes, yes, of course," the man responded, and flagged his partner to come get us. We were led away from the excited crowd and toward the privacy of the squad car. On the way I retrieved Vincent's coat and draped it around him.

We scooted into the backseat of the squad car, and the cop shut the door behind us. We were finally alone, and I turned to Vincent, who was holding my tissue to his head. "Are you really okay?" I asked him, reaching up to gingerly pull his hand away from the wound. "You might need stitches."

"Do you have a mirror?"

I handed him a compact from my bag, and he held it up to the light, inspecting his wound. "A butterfly bandage will hold it fine."

"And besides that?"

"I might have a bruised rib. JB will send for a doctor once we're home. I've got a couple weeks until I'm dormant, and then my body will heal itself. I can wait. I promise, Kate. I'm fine."

He leaned back on the headrest and closed his eyes.

I sat with my head on his shoulder and my arm around his chest and wondered what might have happened had things gone differently.

What if Vincent hadn't been fast enough and one of those people had been killed? What if in attempting to reach the truck, Vincent had been the one mowed down? Instead of sitting in the back of a squad car, I could be kneeling over his mangled body. He had been just inches away. It had been so close.

I closed my eyes and tried to focus on what *was* instead of what *might have been.*

SEVEN

WE SPENT OVER AN HOUR WAITING IN AN OFFICE at the police station before giving our depositions. The official investigation had begun by that point, and the officer who eventually turned up explained that they had discovered a medical card in the driver's wallet saying that he was epileptic. Once they contacted his wife, she admitted that he had recently stopped taking his medication.

"He was unconscious by the time I reached the vehicle," Vincent confirmed.

"He was unconscious, sitting at the wheel?" the officer asked, scribbling in a notepad.

"No. He had slumped over and was lying down on the seat. His foot was no longer on the accelerator."

A row of three small butterfly bandages decorated Vincent's forehead, the result of a paramedic's ministrations while we sat in the back of the cop car. When the officer looked up from his writing, Vincent tested the wound gingerly with his fingers.

The man saw the gesture and closed his notebook. "I've been instructed not to keep you long. And to apologize for the wait before we got to you. It was inexcusable."

From the way the man had bustled in all of a sudden, stumbling over himself to make us comfortable and offering up restricted information on the investigation, I assumed that Jean-Baptiste had been in touch with one of his police department contacts.

"Even though you have repeatedly refused to be taken to an emergency room, I do think you should see a doctor," the man continued, looking concerned. "If for nothing else, you could use a few stitches on that head wound."

"Thanks, Officer. At this point I just want to get home. This whole thing has really shaken me up." I tried to refrain from smiling as Vincent played up his I'm-just-a-nineteen-year-old-regular-guy act.

The policeman nodded and, resting his pen on his notebook, walked around the desk to face us. He extended his hand, but when Vincent winced at the effort of raising his arm, he quickly withdrew it and instead clapped him carefully on the shoulder. "I just want to commend you for your heroic actions today, Monsieur Dutertre."

I pursed my lips to stop another grin. Vincent must be a pro by now at creating random false identities at the drop of a hat.

"Promise me you'll convince him to see a doctor," the policeman said, turning to me. "Today."

I nodded, and we followed him out of the office and through the mazelike *préfecture*, shaking hands again once we were in the lobby.

"Let's go," Vincent said as we reached the front door, and heading down the building's grand staircase, we jumped directly into the backseat of a waiting car.

"Gaspard notified us of your acrobatic feats, Vin. Very James Bond. Nicely done," Ambrose said as he pulled away from the curb. Vincent slumped down to put his head on my shoulder. "How you feeling, man? Clinic or home?"

"Feeling rough. I probably cracked a rib, but I don't need a doctor." *Nice*, I thought, feeling slightly stung. *For me the rib was bruised.* When would Vincent stop trying to protect me from the harsher realities of his existence?

"When are you dormant?" Ambrose asked.

"Got a couple of weeks," Vincent said.

Ambrose peered at Vincent's face in the rearview mirror. "Can that head wound wait till then?"

"I'm fine. Seriously."

Ambrose shrugged. "Too bad we don't scar. That doozy would amp your toughness quotient by about a hundred percent. Have the girls swooning in the streets."

I leaned forward to give his shoulder a playful push.

"*Not* that that's what Vincent's trying for, of course," Ambrose backpedaled, holding one hand up in surrender. "It's just the first thing that would have crossed *my* mind. If I were in his place."

I shook my head and laughed. "Incorrigible. You are truly incorrigible, Ambrose."

He smiled his blinding white smile. "I try, Katie-Lou."

* * *

Back at La Maison, a group of revenants was assembled for an informational meeting on numas with Violette, and as we arrived everyone gathered around to hear the details about the dramatic rescue. What with the mass inquisition and the large buffet lunch that Jeanne had laid out, it wasn't until late afternoon that Vincent and I finally got a moment of peace.

We were settled in his room, sprawled on the couch in front of a crackling fire. Vincent's eyes were closed, and he seemed to be dozing off.

I didn't want to disturb him, but something had been bothering me ever since the accident that morning. "I know you're tired, but can we talk?" I asked, brushing his hair off his face with my fingers.

Vincent opened one eye and looked at me warily. "Should I be scared?" he asked, only half joking.

"No," I began, "it's just about this morning . . ."

I was interrupted by a polite tapping at the door. Vincent rolled his eyes and roared, "What is it now?"

The door opened, and Arthur leaned in. "My excuses. Violette had just one more question about the beheading of Lucien . . . ," he began.

"I have already told Violette every single detail of every numa encounter I have ever had," Vincent said with a groan. "I need one hour alone with Kate. Just one hour, and then I will join you and tell her everything I know. Again. Please, Arthur."

Arthur nodded, frowning, and closed the door behind him.

65

Vincent looked back at me, began to speak, and then shook his head and stood up. "In five minutes someone else will be back here, bugging us again. Let's go somewhere else. Put on your coat."

"Are you feeling strong enough to go out?" I asked as he threw on his coat and scooped some blankets out of a cupboard.

"We're not going out. We're going up." Taking my hand, he led me to the second floor, and then up another, smaller staircase at the far end of the hallway.

"What is this?" I gasped as we stepped through a trapdoor and onto the roof. Vincent lowered the door panel into its place in the floor and flicked a switch near the ground. White Christmas lights snapped on, illuminating a roof patio arranged with outdoor furniture: tables, chairs, and reclining lounge chairs.

"This is where we hang out during the summer. It's better than the courtyard garden. Less shade. More wind. And a decent view."

The whole city was spread out around us, the midwinter nightfall settling in early. Even though it was barely five o'clock, the sky was already changing from cotton candy pink into a rash of brilliant red in one of Paris's spectacular early-winter sunsets. Lights began twinkling from the buildings. "It's so magical up here," I sighed, drinking in the view.

I finally tore my eyes from the scene and turned to see Vincent standing just behind me, hands in his pockets. "So what did you want to talk about?" he asked, concern flickering across his face.

"What's wrong?" I asked, curious. "You look worried."

"Judging from the past, when you ask if we can talk instead of just going ahead and talking, I know I'm in trouble."

I smiled, and reached out to take his hand and pull him closer. "Fair enough. Okay, I was just wondering . . . this morning, before you ran for the truck, it looked like you were hesitating. Trying to make a decision. And it seemed like I was a part of that decision."

Vincent was silent, waiting for me to draw my own conclusion.

"You were going to go for the pedestrians first, to try to throw them out of the way, weren't you?"

"That was my instinct, yes." His face was blank. Unreadable.

"And why didn't you do it?" I asked, a cord of suspicion drawing tight in my stomach.

"Because there was a strong possibility of my own death if I took that route. And I promised you not to die."

I exhaled, surprised to find I had been holding my breath. "That's what I was afraid of, Vincent. That hesitation cost you a few seconds. What if that had been too much?"

"But it wasn't, Kate," he said, looking uncomfortable.

I put my arm through his and walked with him to sit on the edge of a large wooden sun bed that was pushed up against a low brick wall.

"Vincent, about our deal—you know, your promise to me—all along I've been regretting it, because I thought it was going to be too hard on you——"

"I told you, I can stand it," he interrupted me, frowning.

"And I have total faith in you. But whether or not you can stand it . . . I've been feeling like it was wrong of me to ask it of you."

"You didn't ask me to do it. I'm the one who offered," he said defensively.

"I *know*," I pleaded. "Just let me talk."

He sat, waiting to hear what I would say. Looking very unhappy.

"This whole time I've been worried about what your promise not to die meant for me. And for you. But I never thought about what it might mean for those people out there whose lives will be at risk. Someone might actually die because of me, Vincent. Because of my weakness."

He leaned forward and rubbed his forehead, squeezing his eyes shut, then turned to look me straight in the eyes. "Kate, it's not a weakness to be traumatized by death, especially after experiencing your own parents' death. It's not a weakness to want a normal relationship—one where you don't have to watch your boyfriend be carried home in a body bag a couple of times a year. No one is going to die because of *you*. I can still save people without dying. I just have to be more cautious."

"But you had to go against your instincts today. Isn't that risky?"

"Honestly, Kate, yes. But I was able to come up with a plan B. You saw . . . it was probably an even better plan to stop the truck, since it would have hit a car or maybe someone else if it had kept going. So in this case, not following my instinct was a good thing." He looked like he was trying to convince himself.

I hesitated. "Maybe that's why JB doesn't encourage human-revenant relationships. Because that's kind of what it comes down to, isn't it? If you're concerned about me, it will distract you from saving other people."

Vincent's face grew dark. "You mean more to me than anyone

else, and I will not apologize for that."

I felt chilled, but not from the winter air. "Are you saying that my life is more valuable than other people's? That, say, my one life is worth a couple you could have saved if you hadn't been worrying about me? Because, honestly, that would be pretty hard to live with."

Vincent took my hand back. "Kate, how long is a human life?"

"I don't know . . . eighty to ninety years, maybe?"

"And you are seventeen. This is horrible to say, but . . ."

His meaning dawned on me slowly. "I only have another sixty or something years to live. Tops. So you only have to hold out for that long."

His silence was as good as a yes. "During those years, the chances of a human dying because I *don't* will be slim to none. I always walk with my kindred, and if there's ever a life-or-death situation, they can be the ones to make the sacrifice.

"From my point of view, the time you and I have together is short. After that . . . I can spend the rest of eternity making up for lost lifesaving time, if that's how you want to think about it."

We sat in silence, the images called up by his words too disturbing for me to talk about out loud.

"Okay," I said finally. "Even so, Vincent, we're still left with the fact that you're going to spend the rest of my mortal life suffering. I'm sorry, but that doesn't sound like a cake-and-ice-cream lifetime to me. To be honest, it makes me want to call off our agreement."

His eyes opened wide. "No."

"I don't like to think about you going against your nature for me. I don't want to watch you suffer. Your dying for people—like you're supposed to—is the easiest solution to this whole mess. And I'm strong, Vincent. I think I can take it." The quaver in my voice gave me away.

A look of determination replaced his astonishment. He scooted closer and wrapped his arms around me. "Kate, knowing you, just thinking of my deaths will make you pull back from me. So please don't give up on this plan yet. Not before you give me the chance to figure things out. I'm working on a solution. A way to make it all work. Give me time."

As he held me, the last remaining threads of my resolve snapped. I shrugged, feeling powerless. "Vincent, if you think you can come up with something that will solve all our problems, then for God's sake, do it. I'm just saying I'm releasing you from your promise, not that I'm leaving you."

"I'm afraid you will leave me—for totally understandable self-preservation purposes—if you think I'm going to die," Vincent insisted. "So I won't. Our agreement is still on. Okay?"

I nodded, feeling awash in a sense of relief while at the same time kicking myself for it. "Okay."

Pulling back to see my face, he smiled ruefully and fingered a strand of hair that had fallen across my face. "Kate, I admit that we aren't in the easiest of situations. But are you always this . . . complicated?"

I opened my mouth to say something, but Vincent shook his head, grinning. "Actually, don't answer that. Of course you are. I wouldn't be so totally into you if you weren't."

I laughed. And just like that, the force field of fear and worry dematerialized and I was kissing him. And he was kissing me. And as we touched, everything suddenly seemed very simple. It was just Vincent and me, and the world and all its complicated problems lost their importance. I pulled him closer to me.

"You're . . . ," he began.

"Yes?" I said, tilting my head toward his.

"Hurting me," he gasped, clenching his teeth.

"Oh no, what did I do?" My hands flew to my mouth.

He pressed his hand to his chest and tested it gently. "I forgot about the rib," he said. We looked at each other for a second, and then both started cracking up, Vincent laughing carefully, his eyes scrunched up in pain.

"I guess I don't know my own strength," I joked, and leaned toward him again, holding him more softly this time and losing myself in the kiss. And then, in what seemed like seconds later, we were in the middle of the sun bed, Vincent lying down and me hovering above him on hands and knees with my hair draped around his face, sealing out the world. We were in our own mini universe. He reached up to hold my head in his hands as our lips met in a kiss that communicated everything we hadn't been able to express with words.

Vincent kissed me like it was his very last chance to touch me. And, feeling feverish and wild, I returned his kiss unreservedly.

As if he could tell I was losing myself, Vincent's kisses became softer. He pulled me down so that my body was covering his and every part of us was touching. Lying like that for the longest, sweetest moment, he brushed his lips against mine once more before sitting up, scooting back against the wall, and pulling me to him. I sat between his legs, leaning back carefully on his chest as he held me and we stared up into the night sky at the reflecting gold of the rising moon.

Unfolding Vincent's arms from beneath my breasts, I shifted around so that I was looking into his eyes. I didn't need to say anything. Watching him was enough. But after a moment, he spoke. "Kate, I've spent a lifetime waiting for you. Before I saw you, I hadn't cared for anyone for . . . well, for the good part of a century, and it felt like my heart had been permanently disconnected. I wasn't even looking anymore. And without expecting anything . . . without any hope at all, suddenly you were here."

He raised his hand, and running his fingers from my temples through my hair, he spoke softly. "Now that you are here—now that we're together—I can't imagine going back to the life I had before. I don't know what I'd do if I lost you now. I love you too much."

My throat constricted. He had said the magical three words. Out loud. When he registered my stunned expression, his lips curled up at the corners. "But you knew that already, didn't you?"

My heart became a gooey mess inside my chest, and then he said it again.

EIGHT

IT WASN'T UNTIL LATER THAT NIGHT THAT THE idea occurred to me. I had returned to my grandparents' apartment to find that they had left for a dinner party. Mamie had stuck a note to the fridge with dinner instructions. I pulled out the plate of leftovers she had prepared for me and sat at the table for a few minutes, picking at it distractedly as a plan took form in my mind.

Vincent had said he was trying to come up with a solution for our quandary. Well, why did I have to sit around and wait for him to come up with all the answers? Maybe I could do some research myself. I was living in an apartment with a fully stocked antiquities library. It wouldn't hurt to go digging around and see if I could discover something in Papy's book collection.

The previous year I had seen a Greek amphora in his gallery that was decorated with naked warrior figures he called "numina." His startled reaction when I forgot myself and stupidly remarked that the word sounded like "numa" made me suspect that he had come across the term before. And if he had found out about revenants in the course of his research, that book might still be around.

From everything I had heard at La Maison, revenants boasted a long and colorful history. Gaspard was constantly checking his documents for examples of past aberrations. Well, maybe Papy had some books that Gaspard didn't. In any case, if Vincent was searching for an alternative, one might actually exist. And maybe I could find some information he didn't already have.

There was still so much I didn't know. Vincent had told me the basics about revenants, and I had learned more by spending time with him and his kindred. Of course, I had searched for revenants on the internet as soon as I knew what Vincent was. But all I had found were references to the old French tradition of a revenant being a "spirit that has come back from the dead" and all sorts of contemporary spin-offs like zombies and other undead monsters. Nothing that spoke of "real" revenants—the ones I knew.

I asked Vincent once if "revenant" was just the word used in France. He said that most languages used that same word with little variation, because it came from the Latin word *venio*: "to come." So that was what I had to start with: the word "revenant"; a basic knowledge of what they were; the fact that their enemies were depicted on an ancient Greek vase; and . . . nothing else. It wasn't much to go on, but I was determined that if anything revenant-related remained in Papy's library, I would find it.

I left my barely touched meal and hurried to his study. All four walls were lined with shelves. And all the shelves were packed with books. I had no idea where to start. Although some titles were in French and English, that didn't even account for half. I recognized Italian and German, and Cyrillic letters clued me in that some books were Russian. At first glance, I felt completely overwhelmed.

Break it down, I thought. I started at the bookcase closest to the door, pulling up a footstool to reach the highest shelf. *The Church of Hagia Sofia. Architecture in the Ancient World. Roman Architecture and City Planning.* Papy obviously organized his books by themes. The shelf beneath it was the same. As was the next.

Underneath that began a shelf on Chinese funerary statues. And the bottom shelf was all about ancient Asian seals and snuffboxes. That was one whole column of shelves that could be ruled out, and it took only five minutes. This might be easier than I thought.

An hour later, I had narrowed down Papy's entire library to six shelves of interest. Although there were dozens of books on Greek pottery, I wasn't going to pore over all of them to find another example like Papy's numa amphora. Even if I was lucky enough to find one, it probably wouldn't have the in-depth information I needed. No, it was the shelves on mythology that I would focus on.

I began flipping through tomes on Greek, Roman, and Norse mythology. But they were all published in the twentieth century and were the type of books found in any library. Besides listing the major gods, the mythological beings were all the typical ones you'd come across in a Narnia book: satyrs, wood nymphs, and the like. No revenants. Of course.

If they had managed to stay incognito for so long, they wouldn't appear in a mainstream book. I began to skip anything that looked like it had been printed in the last hundred years and inspected more closely those that seemed to have been created on an ancient printing press. Papy protected most of these in archival boxes. One by one I pulled the boxes out, placed them on his desk, and gently went through their contents. Some were just pages of manuscript, and I studied the old parchments for any words that looked like "revenant" or "numa." Nothing.

Finally I got to an ancient-looking bestiary—a type of old-fashioned monster manual. The margins were illustrated with pictures of the mythical beings described on the page. Or so I assumed, since I couldn't make heads or tails of the Latin text.

Flipping past griffins and unicorns and mermaids, I came across a page with an illustration of two men. One was drawn with an evil face, and the other had radiant lines around its head like it was shining. Its entry was entitled "Revenant: Bardia/ Numa."

I shook my head in amazement. Trust Papy to have a book illustrating a species of undead beings who are so meticulous about preserving their identity that they're completely unknown to the modern world.

A shiver of excitement ran down my spine as I tried to decrypt the short paragraph beneath the heading. But besides those first three words, I didn't recognize a thing. I felt like kicking myself for not taking more than a year of Latin in middle school. I pulled a sheet of paper from Papy's printer and carefully copied the text onto it. When I finished, I put the book back in its place, grabbed the Latin dictionary off Papy's reference shelf, and retreated to my bedroom.

Due to Latin's weird verb tenses and the fact that there seemed to be no order to where words appeared in a sentence, I worked on the short text for quite a while. Finally I had deciphered enough to understand that it defined revenants as immortals who are divided into the guardians of life—*bardia*—and the takers of life—*numa*. That both types are limited by the same rules of "death sleep" and "spirit walking." That they take power from their human saves or kills. And that they are virtually impossible to destroy.

Well, nothing new there, I thought with a pang of disappointment. Except for the term "bardia." I wondered why the revenants didn't use it for themselves, since the word "numa" was obviously still current.

I looked back at my notes to translate a paragraph that had been written in smaller script at the bottom of the page. It was just two sentences, and I found them easier to decrypt than the rest, getting them pretty much word for word. As I deciphered them, I felt a chill creep through my body until, when I finished, my fingers felt numb.

"Woe to the human who encounters a revenant. For he has danced with death, being either delivered from or into its cold embrace."

I shivered, and glanced toward the clock as I heard my grandparents return. Midnight. I would have to continue my research another day. But having already discovered something on the first try, I was determined to find more.

NINE

AND LIKE THAT, THE HOLIDAYS WERE OVER AND I was back in school. Junior year had proven to be easy so far, and Georgia, in her last semester of high school, kept me from feeling lonely between classes. But the excitement of being with Vincent and the revenants made this facet of "real life" feel bland. School was just something I needed to get out of the way. I wasn't even thinking past graduation.

Georgia, however, had her future figured out. She would be starting a communications degree at the Sorbonne in the fall. And she had a new boyfriend, Sebastien, who not only *wasn't* an evil killer like her last boyfriend, but had no criminal record that I knew of and was actually really nice. Of course, he was in a band. But you couldn't be a nobody and date Georgia. Glamour and fame were her lowest common boyfriend denominators.

Georgia and I were on our way home after our post-holiday two-day school week and were passing the Café Sainte-Lucie when I heard someone shouting my name. I looked over to see Vincent in the café's front door, waving us over. "I hoped you would pass by," he said. Folding my hand in his, he steered us through the crowded room, where I saw a table full of revenants in the corner.

"Hi," I said, leaning in to give cheek-kisses to Ambrose and Jules as Vincent took two chairs from a nearby table and placed them between him and Violette.

"Georgia, meet Violette and Arthur." I gestured toward the newcomers. "This is Georgia, my sister."

Arthur nodded and stood formally, taking his seat again once Georgia had sat down.

"Let me guess," Georgia said, gawking appreciatively at his gallantry. "If it weren't for that divinely handsome mask, you'd probably look like the crypt-keeper. What are you, like . . . pre-Napoleonic? Friends of Louis XIV?"

Violette gasped and placed a protective hand on Arthur's shoulder. Her shock was offset by his look of amusement.

Ambrose cracked up. "Keep going backward, Georgia. You'll get there in a couple hundred years."

Georgia whistled, impressed. "It seems you have to hang with the geriatrics to find a true gentleman nowadays. Nice to meet you, Arthur."

Violette's ivory complexion turned puce. "Am I mistaken, or does every human in Paris know of our identity?"

Vincent smiled his charming smile at her and said, "Georgia had the distinction of finding out about us the hard way. She was the one who was friends with Lucien."

Violette inhaled sharply. "You are the human who is banned from entering the house."

"The one and only," said Georgia, brushing off Violette's comment with a laugh. "But I've always felt that any establishment that doesn't welcome me with open arms doesn't actually deserve my patronage."

Violette sat there staring at her, seemingly not understanding a word Georgia said.

"Translation . . . JB doesn't want me around—I don't want him around. I have better people to hang out with than stick-up-their-butt centuries-old royal-family wannabes." Georgia pronounced this in such a matter-of-fact way that the words didn't sound like as much of a slam as they really were. My sister—a master of diplomacy. *Oh Lord. Here we go.* I put my hand on Georgia's arm, but she just covered it with her own and stared defiantly at the tiny revenant.

As the meaning of Georgia's words finally sank in, Violette stood abruptly. In a voice low enough so only our table could hear, she sputtered, "Do you know what we do for you, you unappreciative human?"

Georgia looked thoughtfully at her fingernails. "Um, from what I understand, you go around saving people's lives in order to prevent yourselves from coming down with a supernatural case of delirium tremens."

After a second, the entire table burst out in laughter. Violette grabbed her coat off the back of her chair and strode out of the café. Arthur, trying unsuccessfully to stifle his amusement, stood, gave us a little bow, and followed her out.

"Touché, Georgia," Jules murmured appreciatively. "Violette could stand being taken down a notch, but don't expect to be BFFs now."

Georgia gave him a conspiratorial smile. "Hanging with the aristocracy has never been my style."

"So what are you guys up to?" I asked, hoping that the change of topic would shut Georgia up. I was going to have to do some apologizing once I saw Violette again.

"We were seeing Geneviève off," Vincent said, finishing his glass of Coke. "She's gone to the south to stay with Charlotte and Charles. Said she couldn't stand hanging around her house without Philippe in it."

I nodded, knowing how she felt. I couldn't wait to get out of our home in Brooklyn after Mom and Dad died. Everything I looked at reminded me of them—it was like living in a mausoleum.

"Now it's back to work, bringing Arthur and Violette up to speed with the Paris goings-on . . . at least it was until *you* drove them off." Jules winked at Georgia as she smiled demurely and raised her hand to attract the attention of a waiter.

As we left the café a half hour later, Vincent draped his arm around my shoulders. "Come back with us," he urged. "We're having a house meeting since no one's dormant today. It would be good if you were there."

"I'll see you back home," Georgia said. Since she wasn't welcome back at the house, she was clearly letting him off the hook as far as extending the invitation. After enthusiastically kissing each of the boys good-bye, she headed toward Papy and Mamie's.

Ten minutes later we were back in the great hall, just like a couple of months previously when Jean-Baptiste was handing out punishments and rewards after the numa battle and Lucien's death: exile for Charles and Charlotte and acceptance into the household for me.

The two new members of the kindred were seated on a leather couch in front of the fire, heads close together as they whispered heatedly. They seemed to be having an argument. I steeled myself and walked up to them.

"Violette?" I asked.

She peered up at me, seeming as fragile as a porcelain cup. "Yes?" she responded, looking away to nod at Arthur as if dismissing him before turning back to me. He stood and walked over to Jean-Baptiste and Gaspard, who were studying a map off in a corner.

"I just want to say that I'm sorry that my sister offended you. She can be like that sometimes, and I'm not making excuses for her, but I just want you to know that I don't feel the same way she does."

Violette thought for a second, and then solemnly nodded her head. "I would not judge you by your sister's words." She reached out to touch my hand. "What is that phrase you use in English . . . 'Sticks and stones'? I hold no offense," she said in her stilted language.

I breathed a silent sigh of relief. "Can I sit here?" I asked, motioning to an armchair next to her. She smiled evenly and said, "Of course."

"So . . ." I fished for a topic of conversation. "What have you and Arthur been doing for the last week?"

"We have been walking with the others—mainly Jean-Baptiste and Gaspard. They are introducing us to the territories of Paris. Arthur and I have been here before, but things have changed in the last century."

Surreal conversation, I thought for the millionth time. Although I was starting to get used to it.

"Is it weird to be away from your home?" I asked.

"Yes. We have lived in Langeais for a few centuries, so it does feel quite odd to have such a drastic change to one's routine. But, of course, it is for a good cause, helping Jean-Baptiste subdue the numa."

She leaned in closer and spoke earnestly, as if what she was asking was important and confidential. "And you, Kate? How does it feel to be outside of the world *you* are used to—having fallen in with immortals? Do you ever wish you could go back to the normal life of a human girl?"

I shook my head. "No. That life was over for me anyway. At least, that's what it felt like. My parents died around a year ago. When I found Vincent"—or was it when he found me? I wondered—"I might as well have been dead too."

"It is a strange choice for a beautiful, vibrant girl to spend her time with the undead."

She really did sound like an old lady at times. "I feel accepted here," I said simply.

Raising a perfectly shaped eyebrow, she nodded and then took my hand and squeezed it, in what felt like a gesture of solidarity. Girl-to-girl in a house full of men.

"Is everyone here?" Jean-Baptiste strode to the place of authority in front of the fire and looked around the room. "Good," he said.

I felt someone touch my shoulder and looked up to see Vincent standing behind my chair. He gave me a sexy wink, and then fixed his attention on the older man.

"We all know about the drop-off in numa activity since Lucien's death. It's as if they've disappeared. But why? What could they be waiting for?"

"May I?" Gaspard asked, raising a trembling finger and facing us. "They've always been undisciplined in the past. Although Lucien was their leader, he could never seem to stop them from occasionally acting on individual initiatives. But, as we've mentioned, judging from their recent behavior, we suspect they may have a new leader—one who is actually able to keep them under control. And Violette has now confirmed that suspicion." He waved a hand toward the revenant beside me, as if handing her the mic.

"I cannot say that it is exactly 'confirmed,'" Violette piped up. "But there have been rumors. My sources have mentioned a numa from overseas—from America, more specifically—who has begun positioning himself as an international leader."

There were exclamations of surprise around the room. Ambrose spoke up. "I've never heard of something like this. I mean, we have our international Consortium, but the numa? I can't even imagine it. It's not in their nature to work together."

Violette nodded. "I agree that *if* it is true, it is unprecedented. But from what I have heard, the numa in question was a man of great power during his lifetime. People trusted him with their fortunes, and he deceived them all, sending many to ruin and several to suicide."

"How did he die then?" I asked.

"Killed in prison," she replied simply.

"So what's this mean for us?" asked Jules. For once, his expression was serious.

Jean-Baptiste took the imaginary podium. "Violette has her sources, and we hope that they continue to feed her information. But we can begin to contact our kindred elsewhere to see if they have heard anything else on the matter.

"In the meantime, we should strengthen our defenses. Step up our surveillance. And, as I discussed with a couple of you, I am lifting the ban on offensive—" I felt Vincent's body tense behind me, and as Jean-Baptiste's eyes flitted to him, the older revenant stopped in the middle of his sentence, casting the room into an uncomfortable silence.

"May I interrupt at this point?" came a melodic voice from across the room. Everyone stared at its source. This was the first time I had heard Arthur speak: He was constantly brooding away in some corner, scribbling in a notebook. Everyone else seemed just as surprised by this uncharacteristic outburst.

Arthur shot a look at Violette, who clenched her jaw and

glared at him. *Okay*, I thought, *this must have something to do with the argument I interrupted.*

"Perhaps I am stating the obvious, but we are discussing sensitive strategic information in the presence of one who is not of our kind."

What? The blood drained from my face as I felt everyone stealing glances my way. I stared at Arthur, but he avoided my eyes, smoothing a blond lock behind his ear, as if he needed to do something with his hands.

Vincent's hands clamped my shoulders like steel vises. I looked up to see that his face had turned to stone, and had a hunch that if revenant superpowers included shooting flames from their eyes, Arthur would be a revenant barbecue.

Everyone was silent, waiting. Arthur cleared his throat and glanced back toward Violette. Her tiny fingers clenched the arm of the couch, her fingernails digging into the leather.

"Although I allow that humans have interacted with us throughout history, except for the rarest of cases, like our own Geneviève's marriage, serious interaction with humans has always been on an employer-employee basis. I realize that this human has done you a service by killing your foe. But I must question her presence in a tactical meeting involving the protection and survival of our own."

He might as well have slapped me in the face. Tears came unbidden to my eyes, and I wiped them angrily away. Within a second Jules and Ambrose were on their feet, facing Arthur like they were in some kind of gang rumble. Vincent pulled me back toward him as if he could physically protect me from Arthur's words.

Arthur held up his hands in a gesture of innocence. "Wait, kindred. Please hear me out. I do not know Kate as well as you, but I have seen her enough to know she is a good and trustworthy human." He finally dared to meet my eyes, and his look was apologetic. I didn't care. Apology not accepted. "I am not suggesting that she is not welcome here among us," he continued. "Only that she not be involved in this meeting. For her own safety, as well as our own."

There was a cacophony of voices as everyone began speaking—or rather yelling—at once. Jean-Baptiste raised a hand and barked, "Silence!" He looked at each person in the room for a second, as if measuring their feelings in the matter, ending his silent inquisition with me. "Kate, my dear," he said in his noble monotone, which made the "dear" sound anything but endearing, "forgive me for asking you to take your leave from this meeting."

Vincent began to speak up, but Jean-Baptiste raised a hand to silence him. "Just this once, until we settle this matter with our newcomers. I want everyone to feel comfortable with the situation, and Arthur and Violette have not yet had the time to acquaint themselves with your presence here. Would you do me the very great favor of excusing us on this one occasion?"

I shot Arthur the meanest glare I could muster, knowing that it had to be pretty lame: My eyes were red from stifled tears of humiliation. *His* eyes looked empty, but he held my gaze until I broke it. Lifting my chin, I gathered every shred of my tattered pride together as I stood.

"I'll walk you to my room," Vincent whispered, laying a hand on my arm.

"No, I'm fine," I said, backing away from him. "I'll wait for you there." Unable to look at the others, I left the hall.

Instead of going back to Vincent's room, I went to the kitchen, hoping to find comfort from the only other human in the house. I pushed my way through the swinging door into the kitchen, where Jeanne bustled around with trays of food. She put the kettle on the stove as soon as she saw me and came over to give me two energetic cheek-kisses.

"Kate, darling, how are you, my little cabbage?" She held me back and got a look at my red face and eyes. "My dear! What is the matter?"

"I was just kicked out of a house meeting for being human."

"What? But I don't understand. I am very surprised that Jean-Baptiste would take that position after everything that has happened."

"It wasn't Jean-Baptiste. It was Arthur," I said, sitting down at the table. Accepting Jeanne's offer of a Kleenex, I dabbed the corners of my eyes. "He said I might endanger the safety of the household."

"Now, I can't imagine him saying something like that," Jeanne said unsurely, sitting down across from me and pushing a plate of homemade honey-scented madeleines my way. She thought for a moment and then seemed to relent. "Arthur and Violette are . . . how would you say . . . 'old school,' perhaps? They are from nobility. And where they once looked down on the peasants, they now feel the same way about humans. It doesn't mean they aren't good people. It just means they're ... snobs."

I laughed, hearing Jeanne use the derogatory term. She was always so positive about everyone and everything. For her to call Violette and Arthur snobs must mean they were raging immortal bigots.

"They're here to do good work, Kate. Even if they aren't the most pleasant people, they know a lot and have been around longer than anyone else. And seeing their preference for isolation, I doubt they'll stay for long. Before you know it, things will be back to normal."

I nodded, munching on a cookie, and tried to reason that my own pride shouldn't stand in the way of the safety of the group. It's not like I *deserved* to be included in their most secret discussions. I was not a revenant. I was the exception to the rule. Who was I kidding? I didn't belong.

I could feel my mood getting darker by the second. "I'm leaving," I said, throwing my arms around Jeanne's neck. "Thanks. It's nice to talk to someone who understands. Sometimes I feel like I'm living in an alternate universe when I'm here."

"Well, you basically are, *chérie*," Jeanne said as she let me go and tightened her apron. "You won't be staying for dinner?"

"No. Please tell Vincent I went home, and that he can call me later," I said. She gave me an understanding look and threw me an air-kiss from her position in front of the stove as I made my way out.

I wandered through the house and out the front door into the courtyard. Passing the angel fountain, I stepped inside and made my way across the empty basin to its figures. Angel. Human. Two separate entities carved out of one block of marble. I ran my fingers over the angel's arm. It was as cold as Vincent's when he was dead.

TEN

THE DOORBELL RANG AS SOON AS I SAT DOWN ON
my bed. A couple of seconds later there was a knock on my bedroom door.

"Katya, darling. It's Vincent. He's coming up."

"Thanks, Mamie," I said, opening the door. My grandmother
stood before me, dressed in her "going-out" outfit of three-inch
heels and a calf-length skirt. She didn't have an ounce of fat on
her, and her fashion choice boldly flaunted the best legs I had
ever seen on a senior citizen.

"What's wrong?" she asked, zoning in on my expression.

"Oh, nothing," I said automatically, and then, seeing she wasn't
going to move until I answered, I asked, "Mamie, have you ever
been in a situation where you were purposely made to feel like an
outsider? Like you didn't belong?"

Mamie crossed her arms over her waist and gazed at the ceiling. "Your grandfather's family made me feel like that in the

beginning. It was a case of his parents' old money versus my family's new money, and they made me feel like an arriviste."

"But that changed?"

"Yes. When they saw that I didn't give a hoot what they thought about me. I think that was one reason your grandfather fell for me. I was the only woman who ever had the guts to stand up to his mother."

I couldn't help but smile.

Mamie took my hand. Her gardenia perfume hadn't changed since I was a little girl, and the fragrance made me feel grounded. She had known me my whole life. She'd been there in the hospital when I was born.

And even so, I can't tell her what is really bothering me, I thought. I trusted Mamie with my life but couldn't imagine how she would react if I told her what Vincent was. If she even believed me and didn't take me to a psychiatrist on the spot. Her goal was to protect me, and I was guessing that the job of protecting your granddaughter would not involve allowing her to date a revenant.

"This transition must be hard for you," I heard Mamie saying. I refocused on her concerned face. "Moving from Brooklyn to Paris. Starting a new school. Making new friends. It probably feels like you're living in a whole new world. Perhaps a scary one at that."

As I let her hug me close, I thought, *Oh, Mamie, you have no idea.*

* * *

Vincent was waiting in the hallway when I opened our door. His alarmed expression faded when he saw that I wasn't visibly upset. "Kate, I'm so sorry," he said, taking me in his arms. I closed my eyes and let myself bask in the hug for a few seconds before pulling him into the apartment.

"Hello, Vincent, dear," Mamie said, walking up behind us and standing on her tiptoes to give him the customary cheek-kisses. "How have you been?" she asked.

My grandparents loved Vincent, which definitely made my life easier. While they always questioned Georgia about her where-abouts, all I had to do was say I was going out with Vincent and there were no more questions asked. Another good reason not to rock the boat.

"I'll just leave you two alone now," she said after they'd caught up, steering us into the living room and closing the glass doors behind us. The room was crammed with antiques, artifacts, and paintings, and it smelled like a cross between a musty library and a Bedouin tent.

I settled on the couch next to a vase of cut flowers, one of several that Mamie scattered through the rooms, letting you walk through a cloud of freesia or lilac or something else delicious, before moving back into the ancient-odor zone. Vincent positioned himself in an armchair right in front of me.

"I can't apologize enough for what happened back there," he said. "You know that no one else agrees with Arthur."

"I know," I said, though I was aware that Jean-Baptiste hadn't exactly been jumping for joy when he'd officially welcomed me into his house. But since that day, he had been nothing but courteous.

"I just can't figure it out," Vincent said, looking bothered. "Arthur's such a good guy. I mean, even though he and Violette act like they're God's gift to revenants at times, he has never been intentionally exclusive or petty."

"Maybe he was just being honest," I said. "Maybe he actually does think that it's dangerous for me to hear your plans."

"Well, he could have mentioned it before, instead of bringing it up in front of everyone." He brought his hand up to touch my cheek, and I grasped it and pulled it to my lips before dropping it to my lap.

"I'm fine, really," I said, although the humiliation still felt cold in the pit of my stomach. "What *is* up with Arthur and Violette, though? They seem to argue like an old married couple, but I've never seen them touch. Are they together?"

Vincent laughed, and got up to finger one of Papy's ancient figurines that sat atop the fireplace mantel. "They are not together—in the sleeping-together sense of the word." He lifted an eyebrow. "But you kind of got it right with the 'old married couple' reference. Arthur considers himself Violette's protector. They're from the time when women were thought to need protection, of course," he added, grinning.

"Arthur was Violette's father's counselor, and they both died in the same kidnapping attempt. So I guess it's natural that they would stay together all this time, but I know that 'love' is not the nature of their relationship. Codependence, maybe, but not love."

"How do you know that?" I asked, intrigued by the suddenly sheepish look on his face.

"Oh, Violette and I have a bit of a history. I've met her a few times over the years. Whenever Jean-Baptiste found a previously undiscovered text that he thought was particularly important, he had me take it to her for inspection. She wasn't exactly shy about confessing her feelings for me."

I gasped. "Violette was in love with you?"

"Love is a strong word. But yes, she told me she was interested. I couldn't reciprocate. But"—he glanced fleetingly at me, and then back to the figurine—"I was actually tempted to give it a try. I thought it might be my only chance at finding someone to be with."

I realized I was gaping at him. "But Vincent, she's only fourteen. That's kind of . . . I don't know . . . pervy."

"She was in her twenties at the time," Vincent said, pressing his lips together to stifle a smile.

"Oh, yeah. Right," I said, trying to process this weird new information.

"Nothing happened," he reassured me. "At all. But I guess Violette sensed I might be open to it, and that probably encouraged her. We went out a couple of times, but as soon as I realized I couldn't make myself feel something that wasn't there, I ended it. I hadn't actually seen her since then—it's probably been about forty years. I asked JB to send another emissary on those errands."

"She's got to resent me for being with you, then." I recalled Violette's slipup at Philippe's funeral—about revenants who were with humans—and wondered if she hadn't actually said it on purpose. A little jab at the human who had succeeded in doing what she hadn't: capturing Vincent's heart.

"Actually, she's talked to me about you already," Vincent said. "She was pretty gracious about it and congratulated me on finding such a 'lovely young lady.'" His imitation of her voice and ancient speech style made us both laugh. "No, seriously, she seems to really like you."

"So it's just Arthur who's being a jerk?" I ventured.

"Seems like," he said, "even though that's so untypical of him. He took off right after the meeting, obviously to avoid me. Violette asked me to forgive him. She said she had warned him not to bring it up but that he had felt obliged. She was going to talk to him later."

"That was nice of her," I said, warming to the strange girl. "It's over, anyway. I just want to forget about it now."

And as I mentally turned the page on the afternoon's humiliation, something occurred to me. "Vincent, I found something about revenants in Papy's library last night."

"Really?" It was rare that I surprised Vincent instead of the other way around, but right now he looked like if I pushed him with one finger, he would keel right over. "Can I see it?"

I led him to the study, peeking in first to make sure Papy wasn't there. Checking the clock on his desk, I saw that he wouldn't be closing the gallery for another half hour. We were safe.

I pulled the bestiary out of its protective box and, placing it on Papy's desk, turned to the revenant page. Vincent's eyebrows shot up as he saw the illustrations. "Wow, this is really rare, Kate. There is almost nothing about revenants remaining in human book collections."

"Why not?"

He went on staring at the book as he spoke. "Dealers like your grandfather know that if they find anything, they can sell it for a fortune to a group of anonymous buyers. These collectors snatch up anything revenant-related before it even comes on the market." Vincent glanced at me. "JB's one of them. He has stacks of these old manuscripts in his library. I doubt Gaspard's even worked his way through half of them."

"Yeah, well, Papy must really treasure it, then," I said, wondering why he would pass up a good sale to keep the book in his library. Maybe he hadn't seen the revenant page and didn't realize its value.

Vincent's attention was back on the book, and he mouthed the words to himself, following along with his finger. "You know Latin?" I asked.

He smiled. "Yes, it used to be required in schools before people decided that dead languages weren't good for anything. Do you want to know what it says?"

"I actually had an attempt at decoding it last night," I admitted.

"Of course you did," Vincent said, his eyes glimmering with amusement. "I can't imagine you turning down that kind of challenge." He looked back down at the book, and as he read the article aloud in English, I was pleased that I had gotten the gist of it myself. When he was done, I didn't point out the fact that he had purposely skipped the last two lines. If I were in his place, I wouldn't want him to think he was cursed to be with me.

"So what's the deal with the 'bardia' term?" I asked. "If that's actually what you are, why do you call yourselves 'revenants'?"

"Good question," responded Vincent. "I guess it's just kind of gone out of style." He mulled it over for a second. "Actually, it's probably a kind of superiority thing—we think we're the real deal, while the numa are more like deviants. You can ask Gaspard about it, but I think 'bardia' is based on a word that means 'to guard,' so it would actually be the more accurate term for us. It's used in our official documents. But say 'bardia' to Ambrose or Jules and they will definitely look at you funny." He flipped through the book's pages once more before putting it back in its box and placing it carefully in its niche in the bookcase.

"Vincent? When Jean-Baptiste was talking to us today, he said something about going on the offensive. And I felt like there was something you didn't want him to say. Like there was this weird kind of face-off between the two of you before Arthur cut in and voted me out of the meeting. What was that about?"

A strange expression crossed Vincent's face. Pulling me to my feet, he said, "It doesn't matter. And if it ever does, I will tell you about it. But for now, let's talk about something more interesting."

"Like what?" I asked.

"Like where I'm going to take you to dinner tonight," Vincent said, and, grasping me lightly by the hips, drew me toward himself and bent down for a kiss. Any lingering doubts I had melted as quickly as snowflakes over a bonfire.

ELEVEN

I WOKE UP THE NEXT MORNING TO A MIXTURE OF
excitement and dread. I had fight training with Gaspard and Vincent today, and even though I loved the actual fighting, I still felt
way below par with my skills. My first lesson, barely a month ago,
had been a disaster. We had concentrated solely on the sword,
which seemed easy enough when we were walking slow-motion
through moves, but as soon as Gaspard sped things up a notch, I
was useless.

Fighting seemed like dancing to me, and besides not having
much natural rhythm, I've always felt a bit stupid on the dance
floor. This definitely carried over into my lessons. My self-
consciousness made me clumsy, and I was so afraid of looking
like a weak, defenseless novice that I actually became what I
feared most.

However, by the fourth lesson I found myself becoming
engrossed in the movements. It was like my self-hypnosis sessions

in museums or at the river—I let myself zone out, and all of a sudden the moves seemed to come by themselves. It was a kind of yin-yang phenomenon, where my subconscious took over and my brain shut off. As soon as I stopped thinking about what I was doing, everything worked.

The awkward moments were becoming shorter and shorter, and lately it took just a few steps back and forth before the switch flipped and I was on autopilot.

Today will be an autopilot day, I reassured myself as I threw on some jeans and a sweater and made my way blearily to the breakfast table. Papy was already sitting there, dressed for work and reading his morning paper. "Up so early?" he asked, lowering the paper to meet my eyes.

"Exactly why my teacher insists on a lesson at nine a.m. on Saturday, I don't quite get. But I know better than to keep him waiting," I said, pouring myself some grapefruit juice and grabbing a croissant off the counter.

When I had (somewhat hesitantly) told Mamie and Papy that Vincent had gotten me fencing lessons for my birthday, they were delighted—to my astonishment. I hadn't realized how popular the sport was in France, or that it had aristocratic connotations. My grandparents weren't pretentious, but working in the art-and-antiques world gave them an appreciation for anything grounded in history. And what was more historical than swordplay?

Papy went all out and bought me my own suit and épée. I didn't explain to him that Vincent's gym housed a fully stocked armory, or that fencing was just one component of my fight training. He would have to buy a battle-ax, quarterstaff, and a half-dozen other weapons to keep up with Gaspard's training regime.

My grandfather gestured toward a vase of flowers on the hall table. "Found those in the vestibule when I picked up my paper this morning." A brightly colored nosegay was nestled in a small round vase, with a gift-wrapped package sitting next to it. I opened it and pulled out a book entitled *Le Langage des Fleurs*. "*The Language of Flowers*," I whispered to myself and, opening it, saw an inscription on the title page:

> *For Kate. You're already fluent in two languages. I thought a third wouldn't hurt. Your homework assignment accompanies this book. With affection, Violette de Montauban.*

Glancing at the tiny bouquet, I flipped through the pages to look up yellow roses and purple hyacinths and, grinning, shoved the book into my bag and called "*Au revoir*" to Papy.

Once out the door, I looked around for Vincent, my heart beating a little faster in expectation of seeing him waiting for me, leaning up against the park fence like he usually did. Which is why my heart dropped when I saw Jules there instead. I quickly rearranged my look of disappointment into a careful smile, but he noticed anyway.

"Sorry I'm not your boyfriend. And I mean that in all sorts of ways," he said with an amused smile as he leaned forward to kiss me on each cheek.

"Where's Vincent?" I asked, taking the arm he offered as we

headed toward his house.

"He's off doing something for Jean-Baptiste," Jules said, glancing down at the sidewalk as if he was afraid I would read his mind.

Which sent warning bells off in my head.

I thought back to the awkward stare-down between Vincent and JB at the house meeting, and then to Vincent's elusiveness last night when I asked what it had been about. There was definitely something going on that he didn't want me to know.

"And he didn't think I could find my own way to your house?" I asked, feigning nonchalance.

"Yeah, um . . . Vincent's been a bit jumpy lately. About your human vulnerability. With the numa poised to attack at any moment, it's kind of got him spooked."

"Do you think he's overreacting? About my vulnerability, that is," I asked, looking sideways at him. Okay, I was fishing. But I was hoping I could get more information out of flirty Jules.

"Kate, you are totally kick-ass. But you are still made of flesh and blood. Non-reanimating flesh, that is. So I have to say that I get where Vincent's coming from."

I nodded, wishing with all my might that I was as indestructible as them. If I were Charlotte. Or Violette, for God's sake: fourteen years old, and everyone treated her like she was made of steel. *Respect*, I reflected. *It's hard to demand respect when something as tiny as a bullet could remove you from existence. Permanently.*

"So am I going to get an escort to and from school?" I asked, wondering how far Vincent would go with his paranoia.

"*Non*," Jules laughed. "It's just that Violette got a tip-off yesterday that the numa are on the move. She's worried that they might be monitoring our house. It's only because you're coming to our place that Vincent thought you should have an escort. Don't worry: After this morning, you can fend for yourself." And he mock-punched me in the arm. I hit him back . . . hard. "Damn, girl, you pack a mean punch," he teased me, which set off a mock scuffle that lasted the rest of the way to La Maison.

Gaspard was waiting for me in the gym, doing some kind of tai-chi-looking stretching exercises. He finished his movement, gave me a slight bow, and then chatted with Jules while I went to put my padded fight outfit on. It was made of a type of slate gray Kevlar that protected me from the more extreme blades in the revenants' armory. I felt a bit guilty about the expensive, classic-white fencing costume Papy had bought me, which hung untouched in the armory closet. But this higher-tech suit, although it made me look scarily like Kate Beckinsale in *Underworld*, kept me from getting the nicks and cuts that didn't bother the revenants.

Jules whistled appreciatively as I walked over to them and took the sword Gaspard held out toward me. "Kate, you look positively . . . lethal," he murmured.

"I'll take that as a compliment." I smiled, knowing that the outfit emphasized my good points. Too bad I never wore it outside of the armory. *I'll have to be a vampire slayer for Halloween*, I thought.

"As much as I'd love to stay and watch you in action," Jules said, grinning, "I've got to run. Be back in an hour to pick you up." And he jogged up the stairs, closing the door behind him.

I should have jogged right out the door after him. Because the next half hour was unquestionably my worst training ever. Not only was I distracted by thoughts of what Vincent could be up to, but I was used to training with both him and Gaspard. Without Vincent there, ready to jump in every few minutes to let me catch my breath, I finally had to signal Gaspard to stop. "Time-out," I called breathlessly, as he lowered his sword.

I staggered to the edge of the room and slid down the wall, putting my head between my knees as I tried to catch my breath. When I looked up, Gaspard was standing above me, holding out a bottle of water.

"Thanks," I said. "It's a lot harder when Vincent's not here to pick up my slack."

"Is that all it is, my dear? You seem rather . . . distracted today."

I looked at the older revenant, guessing that he would have a hard time flat-out lying to me. "Actually, I was wondering what Vincent was up to this morning. Jules didn't seem to know. Do you?" I asked as innocently as possible, feeling a little bit guilty for prying.

Gaspard eyed me cautiously. "I really can't say," he responded in his formal nineteenth-century style.

Can't, or won't? I thought. *Gaspard and Jules know something I don't. And Vincent says it's not important enough to talk about.* I suspected that Vincent was trying to protect me. To shield me from a situation he didn't want me to know about. I could only imagine that it was something I wouldn't like or there would be no reason for this subterfuge. *I trust him*, I thought. *So why does this one case of secrecy make me want to scream?*

"Okay, I'm ready," I said, pushing myself up off the wall. Gaspard smoothed his hair off his face and readjusted his short ponytail before arranging himself into a fighting stance. I picked up my sword and, with my newly acquired frustration-driven energy, began hacking away at him as if he were Lucien resurrected.

"Now *that's* more like it!" my instructor exclaimed with a smile.

We fought for another half hour, until I backed away from the fight and hung my sword on an empty hook on the wall. I held up my hands and gasped, "That's it for me!"

The sound of clapping came from the stairway. "Brava!" called Violette. She was perched on the steps in a comfortable position that made it look like she had been there for a while. "You are really very good, Kate!"

I smiled and, catching a towel that Gaspard threw me, swabbed the sweat from my face. "Thanks, Violette. Although I have a feeling that with your centuries of experience you're just saying that to be nice."

She smiled coyly, as if I had caught her, and said, "Not at all. For the little training you have been given, you must have natural talent."

"Exactly my point of view," Gaspard affirmed. "So, Violette—do you need me for something?" he asked.

"No. Jules wanted to go to his studio, so I told him I'd walk Kate home and sent him on his way," she said. "Take your time, though."

"Thanks," I said, peeling off the top of my fight suit and exposing my "I Heart New York" tank top beneath. I had been sweating so much, the heavy fabric was starting to make me feel claustrophobic. "And thanks so much for the book and the flowers."

"Arthur behaved so badly the other day, I felt it was up to me to make amends. Did you figure out the message?"

"Yes," I said, pulling off the trousers and adjusting the gray jersey gym shorts I had worn underneath. "Purple hyacinths say 'sorry' and yellow roses, 'friendship.'"

"Very good," she said, delighted. "The hyacinths were in hopes that you will forgive Arthur his insensitivity, and the roses my wish that you and I can be friends."

Even though I didn't want to seem overeager, I couldn't stop a smile from spreading across my face. Charlotte had been gone barely over a week, and already I was suffering girlfriend withdrawal. I had Georgia, of course. But she was so busy with her own social life that it left me with a lot of free time—which Vincent usually didn't mind filling. But now that he was off doing whatever . . . "Hey, instead of walking me home, do you want to grab some lunch with me once I've showered?" I asked.

"Yes!" she exclaimed brightly. "*Grabbing* lunch"—she faltered at the modern colloquialism—"would be lovely. I will wait for you upstairs."

I practically skipped to the shower, where I speed-washed and dressed. "Thanks, Gaspard!" I called as I ran up the steps to the ground floor.

"The pleasure was all mine," he said, smiling slightly as he performed a stiff little bow, and went back to cleaning the various weapons he had pulled off the wall.

Before I could get halfway down the hallway, Arthur appeared, his face buried in a book as he barreled out of a doorway. "Vi," he called, and then looked up and saw me. His face went from normal to freaked out in a second flat, and his forehead scrunched up in a dozen little lines.

"Yes, dear. You were calling me?" Violette glided up behind Arthur, smiling as if no previous weirdness had happened between us and we were all just there for a pleasant chat.

"I just found something in Heidegger that I thought would interest you," he said in a monotone, glancing between me and Violette.

"Kate and I are going out for lunch. You'll have to show it to me later," she said, taking my arm and staring at him, as if daring him to say something.

She wants him to apologize, I thought.

Arthur gave Violette a look that couldn't be translated as anything other than a glare.

"Come on, Kate. We should go," Violette said. I left arm in arm with my defender, but couldn't help glancing back at Arthur. He stood immobile in the hallway, glowering.

"Do not mind him," Violette whispered. "He can be so terribly temperamental. Sometimes I love him dearly. Other times I wish he would . . . how do you say it . . . buzz off?"

I laughed out loud as we walked through the foyer and out the front door.

We sat across from each other in a tiny restaurant, eating steaming bowls of French onion soup while gazing through the window at the covered market outside. The aroma of flame-grilled chicken hung deliciously on the air. And the market stalls were a visual delight, filled to overflowing with seafood, vegetables, and flowers. Behind them, vendors called out to the Saturday afternoon shopping crowd, extolling the virtues of their fruits, while holding out samples for people to taste.

"I do not think I have ever been here before," Violette admitted, after primly wiping a strand of melted cheese from her lips with her napkin.

"It's the oldest market in Paris," I said. "I think it was around four hundred years ago that it was transformed into a market from an orphanage that dressed its children in red. Which is why it's called the *Marché des Enfants Rouges*."

"Market of the Red Children," Violette mused in English.

"You speak English?" I gasped.

"Of course I do," she responded. "I learned it quite a while ago, although I have not had much of an occasion to use it recently. But if you wish, we can speak in your mother tongue. It will be good practice for me."

"Deal!" I said enthusiastically, pausing when I saw her look at me quizzically. "And I'll try to stay away from using slang"—I smiled—"to make it easier on you."

"No, no!" she insisted. "Charlotte was right when she said I needed to be in step with the times. Where better could I learn twenty-first-century language and mannerisms—in English—than from a twenty-first-century American girl?"

"Actually, if you really mean that, I have an idea. Do you like films?"

"Are you referring to the cinema?"

"Yes. Besides reading and hanging out in museums, going to the movies is my absolute favorite thing to do." I scraped the last spoonful of the delicious soup from my bowl and finished off my glass of Perrier.

"Kate, I must admit," Violette said, looking embarrassed. "I have never been to the cinema. It has not been around that long, you know, and I just cannot see the point. Like you, I would rather spend my time reading a book or looking at art."

"But film *is* art! In fact, it's the French who dubbed it 'The Seventh Art.'" I thought for a second. "Do you have anything to do after lunch?"

Violette shook her head with an expression of alarm as she realized what she had gotten herself into.

I reached under the table for my book bag, pulled out a worn copy of *Pariscope*—the weekly guide for Paris events—and flipped back to the cinema section. Scanning the classic film pages, I searched for something that would be worthy of someone's *very first film ever*.

A few hours later I squinted in the bright January sun, as Violette
and I walked out the doors of a vintage-film cinema. Above us
hung a billboard for Alfred Hitchcock's *Notorious*.

"So," I asked, glancing toward her. "What did you think?"

A broad grin—the grin of a fourteen-year-old, for once, instead
of a centuries-wizened old woman—spread across Violette's face.
"Oh, Kate. It was amazing." Her voice was hushed with awe. She
grabbed my hand. "When can we do it again?"

TWELVE

VINCENT CALLED THAT NIGHT, APOLOGIZING FOR disappearing for the day. He had already sent a couple of texts, and from their tone, he was obviously feeling guilty about something and trying to make up for it.

"It's okay, Vincent. I actually spent the whole day with Violette."

"You did?" Although he sounded tired, I could hear the surprise in his voice.

"Yeah, she was supposed to walk me home, but I took her out for lunch instead. What was up with the numa alert, anyway? Jules said some might be lurking around your neighborhood."

"Nothing. It was a bad tip, actually. Violette told Jean-Baptiste to call off the alert tonight. Everything's as it was before: invisible numa ready to jump out when we least expect it."

"Well, you were right about Violette. She's actually really nice. It's just Arthur with the 'humans suck' attitude problem. I think

I'm just going to avoid him as much as possible."

"That's probably a good plan." Vincent sounded exhausted and distracted. Whatever he had been up to today, it had definitely taken its toll. He didn't sound like himself.

"Vincent, I'd better go. You sound beat."

"No, no. I want to talk," he said quickly. "So tell me: What are you doing, *mon ange*?"

"Reading."

"Not surprising," he laughed, "coming from Paris's most voracious devourer of books. Is it something I've read?"

I flipped to the front of the book. "Well, it was published four years after you were born, but was banned for most of your life—existence. At least in its uncensored version."

"Written in 1928 but banned for years. Hmm. Does it have a passage about entering the peace on earth, by any chance?"

"Vincent, you skipped straight to the sex scene! *Lady Chatterley's Lover* is about a lot more than a tumble in the gamekeeper's hut, you know!" I chided jokingly.

"Mmm. Tumbling sounds really good about now."

My heart hiccuped, but I tried to sound calm. "You know, that *is* one of my favorite daydreams. Tumbling with you, not gamekeepers." I grinned, wondering what effect my taunting was having on him.

"Are your grandparents home?" he asked after a pause, his voice sounding suspiciously husky.

"Yes."

He cleared his throat. "Good thing, or I'd have to come over and ravish you on the spot. They *do* talk about ravishing in that book, don't they?"

I laughed. "I haven't gotten to any ravishing parts yet. But ravishing and tumbling . . . I'm not sure I'm available for that, since I have a date with this hot dead dude tomorrow night."

"Okay, I get it. A very wise change of subject." He laughed. "So . . . you haven't forgotten?" I could hear his tired smile over the phone line.

"Forget a date to see the Bolshoi Ballet at the Opéra Garnier? In our own private theater box? Uh, no—I don't think that would be possible."

"Good," he said. "Be there at six to pick you up." These last words were barely audible. It sounded like he was not only tired but in pain. What had he been doing? Now I was past curiosity and entering very concerned territory.

"See you then. Can't wait . . . ," I said, and as I hung up I finished the sentence in my mind: *to find out what you're up to.* If he was as worn down tomorrow night as he sounded now, I might just be able to convince him to talk.

Vincent stood outside my door dressed in his tux, his black hair pushed back off his face in waves. It was like a repeat of my birthday evening: him in his tux and me in the red Asian-patterned long dress he had bought me, worn under Mamie's floor-length black-hooded coat. Vincent's eyes shone appreciatively when he saw me, and once we were out on the street, he gave me a long and delicious kiss.

We parked underneath the Opéra. Although I had seen it several times—as a tourist and during the daytime—the building always took my breath away, looking every bit like a marble wedding cake. Tonight it had transformed into a fairy castle, its warm yellow lights glowing magically through the chilly winter air. We followed richly dressed people walking arm in arm through the monumental doors.

"Have you been here before?" I asked as we walked into the foyer.

"I've come a few times as a fill-in date for Gaspard or Jean-Baptiste when the other was dormant. They always have season passes."

We stepped into the center of the room, and I looked up. "Oh," I gasped, the sumptuous surroundings robbing me of my capacity for intelligent speech. The enormous space was decorated in an over-the-top mash-up of styles—with every single inch of the floors, walls, pillars, and ceiling decorated to the nth degree in gold, marble, mosaic, or crystal. In any other setting it would seem like too much. But here it was stunning.

Vincent led me up the left-hand branch of the grand marble staircase to the second floor, and down a curved hallway lined with dozens of little wooden doors. We stopped in front of number nineteen.

"I didn't reserve the royal box," Vincent explained as he placed his hand on the doorknob. "I didn't think you'd like the ostentation. Everyone's always ogling it, trying to see who's inside. This one's just a good ten-spectator box, but I bought all ten seats and had them clear out the extra chairs for us."

I watched uncertainty flicker across his features and shook my head in disbelief. "Vincent! As if I would even know the difference! Just being here is incredible. We could be sitting in the nosebleed seats and I'd still be over the moon."

Reassured, he opened the door to show a long, narrow passageway papered in dark red velvet and hung with an oval mirror. A narrow fainting couch sat against one wall under a pair of old-fashioned electric lights with flame-shaped bulbs. On the other end of the tunnel-like room was a balcony that opened onto the grand opera, with two wooden chairs set behind a knee-high rail.

"Holy cow. All this is for us?" I asked, feeling like I had just stepped into a romance novel.

"Is it okay?" Vincent asked hesitantly.

I turned and threw my arms around his neck. "It's more than okay. It's incredible." He laughed as, without letting go, I started jumping up and down in a fit of pure joy.

We watched the first two acts of *Prince Igor* sitting side by side in our private box. At first it was hard to concentrate with Vincent next to me, mindlessly tracing circles on my knee as he watched the stage, but after a few minutes the mise-en-scène and costumes swept me away as the dancers performed their acrobatic feats. I lost myself in the spectacle, feeling like I had just awoken from a dream when the curtains closed and the houselights went up an hour later.

"What did you think?" asked Vincent as we stood.

"It's bewitching—all of it."

He smiled, satisfied, and holding his arm out for me, said, "This is the time for the *promenade*." He led me outside our box into the corridor. We followed other couples into a large gilt hall with enormous chandeliers and ceilings painted with angels and mythical figures in a style that reminded me of Michelangelo's Sistine Chapel ceiling.

"Do you want something to drink? A glass of champagne? A bottle of water?" Vincent asked, and I shook my head, seeing that the refreshment line already stretched halfway down the hall.

"I want to use the time to look around," I said, clutching his arm so I wouldn't fall over as I tried to walk and gawk at the same time.

We explored every nook and cranny that the building had to offer, each room opening onto another more exquisite than the last. When we ended up in front of our door, Vincent asked, "Want to see anything else? We have a few moments left."

I hesitated. Although I didn't want to ruin the night by quizzing him on something I suspected he didn't want to talk about, I decided it wouldn't hurt to simply bring it up. "No, let's go inside," I said. Once through the door, we sat on the fainting couch and smiled like kids trying on their parents' clothes.

"This isn't exactly like pizza and a movie at my place. Does it feel weird?" Vincent leaned forward and turned his head to look at me. The way his hair fell across his face as he grinned made the flame already burning inside my chest flare a little brighter.

"Not weird," I responded. "To be honest, you could have taken me bowling and I would be having just as much fun. It doesn't matter what we're doing, as long as I'm with you." As soon as I heard the words leave my mouth, I burst out laughing. "That should totally be on a poster with a fluffy kitten saying it. Cheese factor through the roof!"

"Totally cheesy," he agreed, grinning. "But I was basically thinking the same thing. I've had that feeling ever since I met you." He leaned in and began to nuzzle the skin at the base of my neck.

My eyes closed of their own accord. *Concentrate*, I thought. *Some things are more important than making out with your boyfriend at the Opéra.* "Vincent," I said, pulling back and fixing his eyes with my own. "I don't want to ruin the amazing evening. But it can't wait." I saw him blanch and hurried to get the words out. "You promised not to hide anything from me, but it feels like that's what you're doing with your 'business for JB' or whatever you were doing yesterday. Passing it off like it's not important makes me feel like you think I can't handle it. And that, to me, feels really patronizing." There, it was out. He couldn't avoid it by getting all makey-outie now that the issue was on the table.

Vincent straightened. "Kate," he said, pulling my hand to his lap and pressing it between his fingers. "It's not a question of trust. And it's not a question of not thinking you can handle it. I am in awe of your strength. It's just that"—he hesitated—"I know you won't like it. It's an experiment. And since it might not even work, I was hoping to avoid having to tell you about it."

"I can take it, Vincent. I can take anything."

"I know you can, Kate." His expression was imploring now. "Believe me. But I already hate anything about myself that freaks you out, and this—trust me—is freaky. I'm afraid I would lose your respect if you knew the details. Which is why I just wanted to try it, and check it off the list of possible solutions, and move on. If it actually worked, and that's a really big 'if,' I wanted to present it to you in a way where you could actually see the benefits, weigh them against the distasteful side of it, and help me decide whether I should continue with it."

He watched my face carefully.

"How long does the experiment take?" I heard myself ask, while kicking myself for not digging further.

"Gaspard says we should know after two cycles of dormancy. So just over a month . . . six weeks more."

I looked into his eyes and saw his sincerity. His utter honesty. And his determination to do whatever he could to make us work.

I squeezed my eyes shut and breathed deeply. "Okay. I trust you. But please be safe."

"Thank you, Kate," he said, leaning back against the wall, but keeping hold of my hand. He focused on the ceiling for a few moments, before turning to me. "There's something I've been wanting to ask you about too. Totally different subject."

I smiled wickedly. "*I'm* up for talking about anything."

"Why have you cut all ties with your friends in New York?"

My smile disappeared. "Except that."

"Kate, I totally get the fact that my friends are your friends here. I don't blame you for not wanting to hang out with the kids from school. You say there's no one interesting there, and I understand that you don't want to get attached to people who will leave for their home countries after graduation.

"But your childhood friends—the people you grew up with. The way you've talked to me about them . . . it sounds like you were really close."

"We were," I said, my voice flat. "They even contacted Mamie after I stopped writing, but I had her tell them I wasn't in the mood to talk. They probably all hate me now."

"I think they'd all understand why you fell out of touch last year. It was an awful time for you. You'll never get over your parents' death, I'm not even suggesting that. But you're doing better now. You're coping with life."

"Questionable, since I hang out with a bunch of dead people." My eyes flicked quickly to his. I hadn't meant it as a slam. And from his wry smile, I was relieved to see he hadn't taken offense.

"Okay, you're between worlds. But you've told me you never felt like you completely fit in anywhere. How did you say it? 'Not completely American and not completely French.'

"But that doesn't mean that you should just trash those relationships you had back home. They're part of your past, Kate. We all need a past to root our present in. You can't just live in the here and now."

"Why not?" I snapped, surprising myself by the vehemence in my voice. "Do you know what the past holds for me, Vincent?"

"Death, Kate." His voice softened. "So does mine."

"Vincent, all my memories are built around my family. My parents. After leaving Brooklyn, every time I talked to my friends it dragged me right back into that old life. Everything they said reminded me of home. And it hurt so badly, you can't even imagine." My eyes flitted to his face as I remembered that his parents and fiancée had been murdered before his eyes. But he didn't look angry. If anything, he looked more caring and supportive than ever.

"Okay, you *can* imagine," I conceded. "But Vincent, I'm not a sadist. Inflicting unnecessary pain on myself on a consistent basis is not my idea of staying healthy and sane. I can't be in touch with them. It hurts too much."

Vincent looked down at his hands, weighing his words carefully before he looked back up at me. Without speaking, he traced my jawline with his finger, as if sketching my face's topography. I reached up and grasped his hand, pulling it into my lap and holding it with both hands for comfort.

"I get it, Kate. Believe me, I do. But I just want to put something out there for you to consider. When I died the first time, it was announced in the papers. Everyone knew. I didn't even have a choice about going back to my community—to the people I loved. And I missed that. For years, I practically stalked Hélène's father and sister, making sure they were okay. I couldn't ever show myself, but I watched them.

"I left anonymous flowers when Hélène's dad passed away. And after Brigitte, Hélène's sister, died giving birth to a son, I watched him. He and his family live in the south of France now.

121

I have seen them. His daughter looks like her grandmother. And however weird it sounds, knowing they exist grounds me. Having a link to my past grounds me.

"But I would have given anything to have been able to stay in touch with Brigitte and her father and the other people from my past—no matter how many painful memories that contact would have stirred up. I didn't have that choice. But you do. It might be too early, but I hope you will change your mind someday. I can tell whenever you mention your friends that you still struggle with it. But . . . being in contact with them might actually make you happier."

Pain had been blowing up like a bubble inside me, and at that, it finally exploded. "I *am* happy, Vincent," I growled through clenched teeth. He looked at me, a skeptical eyebrow raised. Realizing how ridiculous that had sounded, I pursed my lips, and then burst out laughing. I leaned forward into his arms, loving him more in that moment than I ever had. He cared for me. Not just because he wanted me for himself. He wanted me to be happy . . . on my own.

The curtains came up, but we didn't move. We spent the rest of the performance kissing and laughing and peeking out at the ballet and then kissing some more.

That night when I got home, I slipped my laptop out of my desk drawer and turned it on. Using the email account I had set up to write to Charlotte, I sent a message to my three oldest friends. *It's me, Kate*, I wrote. *I'm sorry I haven't been in touch. I do love you all. But it still hurts too much to think about my past, and though you don't mean to, you bring it back too clearly.* I wiped a tear away as I typed in one last sentence and then pressed send.

Please wait for me.

THIRTEEN

FOR THE NEXT WEEK, VINCENT WAS TOO BUSY with his project to be able to spend much time with me. Previously, on the rare day we didn't see each other, we had called to catch up at night, and he would give me a complete rundown of his day. But recently he'd begun to carefully skip over bits.

Now that we had talked, I didn't feel as bad about it. And knowing that he had asked for my blessing—in a roundabout way—I felt more supportive of him. But I still worried. Because whatever it was, it was taking a toll on him. His skin's healthy olive tone had begun to look sallow, and dark circles were appearing under his eyes. He was so tired and preoccupied that even when he was next to me, it felt like he wasn't completely there.

At the same time, I couldn't complain about him being any less affectionate. Because he seemed even more so. As if he was trying to make up for everything.

"Vincent, you look awful," I finally said one morning.

"It has to get worse before it gets better," was all he would say.

After a week and a half of watching him rapidly weaken before my eyes, I was getting to the end of my rope. I didn't want to force Vincent to give me more information . . . to put any more pressure on him. And Jules and Gaspard were obviously not going to spill the beans. But that didn't mean I couldn't ask Violette.

Since her Hitchcockian introduction to the cinema, Violette and I had been to several films, each time on her initiative. A couple of days after our first movie date, I received a bouquet of blue and pink flowers and a copy of *Pariscope* with a note attached telling me to look on page thirty-seven. Page thirty-seven was a list of movies. I dug my flower dictionary out of my bag.

The blue flower was monkshood, which meant "danger," and the tiny pinkish flowers were nutmeg geranium: "I expect a meeting." Danger . . . meeting? I looked at the movie listings again and saw, in the middle of the page, *Dangerous Liaisons*. *This has got to be the first time in history that* The Language of Flowers *was used to encode movie titles*, I thought, laughing to myself as I dialed her phone number.

Violette giggled through the whole film, remarking on how the costumes and mannerisms were all wrong, and drawing angry glares from the moviegoers around us. After I convinced her that it wasn't okay to speak out loud in a cinema ("But this is a common entertainment—it is not as if we were at the opera," was her initial response), she limited herself to chuckling and shaking her head at the offending scenes. When I commented afterward about the evilness of the characters, Violette laughed and said, "A perfect example of royal court politics!"

A few days later, the bouquet of bear's foot (knight), lucerne (life), and asphodel (my regrets follow you to death) took me a whole half hour of looking back and forth between flowers and movie listings. When I finally figured out that Violette was using "knight" as a pun, my jaw dropped at the thought of the ancient revenant choosing *Night of the Living Dead*, the most famous zombie movie ever.

We fell into a habit of following up the movie with a café session. But instead of chatting, it felt more like we were trading information: Violette didn't know how to relax. Her default setting was programmed to super intense, and she listened to everything I said with a concentration that intimidated me at first. I finally became used to it, and eventually got her to loosen up to the point where she could laugh about herself.

Violette couldn't hear enough about me and Vincent, and after my initial hesitation, I could tell that it wasn't from some kind of weird, voyeuristic jealousy. Obviously her crush was long gone. She explained that love between humans and revenants was so rare that it intrigued her, and apologized if it was intruding on our personal lives. But when I told her I didn't mind, she enthusiastically dug for every single detail.

It was the way that Vincent and I could communicate while he was volant that seemed to interest her the most. She confessed that she hadn't heard of contact between humans and dormant revenants, besides the very basic intuition that the rare married couples like Geneviève and Philippe developed after decades of living together.

"You know," she said glibly, "that is supposed to be one of the qualities of the Champion."

"What is?" I asked, my heart suddenly beating faster. I had forgotten that Violette was considered an expert on revenant history. Of course she would have heard of the Champion.

She paused, watching me carefully.

"Don't worry, I know about the Champion," I said, and saw her relax. "Vincent told me about the prophecy. Although he didn't know much about it. What does him speaking to me when volant have to do with it?"

"'And he will possess preternatural powers of endurance, persuasion, strength, and communication,'" she quoted. "That is a part of the prophecy."

"Wait a minute . . . endurance? That must be why Jean-Baptiste thinks Vincent is the Champion. He was able to resist dying longer than other revenants his age. What else did you say?"

"Persuasion," she said, "which Vincent has got in excess. He is the one Jean-Baptiste always sends to represent him when there are problems among our kind."

I hadn't known that, either. Although Vincent had mentioned projects for Jean-Baptiste, I had always assumed they were of the legal type.

"Then there is strength. Is Vincent very strong?"

"I've never seen him fight except in training, so I wouldn't know," I admitted.

"Well, the communication thing sure had Jean-Baptiste worked up. The fact that a revenant had volant speech that was strong enough to reach out to a human. When Vincent told him about it, Jean-Baptiste called me right away to let me know. To see if I had any further information on the prophecy that might help verify that Vincent is the Champion."

"And what did you tell him?" I asked, feeling a bit shaken by the whole conversation. Truth be told, I didn't want Vincent to be the Champion. Whatever that meant, it sounded dangerous.

"I told him that he was lucky to have such a talented young revenant living under his roof, but that I seriously doubted that, if there were to be a Champion, it would be Vincent."

"Why not?"

"Lots of reasons," she said with a teasing glint in her eye. "There are several other stipulations spelled out in the prophecy. Conditions of time and location. And believe me . . . it is not here and it is not now. Honestly, the prophecy of the Champion is just one of many ancient prophecies. Most of them have not been fulfilled, and they are probably based on the ranting of oracles or questionable superstitions. Old guys like Jean-Baptiste lap them up like honeyed mead."

I gave her a confused look.

"Fine, like vintage wine. That is a better comparison for Jean-Baptiste, anyway." And then, with a wry grin, she launched into a story about how Jean-Baptiste once sent Gaspard on a wild-goose chase to find some ancient parchment that had never actually existed. She had me laughing so hard that I choked on my latte.

The half a millennia she had spent on earth made Violette a veritable gold mine of good stories and juicy information.

One day, after an evening showing of one of my all-time favorites, *Harold and Maude,* we headed to the Café Sainte-Lucie. Over a shared platter of deliciously runny cheeses and a basket of crunchy sliced baguette bread, Violette told me about the old times, when there wasn't as much animosity between numa and bardia. It was weird to hear her use the ancient term for revenants as if it was common lingo.

At that point, apparently, they considered themselves in the same line of work: the work of life. Preserving life, taking life . . . it all boiled down to the same thing. "It is all about a balance," she said. "In our days, there was open communication between the numa and bardia.

"You know," she continued, leaning forward confidentially, "Arthur has kept in touch with some of our ancient contacts in the numa world, and I am glad for it. My research would have suffered if he had not!" Seeing my shock, she said, "Kate, one cannot cut off a whole subset of our type just because they have gone out of style in recent centuries."

"Your *type*? But you're not even the same kind of creature!" I said, feeling a twinge of disgust at the comparison.

"Ah, but there you are wrong. We are exactly the same kind of creature. What has Vincent told you about how a revenant is formed? Or numa, for that matter?"

"That a human becomes a revenant after dying to save

someone's life. And a human becomes a numa when they die after betraying someone to their death."

"Which is true," she said. "But if you go back a step, bardia and numa are the same thing: revenants. Many, including me, believe that there is a 'revenant gene.' That we are a type of mutation.

"But whatever our origin, everyone agrees that revenants are all born equal: human with a latency to become a revenant. Whether they become bardia or numa all depends on their actions during their human life. And if they are never cast into a situation where they save or betray, they just live out the rest of their lives clueless that they were different from anyone else."

"So a human's not born a numa or bardia?"

"Not unless you believe in the Calvinistic doctrine of predestination." *And once again, she sounds four times her age,* I thought. "But we are not talking theology here. We are talking about human nature. In which case the only answer can be, 'Who knows?' What I *do* know is that the numa and bardia did not used to be the enemies they are today."

"Yeah, Jean-Baptiste said that there used to be a lot more of both in Paris."

Violette nodded and called the waiter to bring us some coffees. "As with most wars, during World War Two many revenants of both ilk were created. And since many held personal grudges against each other from their human lives, there was a massive war of vengeance between the numa and bardia. That all came to an end, though, a decade or so later. And there has been a type of cease-fire ever since."

"Why?" I asked, intrigued by this new information.

She shrugged. "I have no idea. Like I said, Arthur and I have been holed up in our castle in the Loire. I have stayed away from Parisian politics."

"Well, from what I hear, you're the go-to person for anything revenant or numa related," I said. "If anyone would know, it would be you."

"*Touché*," she said, laughing. "I do pride myself on having the inside information on pretty much everything. But I also pride myself on being able to keep a secret. So if I do not tell you something, there is probably a good reason."

"So if I asked you what Vincent was up to . . . ?" I asked with a sly smile.

"I would say, 'Well, whatever do you mean!'" she responded with an equally sly grin.

I had hoped my new friend would be more open with me. Although I knew that if she had, I would have felt bad for going behind Vincent's back to get the information. Her small white hand reached out and touched my own.

"Don't worry about Vincent, Kate. He can take care of himself."

Then it's something dangerous, I thought. Even if she hadn't meant to, she had told me something I didn't know. Now, more than ever, I was determined to find another solution.

A week and a half ago at the ballet, Vincent had said he needed six weeks to see if his experiment had the potential to work. And if it did, I could only imagine that he would continue with it.

Which meant I had just over a month to find an answer to an impossible situation. I just hoped that nothing bad would happen to Vincent before I did.

I jumped as the study door opened, positioning myself in front of the open box on Papy's desk.

"It's just me," Georgia said as she walked into the room, closing the door quietly behind her.

I exhaled, relieved that I wouldn't have to lie to Papy about why I was trolling through his library. He would be overjoyed that I was using it. But knowing his enthusiasm for books, he would be too interested in exactly what I was looking for.

"So what treasure of Papy's deserves a full body block?" she asked, her eyes flitting to the book behind me. I stepped aside to let her see.

"You're reading something in German?" she asked, surprised, as she flipped through a couple of pages.

"I'm not actually sure it's even German," I said, tapping the German dictionary sitting next to it. "Unless it's an old form. It could be a Bavarian dialect, for all I know."

Georgia looked confused. "It's sunny out—for once—and you're spending your free time indoors reading an ancient Bavarian book because . . ." She turned another page to a hand-drawn illustration of a devil-like beast: red skin, horns, and claws. "Ah . . . monsters. May I guess that this has something to do with the particularly hot undead guy you suck face with on a regular basis?"

I leaned tiredly against the desk and nodded. "This is the last book. I've gone through everything in Papy's library that could have something to do with revenants, and found only one that mentioned them. And it didn't tell me anything I didn't already know."

"What are you looking for?" Georgia asked, as I carefully put the book back in its box and slid it into the empty space in the bookcase.

"Honestly? If it were possible, I'd love to find a way to turn Vincent back into a human again. But since it's not, I'll settle for any information that might make things easier for us."

"Hmm," Georgia said pensively. "Normally I'd tease you for talking about magic, except for the fact that we're referring to a reanimated dead guy here, so—hey—I guess anything is possible. Seriously, what exactly are you hoping to find?"

"Vincent told me that the time he resisted dying for a few years—when he got his law degree—he tried yoga and meditation to help ease the symptoms. Gaspard had read in some Tibetan revenant manuscript that that could help. Except it didn't. So I figure I might as well see if I could find something Gaspard didn't already know about. Like an herb or potion or something."

"Hmm," said Georgia, looking off into some invisible dreamworld. "Or maybe bathing naked in the Seine under the light of the full moon"—she glanced up quickly—"in which case, definitely tell me when and where your voodoo's going down!"

I laughed. "Hey, you've got Sebastien! I'm sure you could persuade him to skinny-dip in the Seine if you tried hard enough."

"Of course I could," she said with faux haughtiness. "But who wants a boyfriend with ringworm?"

Georgia was working her big-sister charm on me again. When we were younger, if there was ever anything I needed help with that was beyond her capabilities, she tried the next best thing: distracting me.

"Speaking of boyfriends, we should go out together some night. Vincent hasn't even met Sebastien. And you've been spending all your girl time with zombie Marie Antoinette." My sister made a face. Once she disliked someone, nothing would make her change her mind.

"She's actually really nice," I said, defending Violette.

"She called me an 'ungrateful human,'" Georgia countered. "That kind of says it all, as far as I'm concerned."

"She's just old-school," I said, remembering what Jeanne had told me. "She's not used to seeing revenants mix with us."

"Racist," Georgia insisted, crossing her arms.

"So where should we go with the guys?" I asked, changing the subject.

"Seb's got a concert in a week and a half—two Saturdays from now."

"That sounds perfect," I said. "I'm sure Vincent can come. I mean, he's dormant this weekend, so by then he'll be in good enough shape to go out."

"I can't believe you just said that," Georgia said, shaking her head. "It's just so . . . weird." She gave me a hug and started out of the room, before stopping on the threshold. "Hey, you should check Papy's gallery. He's got a ton of books there."

"Oh my God, I hadn't thought about that!" I exclaimed, my frustration instantly replaced by a little flame of hope.

"Who's lookin' out for ya, baby?" my sister said in a gangster moll accent. Then she gave me an exaggerated wink and closed the door.

FOURTEEN

I AWOKE THE NEXT MORNING, EAGER, FOR ONCE, to jump out of bed and head to the breakfast table. My Papy was there, eating a fresh croissant and drinking coffee from a bowl—which is what hot breakfast drinks are usually served in. Not mugs. Bowls that you hold with both hands as you drink your hot chocolate or coffee. Unless you're drinking an espresso. And then it's in a ridiculously tiny cup.

Grabbing my own bowl, I poured it half-full with coffee and half with the hot milk that Mamie kept in a pan on the stove, and sat down across from my grandfather. "Papy, if you ever need someone to gallery-sit, in case you have a meeting or something, I'd be happy to."

I tried to say it as nonchalantly as possible, but my grandfather eyed me worriedly. "Isn't your allowance enough, *ma princesse*?" I cringed. That was my dad's nickname for me. It had been over a year since he had died, but whenever Papy called me that, it gave my heart a little stab.

Papy noticed. "Sorry, dear."

"It's okay. And I wasn't offering because I want you to pay me. I just thought it would be fun. And I could bring my homework."

Papy lifted his eyebrows. "Well! I'd never get an offer like that from your sister. But coming from an art lover like yourself, I know you're not just trying to be helpful!" He smiled. "In fact, I have a meeting this afternoon—an appraisal of some Greek statuary at a collector's house on the Île Saint-Louis. I was planning on closing the gallery, but if you wanted to come after school . . ."

He didn't even have to finish his statement. "I'll be there!" I said enthusiastically.

Papy's smile was still quizzical, but I could tell he liked the idea. "See you then," he said, rising and patting me fondly on the shoulder. He put on his coat and headed upstairs to say good-bye to Mamie, who had gotten an early start in her restoration studio on our building's top floor.

I smiled to myself as I bit the end off a croissant, humming with pleasure as I did. I had probably eaten hundreds of croissants in my life, having spent every summer here as a kid. And, even so, every time I ate one it was like a pastry revelation. I pulled off a flaky strip and popped it into my mouth and then chased it with a sip of steaming *café crème*.

The fifteen minutes it took for Papy to show me what I needed to know about the gallery seemed to last for hours. But finally he was stepping through the front door into the bright sunlight and giving a good-bye salute with his old-man hat as he disappeared down the street.

As soon as he was out of view, I left the hushed semidarkness of the gallery for the brightly lit office space behind. Visitors had to ring the doorbell to be buzzed through the front door, so I reasoned I wasn't being negligent if I spent a little time away from the desk.

It didn't take long for me to work my way through Papy's gallery library. Most of the books were auction catalogues or twentieth-century scholarly books on art and architecture through the ages. With my recently gained research experience, I could tell they wouldn't contain anything about revenants.

I popped back to the front of the gallery to make sure no one was waiting outside the door, and then made my way to the other side of the space, where Papy had his private viewing room. Switching on the spotlights in the tiny, sumptuous space, I cast around for anything that might be of interest. A few ancient volumes sat on a side table with gloves and a magnifying glass positioned next to them. I slipped the gloves on and opened one of the books. It was a historical document, with lists of goods and dates next to them—it seemed to be a king's or lord's account of tributes paid to him. I turned a couple more pages. More of the same. And neither of the other books had anything of interest.

I stood and thought for a moment. Since Papy dealt only with artifacts, sculpture, and metalwork, when he bought entire estates he often passed the most valuable books and manuscripts to his book dealer friends to sell for him. But during his busy buying seasons, there was often a stash of inventory he hadn't had time to go through, especially the books and prints he would be handing off. I made my way to his stock closet in the back hallway and turned the handle. Locked.

Papy always carried his keys with him, but maybe he kept spares somewhere in the gallery. I returned to the front desk, dug through a couple of drawers, and found a small key taped to the side of one of them, near the back. Carefully unpeeling it, I returned to the closet and breathed a sigh of relief as it slipped easily into the lock.

Inside stood a stack of four boxes labeled ESTATE, MARQUIS DE CAMPANA. Papy had scribbled the purchase date on the side of the box: a few days ago. Knowing him, he had probably put the estate's most important pieces up front and stored the miscellaneous items until he had a chance to research them one by one. I pulled a box out of the closet and opened it. Tiny bundles wrapped in cloth . . . miniature metal god figurines, I saw as I unfolded one. I rewrapped it and quickly replaced it.

The second box was full of tiny plastic zip-lock bags holding bits of ancient jewelry and carved stones—the type that would be set in a ring. *Intaglios*, I remembered Papy calling them, and picked one up to discover a figure of Hercules wearing the lion skin carved into an oval jade. Although I had been around Papy's objects since I was a baby, I never failed to feel a frisson of wonder when I held something made over a thousand years ago.

I knew what the third box held before I even reached inside. My heart beat faster as I opened the flaps. The smell of musty paper poofed out, and I looked down to see a collection of old books. More like hand-bound manuscripts. And though the most fragile ones were in plastic bags, a few sturdier volumes lay loose between them.

Books from a Roman antiquities collector . . . now this could be promising. I picked the first one up. It was an old printed book in German, with engravings of Greek and Roman statuary. I placed it carefully on the floor and reached in for a small book with decorative shapes and swirls tooled into the reddish brown leather cover.

It was the size of the illustrated prayer books I had seen in the Louvre, but much thinner, and as I opened it I saw that it was a hand-penned manuscript, written in the gothic handwriting of medieval monks. I remembered reading about illustrated manuscripts. Some monks spent their whole lives copying books and decorating them. Before the printing press, copying was the only way multiple examples of a book could be made.

This wasn't a masterpiece, like the ones I had seen protected under thick museum glass. It was simple but beautiful, with gold vines and flourishes decorating the edges. The first page was an explosion of leaves and berries, with, at the bottom center, two skulls. *Immortal Love*, it read in French, and the next page was illustrated with a colorful, naively painted image of a man and a woman in medieval clothing holding hands. And even though the painting was simple, I could tell that the woman was elderly—she was depicted with white hair—and that the man was very young: a teenager.

The image had been painted many centuries ago. Maybe even a millennium. I inspected it carefully, taking in every detail. The woman was old, her posture a little bent. And the man was gleaming with youth and health. I would have thought it was an old lady with her grandson, except for the way they stood hand in hand, their heads slightly inclined toward each other in a gesture of solidarity and affection.

I turned back to the title page. *L'amur immortel*, I read again, and then saw a subtitle written in spidery letters below. I could hardly make it out; the ink had worn with the centuries, and the old French was difficult to decipher. "A tale . . . love and tragedy . . . a bar . . . and . . . human . . ." My heart caught in my throat. Could the word be bardia? There was just enough space for it to be. And a *human*?

Oh my God, I had found something. My head spun and then cleared abruptly as the gallery's doorbell buzzed. I got up, a bit wobbly, and raced into the gallery space. A familiar figure stood behind the glass door, tall enough to take up the whole windowpane. He cupped his eyes with his hands so he could see inside. I pressed the door release under the front desk.

"Vincent!" I exclaimed, feeling a twinge of guilt. "How did you know I was here?"

He strode into the gallery, hands in his pockets and an amused look on his face. After giving me a soft kiss, he released me and glanced curiously around the space. "I have my ways," he said. Doing a Vincent Price voice and raising an eyebrow, he quipped, "I always know where you are."

"No, really," I prodded, laughing.

"Well, you see, there's this thing called a text message," he said, deadpan. "And I got one from your phone during your lunch break that told me you were gallery-sitting this afternoon." A hint of a smile curved the corners of his lips.

"Oh, right," I said, lamely shaking my head. This whole situation with Vincent's undercover operations was messing with my mind. It was making me paranoid.

"So what are you doing here?" Vincent asked. "This is the first time I've seen you in the midst of gainful employ. Not that homework isn't gainful."

I was about to open my mouth to tell him the whole thing—to excitedly whip out the book and show it to him—when all of a sudden I hesitated. I didn't want him to see it . . . yet. Not until I had actually figured out what it meant. Maybe it was my pride holding me back, but I wanted to see his face when I set the finished puzzle in front of him, complete with valuable information he couldn't have found somewhere else.

"I was just feeling bored. Thought it would be fun to do something different for a change."

"Bored?" Vincent looked astounded. "In the past week and a half you've gone to a total of four movies with Violette, and you and I have hung out . . . well, not as much as I'd have liked." A flash of guilt crossed his face before he forced it to disappear.

"So what are you up to tonight?" I asked.

"The usual boring revenant stuff," he replied, visibly squirming, and then he sighed and looked me in the eye. "Kate, you know what I'm doing."

"Not exactly." I couldn't help the trace of bitterness in my voice.

Vincent pulled me close and said, "You want to call it off? You say the word."

"No." I shook my head, and Vincent wrapped his arms around me. "I love you, Kate," he whispered. I closed my eyes and nestled in closer to him.

"We're still on for tomorrow night, aren't we?" he murmured.

I pulled back from him and smiled. "Pizza and a movie in our own private cinema? I wouldn't miss it for the world!"

"Yeah, I try to go out in style. Can't have you forgetting about me for the three days I'm dormant."

"As if!" Pulling him to the door, I said, "Papy's due back in a few minutes, and I wouldn't want him to think I was slacking on the job."

"Hey, your Papy loves me," Vincent said.

"He's not the only one," I said, and opening the door, I pretended to push him out onto the street. Closing it securely behind him, I blew a saucy air-kiss through the glass. Laughing, he turned and headed up the avenue toward our neighborhood.

I sped back to the office, slipped the small book into my purse, and then carefully put the boxes back into their places in the storage closet. As I locked it, I heard the key turn in the front door and Papy's voice calling to tell me he had returned.

"I'm in the back," I called, my voice quivering in my panic. I still had the closet key in my hand. How could I get it back into the drawer without Papy noticing? I walked out to the main gallery, and composing myself as much as possible, I gave him a winning smile and asked how his meeting had gone.

"Top-notch property, *ma princesse*." He bustled to the back to hang up his coat. "There's another dealer bidding for it, though, so I'm not sure it's mine yet," came his muffled voice from behind the divider. I quickly peeled a piece of tape off the tape dispenser, pressed the key to the sticky side, slipped the desk drawer open, and reattached it to the spot I had found it. Just as I slid the drawer closed, Papy turned the corner.

"Anything exciting happen while I was gone?" he asked, coming to stand next to me behind the desk.

"Let's see . . . the French president dropped by. Brigitte Bardot. Oh yeah, and then Vanessa Paradis came in with Johnny Depp. They bought a million-euro statue. You know, the usual."

He shook his head in amusement and began scribbling in his appointment book. I kissed him good-bye and tried not to break into a sprint as I headed for the door.

FIFTEEN

AS SOON AS I GOT HOME, I THREW MY HOMEWORK on a chair and sat down on my bed with the book. In the beginning it was difficult. Like reading *Beowulf* in English—there were a lot of words I didn't understand. But gradually, the magic of the story pulled me in, and I felt like I was right there with the characters: Goderic, a nineteen-year-old revenant, and Else, the girl he married just months before he died.

It was Else who was there when Goderic awoke, the day he was to be buried. She gave him food and drink, and he attained his immortality. They learned what he was from a seer who had followed his light.

Else and Goderic became transients, moving every time he died so that the locals wouldn't become suspicious. As she got older, they had to change their story, claiming to be mother and son. After several years Else became sick. Goderic called a *guérisseur* to heal her, and the healer recognized what Goderic was by his aura.

Goderic pled with the man to find a way to let him age normally with his beloved—to resist the powerful desire to die. The *guérisseur* didn't have that knowledge, but told him of another healer who had great power in the way of the immortals.

The next part was full of words I didn't understand. It was phrased in a peculiar style—like a prophecy—but I tried to decipher it word by word. Still speaking of the powerful healer, the man told Goderic, "From his family will come the one to see the victor. If anyone holds the key to your plight, it will be the VictorSeer's clan. He lives in a faraway land, among *les A* . . . . , and can be found under the Sign of the Cord, selling relics to the pilgrims."

My heart skipped a beat. There was a word crossed out. An essential word. After the capital *A*, a thick line of black ink had obscured the rest of the word, making it impossible to know among whom the healer lived. Someone had purposely drawn through it. *Someone who didn't want the healer to be found*, I thought.

I forced myself to keep reading, hoping that the word would recur later, but it didn't. Goderic and Else began traveling north, but she contracted another illness along the way and died in Goderic's arms. He was so distraught that he traveled to the city and hunted down a numa, who "delivered him from life."

By the time I finished, it was two in the morning.

Who knew if there was even a grain of truth in the story? But if there was someone who could help me and Vincent, I wouldn't stop until I found him. However, before I could, I had to locate another copy of the book—a copy that hadn't been tampered with. And I knew just the place to start.

* * *

Although I slept only a few hours, I was wide awake as soon as my alarm sounded. I had set it early so that I could catch Mamie before she went up to her restoration studio and got lost in her work. But when I got to the kitchen, I saw I was too late: Mamie's breakfast dishes were already in the sink, and the white work apron she wore while restoring paintings was missing from its hook by the door.

I sliced a baguette in half, cut it lengthwise, and then smoothed a chunk of salty butter along my bread. A little dab of homemade jam from the quince tree in my grandparents' country garden, and I was holding a traditional *tartine*. Simple but delicious. I wrapped it in a napkin and carried it up the stairs with me.

Walking into Mamie's studio was like entering another world—an oil-paint-and-turpentine-scented world—populated by the subjects of centuries of paintings. Young aristocratic mothers with perfectly dressed children and ribbon-festooned dogs playing at their feet. Mournful-looking cows, cud chewing in the midst of a fog-blanketed pasture. Tiny saints kneeling in front of a cross, with a jumbo-size Jesus hanging on it, bloody and twisted. Anything and everything was in Mamie's world. No wonder I had spent my every free moment as a child up here.

My grandmother was brushing a clear liquid onto the surface of a time-darkened painting of Roman ruins. "Hi, Mamie!" I said, as I walked up behind her and plopped down onto a stool. I took a bite of *tartine* as I watched her work.

She carefully finished her brushstroke, and then turned, smiling brightly. "You're up early, Katya!" She made a gesture that indicated that if her hands weren't full, she would kiss me. I smiled. The all-important first-time-I-see-you-in-the-day cheek-kisses. I would never get used to letting someone get that near my mouth before having the chance to brush my teeth.

"Yeah. I had some stuff I needed to do before school. And I was just thinking about something I heard at the market the other day. I thought you could explain it."

Mamie nodded expectantly.

"This woman was talking about finding a *guérisseur*. For her eczema, I think it was. And I've heard of *guérisseurs*—I know the word means 'healer'—but I don't really understand how they work. Are they kind of like the faith healers we have in the States?"

"Oh, no." Mamie shook her head vigorously and tsked reproachfully. She placed her paintbrush in a jar of liquid and wiped her hands on a towel. From this enthusiastic response, I knew I was in for a good story. Mamie loved telling me about French traditions that I didn't already know about, and the weirder the topic, the more she enjoyed it.

"*Pas du tout. Guérisseurs* have nothing to do with faith, although some claim that their healings are psychosomatic." I laughed as I watched her become animated, warming up to her story. "But I, for one, know that's not the case."

Voilà! I thought. *Trust Mamie to have information on such a bizarre topic.* "What exactly are they, anyway?"

"Well, Katya. *Guérisseurs* have been around for centuries—from the time that there weren't enough trained doctors to go around. They usually specialize in something, like the healing of warts or eczema, or even setting broken bones. The same specialized gift is passed from one family member to another, and once the gift is passed, the previous healer no longer bears the gift. There is always only one *guérisseur* in a family at a time, and each must consciously accept the responsibility in order to inherit it.

"Which is why there aren't that many left. It used to be an honored profession. Now with modern medicine and rising skepticism, fewer people are proud to carry the gifts, and most of the younger generation refuse point-blank to accept it. And when that happens, the gift just disappears."

"Sounds pretty awesome, actually," I admitted.

"Even more awesome when you see it work," Mamie said with a twinkle in her eye.

"You've met a *guérisseur*?"

"Why, yes. Twice, actually. Once was when I was pregnant with your father. I wasn't even three months along, and an old farmer who lived near our country home asked if I wanted to know if it was a boy or girl. Turns out he was a *guérisseur*, and that was his family's gift. That and curing nicotine addiction, if I remember correctly," she said, tapping her lower lip and staring off into the mid-distance.

"And you didn't think it was just a lucky guess?" I asked.

"Out of more than a hundred babies, he was never once wrong. And your own Papy wouldn't have the handsome face he has today if it weren't for another *guérisseur*," she continued.

"Once, when he was burning a pile of leaves, the wind changed and the flames hit him right in the face. Burned his eyebrows and the front of his hair right off. But a neighbor rushed him straight to his mother, and she 'lifted' the burn. Strangest thing . . . she didn't even touch him, she just acted like she was sweeping it off his face and then throwing it away, flicking it off her fingers. And it worked. He had no burns. But it took a while for his eyebrows to grow back."

"Well, that one's a little harder to dispute," I admitted.

"There's nothing to dispute. It works. These people have some sort of power. Just don't ask why or how. It doesn't make any sense. But a lot of important things in this world don't."

Her story complete, Mamie patted the front of her apron and came to stand next to me. "I have to work, dear. The Musée d'Orsay needs this by the end of the week." She brushed my chin softly with her hand. "You know, Katya, you look more like your mother every day."

From anyone else, this would have destroyed me. From Mamie, it was just what I needed to hear. My mother had been strong. Smart. And determined enough to get whatever she wanted, no matter how difficult it proved.

Like the quest I faced now. Bearing my mother's face was a daily reminder that I could be as strong as she had been. And fighting for what I wanted most in life was the best way to keep her alive in my heart.

SIXTEEN

EVEN THOUGH VINCENT HAD TOLD ME HE WOULD
pick me up later in the evening, I went straight to his place after
school. He scooped me up into his arms when he saw me, and
then put me down, worriedly running a hand through his hair. "I
have to take care of a ton of boring stuff before tonight," he said
apologetically.

"I know. I brought homework." I gave him a peck on the lips as
I walked past him into the grand foyer. I had been here a hundred
times already, and each time it made me feel like I was walking into a palace. Which is basically what it was. Vincent held
my hand as we walked down the long hallway to his room, and
crouched down in front of the chimney to build up the fire as I
settled on his couch.

Truth be told, I loved watching Vincent get ready for dormancy. It made me feel more in control, like I was preparing for
these hallucinatory three days myself. There wasn't anything I

could do to help, so at least I could observe.

It was easy to forget what he was as he finished answering emails and checked all the online bills and bank balances he handled for the kindred. He looked like an industrious, hardworking teenager—the rare kind who knows what he wants for the future and is doing everything he can to get it.

That illusion was burst when he put a bottle of water and bag of dried fruits and nuts next to our photo on his bedside table. And I was reminded that *this* was his future—exactly what he was doing right now—for the rest of eternity.

I watched him finalize his predormancy setup. Although Jeanne always made sure there was a tray full of food and drink awaiting each revenant when he or she awoke, Vincent had this primal fear that some catastrophe might happen and she and the others wouldn't be there to leave this critical nourishment. By now I knew how important it was: Without something to eat and drink, the awakening revenant would expire. Meaning Vincent would go from a temporary death to a permanent one.

"So, *mon ange*, do we go ahead with our plans, or would you rather do something different tonight?" Vincent said, nuzzling my ear as I pretended to read my chemistry textbook.

This was my fifth month to experience Vincent's dormancy. The first time I hadn't known what he was, and finding Vincent apparently dead nearly scared me enough to send me to my own early grave. But on the bright side, it also led to my discovery of what the revenants actually were.

The second month was when we discovered that we were able to communicate while he was volant. And after that, we had fallen into a routine. We spent the night before his dormancy doing a pizza-and-movie night in the private cinema in their basement, after which Vincent would walk me home and we would say good-bye. I wouldn't visit the next day—he didn't like me seeing him dead when he couldn't communicate with me. But during the following two days, with Vincent able to travel outside his body and talk with me, we spent every moment together that he wasn't on walking duty with his kindred.

In the beginning I wouldn't let him come to my house while volant. But now I was fine with it. As long as he let me know he was there, the idea didn't creep me out. On the contrary, I loved going to sleep with him whispering in my head. What could be more romantic than hearing your boyfriend murmur beautiful words to you as you're dozing off?

I swore I had better dreams when he was there. I was positive he was putting lovely ideas into my head all night long, but when I mentioned it to him, he said he would never take advantage of a lady while she was unconscious. His playful grin, when he said that, was anything but convincing.

"Movie night, definitely," I said.

Vincent nodded, his face looking more strained than usual. Although he would fall into dormancy during the night, he began to feel weak a few hours before. But this month he looked worse than weak. He looked downright awful.

The dark circles under his eyes now looked like bruises. His skin was wan and drawn, and he seemed as exhausted as if he had just run a marathon. "Vincent, I know I promised not to dig for details on your 'experiment,' but if whatever you're doing is supposed to make you stronger, it doesn't look like it's working very well. In fact, I would say it's having the opposite effect."

"Yeah, I know. Everyone's freaking out about how bad I look. But, as I said, things are supposed to get worse before they get better."

"Well, there's 'worse,' and then there's . . . a black eye." I ran my finger lightly across the bruising.

"In three days I'll be like new again, so don't worry," Vincent said, looking like he was having a hard time taking his own advice.

"Okay." I shrugged in defeat and sat back, crossing my arms. "So . . . what's playing tonight at *Le Cinéma de la Maison?*"

Vincent's encyclopedic knowledge of movies had intimidated me until I reasoned that if I never slept, I would have seen as many films as he had. "I was thinking that, since you hadn't seen them, we could watch either *Scarface* or *Wings of Desire,*" he replied.

I peered at the backs of the two DVD cases he held out. "Well, since I'm not really in the mood for 'bloody drug cartel warfare in 1980s Miami,' an art-house German film about guardian angels sounds just about right."

Vincent smiled tiredly and picked up the phone to order our pizzas.

I checked the time. We had a few hours together before he would take me home. After that, I had a whole day during which Vincent would have no idea what I was up to. Which was exactly how I wanted it.

SEVENTEEN

I STEPPED OUT OF MY BUILDING ON SATURDAY morning, ready for my weekly fight training, to see . . . nobody. And then I remembered Vincent couldn't be there to meet me. Not even in spirit form. He was dead-as-a-doornail dormant today.

I typed in the digicode as I arrived at La Maison, letting myself into the courtyard, and knocked at the door as was my habit when Vincent wasn't with me. Gaspard opened it with a look of surprise, and then fell all over himself apologizing. "Oh, dear Kate," he said, stepping aside and ushering me into the house, "I completely forgot about our practice. I should have telephoned you to cancel. You see, Charlotte called this morning. Charles is gone."

"What do you mean 'gone'?" I responded.

"It seems that he waited long enough for Geneviève to get moved in before taking his leave of Charlotte. He left a note this morning telling them not to worry about him, but that he would not be in contact for a while. That he needed to go somewhere else to get his head 'sorted out.'" Gaspard always sounded awkward when he tried to use contemporary phrases.

"Is someone going to look for him?"

"Where would we even start?" Gaspard replied. "Charlotte and Geneviève will stay put for the moment, in case he decides to come back. Otherwise, I've spread the word among our nearest kin, and I'm sure news will travel. Perhaps we'll hear back from someone who has spotted him." He stood for a moment, looking at the floor as if the tiles held the answer to Charles's whereabouts, and then, shaking himself out of his stupor, said, "In any case, I have several calls still to make, so please excuse me."

"Is there anything I can do to help?"

"No, nothing to be done," he mumbled as he walked toward the double stairway.

"I think I'll stay, then," I called.

"Yes, yes," he said distractedly, disappearing down the hallway at the top of the staircase.

I stood there feeling awful for a moment, wondering what Charles could possibly be up to this time, and thinking of how Charlotte must be going out of her mind with worry. I would write her as soon as I got home.

Glancing down the hallway toward Vincent's room, I had to almost physically restrain myself from going to see him. Even though he'd never know, I decided to be good. This time.

And then it dawned on me. This was the perfect opportunity

to check out JB's library. I waited for a few seconds, until I heard Gaspard's door close, and then skipped up the stairs and made my way to the library.

For me, this room was like book heaven. I had never been in here on my own—only with the whole group during the couple of meetings I had attended in it. And now, here it was, all mine to discover. Thousands of volumes, many of which I assumed contained references to revenants, lined the walls in columns so high that the top shelves had to be accessed by ladders.

Where to even start? I knew what I wanted: the stash of newly acquired books that Vincent had mentioned—those that Gaspard, acting as the Paris clan's unofficial researcher and librarian, hadn't had time to go through yet. I was convinced that if he had seen *Immortal Love*—and had actually read it cover to cover—he would have checked out the *guérisseur* option and Vincent would have told me about it.

I took a few minutes to browse through the shelves, like I had in Papy's library, situating myself in the maze of books. Although there was definitely some sort of order to them, I couldn't tell what it was. However, the spine of each book held a little tag with a reference number typed on it, just like in a public library. After a quick glance around the room, I spotted something that warmed my heart: a big wooden cabinet inset with dozens of tiny drawers. Gaspard kept an old-fashioned card catalogue. I felt like kissing him.

There hadn't been an author's name on Papy's book, so I skipped to the drawers that were catalogued by book title. And to my utter astonishment, there it was—*Immortal Love*—spelled out in old-fashioned typewriter letters. I stood there and gawked at it, incredulous that it had been so easy to find. Underneath the title, Gaspard had typed in French "Illum. manu. 10th century, Fr.," with a Gaspard Decimal System number in the upper right corner. I memorized the number and went searching.

And it was . . . not as easy as I had thought. The book wasn't on the shelf where it should have been, which was full of archival boxes, conceivably holding other illuminated manuscripts. And it wasn't on any of the neighboring shelves. I worked my way around the room, trying once more to get a feel for Gaspard's organization. Near the windows I spied a set of shelves that weren't jam-packed full of books like the others. And upon closer investigation, I saw a small metal plaque attached to the front of the bookcase engraved with the words À LIRE. "To read."

My heartbeat accelerated as I ran my fingers over the spines and noticed that they were organized by number as well. *Thank the OCD gods*, I thought, and then I saw it. The correct number—on the spine of an archival box. I opened it and there it was: bound in the same rust-colored leather as Papy's copy.

I lifted the book out and carefully replaced the box in its spot. Then, carrying it to a small table stacked high with assorted volumes, I sat and opened the cover. There they were, Goderic and Else, holding hands in a portrait that was almost identical to the one in Papy's book.

I had begun turning the pages, carefully, toward the passage about the *guérisseur*, when I heard footsteps approach and the doorknob begin to creak. Panicking, I dropped the book into my bag, grabbed another volume from a stack in front of me, and opened it.

The sparrowlike figure of Violette stepped through the door. "Kate!" she cried, and came over to where I sat to give me cheek-kisses. "What are you doing here?"

"Gaspard canceled my fight training, so I thought I'd just hang out and read."

Violette looked over my shoulder at the book I had opened. "You are reading about snake anatomy?" she asked, confused.

I looked down to see that the page held an illustration of a dissected snake, with Latin terms identifying the different bones and organs. "Um, yeah. I find nature . . . fascinating!" I cringed inside. I sounded like the head of the Geek Patrol.

She closed the book and sat down on the table facing me. "So Vincent is dormant. Would you like to do something?"

I grinned. "I'm actually having lunch with Georgia, but I could meet you afterward for an afternoon showing."

"We can both have a look at *Pariscope* and then telephone each other. Should we say around four o'clock?"

"Perfect," I said, standing. Violette wasn't going anywhere, and I was dying to have a look at the book. I could have read it there, right in front of her, but it would have seemed weird to be hiding something from Jean-Baptiste's collection in my purse. I would just have to return it later. Gaspard had so many volumes on his "To read" shelves that I was sure he wouldn't miss it.

"You are finished with your snake reading?" Violette asked jokingly.

"Um, yeah," I said weakly as I headed toward the door. "See you later then. I'll text you with my top movie picks."

She smiled and waved before heading toward the card catalogue.

I closed the door behind me, my heart thumping away as I felt awash in a tide of guilt. What in the world was I doing? I was sure JB and Gaspard wouldn't mind me using the library, but taking an old, valuable book home with me? I couldn't imagine they would be very happy about that. *I'll bring it back tomorrow*, I thought, and made my way out of the house of the dead and back into the world of the living.

EIGHTEEN

I SAT IN MY ROOM, STARING AT THE TWO OLD
books that lay open side by side on my bed. The word that
had been crossed out in Papy's book was easily legible in Jean-
Baptiste's copy—it was "Audoniens." However, the "Sign of the
Cord" bit had been crossed out so thoroughly that it was impossible to decipher. Both books were needed to fit together the puzzle
pieces: the *guérisseur* lived among the Audoniens and could be
found under the Sign of the Cord.

How strange, I thought. Someone wanted to make this *guérisseur* very hard to find. But not impossible. Well, if someone's
identity was being protected, that must mean that this was more
than just a fairy tale. I just wondered if the healer's descendants
were still around, twelve hundred years later.

So, I was looking for a faraway land (at least far away from Goderic, wherever he had lived) and for a people called *les Audoniens*.
Once I found them, I had to find out what the Sign of the Cord

was. "Selling relics to pilgrims," it said. So probably near a church.

I checked my clock. It was a half hour until my lunch with Georgia—a half-hour away—at a restaurant in the Marais. But Georgia was always late.

Slipping my laptop out of my desk drawer, I typed "Audoniens" into Google . . . and almost jumped out of my chair when I saw what appeared on my screen. "*Audoniens*" was the French moniker for people who lived in Saint-Ouen. Saint-Ouen . . . as in the neighborhood in the north of Paris. Of course, in medieval times it must have been its own town. As Paris grew, it gobbled up all the little towns on its borders and incorporated them into the city. So the healer didn't say "Paris" or "Parisians" because he was referring to the then separate village of Saint-Ouen.

It was so close, I could go there every day if I needed to until I found what I was looking for. Or found that what I was looking for no longer existed. Pushing my luck, I searched for "Sign of the Cord" in English. And came up with a lot of references to spinal cord injuries. There was nothing of interest when I checked in French. I closed my laptop and stuck it back in my desk, then lay JB's book carefully in its own drawer.

I threw my coat on and left the apartment at a jog, with Papy's copy of the book in my bag. I had what I needed, and could at least give his book back today. Hopefully he hadn't had the chance to go through his inventory cupboard and wouldn't notice when I replaced it. Not that he would mind me taking things from the gallery. Papy had always been overly generous with me and Georgia. I just didn't want to draw attention to the fact that the book that I took was all about revenants. He would definitely be suspicious after my "numa" slip last year.

I Métro'd over to the Marais and walked down the tiny street called rue des Rosiers, which was infamous for the World War II roundup of Jews for transport to concentration camps. One Jewish deli still had a bullet hole in its window: the owners left it as a testament to that darkest of times in the neighborhood's history.

I neared the end of the street and saw the three famous falafel shops, lined up in a row. Heading toward the one with the green facade, I spotted Georgia already seated inside. On time. Which had to be a personal record for her.

Over squishy falafel sandwiches smothered in tahini sauce, my sister and I caught up on the last couple of days.

"So it takes your boyfriend being dead for you to come out with me?" Georgia teased.

"Not dead—dormant. And *you're* the one who's so busy I never see you anymore."

"Yes, well, being a rock star's girlfriend takes up all my extra-curricular time." She pretended to do an over-the-shoulder hair toss, even though her hair was way too short to be tossed, and took a big bite of pita.

"Rock *star*?" I teased. "When did he get the promotion from 'wannabe'?"

"Ha, ha," Georgia deadpanned. "You'll see for yourself next Saturday night. Because you *are* coming. So . . . tell me. How's your hunt for Vincent's miracle cure?"

"I actually found something," I said, leaning in toward her and squeezing her wrist excitedly.

"What! What is it?" Georgia's eyes grew big.

I carefully wiped my hands, and then, using a paper napkin to protect it, pulled Papy's book out of my bag. I turned to the first page to show her the double portrait. She studied it for a second and then said, "That is some serious cougar action going on there."

"Georgia!"

"I'm sorry. I couldn't help myself. So, what is it?"

I tucked the book back in my bag and told her the whole story.

"Wow—you booklifted something from Jean-Baptiste's library?"

"Just for a day. I don't know why I couldn't just show it to Violette."

Georgia lifted an eyebrow to show me her feelings for Violette were unchanged.

"Anyway, so now I have this mysterious information to go on, and am going to sleuth around Saint-Ouen looking for some nameless healer whose family might have died out centuries ago."

"Sleuthing. That's so Nancy Drew." Georgia smiled. "Gonna have to get you a pencil skirt and an oversize magnifying glass." Her expression changed from silly to serious in a second flat. "So, what can I do to help?"

"Well, first of all, you can help me return the book to Papy's gallery. Distract him while I put it back where I got it. But after that, I think I'd rather do the sleuthing alone, since I have no clue where I should even look first."

"Deal. But just let me know if you ever want me to come along."

I smiled my thanks. "Oh, and don't mention anything to Vincent. I don't want him to know what I'm doing until I'm sure I'm onto something. He's kind of been . . . doing his own thing that he's not telling me about."

I had meant it to sound flippant, but my voice cracked and gave me away. My sister's eyes filled with sympathy. "Oh no, Katie-Bean. What's going on?"

"It's something he's doing to make things easier on us—some kind of test. But he doesn't want to talk about it because he thinks it will freak me out. Whatever it is, it's not good for him. He looks worn out. And beat up. I'm just afraid it's dangerous."

"Oh, little sister," Georgia said, and leaning over, took me in her arms. She gave me an affectionate squeeze before sitting back and considering what I had said.

"Well . . . first of all, I hope that your instincts are wrong and that Vincent's not doing anything stupid. But secondly, I think you're totally right about striking out on your own, Katie-Bean," she said, petting my arm consolingly. "You've always been the smartest one in the family. If you think you can solve this, then I'm sure you will. And then, when you show up with the answer to all his immortal problems, you'll knock that dead boy right off his feet."

I smiled at her, reassured. Nothing like a sister-sister pep talk for comfort.

Georgia and I pulled the book-replacement scheme off brilliantly, with Papy so surprised to see my sister actually *in* the gallery and acting interested in the antiquities, that I easily excused myself, nabbed the key, and slipped into the back room. I was relieved to see all the boxes were in the closet where I had left them. Papy would never know the book had been gone.

Leaving Papy's, Georgia and I walked up the rue de Seine, past all the minimalist galleries and crowded antique shops. I glanced over at La Palette, the café where I had spotted Vincent with Geneviève last fall. The terrace was punctuated with tall, treelike gas heaters, and all the tables beneath them were occupied.

My eye was caught by a blond boy sitting at a table, talking to a man standing beside him. The table held several open notebooks: The boy had been interrupted while writing. As we got nearer, I saw it was Arthur.

Georgia noticed him at the same time. "Hey, isn't that one of Vincent's friends?" Arthur glanced our way, and he flinched as he registered who we were. "*Bonjour!* Hello!" he called, after a second's hesitation.

"Great. Thanks, Georgia. He looks *really* happy to see us," I grumbled as we crossed the street to stand in front of his table.

The guy talking to Arthur was a handsome older man, probably around Gaspard's age. He looked like someone I knew, but I couldn't quite place him. And there was something weird about him, something just outside my mind's grasp that didn't seem right. When he saw Georgia and me heading in their direction, he tucked his newspaper under his arm and walked quickly away.

"Another friendly acquaintance of the oldsters," I muttered to Georgia, and then I said more loudly, "Hi, Arthur."

Arthur stood politely to greet us. "Hello, Kate. And Georgia, is it?"

"Georgia it *is*," my sister said flirtatiously.

"Yes, well"—Arthur gestured toward his table—"would you like to join me for a coffee?"

"Sure—" Georgia began.

"No," I said, cutting her off. "Thank you, though. We have things to do. In fact, I'm supposed to be meeting Violette soon."

"Ah, yes, for one of your movie dates. Well, she's just up the road shopping." He indicated the direction with a nod of his head, and then stared silently at me, with an expression that looked almost apologetic.

I stared right back, challenging him to say something. If forgiveness was what he wanted, he wasn't getting any from me. "See you," I said after an awkward pause, and, taking Georgia's arm, led her away.

As soon as we got out of hearing distance, she turned to me. "What is wrong with you?" she asked. "He was trying to be nice."

"He also got me kicked out of a house meeting for being human."

Georgia drew her breath in sharply. "He did *not*!"

"He did," I confirmed.

"So they're both racists," Georgia mused. "But the difference is, he's cute. Katie-Bean, doesn't he kind of remind you of . . ."

"Kurt Cobain."

"Totally!"

We were barely out of view of the café when we saw Violette a half block away, inspecting the display in a shop window. Spotting us heading her way, she smiled broadly and waved. "Hello, Kate! Hello . . ." And then she saw who was with me.

"Oh, wonderful. The evil munchkin herself," moaned Georgia. "I'm outta here," she said loudly enough for Violette to hear, and walked off down a side street.

The revenant acted like nothing had happened. "I was about to phone you about our movie."

"Yeah, me too," I said, "but we saw Arthur, and he told us where to find you. We weren't supposed to meet for another hour or two, but if you want, we could go now."

"Absolutely," she said. "My only plans were to sit around with that sourpuss at La Palette and wait for you."

"Sourpuss?" I asked, surprised. This was the second time she'd said something unflattering about her partner. Not that I didn't agree.

"Oh, Arthur can be such a stick-in-the-mud sometimes. I have stayed with him for centuries, but sometimes he makes me crazy." She grinned at me conspiratorially. Laughing, I grabbed her arm and walked with her toward the nearest art-house cinema.

"That was very, very strange," Violette mused as she sipped her coffee.

"I warned you," I said, stirring some whipped cream into my hot chocolate.

"But I thought it was going to have something to do with . . . you know . . . Brazil. I mean, that is what it is called. If they had called it 'Bizarre Alternate Universe,' I would not have chosen it."

I smiled, thinking of the confusion and disgust I had seen on Violette's face during the face-lift scene. Special effects weren't yet in her movie vocabulary. I would make it a point in the future to stick to older, classic films.

"So, how is it going with Vincent? Has he talked to you about things yet?"

"No," I said, my smile disappearing. "And I'm getting a bit worried. Have you noticed how bad he's been looking lately? Whatever he's doing, it's obviously really hard on him."

Violette nodded. "It is probably a case of things getting worse before they can get better."

"That's exactly what he said!" I exclaimed. I sipped my chocolate and shook my head in frustration. "You know, Violette, I've started looking for my own solution."

Her eyebrows rose. "Really? Like what?"

"The same thing he's looking for. Something that will prevent his need for death."

"You are really that upset about seeing him die?"

I nodded. "I didn't react well to Charles's death last fall, and he's not even my boyfriend."

"I guess that *is* the normal human reaction. Especially for someone like you who has been affected by death so recently." She touched my hand lightly in sympathy. "So . . . what are you thinking of?"

"I don't know. I'm just researching it right now."

"Oh, so that is why you were in the library this morning!"

I smiled guiltily. "I actually found something somewhere else—at my grandfather's gallery. A book about a revenant-human couple. It talked about a *guérisseur* who might have had some sort of remedy."

"That sounds fascinating. I would *love* to see it!" she said eagerly.

"I actually just returned it to my Papy's shop." I didn't mention the fact that I had Gaspard's copy sitting in my desk drawer.

"Oh, what a shame," she said. "What was it about?"

"It was this gorgeous illuminated manuscript called *Immortal Love*, and the story was about this couple—the man was revenant and the woman was human. They were going to consult a *guérisseur* who could help them, but then the wife died and the husband had a numa destroy him."

"I have heard about that story before," Violette said thoughtfully. "I have not actually read it, but I have seen it referred to in other texts." She hesitated. "Not to discourage you, but I have to warn you, Kate: Those old legends are usually just that—old legends. They might have a grain of truth in them, but certainly nothing that you could rely on to be helpful."

"You're probably right," I said, wanting to change the subject now. Once I had returned the book, I could show it to her and ask what she thought. Until then, I preferred that she forget about it. The last thing I wanted was for her to go searching for it in Jean-Baptiste's library and find an empty box.

NINETEEN

IT WASN'T UNTIL I GOT IN BED THAT NIGHT THAT I felt it. The loneliness. This was my least favorite day of the month. The day when Vincent was nonexistent. A few streets away, his body lay cold on his bed.

It wasn't like I *had* to see him every single moment of the day. But when I knew I couldn't talk to him—that there was no way to contact him—well, that was when it really got to me.

We hadn't even been together for a year, but it truly felt like Vincent was my soul mate. He completed me. Not that I wasn't a whole person on my own. But who he was seemed to complement who I was.

I leaned my head back against the pillow and closed my eyes. The image of a painting came to my mind: one of my favorite works by Cézanne. It is a small, simple canvas depicting two perfect peaches. The fruits are painted in loose brushstrokes of oranges, yellows, and reds, their vivid colors combined in a way that makes you want to pluck one from the painting and bite into it to experience its tantalizing juiciness for yourself.

But there was something else in the picture that you didn't even notice until you let your eyes drift from the warm colors. The peaches sat on a creamy white plate with a soft blue fabric nestled up behind them. If the peaches had been painted on an empty canvas—fiery colors against a background of pure white— they wouldn't have been believable. But the delicately painted background brought them to life.

That's what Vincent was for me. He gave me context. I was whole in and of myself, but better than whole with him.

But for now, I was alone. I set my mind on what I had planned for the next day, and gradually drifted into sleep.

Good morning, ma belle, a voice said as I opened my eyes. I glanced at my clock. Eight a.m.

Rolling over to my side, I closed my eyes again. "Mmm," I groaned in pleasure. "Good morning, Vincent. How long have you been ghosting around my bedroom?" I spoke my thoughts aloud. It was the only way Vincent could hear me, since mind reading was not a revenant superpower.

Since I woke up. I guess it was a bit after midnight. The words ran through my head like a breeze, bypassing my ears and traveling directly through my thoughts. In the beginning I had gotten only a few words at a time. But now—after a few months' practice—I could understand almost everything.

"Did I snore?" I murmured.

You never snore. You're perfect.

"Ha!" I said. "I'm just really glad you don't have a sense of smell when you're volant. I don't have to jump up and brush my teeth before we chat."

Although I couldn't see him, I imagined he was smiling.

"I miss you," I said. "I wish I could be at your house right now, lying in your bed, keeping you company."

Keeping my cold, hard body company? In my mind, Vincent's voice sounded amused. *When you could be having a conversation with me instead? So—*the next words took a few seconds to come through*—you* do *like my body better than my mind.*

"I like both," I said obstinately. "But I have to say there's something about human touch that seems pretty essential to a relationship. I would not be into dating a ghost, for example."

No ghosts, okay. But revenants are datable?

"Only one revenant," I said, my arms actually aching to hold him against me. I wrapped them around my pillow instead. A flower of desire began blooming inside me as I imagined him lying in bed beside me. "I want you," I murmured, unsure whether he heard my pillow-muffled words.

Desire . . . The airspace in my head was quiet for a whole minute, and then I heard him again. *Desire is a funny thing. When I'm with you—in body—I'm constantly on the defensive. Against myself. We haven't known each other long, and I need you to be sure of what you want before we . . . go further.*

"I know what I want," I said.

Vincent ignored that and continued. *But here, when touching you isn't even an option . . . well, I want you so badly it hurts.*

I sat up in surprise and looked around the room, trying to place exactly where he was. "You've never said that before."

Trying to resist you is like trying to resist dying. It just gets harder the longer I hold out.

I sat there for a minute, stunned by his words. My senses were all on the alert: My fingers tingled and the scent of Mamie's flowers on my nightstand suddenly seemed overpoweringly heady. "You said that dying is like a drug to you," I said finally.

And yet, I choose you instead. I can only imagine that when our time finally comes, it will be exponentially better than any of these short-lived supernatural rewards.

"When *will* our time come?" I asked hesitantly.

When do you want it to?

"Now."

Easy answer, since it's not possible. I could almost hear Vincent's rueful smile.

"Soon, then," I responded.

Are you sure? The words flitted like birds through my mind.

"Yes. I'm sure," I said, my body buzzing, but my mind feeling strangely calm about my decision. It wasn't like I hadn't thought about it. A lot. Sex—in my mind—was something you did with someone you planned on staying with. And there was no question that I wanted to stay with Vincent. Intimacy was the next natural step.

I stayed in bed for another half hour, talking to Vincent. The phone rested on my pillow in case Mamie walked in unannounced. Which she never did. But if that ever happened, it was my excuse for having a conversation with the air.

Vincent was on walking duty for the entire day with Jules and Ambrose, so once he left, I got up, had my breakfast, and took off. I had done my research the day before and had discovered that the Bishop Saint Ouen, for whom the town was named, had died in the royal villa of King Dagobert in 686 CE. It was to this Villa Clippiacum that pilgrims had made their way, and the whole town had been founded around Saint-Ouen's cult.

The royal villa no longer existed, but I found a website saying that it was probably located where a twelfth-century church now stood. I figured I would begin my search in the area immediately around the church, and then work my way outward until I found something.

I took the Métro to Mairie de Saint-Ouen, just above the northernmost edge of Paris's circle—at the twelve o'clock of its watch face—and headed toward the church, using the neighborhood map in the Métro station.

During the fifteen-minute walk, the buildings went from modern glass and tile structures to run-down brick high-rises with satellite dishes attached outside every window. When I finally reached the church, I was amazed to see the squat stone building nestled in the middle of an iffy-looking housing project. Seeing a gang of surly boys leaning on a rail nearby, I headed directly for the church's front door and tugged at it, only to find it locked.

I stepped back to get a better look. The stone facade didn't look very old, but the carving over the lintel was medieval, showing an angel handing a chalice to a queen. To the right of the church was a cobblestone courtyard lined with rosebushes locked behind a white metal gate. On it hung a paper printed with the hours of upcoming masses. "Église Saint-Ouen le Vieux" was typed across the top. This had to be the right place.

The church was perched on a high cliff overlooking an industrial stretch of the river Seine, and I could easily imagine—with its vantage point over water transport—why this location had been chosen for the seventh-century royal villa. *If pilgrims came here to worship, the relic sellers couldn't have been too far away*, I thought.

I glanced around for a church boutique or one of those shops near European holy places that are stuffed with pictures of the pope and postcards of saints. But the only buildings sharing the block with the church were apartments and a retirement home. I began walking away from the church, outward in a zigzag pattern so I wouldn't miss anything. There were no reliquary shops. No signs with cords or ropes.

I even checked the local bars. None of them had a name even slightly resembling what I was looking for, although what did I expect? A pub called "The Cord and Relic"? "The Healer and the Rope"? I didn't exactly expect to see "The Sign of the Cord" spelled out in so many letters, but I found nothing of interest within a good six blocks.

Frustrated, I went back to the church and sat down on its front steps, ignoring the catcalls of the gang of boys and trying to formulate a plan B for my search. A group of three men walked up to a nearby building, knocked on a locked door, and cast suspicious glances at me and the boys as they waited nervously for someone to open it. *I am so out of here*, I thought, feeling distinctly unsafe. As I stood to go, a man with a priest's collar walked out of the gated courtyard. I went after him.

"Excuse me," I said. The man smiled patiently and waited. "Is there some sort of church shop nearby that sells relics or religious items?"

He shook his head and shrugged. "When the church is open for mass, we sell candles and postcards. But I don't know of any shops around here that would deal in what you're looking for."

I thanked him and, disheartened, began walking away.

"You know, you could always try the Marché aux Puces," he called after me.

The Marché aux Puces. Paris's famous flea market. It was less than a half-hour walk from here. Of course, it hadn't even existed a thousand years ago, but maybe *something* had. Something that could have remained. Or relocated. The market was *the* place in Paris where you could find almost anything, so . . . why not?

It was already past noon, so I picked up a panini in a shop and ate it while I walked, knowing full well that eating lunch on the street in Paris is an etiquette no-no. As I munched my sandwich, people I passed wished me *bon appétit*, which was a teasing way of saying, "You should really be sitting down to enjoy your meal."

As I hit the edge of the huge mile-square area that the market comprises, vendors with folding tables holding junk—not even the usual flea-market-style "junque"—started to appear, selling everything from gross old plastic potty seats to car parts. The closer I got to the market's center, the better the goods got, until actual market stalls and tiny shops began to appear, jam-packed with everything from wooden African masks to vintage seventies lava lamps to crystal chandeliers. The smell of incense and furniture wax blended with the sharp sting of sautéed onions as I passed one of several food stands dotting the market.

I scanned the shop signs as I went, looking for any cordlike symbols. *Maybe a workshop that used to house a rope maker*, I thought. But there was nothing like that hanging above the antiques stores I passed. Finally I stopped and asked a vendor if he knew of anything that had a sign of a cord. He rubbed his chin and shook his head. *"Non."*

"Well, is there anyone in the market who specializes in relics? Like . . . religious items?" I asked.

He thought for a moment. "Down that way there's a store that isn't really a part of the market. It's more a shop, with regular opening hours. So it won't be open on a Sunday, but you can have a look." He gave me detailed instructions on how to get there, even though it was just a couple of blocks away. I thanked him with a grateful smile and headed in the direction he had pointed.

It was a tiny shop located on a street corner, flanked by an antique doll store on one side and, down the adjoining street, a vintage clothes boutique. The facade was painted bottle green, and the windows were lined with shelves packed with religious statues in every material imaginable: wood, marble, metal—even bone. There were crucifixes of all sizes and flasks of holy water "from the blessed springs of Lourdes," as the tags read. The shop behind the display was dark. As the vendor had guessed, they were closed.

I backed up to get a better look at the building and noticed an antique, weather-worn wooden sign hanging above the door. On it, a carved raven perched atop the words LE CORBEAU. A light was trying to go on in my head, but I couldn't quite flip the switch.

I read it once again and had a mental flashback to the passage from *Immortal Love*, with its Gothic-style letters that were so hard to read. And suddenly it clicked, and my heart began beating a million miles an hour. *Le corbeau*, "the raven." Not *le cordeau*, "the cord." I had misread the ancient letters in the book and had been looking for the wrong sign the whole time.

Could this possibly be the place I was looking for? It sold relics . . . under the sign of the raven . . . among the *Audoniens*. But this building could only be a few hundred years old, tops.

I didn't know what to think. But there was nothing else to be done. They were closed. No phone number or opening hours were posted on the door. There wasn't even a number on the building. I checked the sign on the doll shop and the place directly across from it and guessed the store's address from that, writing it down with the name of the street.

A woman walked out of the vintage clothes store and lit a cigarette. She glanced over at me. "He'll be back on Tuesday," she called. "Tuesday through Friday."

"Thanks so much!" I called back.

Well, I had two days to wait. And only an hour or two before Vincent was going to be off walking duty. *I hope he doesn't mind hanging out in my room*, I thought. After my busy weekend, I was going to have to spend the whole evening doing homework.

TWENTY

MY PHONE RANG ON TUESDAY MORNING AT THE exact second my alarm went off. I checked the caller's name and then answered. "So, Mr. Punctual, how are you feeling?" I asked.

"Alive. Again. And I've been waiting for an hour to call. Didn't want to wake you before your alarm." His voice was like a long, cool drink of water to my affection-parched soul.

I smiled. "I don't have time to stop by before school. And you're probably too weak to move. In fact, are you feeling better?"

"Yeah, I haven't gotten out of bed yet. But I looked in a mirror, and I look normal again."

"Well, that's a huge relief."

"I know, but it doesn't mean I can't stop. Just four more weeks to go, Kate. So I was calling to say . . . I won't be able to see you tonight." My heart dropped. After Sunday's heartfelt conversation, I so wanted to see him in the flesh. To know that what we had talked about hadn't just been a dream.

"Can't you do whatever it is tomorrow?"

"I'm sorry, Kate. It's really important that I get to it as soon as I'm able."

I was starting to feel at the end of my rope with this whole project. "What do you want me to say?" I snapped, and then sighed. "Please try to be safe, whatever you do."

"Thanks for understanding." Vincent's voice was apologetic.

"I *don't* understand, Vincent."

"You will soon. Everything's going to be fine—I swear."

Yeah. It will. Because I'm going to find another way.

My mood remained dark for the entire school day, and as soon as my last class was over, I booked it to the flea market. It took me a full hour, counting the bus, and the two Métro changes, but finally I was there, standing in front of the little green shop, which was . . . closed.

I had looked it up on the internet, and there was no listing for anything called Le Corbeau. I even Google-mapped it, sifting through the businesses listed in the area near its address. I could see the front of the building on the street view, but there was no mention of the store. It didn't show up in Yellow Pages searches for religious items. There was no trace of it online.

I had wanted to call ahead of time to make sure they were open—always a good thing to do in France. Shop owners are capricious, opening and closing at their whim. There had been many occasions when I'd schlepped halfway across town only to find locked doors and a sign reading, *Temporarily closed.*

Or no sign at all. Like now.

However, the lights were on in the vintage clothes store. An old-fashioned bell jingled above my head as I opened the door, and I got a whoosh of air in the face that smelled like the inside of old suitcases. "*Bonjour, mademoiselle,*" came a voice from behind a rack of crinolines. The woman who'd been outside smoking the other day stuck her head over the rack and peered at me expectantly.

"Hi. I was just wondering if you knew about the shop next door—Le Corbeau or whatever it's called. When will they be open?"

The woman stepped from behind the rack and rolled her eyes. "Them? Oh, you never know. When they're *supposed* to be open and when they're *actually* open are two very different things. They asked me to keep an eye on the place while they're gone. They left yesterday—for a couple of weeks, they said. Maybe more."

Two weeks? I didn't want to wait that long. But what choice did I have? "Do they have a phone? I could call before I come next time."

"Nope. Nothing listed, at least."

I sighed. This trip had been a massive waste of time. Or . . . had it? "So who are the owners?" I asked, determined to learn something. Anything.

The woman put her hands on her hips authoritatively, in a pose that practically screamed Gossip Queen. "It's a man and his elderly mother. They're kind of . . ." She circled her index finger around her temple in the universal gesture for "crazy."

"Are they . . . *guérisseurs*?" I asked hesitantly.

She straightened and raised her eyebrows as comprehension dawned. "So *that's* why you're so eager to find them! What . . . you've got migraines? Or warts?"

"Excuse me?"

"Migraines and warts—that's what the old lady specializes in."

"Oh," I said, my heart beating wildly. There was a *guérisseur* managing the relics shop—I was on the right track! My thoughts raced ahead, and it took a concentrated effort to pull them back to the conversation. "Um, migraines . . . I have migraines."

"Well, then you come back. She'll fix you up. I had my aunt go to her. Used to have migraines so bad they had to take her to the hospital three or four times a year. But ever since she saw the old lady, she hasn't had one."

"And the son? Is he a *guérisseur* too?"

"Well, you know how it works. He's probably next in line for the gift. When she gets tired of using it, she'll pass it on to him."

I thought about what Mamie had told me. "I heard that *guérisseurs* are becoming rare because the younger generation doesn't want to take on the gift."

"Oh, he'll take it, all right. I guarantee you. Like I said, they're both kind of . . ." And she made the crazy sign again. "While he's waiting for her to 'retire,' he takes care of the store . . . and his mother. A good son. Unlike mine"—she shook her head in desperation—"who is a total loser. Keeps having run-ins with the police."

"Ah, thanks for the information," I said, quickly extricating myself from what threatened to be a long and painful conversation. I waved as I left, and she waved back, calling, "Come back in two weeks. Two and a half, maybe, just to be safe."

The next Saturday, just after noon, I was lying in Vincent's room when I got a call from Ambrose. "Guess who I ran into, Katie-Lou? Or who ran into me, rather, and has appropriated my café table until I agree to comply with her wishes."

I smiled. "Pass Georgia the phone."

My sister's voice, complete with fake Southern accent, came across the line. "Hi, little sister. My lunch date bailed, but fortunately I ran into this hunk o' burnin' love, and he has gallantly offered to escort me around town today. I hadn't planned on doing anything really, but I figure it would be a waste not to show him off."

I could hear Ambrose's voice from behind her. "I told you I was busy today. No offense, but I have other things to do than take you to an afternoon-long artist-studio tour."

"Oh shush," I heard my sister chide. "You know you want to. With all the cute hip art chicks we'll meet, you'll be thanking me in a few hours."

I laughed. "Where are you?"

"At the Café Sainte-Lucie. Oh, and Ambrose said you would all come along to Sebastien's gig tonight." Damn. I had totally forgotten to tell Vincent about the concert.

"I did not!" I heard Ambrose's retort. "I only said I would ask Vincent. . . ."

"Tell Vincent Ambrose wants to go," Georgia said, ignoring him. "Oh, and tell Jules and Arthur to come too. Seb's group's opening for a really good British band. I can get everyone in."

"Please don't tell me it's anywhere near Denfert," I said, recalling the numa-infested neighborhood where Lucien's club had been.

"Nope. It's on rue des Martyrs near all the other live-music venues. Just south of Montmartre," she responded. "Ambrose wants the phone back."

"I just want to make it clear that I didn't commit us to anything," Ambrose boomed in his baritone voice. My phone beeped as another call came through. It was from Georgia's number. I put Ambrose on hold.

"I wasn't through talking." I heard her giggle as Ambrose grabbed her phone away. "Just make sure you're there. Nine p.m. Divans du Monde," she yelled as both her and Ambrose's numbers disappeared off my screen.

"You think Ambrose is safe in the hands of your force-of-nature sister?" asked Vincent from across the room. I was lying on his couch with a Modern European Society textbook propped on my chest. It was a part of my deal with Papy and Mamie: I could spend most of the weekend at Vincent's house as long as I got my homework done.

Since I had no clue what I would do after high school, I had forbidden Vincent to bring up the topic. But I assumed it would include some sort of higher education. And now that I had a good reason to stay in Paris, I needed to keep my grades up to have my choice of universities. Even so, a year and a half seemed a lifetime away, and with Vincent nearby, it was hard to stay focused.

"Georgia's just manipulated us into going to hear her boy-friend's band tonight," I said, settling back into my history book.

"Great idea," Vincent responded, looking back down at his laptop. "Arthur and Violette need to learn to loosen up."

I didn't mention that Georgia had left Violette out of the invitation—purposely, I was sure. Maybe a night out with Georgia would clear things up between the two—if they could both remain civil throughout the evening. I thought of their opposing personalities and squirmed.

"Besides, I haven't met Georgia's new man yet," Vincent continued. "I should have already checked him out by now for numa connections."

I couldn't tell whether he was joking or not. "Besides his tragic hipness, he seems pretty harmless," I said, turning a page in my book. I gave him a playful grin and said, "Come here for a second."

"Oh no you don't," he responded, his lips curving mischievously. "I have to finish this email to Charlotte, and you have to finish your European history."

"But dating you is like having my own walking, talking history book. I don't need to study. I didn't even research my last two papers. I just sat back and listened to you talk."

"Yeah, well, your teacher might find it a bit suspicious if you dragged me along to feed you answers on the exam."

"Hey—that's a really great idea!" I said, meaning it. "What if you're volant during finals?"

Vincent shook his head in despair and turned back to his screen.

"No, really, come here just for a minute," I said innocently. "I have a really important question about the Second World War."

"Okay," he sighed. He pressed send and closed the laptop, then came over to sit next to me. It had been only a few days since his last dormancy, and already the dark circles were starting to form under his eyes. His fatigue lent an air of fragility to his normally bursting-with-vitality demeanor. It made me want to protect him from whatever was hurting him. As if reading my mind, he eyed me carefully. "So . . . what's the question?"

Tearing my eyes from his face, I glanced back at the page for inspiration. "So I'm reading about the Resistance fighters who would ride their bikes from Paris out to you guys—the Maquis—in the countryside to pass you orders from the central command."

Vincent nodded. "It was dangerous. Messengers were sometimes caught. So they chose people who wouldn't be suspected by the German soldiers. Women and children were often given the job." He hesitated. "So what's your question?"

"It's kind of specific," I said, playing for time as I searched for something to ask. His proximity was what I wanted, but it sure didn't help me focus.

Vincent's eyes narrowed, and a doubtful smile formed on his lips.

"Um, did you Maquis guys ever get lonely while you were hiding out in the forests and planning ambushes on the Germans?" I reached out my hand and began playing with the back of his hair as I slowly pulled his face toward mine.

"What does this have to do with your homework?" he asked skeptically.

"Nothing," I replied. "I was just wondering what would have happened if I had been this sexy Resistance messenger who came from Paris to meet you in the woods. At night."

"Kate," Vincent said, eyes wide with amused bewilderment. "This is the lamest procrastination scheme I have ever heard. It almost counts as entrapment."

"So, I ride up on my old wartime bike to your camp," I continued, ignoring his protest. "Keep in mind, you haven't seen another human for weeks. What do you do, soldier boy?" I said, doing my best Greta Garbo impersonation.

Vincent leapt on me, pushing me backward onto the couch and kissing me enthusiastically all over as I dissolved into a fit of hysterics.

TWENTY-ONE

VIOLETTE AND ARTHUR WERE WAITING FOR US next to the club's front door. Dressed appropriately for a night out, Arthur, for once, looked his original age. He wore a band T-shirt lent to him by Vincent, over some black jeans. Without his regular button-up shirt and ascot, he was actually pretty hot. *Too bad he's an aristocratic snob*, I thought as I saw Georgia look him over appreciatively, managing to completely ignore Violette's presence as she did.

The little revenant walked up to me and kissed my cheeks. "We have not had a movie date in a whole week!" she said, reprimanding me with a joking smile.

"I know. We have to plan something soon."

She glanced at Vincent, who was standing next to me talking to Arthur, and then back to me. From her expression, I could tell she wanted to ask me something. I took a step away from him and lowered my voice. "Yes?"

"I had been thinking about that book you found at your Papy's place. The *Immortal Love* one. Gaspard actually has a copy of it, but it's missing. Do you happen to have it?"

I felt my face redden. Damn! Once I had gotten what I needed from it, I had totally forgotten about the book. *Why can't I just tell her? Because I'd look like a thief.* "No," I answered.

"Paris's revenants use Jean-Baptiste's collection like a lending library: They never leave a note when they take things. It's so frustrating!" Violette actually stomped her foot like a spoiled child, and I had to press my lips together hard not to laugh.

"Come on!" my sister yelled from where the bouncer was checking his list. I breathed a sigh of relief.

"Let's go," Vincent said, taking my hand as the bouncer held the door open and we filed into the darkened room.

Our group stood near the front of a packed room, watching Sebastien's band play on a raised stage draped with leopard-skin curtains. Between us and the band were a pack of teenage girls, dancing and watching the musicians adoringly.

Jules had brought a date—some gorgeous foreign model-looking type. They had walked in soon after we arrived, her cattish eyes looking sleepy as she poutily scanned the crowd from the protection of his arm.

"This is Giulianna," he offered, introducing her as I joined them at the bar.

"*Ciao*," she said, and turned to order a drink.

As Jules gave me cheek-kisses, he whispered, "She has nothing on you, of course, Kates. It's just that you're so very . . . taken." He winked and put his arm around the Italian bombshell, leaning in to yell his order to the bartender.

"You okay, Ambrose?" I asked, picking up the Perriers I had bought. He leaned tiredly against the bar with a tomato juice in one hand.

"Gonna be dormant later tonight," he said. "Plus, I think I've met my match with your sister. I haven't felt this exhausted in decades."

I gave him a knowing smile and carried the drinks back to where Vincent stood with Georgia. "I see some friends," she said. "Be back in a few." And she disappeared into the crowd.

Vincent looked tense as I handed him his drink. "Is something wrong?" I asked.

"No," he said. "It's just that I always feel exposed when we go places like this without someone volant along to scope out the surrounding area." He tried to look more relaxed and even started nodding along to the music, but I could tell he was worried.

"It's a safe enough neighborhood, isn't it?"

"Normally I would say yes. But it seems like we've been playing without any rules lately." He caught my look. "Don't worry—I'm sure everything's fine."

When I had filled Georgia in about all things revenant after the fateful showdown with Lucien, she had sworn not to tell a soul. I knew their secret was safe with her. Although my sister had her faults, when she made me a promise, I knew she would keep it.

And as far as my hanging out with a group of immortals, all she cared about was that they were nice to me.

So when Georgia introduced everyone after the show, it was clear that Sebastien didn't have a clue what Vincent was. And Vincent, after almost a century of practice, was a pro at acting human.

Georgia gave me a happy check-it-out-our-boyfriends-get-along look. I turned to say good-bye to Jules and Giulianna, who were leaving with a tired-looking Ambrose, and then checked my watch. It was almost midnight. In a few short hours he would be lying on his bed, stone-cold dead. No wonder he hadn't brought a date.

The bartender locked the front door behind them and began cleaning up as we stood around and waited for Sebastien to unplug amps and finish things up with his band. "I know you wanted to go out after, but it's taking them forever," I finally told my sister. "I think we're all ready to leave."

"Just a sec," Georgia said. She skipped over to where Sebastien and his group were working, gave him an enthusiastic kiss, and began making arrangements. I glanced around to see Violette and Arthur standing against the wall, looking like they'd rather be anywhere except here. If they had enjoyed the evening, they sure weren't letting it show. As we made our way to the back door, they followed silently behind.

"So I'm meeting Seb and his band at a bar just a few blocks away. Wanna come?" Georgia asked, directing the question at me and Vincent and ignoring the fact that the others were even with us.

"What do you feel like, Kate?" Vincent asked, putting his arm around me as we exited the building and began walking down the tiny cobblestone alleyway toward the main street.

"I'm pretty tired," I admitted.

"We'll walk you to the bar and wait till Sebastien arrives," Vincent said, throwing his free arm around my sister.

"I won't say no to a revenant escort," she said, "not that this neighborhood's dangerous or anything."

"I beg to differ," came Violette's voice from just behind.

We turned to see four dark shapes walking toward us down the alley. A wave of ice-cold fear washed over me. *Numa.* After two months of near invisibility, here they were, looking larger than life as they bore down on us with a steady but rapid pace.

Vincent and Arthur drew their swords from their coats so quickly that I didn't even see them move. *It's a good thing it's winter*, I thought. *Where would you hide a two-foot rapier wearing shorts and flip-flops?*

Vincent handed me his sword and drew another from inside his coat, before shrugging off the garment and throwing it to one side. I saw Violette's blade flash under the lone streetlight as she dropped her down-filled coat to the ground. She too had come prepared.

In my peripheral vision, I saw Georgia start to panic as she tried the doors of the adjoining buildings, pulling forcefully at their handles. She shrieked a curse as she realized that everything was locked. "Stay behind us," I yelled with a shaking voice, just as the first two numa arrived and began swinging their swords at Vincent and Arthur.

I knew what I was supposed to do. We had gone over it in my weaponry lessons. As the least experienced, I was expected to act as the second line of defense. If forced, I should fight. If not, I should stand behind Vincent or anyone else who had already been doing this for several lifetimes. I held my sword in front of me, bouncing nervously on the balls of my feet, ready to spring if I needed to. *Be calm*, I thought, pushing the fear into a far corner of my mind. *Get into the rhythm.*

Vincent had led his numa to one side of the alleyway and was fighting it with a fury that made my blood feel like it was shooting instead of flowing through my veins. Once again, I saw him as the avenging angel that he had been for much of the last century.

Violette had faced off with another numa, using the same martial arts skills I had seen Charlotte practice to make up for the drawback of her tiny frame. Her assailant was struggling just to keep up. She would have the advantage in no time.

Arthur was fighting the other two numa, using himself as a shield to keep them away from me and Georgia. I assumed that his strategy was to stall until either Violette or Vincent could dispatch their foe and join him to even up the odds. He seemed to be succeeding until, with one concerted effort, the two attackers pushed past his blade and leapt by him to land right in front of me.

I held up my sword just in time to meet the numa's as it crashed down toward my head, and then jumped aside to let him follow through. His blade slid down mine, and the tip smashed the ground. Arthur dashed past me toward Georgia, following the second numa who had gone straight for her. I didn't have time to glance her way but knew that Arthur could defend her better than I could. I had my own numa to concentrate on, and only two seconds to skip backward away from him as he recovered his balance.

I can't do this. As the thought flashed through my mind, I had a panic-induced out-of-body experience. I felt like I was up in the air looking down at myself: a teenage girl standing in an alley-way brandishing a sword at a man almost twice her size. *I can't,* I thought again. *I'm too afraid to move.*

My enemy righted himself and started toward me. I looked up into his cold, murderous eyes, and that was all it took. I felt the adrenaline coursing through my veins and my heart thumping in my chest. And suddenly I was in the zone. With a yell that I didn't realize was coming from my own throat until it stopped, I began moving, slashing, dancing backward and leaning from side to side to avoid his flying sword before lunging back toward him and chopping at his torso. He was able to match each of my moves, but I also met his.

Time stood still as our battle raged on, until all of a sudden my foe was down on the ground. Vincent stood behind him, his sword run through the numa's chest.

I instinctively swung around, my sword held before me as I scanned the alleyway for any remaining danger. Violette stood a few yards away, pushing her foot against a crumpled heap on the ground, using her weight as leverage to pull her sword out of the motionless body. Vincent had taken out his own enemy as well as mine.

And Georgia was sitting curled up in a little ball inside a doorway, as Arthur dragged himself down, back to the wall, into a sitting position next to her. He held his upper arm in his hand, blood flowing freely through a large tear in his shirt at his shoulder. He kicked at something next to his foot, and his slain numa's dismembered head rolled away, settling to rest against its body.

I ran to Georgia as she uncurled. As if in a daze, she stretched a hand toward Arthur. "Are you okay?"

He looked surprisingly strong for being badly wounded as he glowered at the decapitated body. "I'll be fine," he growled.

The others rushed over. Vincent took a look at the wound and then pulled off his T-shirt and wrapped it around Arthur's shoulder, binding it tightly underneath the arm.

Violette smoothed her hand comfortingly through Arthur's hair and pulled out her phone. "Jean-Baptiste? They are back in action. We have four dead numa here—up near Montmartre. Should we just leave them, or do you want to send someone for the bodies?"

She made arrangements while Vincent went to pick up their abandoned coats.

"You should probably come back with us to La Maison," I said to Georgia. As I helped her to her feet, I glanced up at Vincent, who was back, slipping his coat on as he stood over us. He shook his head and gave me a helpless shrug. I had forgotten about Jean-Baptiste's injunction against my sister's visiting the house. *Damn his rules.*

"I'd rather go straight home," she said, solving my quandary.

"I'll walk the two of you to a taxi," Vincent offered, helping her along. Georgia was shaking so hard she could barely stand.

"Is Arthur going to be okay?" she asked, addressing Violette directly for the first time that night.

"He will be dormant in a few days. After that his wound will heal," she responded with the assurance of someone who had lived through this type of experience before.

Once on the main street, Vincent packed us into the back of a taxi. "Go straight home—don't stop anywhere along the way," he called as the taxi drove off.

Jules was waiting outside our building when we arrived. He opened the taxi door and helped us out, and then leaned in to pay the driver. "I heard you were incredible," he said, leading the way to our front door.

"What?" I asked, confused.

"Superhero Kate, fighting off the numa," he replied, admiration glowing in his eyes. He swung his arm around my shoulder and pulled me to him.

Having been so worried about Georgia and Arthur, I had completely forgotten about my performance in the alley. *I fought a numa*, I marveled. *And this time I did it without Vincent possessing me.* I shook my head in wonder, before glancing back at Jules and admitting, "It wasn't me who killed him. Vincent did the honor."

"He told me you kept the guy at bay until he was able to get to you. That's pretty amazing for only a couple of months' training. But then again, I was already fully aware of your awesomeness." He murmured this last part as he opened the door. Georgia staggered silently past him into the front hall and pressed the button for the elevator.

"She was so close to being killed," I said. "Arthur barely got to her in time to save her life."

"Vincent told me." Jules nodded. "Make sure she rests the next couple of days. She'll be pretty weak—Arthur will be getting all her energy."

"What are you talking about?" I asked.

"So . . . you don't know all our secrets yet!" Jules responded with a wry smile. "Just ask Vincent about energy transfer. And make sure Georgia rests while she gets over her shock."

He turned to leave, stepping down from the door to the pavement.

"Hey, what happened to your date?" I asked.

"I've got my priorities," he said, running his fingers through his hair in a debonair gesture. "And keeping you alive, Kates, is a bit higher up on my list than a late date with a pretty *signorina*."

"Glad to know you care." I smiled and, hesitating for just a second, stepped down from the doorway and gave him a good old American hug before turning to follow my sister.

TWENTY-TWO

I PEEKED INTO GEORGIA'S ROOM THE NEXT MORN-ing. She was sitting propped up in bed, flipping through a music magazine. Her hair was sticking straight out, and her regular peaches-and-cream complexion was verging on kiwi-and-stale-milk.

"There you are," she said as I plopped down on the end of her bed. "You're usually up at the crack of dawn."

"Yeah, well, fighting monsters in a dark alleyway at midnight seems to have taken a bit out of me," I said, my shoulder muscles burning as I cautiously tested them. "How are you feeling?"

"Like warmed-over crap," she said. "I have absolutely no energy and was hoping you'd come in so I could hit you up for breakfast in bed."

"Is that right?" I exclaimed, laughing. "Well, I guess I can accommodate, seeing you were two inches from being taken out by an evil zombie last night."

"And rescued by a good zombie?" She smiled.

"If you want to get technical, yeah," I said with a grin, and then got up and walked to the door. "Jules warned me that you'd probably be in shock and should rest. I would spend some quality time in the bathtub if I were you. It's my personal choice for post-traumatic stress. But first, I'll get us breakfast."

I returned five minutes later with a tray for both of us, and sat on the floor with my back against Georgia's dresser while I ate a bowl of cereal. She munched pensively on her toast for a few minutes and then said, "So tell me more about this Arthur guy."

I set my bowl on the ground. "Oh no, Georgia. Please do not tell me you're crushing on Arthur just because he saved your life last night."

"I didn't say I was crushing on him. I'm simply interested in who he is. Will you allow that, Miss Protector-of-the-Undead?"

I rolled my eyes. "I don't really know much about him. He and Violette knew each other in life—she was one of Anne of Brittany's ladies-in-waiting, supposedly, and he was one of her dad's counselors . . . at least that's what Charlotte said. Which would mean they're aristocrats."

"Oh believe me, it shows." Georgia smirked.

"They both died around 1500, so he's really ancient. And they've been living in isolation in this Loire Valley castle for a really long time."

"What's he like?"

"Honestly, Georgia, I don't know," I conceded. "After he said that humans shouldn't be allowed in revenant meetings—right in front of me—I haven't really felt like getting to know him. The chip on my shoulder's pretty much superglued there."

Georgia smiled. "Are he and Violette . . . together?"

"I thought they were. She acts really possessive of him. But Vincent said it's platonic. Platonic but codependent. Sounds like a healthy relationship."

"He looked really hot in that T-shirt last night," Georgia mused, taking a sip of coffee.

"Georgia!" I shouted. "You have a boyfriend. And plus, you've said it before yourself: You don't *do* dead guys. You're not even allowed in their house!"

"I'm not *doing* anything," she said. "Especially not today." She leaned back against her headboard, looking a little weaker than before.

"I can't even believe we're having this conversation," I said, shaking my head. "He's five hundred, for God's sake! Plus he has this love-hate relationship with humans. There's no way he'd look twice at you."

Oh no, I thought. That was totally the wrong thing to say to my sister. She was going to see him as a challenge now. I changed the subject fast. "Anyway, what's wrong with good old Sebastien?"

"Nothing's wrong with him," she said, gazing dreamily at the ceiling. Her expression suddenly changed to alarm. "Nothing except . . . oh my God, Kate. I ditched him last night and never called! Quick—bring me my phone. It's in my bag."

I picked up the breakfast tray as she was babbling some ridiculous explanation of why she hadn't shown last night to Sebastien's voice mail. At least she was still concerned enough about him to make an effort, I reassured myself. The interest in Arthur was just one of those hero-worship infatuations. Knowing Georgia, she'd forget about it by lunchtime.

Vincent and I sat side by side, peering at the over-the-top gore of Géricault's famous painting *The Raft of the Medusa*. He had convinced me to take him to the Louvre, even though it was a weekend and packed with people. "I want you to teach me about art so I can understand why you're so affected by it," he had said. Which was so romantic that before it was even out of his mouth, I was pulling him down the street in the direction of the museum.

We sat in one of my favorite rooms—one that contained melodramatic historical paintings on canvases as big as king-size beds. The sensational scene before us seemed oddly appropriate as a backdrop for a discussion about undead superpowers.

"So what's the story with this energy transfer thing?" I asked.

"Energy transfer?" Vincent repeated, confused, his eyes glued to the scene before us. He seemed to be studying it in a problem-solving way. The decomposing bodies didn't seem to bother him—I could tell he was just juggling the geometry of the live humans in his mind to strategize how many he could save in one go.

"Yeah. Jules mentioned it last night. He said something like Georgia would be weak because Arthur would have her energy. What's that mean?"

Vincent tore his gaze from the painting. "Well, you know why we die for people?"

203

"Besides out of the kindness of your nonbeating hearts?" I joked. Vincent took my hand and held it to his chest. "Okay, your beating undead heart," I corrected myself, reluctantly pulling my hand away. "If you die saving someone, you reanimate at the age you lost your human life. It's a compulsion meant to preserve your immortality, right?"

"Right," Vincent said. "But you know we only die occasionally—maybe once a year in times of peace. Most of our 'saves' don't necessarily involve dying. Did you ever think about why we would spend our immortal lives watching over you if there wasn't a solid enticement? Whatever you've heard about superheroes, none of them are out saving the human race just because they're really nice guys."

I immediately thought of Violette. Of her and Arthur holding out until their sixties until they died for someone, and then only doing it because Jean-Baptiste needed them. They didn't seem to love their job, to say the least.

Vincent turned his body toward me and linked his fingers through mine. "Imagine that everyone has this kind of life energy inside."

I nodded, picturing all the tourists walking around the room with a glowing cloud inside them.

"So you know how, when someone's been in a near-death situation, they sometimes suffer post-traumatic shock? Well, try to picture it as that energy, or life force, being temporarily sucked out of them."

Remembering my own brush with death the previous year, I

said, "After I barely escaped being crushed by the side of the café, I was pretty weak and shaky for a couple of days."

"Exactly," Vincent said. "So if a revenant is responsible for the rescue, the energy or strength that has been figuratively 'sucked out' of the would-be victim is literally infused into the revenant for the hours or days that it takes the human to recover."

I thought about it for a minute, and then stared at him in surprise. "So when you and Charlotte rescued me, you guys got my energy? And same for Arthur with Georgia?"

Vincent nodded.

"And what about the girl who almost got run over by the truck the other day? I saw her afterward, sitting in shock by the side of the road."

"Which is why I was able to stand up and walk away from the accident scene," he confirmed. "That transfer of energy makes us physically stronger. Our muscles, hair, nails, everything goes into overdrive. It's a rush—like a hit of power for us." He watched for my reaction.

"So, basically what you're saying is that I'm going out with a druggie zombie with a death wish. Who used me for my energy. Well"—I gave him as serious a look as I could muster—"I guess I could do worse."

Vincent's laugh turned several heads, and we stood to leave before we drew any more attention to ourselves.

"So Arthur's going to be okay?" I asked as we passed the gigantic tableau showing Napoleon's coronation.

"Yep, thanks to Georgia loaning him her strength, among

other reasons"—and at this, Vincent turned his eyes from mine in an incredibly suspicious gesture—"he's actually not in any pain and has his full strength."

What was that about? I thought, my curiosity piqued. But I had to drop the thought to refocus on what he was saying.

"But his wound won't heal completely until he's dormant. And since it's pretty serious, he'll probably be laid up in bed a whole day after he awakes."

"Why?"

"The more severely wounded you are before dormancy, the longer it takes you to recover," he stated, shrugging as if it were mere logic. "If a severed limb is reconnected during dormancy, we could need another day or two of recovery after awaking. Regenerating body parts lays us up for weeks."

Eww. Although I wanted to know everything about the revenants, sometimes the details Vincent gave me fell into the TMI category. Like now. I tried not to visualize what he had just said, and thought instead about the repercussions. As we walked out of the museum and headed toward the bridge crossing the Seine to our neighborhood, I mulled it over.

The revenant-human relationship was symbiotic—to say the least. Humans relied on revenants (however unknowingly) as we would on doctors or emergency workers: to save our lives. Revenants needed humans not only to keep them existent, but to ease the emotional and physical pain imposed by their particular lifestyle. *Or deathstyle, rather,* I thought in a flash of morbidity.

Without revenants, humans would still exist . . . many would just die a lot earlier. Without humans, revenants would cease to exist. Not to mention that they started out human in the first place.

The system had been working for a long time. Problems only arose when something out of the ordinary happened. Like a human and a revenant falling in love. And, once again, my mind returned to our plight. If I was going to see the *guérisseur*—that is, if I ever showed up when she happened to be there—I needed to know what to ask. Since Vincent was in an explaining mood, I decided to dig a bit deeper.

"So, how does it work? Can a revenant ever die—of natural causes—and just . . . stop existing?"

"Strictly speaking, it's possible," he said. "But no one can withstand the temptation to sacrifice themselves at the end."

"Wait, I thought the older you get, the less you suffer," I said, confused.

"Up to a point, and then when the time for a regular human death approaches, it's like the pendulum suddenly swings back and the suffering is greater than ever." I shivered, and noticing, Vincent put his arm around me and pulled me close as we continued to walk.

"Gaspard told me once about this Italian revenant he knew—Lorenzo something. The guy was centuries old and barely felt the pull of dying anymore. At one point, all the deaths and rescues he had experienced in his existence got to be too much and he decided to sequester himself. He went and lived like a hermit in this isolated hilltop retreat. And it wasn't until decades later that he had a message brought to his kindred that he needed help.

"They came and got him—he was in his eighties by then—and had to help him find someone to save. He said that his physical and mental suffering had come on like a tidal wave—within the space of a few days. The craving to sacrifice himself for someone was too great to let him just lie down and die, which was all he wanted."

We were both silent for a long time as the implications for our own story sank in.

Whether or not Vincent or I found a way to keep him from suffering, we couldn't avoid one of several tragic endings. And if he managed to live as long as I did, someday he would get to that point that no revenant could pass—at eighty years old, or whenever. He would sacrifice his life for someone else's and wake up three days later at eighteen. I would die and he would remain immortal. There was no getting around it.

Sensing my hopelessness, Vincent pulled me to the side of the bridge. We stood hand in hand, watching the water surge forward in tiny, quickly moving whirlpools. The perfect metaphor for the unstoppable flow of time.

TWENTY-THREE

THE NEXT DAY, VIOLETTE TEXTED ME AT SCHOOL, asking if I wanted to go to a movie that night.

> Me: Too much homework. Sorry!
> Violette: Then how about coffee?
> Me: Perfect! After school. Sainte-Lucie.
> Violette: I'll see you there.

I smiled, thinking of how her English was coming along. She was actually using contractions! In just a few short weeks, she had begun to sound more like a normal teenager and less like a dowager duchess. And when I heard her speak French with the others . . . well, she definitely was picking up more "street" expressions.

She was already seated when I arrived at the café, and stood to greet me with a huge smile on her face. Kissing my cheeks, she exclaimed, "Kate! You were so amazing Saturday night!"

We sat down, and she continued to gush, but in a softer voice so the people nearby couldn't hear. "I still can't believe how well you fought after just a couple months of training. We told Gaspard about it, and although he insisted he couldn't take any credit, I could tell he was really proud."

"You were pretty awesome yourself!" I said, meaning it. "That guy was so much bigger than you, and he never even had a chance."

She waved away the praise like it had been nothing. "So . . . what did you think about Vincent? Wait—*monsieur*?" She flagged down a passing waiter so I could order a hot chocolate. I leaned back in toward her.

"He was incredible. I'm glad he got my numa when he did, though. I don't know how much longer I could have fought him off."

She hesitated, watching me.

"What?" I asked, her expression planting a seed of worry in my chest.

"He didn't seem to be operating at one hundred percent, I thought," she replied quietly. "He has those circles under his eyes. And he's so sallow-looking. I mean, he battled like the expert fighter he is, but he just didn't seem to have much physical strength."

I looked down at the table. "You're right, Violette. I mean, I've only seen him in practice, but he could probably have taken those guys on by himself if he weren't . . ." My voice trailed off.

"In bad shape." She finished my sentence for me, and touched my hand. "That's what I thought. But I wanted to get your reading on it since I don't know how he usually performs. I hadn't realized how much his project was affecting him until I saw him fight. Don't worry about it, though. Things will get better," she said gently. "But how about you. Any progress?"

"Zilch," I answered.

She pursed her lips pityingly and sighed. "Don't worry, Kate. I'm sure things will get better." Although she didn't look it. Unsure. Worried. Troubled, maybe. But I didn't see "sure" anywhere on her face.

Just then my chocolate arrived. I sipped the steaming froth off the top while inhaling the rich aroma of cocoa, and wondered for the hundredth time why Vincent couldn't just be a normal human boy.

"Good morning, *mon ange*! Where's your dress?" Vincent called, from where he was leaning against the park gate across the street from my front door. Instead of his regular jeans and jacket, he was wearing a suit and tie. And, oh man, did he look yummy. I stood there in my workout gear and looked him up and down.

"It's time for fight training. What's with the suit, Mr. Wall Street?"

"Didn't you get my text?"

I pulled out my phone to see a message from Vincent logged at three a.m.: *Dress up tomorrow. I'm taking you to a formal event.*

"Formal event?" I asked, my eyes widening. "What kind of formal event takes place on a Saturday morning?"

"A wedding," Vincent said simply.

"You're taking me to a wedding?" I asked, aghast. "Why didn't you tell me before three o'clock—the morning of?"

"Because I wasn't sure I wanted to take you."

My expression must have said it all, because he rushed to explain. "That's not what I meant. I meant I wasn't sure I wanted you to see a revenant wedding. You and I are already dealing with so much right now, I thought it might bring up too many . . . issues."

"So why did you change your mind?" I asked, not quite mollified.

"Because I decided that avoidance wasn't the answer. I promised I wouldn't keep anything from you that you should know. And you're already letting me break that promise . . . temporarily.

"A wedding might be information overkill, but"—he looked down and fiddled with his tie—"at least you'll know more about the world you're getting involved in. I owe you that."

I stood there stunned for a moment, before reaching up to kiss his cheek. "I think I can handle it, Vincent. Thanks for . . ." I didn't know what to say. "Just thanks."

"How long will it take you to get ready?" he asked, brushing my hair back from my eyes with his fingers. "You already look perfect."

I blushed, not wanting to admit that with a houseful of revenants living right down the street from us, seemingly popping up whenever I turned the corner, I never left the house now without making sure I looked okay. "Honestly, ten minutes. Just let me find a dress and shoes and I'll be right back."

"Fine," he said, looking at his watch. "We've got plenty of time."

An hour later we walked into the lower chapel of Sainte-Chapelle, an eight-hundred-year-old royal church that stands a few blocks from Notre-Dame Cathedral on the island in the Seine called the Île de la Cité.

"The wedding is *here?*" I gasped as Vincent took my hand and led me up a minuscule winding stone staircase into the nave. And as soon as we entered the room, I began to feel that same heady sensation of sensory overload—a dizzy feeling—that I had experienced the handful of times I had visited the chapel as a tourist. Because the space was just that unexpectedly overwhelming.

The ceiling was higher than the length of the room, its decoration so distant it was barely visible. But it wasn't the palatial height that took my breath away—it was the composition of the walls. Fifteen stained-glass windows, each fifty feet high, were set into the entire vertical surface of the chapel. The room was basically all glass held together by skeletal stone columns. The light that filtered through was a blue so deep it appeared purple, and the thick glass looked like precious stone. The overall effect made me feel I was a tiny gold figure inside a Fabergé egg, with my entire world encrusted in jewels.

I took a deep breath to stabilize my tap-dancing heart and wrapped my arm through Vincent's. "How in the world were they able to reserve this for a wedding?" I whispered, as we moved toward the group of people assembled at the altar.

"Connections," he whispered back, giving me a sly grin. I shook my head in wonder.

As there were no chairs, the group of thirty or forty revenants—several of whom I recognized from New Year's—was standing. We headed toward Jules and Ambrose, who took a break from talking to Jean-Baptiste and Violette to make appreciative comments about my appearance.

"Wow, Katie-Lou. You sure do clean up well. I barely recognize you out of jeans and Converses," Ambrose said, giving me a hug. Jules just shrugged and said, "Not bad," in a flippant voice before lifting his eyebrows and stroking his chin comically.

"Where's Gaspard?" I asked.

"Dormant," Vincent said. "And Arthur awoke during the night, so he's still in bed."

I nodded and looked toward the priest, who had begun addressing the crowd. "Dear ones," he began, "we have gathered together today to celebrate the union of our brother Georges with our sister Chantal."

I raised an eyebrow at Vincent. "Is he . . . ?" He nodded—the priest was one of them.

Vincent pulled me in front of him so that I could see better, resting his hands on the waist of my plum-colored knee-length dress.

The bride was stunning, wearing a traditional full-blown wedding gown with the works: veil, long train, and yards of creamy satin. She was twentieth century all the way, whereas the groom looked like he was from a much older time. He was dressed like one of the three musketeers, with ruffled collar, velvet waistcoat, and trousers that ended under the knee, just above where his long boots started. But instead of looking silly, he looked . . . dashing. I couldn't help wondering if he had walked here wearing that.

"What's up with d'Artagnan?" I whispered to Vincent.

"People usually wear the clothes of their era when they marry. It's revenant tradition."

I smiled, unable to keep myself from watching out of my peripheral vision for his cohorts to swing in on ropes through the chapel windows, donning feathered hats and brandishing swords.

The priest followed the wording of a regular wedding ceremony, punctuated by an occasional piece from a string quartet. The music drifted around the room like a symphonic mist, giving an even more otherworldly effect to an extraordinary event. When they got to the vows, the bride and groom faced each other and promised to be loving and faithful "so long as we both exist." *Well*, I thought, *that's an interesting twist*.

My thoughts percolated with the implications of what was happening. When humans married, they were already promising a lot by vowing they would stay together for several decades. This couple was stating, before their kindred, that they wanted to stay together . . . forever. Or at least for a *really* long time.

As the ceremony ended, the couple kissed, and then, taking each other's hand, led the rest of the group down the stairs and out of the chapel. Once on the street, the procession walked the ten minutes to the tip of the island, went down some stairs, and arrived at the Place Dauphine, a paved, tree-lined park jutting out into the Seine. A large white tent had been erected, with gas heaters warming the space inside.

Vincent and I took plates of food and walked out of the tent to sit on the edge of the quay, which had been lined with soft blankets for the occasion. We dangled our legs over the water and silently picked at our tenderloin and potatoes gratin.

"No questions? Comments? Existential pondering?" Vincent said finally.

"I have so many thoughts going through my head right now, that I don't even know where to start," I said.

"Start basic then, and save the existential for later." He set his empty plate on the blanket next to him and looked at me expectantly.

"Okay. Who are they—the bride and groom, I mean?"

"Georges and Chantal. He's eighteenth century, she's 1950s. He's French, she's Belgian."

"How did they even meet then? I haven't heard of you guys traveling much."

"They met at a convocation—a meeting of our Consortium that takes place every few years. Representatives from all over the world come to the big ones. We usually just go to the European meeting."

"An international meeting of revenants? Like the undead United Nations?" I curbed my laughter, seeing Vincent's solemn expression.

"It's an ancient tradition. The meetings are top secret, of course—for the obvious security reasons. Otherwise it would be like offering ourselves up as numa bait."

"And that's where the bride and groom met? At a political convocation?"

"Yeah. Besides being an informational meeting, it has an ulterior function of being a matchmaking opportunity. It's hard to meet a partner when your social circle is so limited."

Charlotte had once said that to me. It was the reason she used for why she didn't have a boyfriend. Of course, now I knew it was because she was in love with Ambrose, and had been for years. I wondered briefly how she was doing without Charles. We had emailed a few times, but I hadn't heard from her since her twin had run off.

Vincent began idly playing with my fingers, pulling my thoughts back to the here and now. "Do most revenants have partners?" I asked. "I mean, Ambrose and Jules seem to be happy with their single status."

"They're still 'new.' Them wanting to settle down would be like a modern-day teenager wanting to get married. Why commit to one person when you've barely started experiencing life? Or afterlife"—he corrected himself—"whatever."

"You don't seem to mind settling down for one girl yourself," I teased him, and then suddenly felt self-conscious.

Vincent smiled. "I'm different. Remember? I was on the verge of getting married while I was still human. Maybe I'm just a committed kind of guy," he said, leaning pensively over the water before turning his head to look at me.

"To return to the subject," he said, giving me a shy smile, "after a few hundred years of bachelorhood, people like Georges often want someone to be with. I guess that's one part of our basic humanity that remains with us after death. The need to love and be loved."

"Well, what about Jean-Baptiste? He's still single."

Vincent looked back at the water and grinned. "He's just not very demonstrative with his affections."

"What?" I exclaimed. "Jean-Baptiste has a girlfriend?"

He raised an eyebrow and, giving me a sideways smile, shook his head.

"A mistress then? A boy . . . oh!" I said, as the truth finally dawned on me. "Gaspard!"

Vincent gave me a broad smile. "Don't tell me you didn't think of that before."

I shook my head. But now that I knew, it made absolute sense. They were perfect for each other.

Vincent jumped up and took our plates to the tent. Returning to sit next to me, he said, "I have something for you, Kate." He reached into his jacket pocket and opened his hand to reveal a tiny red velvet drawstring bag.

Loosening the strings, he pulled out a pendant on a black linen cord and placed it gently in my palm.

It was a gold disk the size of a dollar coin, and it was edged with two circles of tiny gold pellets, one nestled within the other. Set in the center of the disk was a dark blue triangular stone with a smooth, slightly rounded surface. And in the space between the stone and the rows of pellets were decorative gold wires curved into the shape of flames. It looked ancient, like the Greek jewelry in Papy's gallery.

"Oh my God, Vincent. It's so gorgeous." I could barely speak, my throat was so choked with emotion.

"It's a *signum bardia*. A signal to revenants that you are attached to us. That you know what we are and can be trusted. Jeanne has one—she never takes it off."

Tears welled in my eyes. Clutching the pendant tightly in my hand, I threw my arms around Vincent's neck and hugged him for a few seconds, before letting go and wiping my tears away.

His smile was hesitant. "You like it then?"

"Vincent, 'like' doesn't quite do it justice. It is beautiful beyond words. Where did you get it?" I asked, unable to tear my eyes from the exquisite piece of jewelry.

"It's from our treasury."

I glanced quickly at him. "So it's Jean-Baptiste's?"

Vincent smiled reassuringly. "No. Although it's kept in his house, the treasury belongs to France's revenants. The pieces have been passed down for millennia. This one is logged into our records as last being used by one of our emissaries to Constantinople in the ninth century."

My eyes widened. "Are you sure I should have it, then? I mean, is it okay with everyone?"

"I showed it to Jean-Baptiste and Gaspard, and they congratulated me on my selection, agreeing that it was the perfect choice for you. It is yours now—you don't ever have to give it back. At least, I hope you won't." His grin was lighthearted but his eyes were earnest.

Wow. I looked back down at the pendant and traced the flames tenderly with my finger. Vincent studied it with me. "There are a lot of different interpretations of the symbols—whole books have been written about *signa bardia* in general—but the pyramid is supposed to mean life after death, and its three corners signify our three days of dormancy. The flames represent our aura and the only way we can be destroyed. And the circle is immortality."

I just looked at him, unable to believe that this ancient pendant, symbol of Vincent's kind, was mine. He took it from my hand and gently looped its cord over my head. His expression when he leaned back to look at me was as priceless as the piece itself.

"Thank you."

"I would say 'you're welcome,' but I can't take all the credit. This isn't just from me to you. It is from all of us to you. I know how upset you were when Arthur made you feel like you weren't one of us. I want you to know that you aren't an outsider. You aren't a revenant, but you are still one of us. This *signum* means that you are kindred."

I leaned into his arms. And as he nestled my hair with his cheek, I closed my eyes and wished that nothing would ever change. That time would stop and we could stay like this forever.

TWENTY-FOUR

THE TWO WEEKS THAT HAD PASSED SINCE I HAD
last been to Le Corbeau had seemed to stretch on forever. But
finally it was Tuesday, and I was ready to dart out of my last class
to go directly to the relic shop.

So when I walked out of the school's front gate and saw Jules
waiting for me, I felt like someone had just taken my wrists and
slapped a pair of handcuffs on them. "Jules," I said with undis-
guised disappointment, "what are you doing here?"

"Nice to see you, too, Kate," Jules said, obviously amused.
"Your boyfriend has asked me to be your bodyguard this afternoon."

"He what?" I exclaimed.

Jules moved forward to kiss my cheeks, and I leaned backward so he couldn't reach me, which made him laugh outright.
"Hey—don't blame this on me!" he said, backing away with his
hands up in the universal "I surrender" gesture. "Vincent gets

to handle the dangerous missions while I guard the damsel in distress."

"I am *so* not distressed. But I did have something I wanted to do . . . on my own." And then his words sunk in. "What dangerous mission?" I asked, searching his face.

"Ah! I finally get your undivided attention." He grinned. "Could I tell you more once we are in the car and out of the bus lane?" Jules motioned to the BMW, which was parked illegally a few yards away. I saw a bus approaching, flashing its lights for him to move, and hurried to jump in before the bus driver could make a scene.

"Are we waiting for the ever-effervescent Georgia?" Jules asked as he slid behind the wheel and put the car in gear.

"No, she's got drama club till six," I answered absently, my mind on what Vincent could be doing.

I waited until he was off and said, "Okay. I'm in the car. Now spill!"

As we drove, Jules told me that the revenants who were house-sitting for Geneviève had called Jean-Baptiste that morning to inform him of a break-in. While they had been out, someone had entered the house and turned the rooms upside down. The door had been forced, the lock broken. But nothing seemed to be missing. Jean-Baptiste and Vincent had gone to investigate.

"And all that means I get a guard because . . ."

"Because everyone is wondering if this means the numa are back on the move, so Vincent was worried about you. And since

JB insisted on him going along to Geneviève's, I volunteered to pick you up," Jules said with a satisfied smile, keeping his eyes on the road. "So where is this thing you wanted to do? I'll take you."

"It was a private errand. But I'll do that another time," I sighed. My stomach twisted with anxiety as I wondered when I'd have another opportunity to visit the shop. "So, how about you take me to Vincent?"

"How about I take you to my studio? Much less dangerous. Plus, I need a model and you could sit for me."

"You want me to sit for a portrait?" I asked, stunned.

"Actually, at the moment I'm concentrating on full-length reclining nudes, in the spirit of Modigliani," he said. He was making an effort to keep a straight face.

"If you think for even a second that I'm going to take off my clothes in front of you, Jules . . . ," I began.

He burst out laughing, slapping the steering wheel with his hand. "Just kidding, Kates. You're a lady. I wouldn't ask you to compromise your purity like one of my paid models—a bunch of low-heeled strumpets, the lot of them!"

After I'd seen a half-dressed model posing in Jules's studio, Vincent had told me that the girls were usually university students needing cash for their school expenses. A far cry from "low-heeled strumpets." Jules was trying the guilt-trip method of attack. And it was working.

"Okay, I'll pose for you," I conceded. "But under no circumstances will any article of clothing leave my body while I am in your studio."

"And if you're elsewhere?" he asked, breaking into a sly smile.

I rolled my eyes as we drove over the bridge and the Eiffel Tower came into view.

I inhaled deeply as we walked into his studio, taking in one of my favorite odors—the smell of wet oil paint. I had breathed in that same air since I was a small child, whenever I visited my grandmother's restoration studio. In my mind the smell was indelibly associated with beauty. My eyes followed my nose expectantly, knowing that a reward must be right around the corner.

And what a reward! The walls of Jules's studio were filled with color. Primary-hued geometric cityscapes and nudes painted in luscious pinks and flesh tones. My brain shifted into art mode. Surrounded by all that beauty, I felt whole. Fulfilled. Like a light had been switched on inside me, illuminating all my mind's dark, musty corners.

My reverie was interrupted by a crashing sound from the next room. Jules rushed past me before I could even react, having grabbed a sword from an umbrella stand, and hurled himself through the doorway. I heard a howl and, by way of the connecting door, saw a man leap into the air.

Time stopped as I watched him suspended in space, unable to believe what I was seeing, before I was jolted back to reality by an earsplitting crash as his body hit the large plate-glass window and disappeared outside. I ran to the now-jagged opening, my shoes crunching splintered glass beneath them, and saw the man land on his feet on the cobblestone pavement two floors below. Unshaken by the fall, he brushed himself off and then, holding his hands to his torso to staunch the flow of blood from a wound, he ran across the courtyard and out onto the street.

I spun to see Jules standing with a bloody sword in hand, staring at the broken window. Next to him, a small desk was covered in art books and gallery brochures, which were strewn as if someone had thrown them all up in the air and let them land where they would. The desk drawer lay on the floor, empty.

"Did he . . . ?" Jules began, unable to finish his question.

I nodded. "He landed on his feet and ran off. But I think you got him," I said encouragingly. "He was holding his side when he ran away."

"What was a numa doing in my studio?" Jules murmured, looking shell-shocked. "And how the hell did he get in? The window and the door both have top-quality locks."

Amid the glass shards, I spied a glint of metal. Picking my way carefully toward it, I bent to fish out a tiny silver set of tools strung on a chain. They looked exactly like the type of thing that could pick a door lock. I held them up for Jules to see. As he stared, his face turned a strange shade of purple. He pulled his phone out of his pocket and hit speed-dial.

"Vince? Yeah, she's here. Just listen! They came here, too—to my studio. . . . Only one—he got away. No, she's fine. Yes, I'm sure." Jules passed me the phone.

"Kate, are you okay?" Vincent was speaking in the controlled tone he used when he was hiding panic.

"I'm fine. The guy didn't even notice me. Jules went straight for him and he jumped through the window."

"I'll be right there."

"There's no reason, Vincent. We're both okay. Finish what you're doing—I'm going to see you tonight anyway."

"We *have* to come. See if we can figure out what he was looking for. We're probably only twenty minutes by cab, so just stay put. I have to see you to believe that you're safe. Could you give the phone back to Jules?"

Jules listened as Vincent spoke for a moment, and then, putting the phone back in his pocket and shaking himself out of his stupor, he looked up at me as if he had finally noticed that I was there. Dropping the sword to the floor, he strode over and took my shoulders in his hands, gripping me a little too hard. "Kate, you're fine? You didn't get cut anywhere?" He searched my face.

I was so stunned by his intensity that I couldn't speak. Jules was always joking around me, teasing me, but now his wide eyes held my own transfixed, and his expression couldn't be more serious. I shook my head and managed to utter, "I'm not hurt."

He exhaled as he registered the fact that I hadn't been touched and, grasping me to himself, hugged me so hard I couldn't breathe. After a few seconds, his grip loosened, but he didn't let go until I finally moved, pulling back gently as I said his name.

His hands dropped to his sides, but he stayed—his face inches away from my own and his warm breath soft on my skin—for what seemed like forever. Then, abruptly, he turned and strode out of the studio. I heard his feet on the wooden stairway, and watched out the gaping hole of the window as he crossed the courtyard and stood motionless by the stone doorway to the street, waiting there for the others to arrive.

TWENTY-FIVE

ONCE AT THE STUDIO, VINCENT AND JEAN-BAPTISTE had combed it for clues while Jules and Ambrose nailed a big board of plywood over the gaping window. Now we were in the car on our way back to La Maison for what JB was calling an "emergency meeting."

My phone rang. Seeing Charlotte's name on the screen, I answered immediately. This was the first time in over a month that one of us had actually picked up the phone to call.

"Hi, Charlotte!" I said, trying to clear my voice of the tension that was weighing on everyone in our group.

"Kate," she responded, sounding as if she were just next door instead of on the other side of the country.

"How are you?"

"Fine. I had to call you, though—I heard from Charles last night. He's in Germany, living with a group of revenants in Berlin. And he's okay!"

"Oh, Charlotte. You must be so relieved."

"I can't even tell you. I was practically giddy when he told me he was safe, and then I started yelling at him for not calling before. But we're okay now."

"I'm so glad to hear that. See! All those names you were calling him were . . . well, they were still mostly true."

Charlotte laughed; then her voice became serious. "Actually, Kate, the guys he's staying with got a tip that big things are going down with the numa in Paris. He said he wasn't ready to talk to the others yet, and asked me to warn JB."

"Well, he's just in time. Did you hear about what happened to Geneviève's house?"

"Yeah. Jean-Baptiste called this morning to ask if there was anything in her house that a numa could be after," Charlotte affirmed.

"The same thing just happened in Jules's studio a couple hours ago."

She gasped. "Oh, Kate. I wish I could come back. There's no reason for me to stay here now that I know that Charles isn't going to be showing up on the doorstep at any moment."

"Then why don't you?" I asked, glancing at Vincent, who was sitting silently beside me in the car.

"It's Geneviève. She doesn't want to go back to Paris. And I can tell that being here, far away from her memories of her life with Philippe, is helping her. I can't just ditch her, and I don't want to suggest something that's going to set her back. But with everything going on there, do you think Jean-Baptiste needs me?"

"I don't know, Charlotte. It seems like pure chaos here for the moment. If Geneviève needs you there, it might be better for both of you if you stay."

She sighed. "You're right. I'll bring it up with Jean-Baptiste anyway just to be sure. But Kate?"

"Yes?"

"I'm so glad Charles is safe."

"I know, Charlotte. Me too. It's good that he's with other revenants," I said. *And not with numa*, I thought, knowing that Charlotte had feared the same thing.

Once again, we were assembled around the massive hearth in the great hall. Jean-Baptiste explained what they had found at Geneviève's and Jules's, which was basically nothing. However, it was obvious from the items that had been disturbed that the object of the break-ins was some sort of document. But neither Geneviève nor Jules could imagine anything the numa would want to steal from them.

"I have racked my brain," said Jean-Baptiste, placing two fingers on his brow for emphasis, "and can't think of one thing among our paperwork that would be of any interest to our enemies."

"How about banking information?" Violette asked. "Maybe they're looking for account numbers or something."

"Well, that's an idea," said Jules. "But we're paperless now—all our banking is online. And even if the numa weren't already rich off all of their underworld dealings, I doubt our bank accounts would be their first target if they needed some extra cash."

Violette frowned.

"May I?" Gaspard asked. He was so overly polite that he never cut into a conversation without asking permission first. Jean-Baptiste nodded at him. "Although I agree that we must focus on discovering what they *might* be after, we should not rule out the fact that this might merely be a diversion. They may be attempting to draw our attention away from some larger plan they are carrying out."

I spoke up. "Charlotte mentioned something on the phone when we were on our way here." Everyone turned toward me. "Charles called her. He's in Berlin, staying with a group of revenants. He phoned to warn her that they had heard rumors that something big was happening with the Paris numa."

"Yes, she called me too—" Gaspard began, but was cut off by Violette.

"Why didn't I hear anything about this?" she exclaimed, her face pink with emotion, signaling that she was officially pissed off.

"I—I was going to consult with you later, Violette," Gaspard stuttered. "But Charlotte just phoned me last night, and with the break-ins this morning, there was so much going on."

Violette pressed her temples in exasperation. "*How* am I supposed to be helping out if people withhold such important information from me?"

Everyone stared at her. Ambrose rolled his eyes toward me and mouthed the words, *Drama. Queen.*

She glanced around at us, as if she had just noticed we were all there, and then looked back at Gaspard. "I'm sorry," she said. "I've just been trying so hard. Digging wherever I could, and hitting a brick wall everywhere I turn . . . when there's information sitting right in front of us." She stood and walked to Gaspard, placing a dainty hand on his arm and leading him away from the group.

"Now what did Charlotte say, exactly?" she quizzed him as they left the room.

On the other side of the hearth, at the edge of the group, Arthur sat in an armchair, shaking his head tiredly like the long-suffering husband of a temperamental spouse. He pulled a pen and notebook out of his jacket's inner pocket and began to write.

I squeezed Vincent's fingers. He was sitting in front of me on the floor, his elbow propped on the couch so that he could hold my hand. He glanced up, and I inclined my head toward Arthur. "Is he taking notes?" I whispered. Vincent's eyes traveled across the room. "No, he's writing," he responded.

"What do you mean?" I asked, intrigued.

"He's an author. Of novels." Vincent laughed at the astounded look on my face. "What, you didn't think we could have careers that didn't involve saving lives? Arthur and Violette have to do something with their time. They don't even own a TV."

"What does he write?"

"Well, have you heard of Pierre Delacourt?"

"Yeah, the historical thriller guy? I actually think I read one of his books in an airport once. That's Arthur's pen name?"

Vincent nodded. "That and Aurélie Saint-Onge, Henri

Cotillon, and Hilaire Benois."

My mouth dropped open as I realized that the writer behind some of the most famous pseudonyms in French literature from the last couple of centuries was sitting across the room from me, scribbling in a notebook.

"This train wreck of a meeting is adjourned," snapped Jean-Baptiste, drawing attention to the fact that no one was paying attention to him anymore. "I will speak to each of you individually about what I need you to do. Vincent," he said, walking over to us, "I need you to fly to Berlin tomorrow. Talk to Charles's source. Find out everything they know and where they're getting their information." Vincent nodded, and Jean-Baptiste moved on to Jules.

"Wow, just like that and you're off," I said. "How long do you think you'll be gone?"

"I would guess a couple of days. It'll depend on what I find when I get there. How much information there actually is. Although I have a feeling that part of the reason JB is sending me instead of just phoning is to have someone check up on Charles."

I nodded, and although I felt a twinge of sadness that he was going away—so much had been going on that we had barely had time to catch up since he'd been dormant—I also felt a sense of relief. Because the only thing on my mind right now was when I could get to Le Corbeau.

TWENTY-SIX

WHEN GEORGIA AND I LEFT OUR BUILDING THE next morning to see Jules waiting for us in his car, my heart did a little leap. Vincent must have already left. I checked my phone to see his good-bye text, and the heart-leap became a staccato patter. Today was my day.

"So what's up with the chauffeur service?" I asked as I jumped into the front with him while Georgia settled in the back.

"Vincent would have been here this morning, but he had a flight at six a.m. Which means he was at the airport at five."

"Good thing you guys don't sleep," I said.

From habit, Jules's eyes flicked to the rearview mirror to see if Georgia had heard. And then I saw him remember—*She already knows*—and he relaxed again.

He does *think of me as one of them now*, I mused, and I smiled as I touched the pendant hidden under my shirt.

"That's actually not my question. What have we done to

deserve a ride to school? Were there more numa attacks during the night?"

I meant it as a joke, but Jules's unchanged expression informed me that I had hit the nail on the head. "No!" I gasped.

"Yes, two other revenant homes in the Paris area were ransacked—one last night and the other early this morning, both times when the occupants were out."

"So what's that have to do with us?" piped up Georgia from the backseat. "Not that I don't appreciate door-to-door service to high school, of course."

Jules peered at Georgia in the mirror. "That attack after your boyfriend's concert, followed a week later by four break-ins by our enemies, all adds up to the fact that the numa are back in action. And Vincent is worried that you, Kate, could be a target."

"Why me?"

"The numa know he's JB's second, and they know you're with him. Kidnapping you—or worse—would be the perfect way to provoke him. Vincent just wants someone to keep an eye on you until he's back and can do it himself."

That was a lot to process. "I feel like saying that I can fend for myself. But after facing off with those guys in the alley, I think I'll just thank you for the offer and shut up about it."

"So, Jules," Georgia said, leaning forward, "not that I'm not appreciative that you are protecting my sister from evil murderous zombies. But since that conversation's run its course."—she paused for effect—"Kate tells me that Arthur is a writer."

To my dismay, my sister had not given up on her crush on

Arthur. And ever since she and Sebastien had broken up the previous week, she had mentioned the revenant at least once a day.

"He asked about you, actually," Jules said matter-of-factly.

"He *did*?" Georgia purred. "Do tell!"

"He was just wondering if you had recovered from the trauma of your numa attack. He saw you on the street the other day and said you looked well."

"Looked *well*? I wonder if that means 'looked hot' in fifteenth-century speak?"

"And she's off," I murmured, drawing a laugh from Jules.

"No offense," he continued, "but I think what interests him is that Violette seems to hate you so much. It provides entertainment for that otherwise dull practically-married-without-benefits life of his."

"Mmm . . . benefits," Georgia said, rolling the word around in her mouth like it was candy. "Be sure to mention to Arthur that I'm single again, you know, when the topic of me comes up."

I shook my head, and Jules burst out laughing. As we pulled up to the school, and Georgia got out of the car, I leaned over to him. "Can you wait for a minute?" He nodded, looking confused, as I stepped out of the car.

"Georgia, I'm skipping today. Can you cover for me?"

My sister eyed me curiously. "This is so unlike you that I'm assuming it must be of vital importance. Like Nancy Drew–style sleuthing for questionably existent healers kind of importance. Hmm. What'll you swap for my silence?" She smiled craftily.

"Okay, okay. I'll make sure Jules puts in a good word with Arthur."

"Make it a date with Arthur, and I'll write you a sick note signed by Mamie."

I laughed—"I'll see what I can do"—and turned to get back into the car.

"Hey, Kate," Georgia called, her voice serious now. I hesitated. "Be careful, whatever it is that you're doing."

"Promise," I said, throwing her an air-kiss and lowering myself into the passenger seat.

"What's up, Kates?" Jules said unsurely, fiddling with the radio dial.

"A day trip," I said.

That got his full attention. "Where to?"

"To Saint-Ouen."

"You're skipping school to go to the flea market? Does Vincent know you're doing this? Wait . . . don't tell me. Of course he doesn't or you'd wait till he got back to go."

"Did Vincent ask you to guard me today?" I asked. Jules nodded. "Well, I'm going to Saint-Ouen. So you can either drop me off at the Métro station or take me there yourself. Whatever your guard-sense feels is right."

Jules's lips formed an amused smile. "Kates, has anyone ever told you that you are one persuasive girl? Are you on the debate team at school?"

I shook my head.

"Pity," he said as he put the car in gear. Swinging it around to face Paris, he gunned the motor and we were off.

***

"Jules?"

"Um . . . hmm?"

"How did you die?"

We had been stuck in traffic on the Périphérique for a half hour. Up to now our conversation had consisted of small talk— which meant in the revenants' case things like how Ambrose and Jules had recently saved people in a tourist bus that drove into the Seine. But I had been wondering this for a while, and sitting in gridlock felt like the perfect time to ask.

"I mean, you told me you died in World War One," I continued, "but did you die saving one particular person, or was it more the abstract fact that you were defending your countrymen as a soldier?"

"There aren't any abstracts in becoming a revenant," Jules replied. "Just fighting in a war doesn't count. If it did, there'd probably be a lot more of us."

"So who did you save?"

"A friend of mine. I mean, not exactly a friend, but another artist whose group I hung out with in Paris before the war. Name was Fernand Léger."

"*The* Fernand Léger?" I gasped.

"Oh, you've heard of him?" There was no hint of sarcasm in his voice.

"Come on, Jules. You know I love art."

"Well, he wasn't as famous as the others in his group: Picasso, Braque, Gris."

"He's famous enough for me to know him. And wasn't it his gallery at the Museum of Modern Art that I saw you hanging out in last summer? You know . . . when you pretended you were someone else because I recognized you from the subway crash?"

Jules grinned at the memory. It was his postmortem appearance that had sent me running back to Jean-Baptiste's house to apologize to Vincent, only to find him dead on his bed. Which led me to my discovery of what he was. A historic day in the life of Kate Mercier, to be sure.

"Yeah, he's got an unrecognizable portrait of me hanging in there. Not very flattering. I look like a robot. Actually more like a robot-skeleton. Which is understandable, I guess, since I was dead by the time he painted it."

"Are you talking about *The Card Players*?" I asked in awe.

"Yeah. There was a lot of downtime in between fighting. We played a lot of cards. After the war, when I was volant this one time, I overheard him telling someone that the soldier on the right was the one who saved him. But I still can't see a resemblance for the life of me." Jules cracked a smile at his own joke.

"How did it happen? I mean the saving bit?"

"Gave him my respirator during a German mustard-gas attack. Once I was down, the enemy came through and shot all of us who were on the ground."

What an awful way to die, I thought. Although I was horrified, I tried to make my voice sound matter-of-fact so that he would keep on talking. "Why did you do it?"

"I was young and he was an older, established artist. I respected him. Worshipped him, in a way."

"Even so, how many starstruck kids would give up their life for their hero?"

Jules shrugged. "I've talked about it with other revenants. We all feel like in our human life there was something inside us that was almost suicidally philanthropic. It's the only characteristic we all have in common."

He was silent after that, leaving me to wonder if I would have what it took to give my life for someone else. I suppose it was something I wouldn't know until I was there, on the spot—looking death in the face.

Twenty minutes later, we pulled into a parking lot a few blocks away from Le Corbeau.

"Are you going to tell me what this is about?" Jules asked for the fortieth time.

"Nope," I said as we got out of the car. Spying a tiny café nearby, I gestured to it and said, "But you can wait for me there."

"The answer to that command is '*Non, madame la capitaine.*' Not on your life am I letting you go on some unknown errand— one you obviously don't want Vincent to know about—on your own. You guilt-tripped me into bringing you here by appealing to my sense of duty in guarding you. Now you've got to live with what you asked for."

We stared each other down for a few seconds. But when I saw he wasn't going to budge, I nodded, and we began walking in the direction of the shop. It was actually nice to have him along, because I was starting to feel nervous—unsure of how I would handle things when I got there.

From a block away I could see that the lights were on, and my heart started pounding like crazy. The carved raven atop the sign seemed to regard us menacingly as we neared. We came to a stop outside the door, and Jules turned to me with the most incredulous look on his face. "You dragged me halfway across Paris to buy a"—he peered at the window display, and then back at me—"a plaster Virgin Mary?"

"No."

"Then what?" He glanced back. "A Pope John Paul night-light? Kate, what the hell are we doing here?"

"The question is, 'What am *I* doing here?' and the answer is, 'It's none of your business, Jules.' I'm sorry for dragging you along, but there's something I need to do. And I would rather you wait out here."

"What?" Jules shouted.

"I have to talk to the owner about something. If I'm wrong about it, I'll be back out in a second. If I'm right, it might take a little more time. But it's something I want to do myself."

"Kate, I honestly don't know how Vincent puts up with you. You are . . . infuriating."

"But you'll do what I ask?"

Jules ran his hand through his curls, looking very unhappy. "I'll give you fifteen minutes. If you're not out, I'm coming in to get you." And he stalked off to sit on the step of a boarded-up storefront across the street.

TWENTY-SEVEN

I PUSHED THE DOOR SOFTLY. WHEN IT DIDN'T budge, I put more force into it, practically bursting into the shop when the sticky door finally gave way. I glanced around self-consciously to see a room chock-full of stuff, even more crowded than the window displays. And from the looks of things, I could tell they had put the cheap inventory in the windows—probably to discourage theft—because surrounding me were the most interesting objects I had ever seen outside a museum.

A very old ivory Madonna—the sway in the hip on which she balanced her child following the natural curve of the elephant tusk—sat next to an ornate box—a reliquary—with a realistic metal finger attached to the lid. Old coins with images of saints on them, antique rosaries hanging from every available protrusion, and crucifixes made of precious metals and stones. Although each piece was individually beautiful in its own way, with all of them amassed chaotically together in such a small space, the place felt seriously creepy. Like a tomb stocked with goods for the afterlife.

I stared at the front desk for an entire second before I realized that someone was behind it—staring right back at me. He stood so unnaturally still that when he spoke, I jumped. "*Bonjour, mademoiselle*. What can I do for you?" he said in a slightly accented French.

My hand flew to my heart. "I'm sorry," I gasped. "I didn't see you there."

His head tilted slightly sideways at my words, as if he found the idea of someone being surprised by a speaking statue curious. *What a strange man*, I thought. With his slicked-back, dyed-black hair and the huge eyes that projected surreally from bottle-thick glasses, he looked like a cartoon version of the store's avian namesake. *Serious creep factor*, I decided, shuddering.

"Um . . . someone told me that I could find a *guérisseur* here?" I said, my voice coming out embarrassingly timid.

He nodded oddly and stepped from behind the desk to display a skeletal frame dressed in strange, old-fashioned clothes. "My mother is the *guérisseur*. What ails you?"

I thought of my conversation with the woman in the next-door shop and blurted out, "Migraines." There was something about this man—about this whole situation—that made me very nervous. If meeting the revenants was like traveling to a strange new country, this made me feel like Neil Armstrong, touching his toe to the virgin surface of the moon.

He nodded in comprehension and lifted a stick-figure arm to gesture toward a door at the back of the room. "This way, please."

I wove my way through stacks of old books and waist-high statues of saints, and then followed him up a steep and winding set of stairs. He disappeared through a door on the landing, and then reappeared, waving me inside. "She will see you," he said.

Upon entering the room, I noticed an elderly woman sitting by a fireplace in a worn green chair, knitting. She glanced up from her work and said, "Come, child," nodding to an overstuffed armchair facing her own. As I stepped into the room, the man left, closing the door behind him.

"I hear you suffer from migraines. You are young for that type of affliction, but I have cured children as little as five years old. We'll fix you right up."

I settled myself in the chair.

"Now tell me about the very first time you experienced this problem," she said, continuing her knitting.

"Actually, I don't have migraines," I said. "I came to talk to you about something else."

She looked up, curious but not surprised. "Do tell, then."

"I found this really old manuscript. *Immortal Love*, it was called. It talked about a *guérisseur* living in Saint-Ouen who had special abilities regarding . . . a certain type of being."

Although I had planned my speech ahead of time, it wasn't coming out right. Because now that I was here, I wasn't at all sure of myself. Even though everything seemed to point to this being the right place, honestly . . . what were the chances that this old lady was the descendant of the healer in the book? After all these years? And out of the thousands of *guérisseurs* that must exist in France?

The woman's needles stopped their clicking, and she stared at me, giving me her full attention for the first time. Suddenly I felt extremely foolish. "A certain type of immortal being . . . called a revenant," I clarified.

She stared for another second, and then, placing her knitting in a tapestry bag next to her chair, she put her hand on her chest and leaned forward. At first I thought she was having some kind of attack. And then I realized she was laughing.

After a few seconds she stopped to catch her breath. "I'm sorry, dearie. I'm not making fun of you. It's just that . . . people think that we *guérisseurs* are magic, which leads to all sorts of misconceptions. And I know that the shop below must add to my mystique—all the religious artifacts make locals think I'm a witch of some sort. But I'm not. I'm just an old lady whose father passed a simple gift to her: the gift of healing. But that's all there is to it. I can't conjure up spirits. I can't cast evil spells on your enemies. And I don't know anything about . . . immortal whatever they are."

I felt my face redden, not only from shame but from the weeks of pent-up expectation that had been mounting inside me. Which had all just run headfirst into a brick wall. My eyes stung, and I took a deep breath to keep myself from crying. "I am so sorry to have bothered you," I said, and stood to go. "Um, am I supposed to give you something for your time?" I began fishing in my purse.

"*Non*," she said sharply. Then, her voice softening, she said, "All I ask is that you write your name on one of those cards, and place it in the dish. That way I can send you good wishes in my prayers." She nodded to a stack of index cards on the table next to my chair. I scribbled my name on the card and leaned over to place it in the bowl. And froze.

Painted on the inside of the dish was a pyramid inside a circle. A pyramid surrounded by flames. I spun to see the old woman sitting immobile, staring at me with one eyebrow raised. Waiting.

I thrust my hand inside my shirt, pulled out my pendant, and held the *signum* out for her to see.

She sat there stunned for a second, and then stood to face me. "Well, if you had shown me that when you arrived, we wouldn't have had to go through this charade, my dear," she said, her expression changing from distant and professional to complicit and friendly. "Welcome, little sister."

It felt like a dozen bees were buzzing around in my head as I sank back down into the chair. I couldn't believe it: Was this really happening?

"Are you okay, *ma puce*?" she said, looking worried, bustling over to a sideboard where she poured me a glass of water from a pitcher. She set it on the table next to me and then sat back down.

"Yes!" I said, a little too loudly, my voice sounding strange to my still-ringing ears. "Yes, I'm fine. I just . . . I'm so surprised that you're really . . ." I didn't know what else to say, so I just shut up and waited.

"Ha! Yes, I am really. Or rather, my family is. Although I've never been consulted on the subject of revenants. It's been a few hundred years since one of us has. So this is quite exciting for me, really." Her eyes sparkled, as if to prove it. "You must have found both of the books?"

"Um, yes. How did you know?"

"Ah, well, we had a bit of a problem back in the eighteenth century. Some of the baddies—the numa, they're called—got their hands on one of the books and came to find us. Very nasty occasion, that was. So my ancestor took possession of it and tracked down the nobleman who owned the only other existing copy. They are the ones that did that little bit of ink work on the two manuscripts to make us hard, but not impossible, to find. We do have our purposes," she clucked proudly. "You don't happen to have the books with you, do you?"

"No," I admitted.

"Well, that's a shame. I would have loved to see them. All I've got is a handwritten copy of the text that my ancestor made. We couldn't exactly keep the originals. That would be a bit counterproductive, wouldn't it?"

"Um, yes," I said, working hard to keep my thoughts moving as rapidly as she was throwing out new information.

"So, tell me . . ." She waited.

"Kate. Kate Mercier."

"Tell me, Kate Mercier, what have you to ask me?" She spoke the words as if they were a formula she had been told to follow.

"I . . . I'm in love. With a revenant."

The woman's face dropped. "Oh, my dear."

Her look of pity only bolstered my resolve. "He's still young: He's only been a revenant for eighty-five years. So the compulsion to die often is still really strong. I love him. But I'm not strong enough to stay with someone who dies the gruesome deaths they do . . . over and over again."

"Very few would be, my dear. Unless you cast all feeling from your heart, it would be a terribly traumatic life for you. And if you were able to succeed in numbing your emotions to that extent, well, you wouldn't be the same sensitive girl that you are now—the girl that he fell in love with."

I thanked her silently for understanding. "I'm searching for a way to ease the suffering that comes with his resisting death. So that he can hold out for longer. Perhaps for my lifetime," I said, but in my mind the words were, *Until I die.* "I don't want him to suffer for me."

"I understand," she said, sighing. "But I must tell you, I don't have any kind of mystical cure sitting around. No bottle of healing unguent or potion hidden away in a cupboard. As you remember, the boy in the story never made it to my ancestor in the end. But after the story was passed to us, the gifted ones in my family have, over the ages, written down their thoughts on this and other matters.

"I will have to find my records, Kate, to see what I can come up with. There are things I know about the revenants. Secrets I've been given. But none of them would provide a solution to your particular problem. You have chosen a hard path, and I do not envy you that. But I will do my best to find something to ease the suffering—for both of you."

She stood and walked to the door. "Let's go downstairs," she said. I followed her down and into the shop, where we came to an abrupt halt as we took in the scene before us.

Jules stood in the middle of the room, the tip of his drawn sword pressed to the chest of the bottle-glassed man, who looked like he had shrunk a foot under the revenant's fierce gaze.

"I—I don't know what you're talking about," the man was stuttering. "There's no one here but me!"

"I know the girl is here, now take me to her!" Jules roared, and pressed harder with the sword, trapping the man against the front desk.

"Jules, stop!" I yelled.

Both men turned, and Jules dropped his sword, slipping it into its sheath as he walked quickly in our direction.

"Kate. Are you okay?" he asked, reaching for me.

"An aura like a forest fire," said the old woman, staring at Jules. "You are one of them." And then, slowly, she curtsied as if he were visiting royalty.

"What the—" Jules said, astounded.

The lady stood and held out her hand for Jules to take. "I am Gwenhaël, and this is my son, Bran." She gestured toward the bug-eyed man, whose hand was clutching his chest as if Jules had actually wounded him.

Jules threw me a *What the hell is going on?* look, and cleared his throat uncomfortably.

"Is this the boy in question?" the woman asked.

"No," I answered.

"Well," she responded, studying Jules's face as if trying to memorize everything she saw for future reflection. Jules raised his eyebrows and looked at me pointedly.

"We are honored to have your visit, sir," she said finally, and then turned to me. "As we are to have yours, dear Kate. Give me a week and then come back. That will give me time to go through all my ancestors' texts. Maybe I will have some information that can help you."

"*Merci, Madame . . .*"

"Just Gwenhaël," she responded, and patted my hand. "I will see you in a week."

Keeping a careful distance from Jules, Bran handed me a card with only a telephone number printed on it. "You can call before you come. Save you a trip. Good-bye," he said, giving us a quick bow and then staring at us with his huge, reflected eyes as we stepped out of the store and into the street.

We had barely taken three steps before Jules turned to me. "Do you plan on telling me what that was about?"

"No," I responded stubbornly.

"Then you plan on telling Vincent about it?"

"At some point, yes."

Jules shook his head. "You were in there for twenty-five minutes. You could have at least waved from the window to let me know you were okay." He looked angry, but I could tell it was because he had been worried sick.

"I'm sorry," I said, meaning it.

We got into the car, and Jules pulled out of the parking lot and headed south. After fifteen minutes of silence, he spoke. "Kate, you have to tell me what you were doing back there with that crazy old lady and Raven-boy."

"Raven-boy?"

"Bran. It's a Breton name that means 'raven.'"

Okay.

"Kate . . . how did that woman know what I was?"

"She's a *guérisseur* whose family has links to the revenants."

He paused, absorbing that information. "And you were there because . . ."

"I'm trying to find a way to help Vincent. So that he doesn't have to finish this stupid experiment he's doing at the moment. Whatever it is looks like it's hurting him, not helping him."

This seemed to defuse his tenseness, and his voice became softer. Understanding. "Honestly, Kate, I don't even know what to say. I don't think that you realize what you're getting yourself into by exploring our world like this . . . by yourself. Those people could have been dangerous. They *could still* be dangerous. Everything having to do with revenants is. Because everything that has to do with *us* also includes the numa. Those people could have ties with our enemies."

"They don't, Jules. I'm sure of it. Gwenhaël even mentioned that her family had had a problem with numa hundreds of years ago."

"WHAT? You see, Kate?" Jules yelled, banging his hand on the steering wheel.

"They aren't aligned with the numa, Jules. They're on your side. The revenants' side. *Our* side. And I was never in danger."

"And how do you know that from a twenty-minute chat?" Jules asked, his words short and clipped.

"I just know."

"If the numa knew where this family of *guérisseurs* was hundreds of years ago, they might still know where they are now," he said softly, almost to himself. He glanced at me, and then turned his gaze back to the road.

"Kate," he said, weighing his words. "I care about you. You don't even know how—" He cut himself off before he could finish and placed his hand on mine. I felt its warmth for one long second before he squeezed tenderly and moved it back to the steering wheel. "And what you're doing right now scares the hell out of me. Swear that you will not put yourself into a dangerous position like that again. Not by yourself. Not without warning one of us what you're doing."

"I swear," I said.

"I'm not sure if I believe you, but I've said my piece." He glanced over at me and then back at the road, gritting his teeth. "So, Kate. You think of me as a friend, right?"

I nodded, wondering what in the world could be coming next.

"Then why did you involve me in something like this? Vincent is the person I am closest to in this world. When he finds out I took you to that place, behind his back, he is going to go ballistic. And he won't be mad at you. He'll be mad at me."

"You're not going to tell him?" I gasped.

"No. I'm going to leave that to you."

"Well, I *will* tell him," I said, suddenly feeling defiant. "As soon as I have more information. While he's making himself look like an anemic insomniac, I'm not just going to sit on my butt and wait for him to come up with a solution to our problems."

As we pulled up in front of my house, Jules looked at me with a strained expression. "Kates, I've got to give it to you—you are one determined, ballsy chick. But if you ever plan on doing something that's going to piss Vincent off, leave me out of it." It was his tone of voice, his obvious loyalty to his kindred, that got to me.

"I swear I didn't think it through before I asked you to do this," I said, choking a little on the words. "The last thing I want to do is cause a problem between you and Vincent. I *am* sorry for that part, Jules."

He nodded his acceptance of my apology. "Out," he said with a tired smile.

After pulling myself from the car, I leaned back in and said, "Thanks," and gave him a peck on the cheek.

"Aren't your grandparents going to wonder why you're home so early?"

"Papy's at his gallery, and Mamie's working on a weeklong project at the Louvre. Unless you tell them, they'll never know."

"Okay, see you tomorrow morning, seven thirty sharp."

My smile was difficult to pull off with the lump in my throat. "So you'll still guard me?"

"With my life." He gave me a one-handed salute, put the car into gear, and drove away.

TWENTY-EIGHT

VINCENT PHONED THAT NIGHT WHILE I WAS doing my homework. "*Guten Tag*," I said. He responded with a flood of German words, pronounced so quickly that even if I spoke German, I doubt I would have understood. "Um, *danke*? *Lederhosen*? Sorry. That's all I can add to that conversation. So, getting off the topic of leather Alpen-wear . . . did you find Charles?"

"Yes, I did. I'm here in the house with Charles and the kindred he's staying with." From behind Vincent, speed metal was pumping so loudly that I could barely hear his voice.

"Why don't you go outside?" I yelled into the phone.

"I *am* outside," he said. "Just a sec." And I listened as the music got farther and farther away. "Okay. I'm down the block now. Can you hear me?"

I laughed. "Just what kind of German 'kindred' have adopted Charles?"

"Well, I can definitely say that it's a big change from Jean-Baptiste's house."

"Is Charles okay?"

"He's not only okay. He actually seems happy—for a change. Although he feels pretty bad for abandoning Charlotte. He's just not ready to come back yet. And believe it or not, I actually think this place is good for him."

"That is great news!"

"Yeah. Now we just have to track down the revenant who gave Charles's group the information. They don't really know him that well, so they aren't sure where to find him. I'll probably be here another couple of days. And then I was thinking I should go to the south to see Charlotte. Fill her in on how Charles is doing and see how she and Geneviève are getting along."

My heart plummeted. "So you won't be back until next week, then."

"Well, I was actually hoping that you'd come along with me. I thought you'd enjoy seeing Charlotte, and—more selfishly—I've been wanting to get away with you. To take you somewhere for once."

My heart stopped its descent and shot back up, lodging in my throat so I could barely speak. "Us? Go on a trip? To the Côte d'Azur? Really?"

"Do you think your grandparents would be okay with that?"

I tried to compose myself, but my lungs insisted on hyperventilating. "Oh, Vincent, that would be so amazing! And if we're staying with Charlotte and Geneviève, I know Mamie and Papy won't mind."

"Then it's a plan. I'll make sure I'm back from Berlin by Friday.

If we take a four p.m. train, we'll be in Nice by ten that night. And we can come back Sunday evening. It only gives us a day and a half there, but I wouldn't want you to have to skip school."

My face flushed. What would he say if he knew that I *had* skipped school—to do something he might not be happy about? And had made Jules my accomplice. Make that *when* he knows. *I'm going to tell him*, I thought. *I just have to find the right time.*

On Thursday, I asked Jules to make a detour at La Maison on the way home from school.

"What—do you miss Vincent so much you're just going to hang out in his room?" he teased.

"No, I actually borrowed a book from Jean-Baptiste's library and keep forgetting to return it." *Okay, why was that so easy to say to Jules when I couldn't to Violette?* I wondered.

"Ooh—beware . . . you risk the wrath of Gaspard, Guardian of the Books. Which, I can assure you, is truly something to fear," he said, narrowing his eyes and lifting his eyebrows dramatically.

I laughed. "I'm sure he wouldn't have minded if I had asked. But since I didn't, I wanted to return it before he notices it's gone."

"You are a very conscientious young woman," Jules quipped, and I play-punched him in the shoulder. He waited for me in the car as I ran into the house, and seeing no one around, I went directly to the library.

The door was open, so I fished the book out of my bag and unwrapped it from the scarf I had used to protect it from stray pens and hairbrushes. I had just pulled the box off the shelf when

I heard someone clear his throat. Whipping around, I scanned the room to see Arthur sitting in a corner—pen and notebook balanced on his knee and a pile of open books scattered around him.

"Hello, Kate," he said.

"Uh, hi, Arthur," I replied, slipping the book into the box and replacing it on the shelf as quickly as I could. As if I went fast, he wouldn't notice. Silly me.

"What've you got there?" he asked.

"Oh, just a book I found the other day," I said, trying to sound lighthearted, while knowing full well that I was the worst actress in the world. I was practically radiating guilt vibes.

"About what?"

Suddenly my mood switched and I thought, *What business is it of his, anyway*? "It was about werewolves. No, wait . . . maybe it was vampires. I wouldn't know. I'm just a clueless human, and it's so easy for me to get all of you monsters mixed up."

He stood and took a step toward me. "Kate, I apologize for humiliating you in front of everyone. I really didn't"—he hesitated, weighing his words—"want to. But it is true that there is information that humans shouldn't possess. Things we discuss in our meetings. Even the books in this library. Not because you don't deserve to. But because it could put you in danger."

Furious, I held my hand up in a "talk to it" gesture. "Don't even get started, Arthur, because I don't want to hear it." I fingered the *signum* under the fabric of my shirt, as if drawing strength from the fact that at least *one* revenant—the only one who really mattered to me—thought of me as kindred. And then the dam burst.

"You might be from a time when humans were looked down on by beings like yourself. A time when men were the only ones considered smart enough to educate"—I gestured toward his pile of books—"and girls like Violette had to have protectors. But this is the twenty-first century. And I've got this"—I pulled out the *signum* and held it up for him to see—"that says I'm kindred. And I've got this"—I pointed at my head—"that says I'm as smart as you. And I have this"—I held up my middle finger—"that says go to hell, you immortal bigot."

And with that I spun around and stomped out the door, filing the expression on Arthur's face in a mental folder labeled "Kate's Proudest Moments."

Friday afternoon Vincent and I arrived at the Gare de Lyon to find pure chaos. The railroad employees were on one of their frequent strikes, and only one out of three trains was scheduled to leave. We checked the departures board to find our train.

"Canceled," read Vincent. Seeing my face fall, he squeezed my hand. "Don't give up yet. Let's see when the next train is." He worked his way down the list, mouthing the names of the destinations silently to himself until he found it: "Paris–Nice: tomorrow morning, getting in at two in the afternoon."

"Oh no," I groaned. "We won't even be there for twenty-four hours . . . that is, if there even *is* a train back when we need it." I looked from the board to him. "How long does it take to drive?"

"Eight and a half hours if we don't stop and if there's no traffic. On a Friday night we wouldn't make it in less than ten. So driving's not an option." He thought for a moment and then pulled out his phone and began texting. "I have an idea," he said. "Let's find a taxi."

A half hour later we were at Le Bourget Airport, boarding a tiny private jet. "It's Jean-Baptiste's. We only use it in case of emergencies," Vincent yelled over the noise of the engine as we walked up the stairs.

"I'm sure! It must cost a fortune each time you go somewhere!" I said, and stepped into the eight-person cabin.

"It's not actually that," Vincent said. "It's justifying the carbon footprint."

Trust a supernatural whose mission is saving the human race to think green, I mused while looking around myself in spoiled delight.

An hour and a half later we landed in Nice. Charlotte was waiting for us at the arrival gate. As soon as we stepped past airport security, she put an arm around each of us, squeezing us into a sandwich hug.

"I cannot tell you how good it is to see your faces. Much longer without my friends and I would have come to Paris, so thanks for saving me the trip!"

Her eyes shifted from my face to Vincent's, and she gasped. "Oh my God, Vincent. You look awful!" She raised a finger to trace the bruiselike patches under his eyes. It had been almost three weeks since Vincent had been dormant. He already looked as bad as he did at the end of the last month, and he still had one more week to go.

Though he claimed he was hopeful his experiment was working, I didn't want it to go on any longer. Next week I would talk to Gwenhaël, and if she had come up with some alternative plan, I would ask Vincent to call off this awful experiment.

"Look at *you*!" I exclaimed, changing the subject. Her hair had grown out to shoulder length. "I only saw you six weeks ago. How in the world did you grow your hair out so quickly?" I asked, and then laughed, realizing who— or *what*, rather—I was talking to.

Charlotte giggled. "Geneviève and I haven't just been on vacation here. And I have a feeling that Vincent and you don't talk about hair care. When we're busy saving people, getting all that transferred energy, we have to get a haircut about once a week."

"Doesn't your coiffeur catch on?"

"I have four in Paris," Charlotte responded, "and use them on a rotating basis so no one notices."

Just one more detail I would never have thought of, I mused, wondering if there would ever be a point where I would stop being amazed and the whole revenant thing would be old hat.

We made our way arm in arm through the small airline terminal and into the early evening darkness outside. It was chilly, but not as cold as in Paris. I took a deep breath. The air had a slightly salty seaside flavor.

Geneviève was waiting for us at the curb in a bright red Austin

Mini. She leapt out of the car when she saw us and ran over to squeeze me enthusiastically. "It's so good to see you!" Leaning in to kiss Vincent, she shuddered. "Vincent, I've just got to say it: You look terrible. Let's get you guys home." And she hurriedly slid behind the wheel.

Charlotte and I sat in the tiny backseat, while Vincent took the passenger side, his legs folded so tightly that his knees were practically at his chest. Although it was dark, a million tiny lights lit the highly populated coastline between Nice and Villefranche-sur-Mer. We drove along the beach before continuing onto a treacherous-looking two-lane road scaling the sheer cliffs that overlooked the sea.

Twenty minutes after we left the airport, we pulled off the main road onto a steep drive and up to a glass-and-wood house perched on the side of a hill. It looked more like a contemporary art museum than a home.

"Here we are!" crowed Charlotte enthusiastically as we winched ourselves out of the tiny car. "And you got here just in time for dinner."

"Come in, come in," said Geneviève, waving us through the front door.

I turned to Vincent, who was watching my face carefully. "This is amazing. Thank you," I murmured, going up on tiptoes to give him a kiss.

"My pleasure," he said. It was a strange and new feeling seeing him outside of his regular Parisian setting, and I could tell he was thinking the same about me.

The house couldn't have been more different from Jean-Baptiste's *hôtel particulier*. The architecture's twentieth-century minimalism was echoed by the furniture: the whole effect meant to emphasize the view outside. I walked across the room and pulled aside a sliding glass door to step out onto an enormous wood terrace balanced high above the ground and facing the sea. We were practically overhanging the ocean. The twinkling lights of the town of Villefranche-sur-Mer stretched out beneath us, wrapped around a U-shaped harbor with a battalion of luxury yachts moored offshore.

"I can't believe you're living here," I said to Charlotte, who leaned against the waist-high guardrail beside me. "It's like you've got front-row seats to the most beautiful place on earth!"

"I *know*!" she replied, looking out toward the sea. "It's like living in a dream. I shouldn't complain about being away from home. It's just that I miss everyone."

"Well, we're here to cheer you up," I said, wrapping my arm comfortingly around her and realizing with a sharp poignancy how much I had missed having her around. Violette was a fun friend to go out with. But we hadn't connected the way Charlotte and I had. With Violette, friendship was an effort. With Charlotte it was the most natural thing in the world.

We ate dinner in a glass-enclosed dining room adjacent to the terrace, our chairs arranged in a half circle before the spectacular view.

"So, tell me about Charles," Charlotte said as soon as we sat down.

"He's doing well, Charlotte." Vincent's voice was both comforting and honest. "Apparently, he met someone from Berlin a few years ago at a convocation and decided to look him up."

"Hey, I remember that guy. Charles was fascinated by him. He was kind of . . . punk. Blue hair and lots of piercings."

Vincent raised an eyebrow. "Yeah, they all look like that in that particular clan."

"Charles, too?" Charlotte's eyes were wide.

He laughed. "It actually kind of suits him."

"What!" Charlotte gasped. "Did you get a picture?"

"No, I was kind of too busy carrying out a mission for Jean-Baptiste to photograph Charles's hair."

"We don't care about his hair," Geneviève said, laughing. "Tell us how he is. What he's doing there. When he's coming back."

"See, this is why I think he's in exactly the right place." Vincent leaned forward, speaking eagerly. "That particular clan in Berlin is made up of young revenants, who at some point all became disillusioned with our mission. Bitter about our fate. The place is like an undead Alcoholics Anonymous. They have meetings all the time where they talk about their feelings.

"And their leader is really motivational. Always going on about how revenants fit into the whole cycle of life. That we're angels of mercy, allowing humans who haven't lived out their destiny to survive until they can. So when Charles and his kindred walk, it's like they're truly on a mission. They're so psyched about it . . . it's really amazing to see."

Charlotte was closing her eyes as she listened, imagining it. When Vincent finished, she gave a rueful smile. "I can't even tell you how good it is to hear you say that. It's been awful not knowing where he was or what he was doing," she said. "He never really recovered from his depression after the whole thing with Lucien, and I was afraid that he was going to do the same thing again: find some numa to destroy him. But I figured he had intentionally gone somewhere far away this time, where it wouldn't put the rest of us in danger."

Geneviève spoke up. "Maybe our little group is too tight for him in Paris. He didn't have room to grow—to find himself. It *is* pretty intense living with the same people for decades."

"You're right," said Charlotte. "Being on his own is obviously what he needs right now. But . . . do you think he'll come back?"

"Honestly? I don't know," Vincent said.

There was a minute's thoughtful silence, and then I asked, "How are *you*, Geneviève?"

"I'm taking it one day at a time," she responded, her eyes losing their sparkle. "Charlotte does a good job distracting me. It would have been hellish to have stayed in Philippe's and my house in Paris. The new scene is good for me, and we're close to Nice, where a group of around a dozen of our kind have been living for a while."

"Anyone interesting in the group?" I teased Charlotte.

She shook her head. "Interesting friend-wise, but no one special. My feelings haven't changed." She glanced quickly at Vincent, who looked away as if to give us some privacy.

We talked into the night until I could barely keep my eyes open. "Sorry, I'm beat. I know you guys will be up all night but I, for one, need a bed."

"I picked out your bedroom," Charlotte said. "I'll show you where it is."

"I'll come check on you later," Vincent said with a sexy wink as I rose to follow Charlotte out of the room.

"Wow," was all I could say as I put my bag down next to a king-size bed facing a floor-to-ceiling window with a harbor view.

"Nice, no?" Charlotte grinned.

"This is perfect, Charlotte. Thank you so much," I said, hugging her. "I really do miss you."

"And I miss you," she said. "All of you." She looked out the window at the sea, and her sadness was tangible.

"Does he ever call?"

Charlotte took a deep breath, and then said, "Ambrose calls all the time. Just not for me."

"What?" I exclaimed, and then it dawned on me. "No!"

"Yes. I mean, it's innocent. So far. Geneviève just thinks he's being nice. Caring. But he confessed it to me. He said he'd been in love with her for decades. Ambrose thought that when Philippe died he might have a chance at winning her heart. He asked me not to say anything. He doesn't want to rush her, because he knows it will take time for her to get over her husband's death. He's just so in love that he wants to know how she's doing all the time."

"Oh my God, Charlotte. That's just awful."

"Awful for me. But maybe not awful for them. Who knows? Maybe Geneviève will fall for Ambrose someday."

I took her in my arms again, and as I hugged her, she started crying. "Oh, Kate," she whispered. "I wanted him to choose me."

"So did I, Charlotte. I've been hoping for that this whole time. It's really not fair. You would be perfect together."

"I thought so too." She sniffed and wiped her tears away. "But I can't think like that now. I love Geneviève and I love Ambrose, and if they could be happy together, then I would never get in their way."

Charlotte gave me another squeeze and then left me alone. I didn't even bother getting undressed. Wondering why life—or death, in Charlotte's case—couldn't be easier, I lay down on the bed, closed my eyes, and let the sound of the waves lull me into unconsciousness.

TWENTY-NINE

THE NEXT MORNING I AWOKE TO SEE VINCENT lying beside me, watching me sleep. *"Bonjour, mon ange,"* he said, playing with a strand of my hair. Then, rolling over, he plucked something out of a bowl on the bedside table and, before I could see what it was, popped it into my mouth. I bit down in surprise. And my mouth was filled with the sugary sweetness of a strawberry.

"What—" I began, but couldn't talk around the berry.

Vincent tried not to laugh. "When I was volant, you made such a big deal about not having to brush your teeth before talking to me that I thought I'd run a better chance of getting a first-thing-in-the-morning kiss if I spared you the indignity of morning breath."

"So now I have strawberry breath."

"My favorite," he responded with a teasing smile.

"Wanna try?" I proposed, and leaned forward for a kiss.

"Mmm," he said, nodding thoughtfully. "Good. Good. But just for the record, I think I prefer Kate au naturel."

I laughed and put my arms around him. "This is the best, waking up next to you."

"We've spent the night together," he replied, "when I've been volant."

"Yeah but I couldn't do this," I said, and pressed my lips back to his. He took my head in his hands, returning the kiss, and then, wrapping me in his arms, he pulled me toward him. Our limbs wound themselves around each other's until our bodies were completely tangled, and I couldn't feel the point where mine stopped and his started.

His hand moved inside the back of my shirt, and the novelty of his warm skin brushing against mine sparked a powerful longing inside me. I didn't want him to stop until he had marked every inch of my body with his touch. And as he continued, it felt like I was expanding. Like my body was too small to contain me and I would burst out of my skin like a supernova.

"Kate." Vincent's voice sounded like it was coming from a distance. "Are you ready for this? Do you want it to be now?"

"Yes," I said automatically, and then, opening my eyes, I hesitated. Vincent had sat up and begun pulling his shirt over his head, and I saw that his chest was marked with bruises—bigger, darker facsimiles of the ones under his eyes. And although they didn't repel me—if anything, they triggered something in me that wanted to take care of him—they were shocking enough to clear away the mist from my passion-muddled thoughts.

We're both hiding something. The words flashed through my mind with a clarity that made me wonder if they had been spoken out loud.

It was true. We were both keeping something important from the other. And suddenly it seemed dishonest for our bodies to join when our spirits were divided. *That's not how I want this to start,* I thought, and as he folded me back into his arms, I said, "Wait, Vincent. I'm not . . . I'm not ready yet."

Vincent's grasp on me loosened. He paused, then moved his mouth next to my ear. "That's okay," he said, his hot breath on my skin making me shudder. "I've waited this long for you—I'm in no rush. We'll have all the time in the world."

We lay there motionless for a few minutes as I savored the sweetness of feeling his body pressed against my own. Finally we eased apart enough to look into each other's eyes. "Kate. Don't cry." Vincent looked concerned.

"I'm not," I said, and then realized that my eyes were filled with tears.

I wasn't crying from frustration: My desire for Vincent wasn't only physical. It wasn't confined to the here and now. I wanted him, body and soul. And I wanted the hours we had together to be full of life and love and joy at having found each other.

But looking at the boy lying inches from me was like being laughed at by misery and death. Besides the bruises on his chest, his lovely face was marred by the pallor of exhaustion and the circles under his eyes. And although he was still stronger than any boy I knew, his strength had been markedly sapped.

Seeing him waste away before my eyes was making our future feel even bleaker than ever. This was not how things were meant to be. We had avoided it for long enough . . . now it was time to talk.

"You did *what*?" Vincent said, aghast.

We sat facing each other in the middle of the bed. I grasped his hands firmly between mine, unsure if my death grip was meant to keep him calm or provide myself with the support I needed to spit the story out.

"Vincent, are you even hearing me? There is a *guérisseur*. A long line of *guérisseurs*, actually, who have had a special relationship with revenants. I am positive that Gaspard doesn't know about them. Because the healer said it had been centuries since her family had even seen a revenant. This is *new* information. She might actually be able to help us."

"Kate, how could you even think of doing something like that without me? You could have been in serious danger. This is *my* world we're talking about here. A world where death is always present."

"It's my world now too."

That shut him up. And I took advantage of his silence to tell him the whole tale, beginning with finding the references in the books to tracking down the shop to seeing the *signum* in the *guérisseur*'s bowl and what followed. As I finished my story, I saw the glimmer in his eye. If it wasn't an actual glimmer of hope, it was at least a glimmer of interest.

"Okay, Kate. I agree that this could be promising. But I wish you had told me about it before. I can't help but freak out when I think of you going alone to see someone who could have been a complete wacko. You could have been hurt . . . or worse. And I would never have known where to find you."

"Jules came with me," I said, trying to sound firm, but the confidence that I had begun the conversation with was quickly fading.

"JULES?" Vincent responded, incredulous. "Jules took you to see this *guérisseur*?"

"Well, he didn't exactly know where he was taking me—or why—until after it was all over."

My heart sank as I recognized the expression on Vincent's face. It was a look of betrayal, as he realized that his best friend and his girlfriend had done something behind his back.

"Vincent, stop!" I insisted. "I talked Jules into it. If there's anyone you should be mad at, it is me. If it helps at all, Jules was furious and said if I didn't tell you about it, then he would. I did *not* do this with the express purpose of deceiving you, Vincent. I did it to help *us*: you and me."

"I am already doing everything I can to help us." Vincent's eyes flashed with anger.

"What? What is it exactly that you are doing?" I said, my voice rising. "Because from what it looks like to me, whatever you're doing is causing you more harm than good."

"That's because you don't understand how it's supposed to work," Vincent shot back, rubbing his temples in frustration.

I touched his knee. "Then explain it to me."

Our eyes met, and we held the gaze for a long while before he exhaled. "Fine. Just give me a little time to think. But we'll talk tonight, I promise."

THIRTY

THE MORNING PASSED QUICKLY, WITH THE FOUR of us wandering lazily through the little town and across the abandoned winter beach. After a lighthearted lunch, during which Geneviève banned any serious or depressing subjects, we headed to the harbor to where a sleek blue speedboat was moored between massive luxury yachts.

"Wow, I wonder whose that is," Charlotte remarked. Then, leaping over the railing, she plopped herself down in the driver's seat. "All aboard!" she yelled, and then cracked up when she saw my expression. "Don't worry, Kate, it's ours." She patted the seat next to her. "Come on!"

We spent the next couple of hours speeding up and down the coast, the landscape shifting rapidly from magnificent beaches to vertiginous cliffs towering over the sea. Vincent leaned toward me at one point and said, "I don't think I've ever seen you look this ecstatically happy before."

"It's the closest thing I can think of to flying," I admitted.

"To-do list with Kate," he said to himself, looking satisfied. "More speedboats."

After dinner that night, Vincent stood and took my hand. "If you'll excuse us, I'm going out with Kate," he told Geneviève and Charlotte. We walked down the steps from the terrace, past a covered swimming pool, and through a gate into the trees. After a minute, we reached a rocky outcrop with a perfect view of the bay.

"I've been coming here as long as I've known Jean-Baptiste," he said, settling himself on the edge of the cliff and lifting his hand to pull me down next to him. "It's his favorite home-away-from-home. He had it built in the 1930s, after he saw photos of Le Corbusier's buildings. The house is amazing, but I've always come here—to this spot—when I needed to stop and remember what life was about." He wrapped an arm around me and we sat quietly, our legs dangling over the side of the rocks, watching the lights of the boats shimmer on the water.

"Close your eyes and tell me what you hear," he said, and waited.

I smiled. "Is this a game?"

"No, it's a meditation."

I shut my eyes and calmed my breathing, letting my senses take over. "I hear waves crashing. And the wind in the trees."

"What do you smell?"

I switched senses. "Pine trees. Brine."

He took my hand and ran my fingers over the stone we sat on.

I responded without him asking. "Cold, smooth rock with little indentations all over, the size of my fingertips." Opening my eyes, I breathed in the chilly sea air and tasted its pure flavor—such a change from the city air of Paris.

I felt nature move around me and through me, as my pulse slowed to the rhythm set by the crashing waves and staccato sea breeze. Our two insignificant human bodies became indecipherable from the titan agelessness of the elements around us. As we sat in silence, I knew Vincent was experiencing the same mesmerizing calm as me. Finally he spoke.

"You know how you meditate in front of paintings? Well, I do it in nature, when I need to remember that my universe isn't fantasy fiction—that I still exist in the real world. And that my immortality isn't some cosmic joke. This is the purest place I know. And what I feel here is the closest I've felt to happiness in all the years after my death.

"But now I have something that blows that feeling out of the water. Every time I need a hit of joy, I think about you. You are my solace, Kate. Just knowing that you are in this world, everything makes sense."

He leaned forward and, smoothing my hair off my face, gave me a short, sweet kiss before continuing.

"I want us to work, Kate. That is why I've been searching for something—anything—to make our time together as easy as it can be. Without the pain that my regular revenant existence—that my deaths—would bring. And, although things might not look great on the surface, I do think I've found it."

Although my heart leapt at his enthusiasm, a feeling of dread quashed my joy. This was going to be worse than I had imagined. Vincent was approaching the subject way too carefully, and the look in his eyes said he was worried about how I would take it. *Here it comes*, I thought, and braced myself.

Vincent held my gaze. "You know how dying for humans satisfies a need within us? That saving people is our very purpose for being?"

I nodded, a bud of fear blossoming in my chest.

"Ancient texts call that 'lifestyle' the 'Light Way,'" he said. "It is the natural order of things. It wipes the slate clean, giving us a year or so before we start feeling the pull again.

"But there is another way to assuage the need to die. It's called the 'Dark Way.' It's a temporary cure, and doesn't bring us back to our death age. But some have been known to use it as a method to resist . . . when there is a dire enough reason to."

I shivered, knowing that whatever it was, I didn't want him to be doing it.

"Remember the energy transfer that Arthur got when he saved Georgia?"

"Yes."

"Well, with the Dark Way the same principle applies, but in reverse. When a revenant kills a numa, we are temporarily infused with their energy."

This is very, very bad, a voice inside my mind told me. Shuddering, I forced it to shut up and listen.

Vincent continued. "Historically speaking, there's a good

reason for this: If a wounded revenant is able to kill a numa in battle, the immediate power surge gives him enough strength to escape to safety. You saw how strong Arthur was after killing that numa in the alleyway. He got right up to his feet after sustaining a pretty serious wound. Since he received the numa's energy, as well as the strength from saving Georgia, he didn't suffer at all."

I nodded, trying to wrap my mind around it. Even though most of the revenants' rules for functioning sounded strange at first, they all had some sort of rational purpose behind them.

"So that's one short-lived benefit of killing a numa. But on top of that, if the revenant hasn't died for a while, it also alleviates that desire to die—scratching his itch, you could say.

"For one pursuing the Dark Way, killing numa on a regular, continual basis not only scratches the itch but prevents it. Completely. At least that is what Gaspard and Violette have concluded from the old texts. We don't actually know of anyone who has tried it in recent times."

"Why?" My voice was hollow. "Because it's dangerous?"

"It's not dangerous in and of itself."

"Then why?"

"The idea itself is unappealing." Vincent sighed deeply. He *really* didn't want to talk about this. "Humans are good by nature. When we get their energy, it's that positive power of their innate goodness that we're infused with. Numa are evil, and so is their energy. So when we kill them, it's the negative power of their rage that's transferred."

"That . . . evil . . . numa power . . . has been going into you?" I tried to hide the disgust in my voice. Vincent had been right to assume that the idea would freak me out. I wasn't only freaked. I was deeply, intensely disturbed.

He nodded, quickly adding, "But it's not like their character can rub off on me or anything. It won't change me . . . make me evil or whatever. It just has these unfortunate side effects"—he touched the mottled shadow under his eyes—"but they're not going to last. They mean my body is building up resistance."

"Then why are you in an even more awful state this month than last?" I exploded. "If you're building up resistance, shouldn't it be getting better, not worse?"

"The texts say that it will work."

"Damn the texts, Vincent."

I rose to my feet, and Vincent followed my lead. "I have to walk," I said, feeling like moving would disperse the storm clouds inside my head. I felt overwhelmed. And scared. And I honestly didn't know what to think anymore.

"Let's go to the beach," Vincent said, and taking my hand, he led me down the hill until we were walking on the sand, the tide lapping just a short distance from our feet. I couldn't look at his face, and kept my gaze on our feet as we walked.

"Killing numa is an honorable thing," he said finally. "We just don't usually hunt them down and kill them for the pure purpose of achieving the Dark Way. But only because we are programmed to save humans—that is our primary reason for being."

I felt so cold that my teeth were chattering, but I tried to keep my voice calm. "Even if absorbing nasty"—I grimaced—"numa energy isn't dangerous, doesn't it worry you that all the numa in Paris are going to be after your head?"

"I pick them out when they're on their own, and make sure that no one sees it happen. We destroy the bodies with fire, so there isn't a trace left. As far as the numa know, their members are merely disappearing, not being slain."

My horror was now tangible. It wasn't just my teeth chattering—my whole body was trembling. "How long has this been going on?" I asked.

Noticing my shaking, Vincent pulled me to a stop and tried to draw me close to him, but I resisted. His forehead wrinkled in frustration. "Since just after the New Year," he answered. "Six weeks. A few numa each week. Jean-Baptiste and Gaspard gave their approval, since they needed the surveillance work done anyway."

"Do the others know about this?"

"One of their conditions was that I only do it while walking with the others. So, yes—Jules and Ambrose have been helping me." Vincent looked steadily into my eyes.

"You've been hiding this from me because you were worried that it will change the way I think about you." I watched him carefully.

His silence and the vulnerable look on his face confirmed my hypothesis. "So does it?" he asked.

"I'm calling this off," I said, avoiding his question. "This is going way too far."

"Kate, if this works, it's our answer. I'll be able to avoid death until..."

"Until I die," I filled in the gap.

Vincent shook his head as if to banish the thought from his mind. "Isn't the death of numa better than my own?"

"That's not the issue. You risk being permanently dead if something goes wrong. If they catch you, they will destroy you. That is, if this Dark Way black magic doesn't destroy you first with its scary side effects. Just look at you, Vincent. There has to be another way for us besides your single-handedly becoming the Numa Slayer."

"Well, there's not," Vincent said with finality.

"What about my *guérisseur*, Vincent? You obviously haven't investigated every possibility out there. And I'm not going to sit back and let you risk your immortal existence just for a chance that you and I can have a few good years together. At least you've got to let me search for an alternative. Something safe. As you yourself said, my life is short. Just a blip out of the centuries— who knows, the millennia, even—that you will live. You're not going to risk all that for me."

By this point we were facing each other on the beach, hands by our sides and fists clenched. As if echoing our emotions, the ocean wind picked up and blew a spray of seawater high in the air, showering us with ice-cold droplets that ran down my face like tears. Vincent took my hand and led me farther from the water, and then clasped my shoulders, pleading now.

"Without you, my immortal existence—as you call it—it's just survival. That's what it's been so far, at least. But with you, Kate, I'm not just surviving. I'm actually living. I'd trade this one second with you"—he closed his eyes and brushed his lips against mine—"for a thousand years without you. And if I can stretch this second out to last a few decades . . . well, having my immortality extinguished seems a very fair trade."

"I hate the thought of that energy being inside of you. And I can't even bear the thought of what would happen if some vengeful numa caught you," I said, determination running hot through my veins. "Finish this crazy experiment if you have to, but I will be looking for another way. If this *guérisseur* can't find a solution, I'm just going to keep on searching."

Vincent cocked his head, studying my face. "If that's the way you feel, then we'll both search. And when you return to the healer's next week, I'm going with you."

We stood for another minute—half-angry, half-relieved. Nothing had been resolved, but at least we were harboring no more secrets. So why did I feel further away from him than I ever had?

We ran back up the hill and escaped the wildly whipping ocean wind for the calm of the house. "Vincent?" I asked. "Stay with me tonight."

I fell asleep with my fingers resting on Vincent's cheek, and woke up twice during the night to see him lying on his back, watching the ceiling as I slept.

In the morning when I woke, he was gone. I walked into the

kitchen to see him making coffee, a pan of eggs bubbling on the stove. Charlotte and Geneviève were already at the table, drinking coffee and eating croissants.

"Not even a cuddle?" I whispered as I gave him a good-morning hug in the kitchen.

"I might be supernatural, but I'm not made of steel, Kate," he said, smiling. "And unless you changed your mind in the last twenty-four hours, I thought it safest to be in another room when you awoke." He leaned in to give me a slow, warm kiss. "Does that make up for it?"

"For the moment," I said, eyeing him coquettishly. He raised an eyebrow, grinning, and I took my cup of coffee from him and headed to the table.

The day passed in slow-paced luxury. We drove into Italy, turning off the coastal road to drive through rolling hills dotted with ruins of ancient villages. Stopping in the medieval hill town of Dolceaqua, Geneviève stocked up on olive oil and Charlotte on amaretti cookies before we headed to a simple but decadent lunch in a tiny five-table restaurant. Hearing the beautiful language spill effortlessly off Vincent's tongue made me long for an extended Italian vacation with him. It was hard not to plan ahead. Hard to remember that we weren't just a normal couple like the people sitting around us.

The weekend had gone too fast: When we got back to the house, it was already time to leave. We picked up our bags and squeezed into the Mini. "I wish we could stay another week," I said, hugging Charlotte and Geneviève outside the airport.

"Come back whenever you can. As often as you can!" Charlotte said.

"Don't worry," Vincent said. "Kate won't need much convincing."

And waving good-bye, we made our way across the tarmac to where our plane waited to take us home. Back to reality.

THIRTY-ONE

I DRIFTED THROUGH THE NEXT DAY ON A CLOUD, my body in Paris, but my mind back in the house in Villefranche-sur-Mer. Memories of the weekend flitted in and out of my thoughts as I tried—and then stopped trying—to focus on my classes, my homework, and everything else that kept me from being where I wanted to be: with Vincent. Preferably wrapped in his arms.

As Ambrose, my Vincent-appointed guardian for the day, drove me home from school, I was so out of it that he had to tap me on the shoulder and tell me that my phone was ringing. It was Papy, and his voice was unusually tense. "Kate, do you think you could come straight to the gallery instead of going home?"

"Sure, Papy. What's up?"

"I just need some help. I'll tell you when you get here."

Ambrose parked across the street from the gallery and waited in the car. I walked in to find Papy talking to two men in police uniforms. He introduced me briefly. "Officers, this is my grand-daughter Kate." The men nodded, and Papy took my arm to lead me a few feet away.

"The gallery was robbed last night," he said.

"What?" I gasped.

"It's okay, dear. Everything was insured. It's just very . . . both-ersome. The store has never been broken into before."

"What did they take?"

"A little bit of everything. All pieces that were easy to carry—none of my statues, thankfully." Papy suddenly looked ten years older. He rubbed his forehead with his fingertips and squeezed his eyes shut. "I was hoping you could watch the shop while I went back to the station with the detective. They're done with the on-site investigation. Now it's just paperwork."

"Sure, Papy," I agreed, and a moment later he walked out the door with the two men, doing his little hat wave at me as they moved out of sight. I phoned Ambrose in the car to tell him that I had to gallery-sit for an hour or two, and he told me he was fine waiting—to take my time.

I looked around at the mess. The glass cases that had been broken were completely stripped of their contents. I tried to remember what they had held. Ancient jewelry, tiny Greek figu-rines, examples of Roman glass. It did seem quite random, as if they hadn't known much about what they were taking, but were just interested in anything small enough to carry. *Hoodlums instead of specialized art thieves*, I thought.

And suddenly a tiny, red-hot needle of panic pierced my heart.

I raced back to the stock closet and saw the shattered door standing open. The boxes inside were scattered, their contents dumped on the floor. I sifted through the books, looking for *Immortal Love*. Piece by piece, I pulled the contents of the closet out into the hallway as I searched until I was sure. The book was gone.

My thoughts returned to the week before, when Gwenhaël had told me about the numa finding the book centuries ago and making trouble for her family. A "very nasty occasion," she had called it.

I fished around in my bag until I found the card that her son had given me. My hand shaking, I dialed the number. He answered on the first ring.

"Bran, it's Kate Mercier. I'm the one who visited your mother last week."

"She's gone." The words sounded so distant I wasn't sure I had heard him correctly.

"What did you say?"

"She's gone. They came this morning, the evil ones."

"Oh my God, the numa got her?" My lungs were sucked empty.

"No. When they came, we hid. They did not find us. And as soon as they were gone, she left."

"Where did she go?"

"Into hiding. She didn't tell me where. If I knew, the evil ones could get that information from me. As it stands, I am useless to them."

"Oh, Bran. I'm so sorry."

"It's not your fault, Kate. It was time. Things happen when

they are supposed to, and as the time of the Victor draws closer, our services will be required. I will stay, Kate, and my mother will return. Let your friends know that we will be here when they need us."

"Bran, I don't understand what you're talking about. What victor?"

"That is why the numa want us. The texts say that my family will produce the VictorSeer."

All of a sudden, I remembered a phrase from the book that had been practically incomprehensible. Something about the *guérisseur* being the one who would see the Victor.

"I still don't . . ."

"The revenants call him the Champion. And we will be the ones to identify him."

It took me a few seconds of realization, and then everything was suddenly, shockingly clear. "Your mother can identify the Champion," I stated, clarifying. "And the numa came looking for her. Because if the Champion is found, the numa will know the identity of the one who will conquer them."

"That is correct. But if they find him before he can overthrow them, they will attempt to seize his power for themselves."

"Seize his power?" I asked, confused.

"The texts state that the Champion's power can be transmitted by force. If he is captured, the one who destroys him will receive his power. As you can imagine, the results would be disastrous."

"And the numa want to force your mother to tell them who it is."

"That is right. But they are misled. It isn't my mother who will find the Champion."

"What do you mean?"

"She possesses our family's theories on when and where it will happen. And some coded clues about who it will be. But as far as identification on sight—the gift of the VictorSeer—my mother claims she doesn't have that capability."

"So will it be you?"

"Me or one of my descendants."

"You *have* descendants?"

"Yes."

I exhaled. "Some say that my boyfriend is the Champion."

The line was silent for a long time. Finally Bran spoke. "My mother has not yet passed me the gift. When she does, I will contact you. Bring your boyfriend to me then. If I am indeed the VictorSeer and he indeed the Champion, we will know it then and there."

I gave him my phone number. And then I gave him my grandparents' number as well. I didn't know how long it would take for him to call me. But I guessed it could be years.

THIRTY-TWO

IT WAS ONLY THREE CALENDAR DAYS AFTER OUR
weekend in the south, but it felt like it had been three weeks. Vincent had worked nonstop with Jean-Baptiste since the moment
we had returned, and I had kept busy with homework and a *Cas-
ablanca* movie date with Violette.

But I had awaited this afternoon with a feeling of anticipa-
tion, knowing that Vincent would be meeting me here at Papy's
where I was working for the afternoon. After the break-in, Papy
had tried to cancel my gallery-sitting sessions, saying it was too
dangerous. But I convinced him that it was doubtful the thieves
would return in broad daylight . . . if they dared return at all.

Ambrose dropped me off after school, leaving only after I
reassured him that Vincent was arriving at any moment. Papy
had invited him to come see the new Greek war helmet he was
bringing back from his appointment, using Vincent's interest in
ancient weaponry as an excuse to invite him to the gallery. But I

knew that neither of them needed the enticement. They genuinely enjoyed the other's company.

I wandered around the gallery, looking at the cleanup job Papy had done since Monday. He had immediately replaced the glass cases, but it would take a while for him to restock them with new inventory. The doorbell rang, and I skipped to the desk to push the button for the door release. But the huge smile that spread across my face quickly faded as I saw that it wasn't Vincent coming through the door. It was two men I had never seen before. And I could tell, before they even said a word, that they were numa.

They were on me in an instant, crossing the gallery in a blink of an eye. They didn't touch me. They didn't need to. They just loomed.

"What do you want?" I asked. The words came out as a squeak: My throat was squeezed shut as effectively as if a boa constrictor was looped around my neck. I instinctively glanced around for something to fight them with, but there was nothing within grabbing distance, and I doubted I could get very far before they would stop me.

"We want to know what she told you."

"Who?" I asked, confused.

"You know who. The old lady healer. What did she tell you about the Champion?"

I blinked in sudden comprehension. "She didn't tell me anything about the Champion."

"We know you talked to her. And now her son says she's gone

and he doesn't know where."

"Although we're keeping an eye on the place to make sure he's not lying," sneered the other, as if this were one big joke.

My fear evaporated and was replaced by fury. "You better not hurt them!" I growled.

They both stared at me, surprised by my outburst. And then, with a low, evil laugh, one stepped forward and grabbed me by the wrist. Hard. "We want to know what she told you."

Just then I heard the lock click, and Papy walked into the gallery, leaving the door open behind him, the huge box in his arms blocking his view. He walked across the room and, setting it down next to the armory display, placed his hat on top and began to shuffle his coat off.

"Papy," I called, my voice high-pitched and unnatural.

He looked up and froze. "Take your hands off my granddaughter," he barked, and began moving toward us.

"Don't move, old man," said the one holding me, and tightened his grip on my arm.

My grandfather stopped, and his eyes narrowed. "You were the ones on the surveillance tapes," he said. "You've already robbed my store. What do you want now?"

"All your granddaughter has to do is tell us what we want to know and we will leave without injury to either of you."

"No," said Papy sternly. "You will leave now or I will be forced to call the police." He pulled his cell phone out of his pocket.

"That won't be necessary," came a deep voice from behind us. Vincent stepped through the open door, his face like the sky before a devastating storm. My captor's partner threw himself across the room, and then staggered backward as Vincent's fist connected with his jaw. He fell and lay motionless on the floor.

The numa holding me jerked me to his side, his hand clamped around my arm like a vise. "We're just having a little chat with your girlfriend. No need for you to get involved."

"Let her go," Vincent said in a lowered voice, his quick, urgent glance at me piercing my heart with its concern. "Let both of them go. Anything you have to talk about can be discussed alone with me."

"But you see, we don't want you," the numa said, his lip curling in mockery. "Not this time."

"What issue do you have with the girl?" Vincent growled.

"You mean, besides the fact that she destroyed our former leader? But that's of no importance now. She has information that we want." The numa raised his free hand to my neck. "So I would advise that you stay where you are while she answers my question—or my hand might just slip."

The feel of his skin against mine made me want to puke. With a gesture prompted more from disgust than from fear, I struggled and managed to kick him hard in the shin, but he only laughed and grabbed me tighter, pulling me firmly toward the back of the gallery, away from Vincent.

The metallic sound of a sword leaving its sheath split the air and brought my captor to a halt. Vincent's eyes burned like coals as he lifted an evil-looking saber.

The numa started in shock, his fingers digging painfully into my skin, and sputtered, "You wouldn't. Not in front of a human!" He glanced toward Papy, whose startled expression revealed that, though he might not have heard the rest of the repartee, he had definitely registered the last few words.

"I would, actually. With pleasure," Vincent replied, and brought the curved sword up into the light as he took a step toward us.

The numa staggered slightly back, dragging me with him. "Why would you risk exposing us and yourself . . . ," he began to ask, his face contorted in confusion.

Vincent's voice was as sharp as the steel in his hand. "Starting here and now, all rules are forgotten. On behalf of your kind, you just declared war."

My captor weighed the situation. And then—just like that—he released his hold on me. Keeping a safe distance from Vincent's blade, he moved toward his fallen partner, who had just begun to stir. Giving him a motivational kick, he shoved him toward the door. Pausing on the doorstep, he glared at me. "We *will* be seeing you again. *Au revoir*, Kate Mercier." And with that, he followed his companion down into the street.

My grandfather sprang into action, slamming and dead-bolting the gallery door and pulling a thick curtain across the windows.

"What did they want?" Vincent asked urgently. He sheathed his sword and tucked it back under his coat.

"The *guérisseur*," I whispered, suddenly feeling crippled by the thought that my actions—however well-meaning—had brought this upon us. Jules had been right. I had walked into their world and brought danger right back out with me.

Vincent saw my expression and reached for me, but froze as Papy's sharp words echoed through the room. "Do not touch my granddaughter." He approached us slowly. Carefully.

And there we stood in the low-lit gallery. Glowing dust motes spiraled upward, lit by the cracks of sunlight spilling in from the curtains' edges. The three of us were motionless, staring at one another as the rows of ancient statues looked on. My grandfather's face held an expression that was completely foreign to it. There was no kindness. No gentility. He stared coldly at Vincent as if he were a complete stranger.

Finally he spoke. "What are you?" The three words were crisp and concise and demanded a response.

Vincent's eyes flickered to me. I saw how Papy was watching him and knew there wasn't any way out. If Vincent's sword hadn't already alerted my grandfather that something was amiss, the numa had definitely exposed us with his words. I gave my head the slightest of nods.

"Revenant," Vincent said, looking Papy straight in the eyes.

To my grandfather's credit, he didn't even flinch. "And those men who attacked Kate?"

"Numa."

The word seemed to freeze in the air and hang suspended between the three of us before exploding on the arrow of Papy's response. "Out."

"Sir, I—" Vincent started, and at the same time I blurted, "But Papy—"

"Out!" My grandfather's voice cut us off. "Get out of here. Out of my granddaughter's life. How dare you expose Kate to mortal danger. How dare you bring these monsters through our door. Get out and stay out."

"No!" I cried, and running to Papy, grabbed his arms and waited until his eyes lowered from Vincent to me. "Papy, no. Vincent's . . ." All my arguments flashed through my mind and fell away as I realized that they were useless. *Vincent was protecting me*, or *It's already too late, the numa know who I am*. Nothing I could say would convince Papy. Because he was right: I *was* in danger because of Vincent. I settled for one true statement—the only one that my grandfather couldn't refute. "I love him."

Papy freed his captive arms and wrapped them around me, hugging me as if he had lost me for years and then found me again. After a second, he held me away and said, tenderly but seriously, "Kate, you may think you love him. But he's not even human."

"*He's* not the bad guy," I insisted. "*They* are."

Papy glanced over my head at Vincent, who hadn't moved. "I know, darling. I know about them. At least I've studied them, along with every other mythical character that shows up in the ancient arts. Although I wasn't convinced that they actually existed." His voice became cold with this last statement, and I pulled away from him to face Vincent.

Vincent's eyes—still locked in my grandfather's gaze—looked

hollow. "Kate, your grandfather's right. My presence in your life has put you in danger."

I felt like someone had grabbed me by the throat. "Stop it!" I yelled. "Both of you—stop right now." I stomped my foot, and both men started as if I had slapped them. Now that I had their attention, I began to talk.

"Papy, Vincent saved my life. He's the one who moved me out of the way of the falling stones at the café last year. If it weren't for him, I wouldn't even be here now for you to be fighting over." My grandfather's face remained hard, but his fists unclenched. Knowing he was absorbing my words, I continued.

"*Grandpère*," I pleaded, "do you want me to be like I was before? Depressed? Grieving? Living in the past with no company besides my dead parents' ghosts? Vincent not only saved my life, he helped me find my way back to the world of the living."

"That's quite an accomplishment for someone who is undead," Papy said dryly.

Vincent just stood there, looking like he didn't know what to say, but his hands were open as if he was trying to beam me support through the five feet of space that separated us. *He's not even worried about himself,* I thought. *All he cares about is how I come out of this.* I launched myself toward him, wrapping myself around his neck, and felt his arms encircle me carefully.

"Vincent, this is my gallery, and I will ask you to leave it now," Papy demanded.

Vincent gently unwound me from him and, taking my hand in his, turned to face Papy. "I would ask that—before you come to a conclusion—you discuss this alone with Kate. I will live by any decision the two of you make together."

Taking my head in his hands, he kissed me lightly on the lips. "I'll call you later," he said softly. Then, giving Papy a polite bow, he walked to the door, flipped the lock open, and disappeared onto the street.

My tears were falling in earnest as I felt Papy's gentle hands on my shoulders. "*Ma princesse*," he said mournfully. "Whatever have you gotten yourself into?"

THIRTY-THREE

PAPY ORDERED ME TO SIT DOWN AND SPENT THE next fifteen minutes closing the gallery early. We were both jumpy on the walk home—waiting for the numa to double back and come for us. I felt like telling my grandfather that sending Vincent away before he could escort us safely to our house might not have been the smartest idea, but by that point I was keeping my thoughts to myself.

Then, halfway there, I saw Ambrose in a phone booth pretending to be deep in conversation, although I knew full well that he never left home without his cell phone. He winked as I walked by, and I suspected that Vincent had provided us with ample protection. When I spotted Gaspard sitting in a café reading a book, and he raised an eyebrow as we passed, I was sure of it.

Once home, Papy and I headed directly to his office. "Kate," he said gravely, as I posed nervously on a leather armchair, "do you even know what Vincent is?"

I nodded. "I know everything, Papy. Or at least, I know a lot. But how do *you* know about them? You can't tell me you just jumped from studying mythological beings to believing they exist. You didn't even blink when Vincent told you what he was."

My grandfather sighed, walked to his bookcase, and, after searching for a minute, pulled out the old bestiary. He laid it on the low, round table between us and opened it, flipping through until he found the right page.

"This, my dear," he said, gesturing toward the book, "is the only record of a revenant in my entire library. I have seen them mentioned in other texts, but as soon as books or works of art concerning revenants come onto the market, they are snatched up for astronomical prices. The buyers are a secret network of private collectors using obviously fictional names and paying in cash. We antiquities dealers know to contact them if we come into possession of anything of that nature.

"None of the dealers talk about the revenant-theme collectors—not even among ourselves; our clients have made it clear that if we discuss their interest with anyone they will no longer do business with us. All literary traces of revenants have disappeared into these buyers' collections. So of course it occurred to me that there might be a reason for the secrecy—beyond an extremely competitive market."

I met Papy's serious gaze with a determined look of my own. He wasn't going to scare me, and he needed to know that.

"There are strange, mystical things occurring in our world that very few people know about. Because my profession necessitates constant detective work into the darkest corners of history, I unluckily happen to be privy to some of them. Most of my colleagues prefer to stick their heads in the sand and pretend that revenants are fictional beings. But I don't agree with them—I suspected their existence. And after what I witnessed today, my suspicions have been confirmed.

"But Kate, these things should remain where they began—in the shadows. Not in my life, dating my granddaughter. I cannot let you see Vincent again. Your parents would have expected me to protect you, and barring you from seeing something"—he hesitated, registering the look on my face—"some*one* who means certain danger for you, is part of the responsibility I have accepted."

"But Papy . . . ," I began, suddenly blinded by an onslaught of tears.

"You are seventeen and still under my guardianship. When you are eighteen you can do what you want, although I will hope that by then you will see things the way I do." His words were delivered with firmness, but I saw his eyes cloud with emotion as he watched me cry. I leaned forward into his arms.

"Oh, dear Kate," he soothed. "I hate to make you unhappy. But I would rather see you depressed than dead."

Back in my room, I picked up my phone and stared at it for an entire minute. For the first time in almost a year I wanted to tap in the number of one of my Brooklyn friends and hear their old familiar voice at the end of the line. But even though I knew I could do that—any one of them would be forgiving enough to pick right up from where we had left off—how could I even begin to tell them about my situation? It was too incredible to describe.

Um, yeah, Claudia? I'm dating this dead guy named Vincent and Papy won't let me see him, because if I do I might be killed by these evil zombies that are out to get him. My friends would think that my grief had driven me mad.

I shook my head in frustration and dialed Vincent's number. His voice sounded calm, but I could tell he was as shaken up as I was.

"What's the verdict?"

"Papy said I can't see you anymore." I couldn't help my voice from wavering.

"What else could we expect? He's a rational man." His voice shifted from cautious to warm. Caring. "Kate . . . I wish I were there with you. Are you okay?"

I sniffed and pushed my palm hard against my forehead to keep the tears from coming. "I'm all right. And I see where he's coming from. But he's wrong."

"He's not wrong about the fact that I bring danger into your life."

"The danger's already here, Vincent. It's too late to think of that. Those numa are after me now. So thinking about it rationally, it's even more dangerous for me to stay away from you. Besides the fact that I don't *want* to stay away from you." My tears won out, and I began to cry. For about the thousandth time in one day.

"It's going to be okay, Kate," Vincent said softly.

I grabbed a tissue and breathed deeply, trying to compose myself. "I owe Papy my respect. But I just can't obey him in this case." Vincent didn't respond.

Something that had been nagging at the back of my mind for the last few hours began to emerge and form into a coherent thought. The whole revenant revelation and anti-Vincent campaign by Papy had overshadowed something important. But now I began to realize the repercussions of something the numa had said, and my heart was suddenly in my throat.

"Vincent—today in the gallery. That numa said something about me killing Lucien." I shivered, although it was about seventy degrees in my bedroom. "How could he know that? No numa were there to witness it, and only your kindred know what happened."

"I was wondering if you had picked up on that," Vincent responded darkly. "I've been discussing it with the others since I got back."

"Could there have been a volant numa spirit accompanying Lucien who returned to tell the others what happened?"

"No—I was volant too, remember? I would have known if someone else was there."

"Then how . . ."

"Only revenants knew about that. It has to be one of our own who shared the information."

"What?" I sat there stunned, waiting for some kind of explanation.

"Ambrose and Gaspard and I have been talking about it. It's the only answer. Somewhere in Paris, a revenant is talking to the numa. Maybe even working in conjunction with them. I'm sure of it. We all are. Not just because of this. The report I got in Berlin was that there was some sort of information leak."

"But why?"

"I have no idea."

"And how did the numa know that I visited the *guérisseur*?"

"They could have been following you. Watching you."

"But Jules was with me. Surely he would have known if numa were around."

Vincent *hmm*-ed in agreement.

"Who else knows I visited Gwenhaël?"

"Well, by now our whole house does. I discussed it with them when you and I got back from the south. And then gave them the update when you told me that she had fled after the numa came to her shop. But I doubt they've mentioned it to anyone else. As far as we're concerned, until her son contacts you to say she's back, that path's hit a dead end."

As he spoke, an idea came to me. I hesitated before voicing my suspicion, knowing it sounded crazy. "But let's say it *is* someone in your house. Arthur made it really clear what he thought about letting a human be involved in revenant affairs when he voted me out of that meeting. And then, when he saw me in JB's library—the day I returned the book—he said that there was information in there that humans shouldn't know about."

"Now wait a minute, Kate," Vincent said forcefully. "If you're saying what I think . . . Arthur might not like the fact that you're as involved as you are in our business, but he would never put you at risk. There is no way he would purposely sell you out to the numa."

"No, you're right," I conceded, feeling worse about my theory sounding stupid to Vincent than I did for falsely accusing Arthur. And then I thought of something else. "Wait, Violette told me Arthur had kept in contact with numa from their past life. She said it was from a time when numa and revenants weren't enemies."

"What?" Vincent said, incredulous.

But I was on a roll. There was no self-editing for me by this point, no matter how weird it sounded to Vincent. "Actually, I saw Arthur talking to this really iffy-looking guy one day, at La Palette. He could totally have been a numa. . . . Now that I think back on it, I'm sure of it. He had that weird thing going on in the air around him."

"What do you mean, 'weird thing in the air'?"

"You know. They all have that kind of thing around their bodies. Like the few inches around them are in shades of gray. Like they've sucked all the color out of the air."

Vincent hesitated. "You can tell who's numa and who's not?"

"Um, yeah. Can't everyone?"

"No, not humans." He thought for a second. "Could you tell with Lucien?"

"No. I don't think so," I admitted, trying to remember. Besides the time he had a knife pressed up against my sister's throat, I'd only seen him in a dark nightclub.

"Then it probably has something to do with when I possessed you. Gaspard keeps asking me if you've had side effects."

Impatient with this unrelated diversion, I continued my theory: "So if you told Arthur that I had been to the *guérisseur*, he could have passed that information on to the numa."

"Kate . . ." Vincent's voice was dark.

"No, not like that. Not on purpose. But if he is in contact with the numa, maybe he let it slip. Maybe he just mentioned it to someone. To the wrong someone."

"Kate. You sound completely paranoid. I know you're scared and you're just trying to figure this all out, but I promise . . . you are looking in completely the wrong direction."

"But Vincent, you agree that only revenants know I killed Lucien."

"The entire revenant community is aware of that. And there are a *lot* of us. Not just the seven who live in our house."

I ignored him and continued. "And out of all the revenants, only the ones in your house knew that I went to the *guérisseur*. And Violette told me that Arthur is in contact with the numa. Who else could it be? And whether or not he meant to put me in danger . . ."

"Whether or not? Kate, stop right there. None of our close kindred would betray us to the numa," Vincent said. "I know you're still angry at Arthur for shaming you in front of the house. And, quite honestly, I am too. But whether or not he is bigoted against humans, he's good at heart, and he is *not* stupid. He wouldn't let your activities 'slip' to a numa if—and I seriously doubt this—he is actually in contact with any of them."

I sighed, wanting to believe him. But I had a feeling. There was just something wrong about Arthur. I didn't trust him. But I couldn't say anything else to Vincent about it.

"Kate, don't worry about this. We're taking care of everything. Jules is volant tomorrow, so he's going to come with Jean-Baptiste and me to begin investigating Paris's revenants on our own . . . to see if we can find the leak. Ambrose is going to take you and Georgia to school."

Good plan, I thought, *except you're looking in the wrong place— your "leak" is living under your own roof.*

Vincent and I said good night and reassured each other that, although we had to be careful not to provoke my grandfather, we would see each other secretly. But when I hung up, I felt anything but reassured. Not that my recent behavior had been the best example, but I hated sneaking around behind anyone's back. And knowing that I would be going directly against Papy's wishes felt like a betrayal of his trust. He had taken Georgia and me in and was doing his best to give us a good life. And I was blatantly disobeying him.

THIRTY-FOUR

AS SOON AS I HEARD GEORGIA GET HOME THAT night, I popped across the hallway and installed myself in her bedroom. "Katie-Bean!" She greeted me with a smile, but her expression quickly rearranged itself into one of concern when she saw my face. "Oh no. What happened?"

"Papy knows."

"Papy knows what?"

"That Vincent's a revenant and that I've got numa after me."

"What do you mean, you've got numa after you?"

I told her the whole story. The meeting with the *guérisseur*. The theft at our grandfather's gallery. The healer's disappearance. And then the standoff between Papy and Vincent.

"You're not going to stop seeing Vincent, are you?" Georgia asked, alarmed.

"No," I admitted. "I'm not. But I won't be able to talk about him anymore in front of Papy and Mamie. And I will probably have to lie about what I'm doing when I'm out. Which makes me feel pretty low. But there's no way I'm going to stop seeing him."

Georgia thought for a moment. "So what are you going to do? I mean, you can't just keep ducking Papy forever."

I settled in at the end of her bed. "I've come up with a plan. It's kind of lame, but . . ."

"Spill," my sister said.

"I thought I would ask Jean-Baptiste to talk to Papy."

"What! Why?" asked Georgia.

"Because Vincent told me JB's part of this group of supersecret revenant-theme collectors that Papy sells to. So Papy might actually listen to him. There are a few outsiders who know what they are—like Jeanne, their housekeeper. So Jean-Baptiste must know how to explain it to humans he needs—in a way that convinces them to do business with him and keep things quiet."

"Doing business with someone and convincing them to let their granddaughter date your undead faux-nephew are two very different things," Georgia said, finally peeling off her boots and tights and getting comfortable on the bed.

"I know," I mumbled, disheartened. "It's a long shot. But what else can I do? In any case, with everything else going on, that's hardly my priority."

"What is the priority, then? And how do you plan on using me to help you achieve it?" Georgia asked, her eyes glittering with enthusiasm. My sister was good at the listening, but even better with the action.

"This is the deal, Georgia. First I have to find out who's been talking to the numa about me. If Vincent and his kindred can take care of *that* problem, hopefully I'll be off the hook with the numa. They didn't seem to care about my killing Lucien, especially since I obviously didn't do it alone. They used the term 'old leader,' so they must have a new leader now. Everyone seems to think so. And they were sent to find out what I learned from the *guérisseur*. So it's not personal—they're not going to hunt me down for the rest of my life.

"Besides—if Arthur is the one talking to the numa . . ." Georgia's eyes bugged, and she looked at me like I had suddenly gone stark-raving mad. I held up my hand in a "just wait" gesture. "*If* he's the leak, then Vincent's whole house is in danger. But when I told Vincent my reasons for suspecting Arthur, he wouldn't even listen to me."

"Well, that's probably because you're insane. Besides the fact that I think Arthur is deliciously dreamy—"

"And your taste has been so reliable in the past," I cut in.

"*Touché*," Georgia admitted. "But I know I'm right this time. I actually had coffee with him this afternoon." She gave me her sly cat grin and pretended she was fanning herself from the memory of his hotness.

"What?" I exclaimed. "He asked you out?"

"Well, not exactly," Georgia allowed. "I just kind of stumbled across him sitting at the Café Sainte-Lucie, and he asked me to sit with him. And since the evil munchkin wasn't there to piss me off, I said yes."

"This afternoon after school?" I asked.

"Uh-huh," she said, eyeing me suspiciously.

"That's when the standoff at Papy's happened. Arthur was probably waiting for the numa to report back to him."

Georgia's mouth fell open. "Um, paranoid much? Earth to Kate: You're losing your grip on reality. Arthur is a totally normal and very nice dead guy. I would be much more suspicious of Violette."

I shook my head. "I trust Violette. If Arthur is behind it—wittingly or unwittingly—she must not know a thing about it. Otherwise she would have told me. We've gotten really close, Georgia. I know you don't like her, but I do."

She patted my arm, as if comforting an invalid. "I think the key word in what you just said was 'unwittingly.' If he does hang with fringe numa types, it's possible he could have given something away. Although I just can't see him buddying up with the evil ones. I seriously don't think that Arthur would hurt a fly. He seems kind of anxiously reserved, but he's such a nice guy I'm starting to suspect he's actually too nice for me. He seemed genuinely upset about having offended you."

"See! He *was* talking about me. And he's probably just pretending to be remorseful to throw everyone off."

"That's enough, Kate. You're on a one-way train to cuckooland."

"I'm going to prove that he's the one."

"Okay. It's a challenge. I'm going to prove that he's not. Especially seeing that if you're right and he's evil, that will mean I'll have to cancel my date with him for Saturday night."

"Georgia!"

"Just kidding," she said, and then under her breath added, "Not really."

A pot of tiny purple-spotted violet flowers sat on the hall table the next morning. Papy lowered his newspaper long enough to nod toward them, and I wondered if he would have been so blasé about it if the card attached had said "Vincent" instead of "Violette."

Heard about your frightful experience yesterday. Let's have coffee later on. Café Sainte-Lucie after school? Kisses, Violette

I pulled my flower dictionary out of my book bag and found the picture of the flowers—they were oak-leaved geraniums. "True friendship," I read, smiling as Georgia walked up behind me. "Those are pretty," she commented, leaning down to smell them.

"They're from Violette," I said, watching for her reaction.

"They look like weeds," she replied, straightening, and went to sit next to Papy at the breakfast table.

"Are you okay?" was all Papy uttered at breakfast, but he said it with a look of concern as he glanced over at Georgia—like he would say more if she weren't there. If my grandfather thought I wouldn't tell my sister everything, then he really didn't know us. Maybe our occasional fights threw him off the scent of just how close we actually were.

A half hour later, we stepped out of the house to see Ambrose waiting for us at the corner, standing next to a black 4x4. "Ladies," he said in a Barry White voice, and stretching his arms in front of him, cracked his thick neck from side to side. "This way, please." He opened the door, and I jumped into the backseat. "And the lovely Georgia?"

"All this yummy muscleness first thing in the morning is almost too much for me to take," she cooed, and gave him a playful wink as she scooted herself into the front seat. I shook my head. If "Flirt" qualified as a foreign language, my sister and Ambrose would both have PhDs in it.

"So where is everyone this morning?" I asked Ambrose as he put the car in gear and headed toward the river.

"Vincent and Jean-Baptiste have gone off to visit the revenants staying in Geneviève's place. You know . . . to dig around to see who tipped the zomboids off to your leader-slaying extravaganza. How's it feel to be Numa Enemy Number One, Katie-Lou?"

"Scary, actually," I confessed. "I thought that your chauffeuring me around for the last week was pretty useless until yesterday."

"Does that mean you're happy to see me for once?" Ambrose said, his teeth gleaming white against the dark-chocolate brown of his skin.

"I'm always glad to see you, Ambrose," I said, knowing that if the same line had come from Georgia it would have sounded as seductive as Mae West.

"How about your oh-so-tempting medieval friend?" Georgia said.

"I suppose you're referring to Arthur and not Violette?" Ambrose replied with a chuckle. "They're both training with Gaspard this morning, before going to visit some of the other kindred on their own. Jules is volant, so I'm going to drop you off at school and walk with him and Gaspard this afternoon before I come back to get you. Stay inside the school gates, will you? We don't need any drive-by numa action while you wait for me on the street."

Ambrose watched as we entered the school grounds, and once we were through the doors, he drove off. Georgia turned to me. "Well? I got the intel on what Arthur's up to. What are we going to do with it?"

"This is our chance," I said. "We know where he is right now. We can stake out the house and see where he goes when he leaves."

"You heard Ambrose. Arthur's supposed to be going somewhere with the Royal Pain."

"Well, what will it hurt to spy on them for a couple of hours? Besides skipping school, that is. This is our only chance not to be followed by the revenants."

"Or the numa, for that matter," Georgia agreed. "Everyone thinks we're in school. We'll have to go now—we don't know how long Gaspard's kick-ass training lasts." She glanced around the hallway, and her eyes landed on an athletic-looking guy carrying a pile of books. "Hey, Paul!" she yelled. "Remember that time you offered to loan me your scooter?"

THIRTY-FIVE

MY SISTER AND I HUDDLED AT THE END OF THE rue de Grenelle, looking ridiculously suspicious as we hid behind the corner, throwing glances every few minutes down the road toward Jean-Baptiste's mansion.

"What time is it now?" I asked, my teeth chattering in the February cold.

"Five minutes after the last time you asked," Georgia growled. "It's eleven oh five and we have been here a total of an hour and thirty-five minutes. How long do your training sessions with Gaspard run?"

"An hour," I said. "But I'm sure that Violette and Arthur can go for longer than me, and we have no idea when they started." My heart dropped an inch as our mission began to seem much stupider than it had within the hallway of our warm and safe school.

"Wait!" Georgia hissed in a dramatic whisper. "The gate is

opening. And here comes . . . it's Arthur! He's wearing a motor-cycle helmet, but I know it's him—he's got on the same leather jacket he wore at the café yesterday."

I struggled to look past her, but she pushed me backward. "Shh!" she insisted, even though we were yards out of his hear-ing range. "He's driving the motorcycle slowly to the end of the block. He's getting off and walking the bike backward onto the sidewalk. Holy cow—he looks like he's hiding!"

Georgia's commentary was beginning to sound hysterical. "What do you mean 'hiding'?" I pushed her out of the way. "I don't see anyone."

"Okay. Far end of the street. Just behind the last building. He's hiding down there."

"Did he see us?"

"No! He didn't even look our way when he came out of the driveway."

"Then why is he—"

"Wait!" Georgia interrupted me. I poked my head above hers, looking around the corner of the building. A taxi had just turned past us to drive down the road and was now parked in front of the *hôtel particulier*. The gate swung open again, and Violette stepped out, peering both ways before jumping into the cab. We pulled back, waited a second, and then stuck our heads around the corner.

The taxi drove to the end of the street and turned left on the one-way avenue. Georgia and I had our helmets on in a second and were on the borrowed scooter, heading down the rue de

Grenelle, as we saw Arthur's motorcycle pull out onto the road a safe distance behind Violette's taxi. We turned left onto the avenue, a few cars behind Arthur.

The next twenty minutes were spent maneuvering our way between cars and trucks, trying to stay out of view even though Arthur never once looked around. His attention was fixed on Violette's taxi, and he was obviously using the same defensive tactics we were to avoid her seeing him. We headed north over the river, and up past the Louvre and across town until we arrived at the steep hill called Montmartre and began inching up its tiny one-lane roads.

"They're heading toward Sacré-Coeur," I yelled, looking up at the white-domed basilica perched on the hilltop. A refrigerated yogurt truck that had served as our camouflage for the last few blocks stopped in the middle of the street, and its driver jumped out to make a delivery. We spied Arthur half a block up, parking his motorcycle at the base of the rue Foyatier staircase—the landmark that pretty much everyone in the world recognizes from black-and-white Paris postcards. Its multiple flights of steep steps are lined with old-fashioned black metal streetlights, and it is so Old Paris–looking that you half expect everyone on it to suddenly break out into an impromptu Moulin Rouge can-can routine.

"Quick!" I yelled. Georgia pulled up behind Arthur's bike and locked the scooter to a lamppost. There were enough people around that even if he turned, he probably wouldn't have noticed us huffing and puffing up the stairs a few flights behind him.

Once he got to the top, he turned right and began jogging toward the far side of the church. The sun was directly overhead, and the church's white stone was blinding in the midday light, making it difficult to follow Arthur's form as he wove in between the groups of tourists and pilgrims lined up to enter the basilica.

He disappeared through the swarms of people around the far edge of the church. Pressing toward him through the crowd, I reached out to touch Georgia and instead grabbed an extremely hairy forearm. A tall man in a "Heck Yeah Cowboys" baseball cap looked down at me with an amused smile. "Well, hello there!" he said in a Texas accent.

"Sorry," I blurted, and cast around for Georgia. I caught sight of her about thirty feet in front of me, being swept along by a crowd led by a tour guide waving an Italian flag. She had just begun to realize I was gone, and turned to look for me when the tour group surged and I lost her again.

Pushing my way out of the group of Americans, I followed Arthur's path, turning the same corner that he had disappeared behind.

I was thrust into darkness as I came around the edge of the basilica onto a deserted stone patio to the side of the edifice. It took my eyes a second to adjust from the brilliant daylight to this sun-hidden courtyard that was empty of tourists and as quiet as a crypt.

The patio was large—the shape and size of a skating rink. Its outer edge bordered a precipice and was sided by iron guard-rails to protect the monument's visitors from the perilous drop.

Hulking statues of saints and angels circled the patio, casting weird shadows in the half-light and creating a distinctly creepy atmosphere. Georgia was nowhere to be seen.

I blinked, looking for Arthur, and saw him nearby, hiding behind a statue. He was staring at some people who were half-concealed in the building's dark shadows. Right in front of me was a larger-than-life figure of an avenging archangel, crouched with sword extended as it fought its invisible enemy. I took Arthur's example and crept behind it, squinting out from under its sword-bearing arm at the figures across the terrace.

A jean-clad girl was speaking authoritatively to two large, menacing-looking men. With a chill, I recognized them as the numa from Papy's gallery.

As the speaker gestured, her head turned slightly. My hand flew to my mouth to suppress a gasp. "No," I whispered. What was Violette doing? She didn't seem to be threatened by the numa. If anything, they seemed to be hanging on her every word.

I glanced over at Arthur. He was looking at the same scene I was, yet he was hiding. I didn't understand.

And then—suddenly—I did.

As a wave of comprehension washed over me, I felt immediately and violently ill. I clutched my stomach and prayed that I wouldn't vomit then and there.

Then a third man stepped forward from the shadows behind the church. It was the man I had seen Arthur talking to at La Palette. And now that I saw what he was wearing—a long fur coat that looked like it had been designed for a Renaissance lord in a costume drama—I knew where I had seen him before. He was the man between the tombs at Père Lachaise cemetery the day of Philippe's funeral. I had been right to be afraid then. Because now, without a doubt, I could tell that the trick-of-light colorless thing going on in the air around him meant just one thing. He, too, was a numa.

He got down on one knee in front of the tiny revenant and, bowing his head, raised her hand to his lips. And just as Violette touched him lightly on the head, bidding him to rise, I saw someone sprint past me into the middle of the terrace. Blinded by the sudden change in light, she called, "Kate?"

I wanted to reach out and pull her to safety. I wanted to somehow warn her to run without giving her away. But it was too late. Because just then Violette turned and saw my sister.

THIRTY-SIX

VIOLETTE CHARGED TOWARD GEORGIA, SEEM-ingly propelled by fury alone.

I was momentarily frozen in place. My brain fought what my eyes said was true. It wasn't supposed to be Violette meeting with the numa: Arthur was the traitor.

Puzzle pieces began fitting together in my mind. Violette's fascination with *Immortal Love* and her frustration when she couldn't get her hands on it. Soon after, revenant dwellings around Paris were ransacked by numa looking for . . . not documents but a book.

Another puzzle piece fell into place: The day after I replaced Gaspard's book in his library, Papy's copy—which must be read along with it to find the *guérisseur*—had been stolen. Someone had put the clues together and sent numa after Gwenhaël. And when they couldn't find her, they had come after me with questions about the Champion. Now it was clear that Violette had been behind it all.

Why was she interested in the Champion? She had acted like the whole story was a stupid old fairy tale. Why did she even care?

Unless she believed it. It was *she* who had offered to come to Paris to help Jean-Baptiste. To live in the same house as Vincent. I thought of her unceasing questions about us as a couple and the way we could communicate. About Vincent and his superior talents. About his waning strength. And suddenly it all made sense. For whatever reason, all Violette had ever wanted was the Champion.

It was with my heart in my throat that I emerged from behind the statue and ran in their direction. Out of the corner of my eye I saw Arthur leave his hiding place and run toward me. I sped up, still unsure of whose side he was on.

But before I could reach my sister, Violette had shoved her violently backward, and pressed her against the guardrail. "What are you doing here?" she yelled, as Georgia glanced fearfully down the side of the precipice and then quickly straightened herself.

"The question should be what are *you* doing here, Little Miss Mata Hari?" Georgia's vehemence made her sound confident, but I could tell she was scared. Violette lunged for her again, but my sister grasped the handrail behind her with both hands and kicked out, landing a blow to Violette's hip.

As Violette stumbled back a few steps from the shock of the blow, I ran to stand beside Georgia, positioning myself defensively with fists raised.

"I guess this means our coffee date is canceled," I said. The betrayal gnawing at the pit of my stomach turned my voice to frost. She just shrugged, demonstrating with one gesture that I was nothing to her. I wanted so badly to rush her, to push her, to demand an explanation. But I had seen her fight before and knew that even without a weapon, Violette was lethal.

There was a movement from behind her as two of the numa rushed out of the shadows toward us. In the same second I saw Arthur, who had been hanging back, leap toward them.

"These humans are mine!" the tiny revenant screamed without even looking over her shoulder. All three men came to a standstill a few yards behind her. Maintaining a careful distance from the numa, Arthur called, "Violette, let the girls go!"

She spoke, never taking her eyes off Georgia and me. "You'd like that, Arthur, wouldn't you? Whatever happened to my old companion, who agreed that humans were barely worth the blood we spilled for them?"

"That was your opinion, Vi. It was never mine."

"I know you, Arthur. I've known you for half a millennium. We're practically the same person. Why didn't you come with me when I asked? We have a new road to follow now."

"I never thought it would be this road, Vi. And I've played your whipping boy for long enough. I said what you told me to about leaving Kate out of house meetings. And I looked the other way when I knew you were in contact with our enemy. Hell, I even dropped off a message from you to that one . . . that Nicolas," he said, pointing back in disgust to where the fur-coat guy stood motionless in the shadows. "You've always used them for information, but I never thought you'd stoop to working with them. Or bowing down to their new-blood American numa overlord, for God's sake."

"There is no American, Arthur," Violette said, with a short laugh as I gasped. "I made him up and claimed to be his emissary. I played an influential bardia in the pocket of a numa in case they balked at obeying me. But they've been following my orders for over a year. If Lucien hadn't botched up the order to bring me Vincent's head, you and I wouldn't have had to endure this whole charade with Jean-Baptiste. The numa take orders from *me* now, and the revenants will soon be overthrown."

"What do you mean they obey you?" Arthur asked, incredulous. "Four numa attacked us in an alleyway. You killed one of them. And you've stood by and watched Vincent destroy more than one."

"Let's just say I had a few troublemakers who didn't want to accept my authority, whom I was more than happy to dispose of. It was very effective in allowing me to measure our Vincent's strength. I do love strategizing, as you well know, dear Arthur.

"But now that everything has been set in order, you can take your place next to me as my consort. Give me your allegiance, and I will forgive your reluctance."

"Never." Arthur's proclamation made him sound like the medieval knight he had once been. Or like his namesake, the king of knights.

Violette gave an enraged growl and—spinning so quickly I barely saw her move—landed a karate-style kick to the side of

Georgia's head, taking out her fury on my sister.

I threw myself on Violette, wishing I had something besides my body to fight her with. A sword. A quarterstaff. Any weapon that I had trained in, since I had never fought hand to hand.

I did my best to remember Gaspard's lessons as I ducked and bobbed to avoid Violette's martial arts–style attack. Although I couldn't get a punch in edgewise, my actions distracted her from my sister, who was cursing loudly as she pushed herself up on her hands and knees. "Run, Georgia!" I yelled. "Get out of here!"

"And leave you to fight alone?" Georgia said indignantly. Out of my peripheral vision, I saw her move into a crouching position and spring back toward us.

I heard the numa fighting with Arthur and knew he was too occupied to help. This was our fight, and though Georgia and I were inexperienced, I bet on the two-on-one ratio giving us the advantage.

My hopes were quickly dashed as Violette's fist connected with my shoulder. I heard something crack and felt a sharp pain as I staggered backward. She used the moment to kick Georgia in the ribs. My sister backed up to the guardrail, her hands pressed to her side and her face contorted in pain.

"I've seen the way you look at Arthur. Did you think you could steal my partner?" Violette asked Georgia in a cold, even voice.

"From what I understand, he's not yours to lose," Georgia said, a bitter smile curving the corners of her mouth.

"How would you know that, you stupid mortal?" Violette said, and spun to glance toward Arthur. Which gave me just the opportunity I was waiting for.

I used my good arm to land a punch to her head. My knuckle crunched hard against her jawbone. She screamed in rage and staggered backward a pace, but seemed otherwise unaffected. Violette was stronger—and tougher—than I could ever have imagined.

Behind her, Arthur was battling the two numa, with Nicolas standing patiently, watching from the other end of the terrace. Jean-Baptiste had said he was Lucien's second. Even though he had offered his fealty to Violette, the noble-looking numa seemed happy enough not to get his hands dirty defending her.

For once, neither side had thought to bring weapons—the numa planning on a peaceful meeting with Violette, and Arthur trusting her too much.

Violette called out: "Alain! Back me up, and take the girl." Before I could defend myself, the smaller of the two numa had defected from the fight with Arthur and was behind me, clasping my arms in a viselike grip. My injured shoulder flared painfully. I kicked and fought, but my captor was so strong it made no difference.

There was no way my sister could take on Violette herself. And no one could come to our rescue, since nobody knew where we were. Violette executed another kick to Georgia's head, and I watched my sister slump to the ground. Despair gripped me. I wouldn't live to see Vincent again. I thrashed one last time to escape my captor's grip.

"Drop her," came a voice from across the terrace. I twisted

around to see Vincent, his dark face contorted in rage, coming around the corner of the church. Without slowing, he passed the giant statue of the archangel and, grabbing its marble sword in both hands, broke it off below the hilt. Swinging it at the head of Arthur's attacker, he felled him with one violent blow, and the stone weapon shattered upon contact.

In his surprise, my captor dropped me. I landed like a cat on all fours and then sprang to my feet. "Kate!" called Vincent, and pulling a sword from beneath his coat, he threw it to me, hilt-first. Time slowed as I watched the silver blade soar through the air and felt the leather grip in my hand as my fingers closed tightly around it. Then it sped up again as I swung upward with all my might and caught the numa under his chin. The blade sliced cleanly through his neck, and his headless body toppled to the ground.

I stood there and watched the head wobble across the stones, trailing blood behind it. For a split second I felt sick, and then I forced myself to stop. *Now is not the time.*

I spun, sword held in front of my face, at the ready. My shoulder hurt so badly now, I had to clench my teeth to hold the position. Before me, on the far side of the terrace, I saw Nicolas running back into the shadows behind the church and Arthur leaping down a darkened stairway after him.

On my left, Vincent was making his way toward Violette, who was squatting down next to an unconscious Georgia. Though she was easily a half foot shorter than my sister, Violette picked up Georgia's limp body in her arms as easily as a mother carrying her child to bed and began lifting it toward the guardrail.

"No!" I screamed, dropping my sword. I started toward them, and then stopped myself abruptly. The slightest movement, and the revenant could drop Georgia over the rail to her death. *In fact, why hasn't she already dropped her?* The thought flashed through my mind, as I watched her hesitate.

"Violette, what are you doing?" exclaimed Vincent. He sounded genuinely confused. I realized that he still didn't understand what was going on. He hadn't suspected her in the least. None of us had. Except Georgia, of course—who was now being held in midair above a precipice. Violette stood like a statue, looking down at the dizzying drop.

Behind us, the numa that Vincent had downed began to stir. Bleeding profusely from the side of his head, he raised himself to his feet and lunged dangerously in our direction.

"Violette, make your numa stop!" I yelled.

Inexplicably, she obeyed me, calling, "Paul, stop." The huge man froze in place. I took a careful step toward her.

"You've never killed a human, have you?" I asked, wondering if this was the reason for her hesitation.

"No," responded Violette, still looking over the drop-off. She eased Georgia's body down, propping it atop the guardrail and letting the metal structure take the weight. All she had to do was let go and Georgia would fall. *Don't drop her,* I prayed. My sister's body already looked lifeless. I blinked back the tears stinging the corners of my eyes.

"Then why now?" I asked.

"You know the formula, don't you, Vincent? If a revenant kills a human . . ."

"She becomes numa," he finished softly.

My mind felt sluggish with panic, but I pushed it to work. Violette hated Georgia. And it seemed clear that she hated humans. What did she care about? The answer was obvious: herself. "You don't want to be one of them, Violette. No matter how unworthy humans are of saving, vengeance against one human is not worth becoming a monster."

Violette swallowed, and then her voice came back as smooth as liquid ice. "Vengeance has nothing to do with it. I never wanted to be what I am. I had my immortal future decided for me at an age when I hadn't even lived life. I'm so tired of being at the mercy of humans to keep me alive. I don't want to save you. My only desire is to possess the power over my own destiny. And once my numa and I have conquered the revenants, Paris will be mine and I'll have all the power I want. My own kingdom to do with what I wish."

"You'll still be dependent on humans to survive as a numa, Violette," said Vincent. "No matter what, you're stuck in a never-ending cycle. You're just trading rescue for betrayal."

"At this point, the latter sounds much more bearable," Violette said.

"And what is this scheme to overthrow us? How do you plan on doing that?" asked Vincent incredulously.

"With the power of the Champion," she said, her eyes narrowing as she stared unflinchingly at Vincent. "Of course, if you had agreed to have me by your side, I wouldn't have had to resort to seizing control. I could have shared your power over all the revenants once you took your rightful place as their leader. But when you made it obvious that you wouldn't come to me by choice, I decided that conquering them with the help of the numa might not be such a bad alternative."

"That's why you propositioned me thirty-five years ago?" Vincent said, staring incredulously at the girl. "Because you thought I was the Champion?"

"Well, it wasn't because of your beautiful blue eyes," she said wickedly.

"You don't know he's the Champion, Violette," I challenged, my eyes darting to my sister. *Don't. Drop. Her.* "That *guérisseur* you tracked down didn't even turn out to be the VictorSeer."

"No, but she had all the information that I needed." Violette's smile slashed like a knife.

"What?" I gasped. "But . . . she escaped you. Her son told me!"

"Ah, but she came back home," stated Violette. "Or so my men here were informing me when your sister interrupted our meeting."

My eyes opened wide in shock. "Gwenhaël. What did you do to her?"

"I, personally, did nothing. But my numa . . . well, it seems they had to go a bit far to get her to talk, and after that there was a little accident."

"You killed her!" I choked, the air leaving my lungs like a balloon stuck with an iron spike.

"As I said, it wasn't me. My men just got carried away. And, although I hadn't planned things to happen quite like this, because of what she told us I am even happier to see you here, Vincent."

"What did she tell you?" Vincent asked, his eyes narrowed to slits.

"Why, that you are the Champion."

"She can't know that. She never laid eyes on me."

Violette shrugged as if that wasn't important. "The information she gave us as good as verified it." She shifted the balance of Georgia's body on the guardrail to lighten her load. *Don't. Drop. Her.* My body thrummed with alarm every time Violette so much as breathed.

"After Kate's visit, the *guérisseur* woman did her research. As I suspected, the timing is right. The place is right." She smirked at me. "I know, Kate, I told you the contrary. But you're so gullible, it was just too tempting."

"And . . . ," prompted Vincent.

"And when she told my men this morning that the Champion was the revenant who killed the last numa leader—that would be you killing Lucien, my dear Vincent—well, that clinched it for me. Congratulations. You are the chosen one."

Vincent raised his hand to his heart. "It just doesn't make sense." The dark blotches under his eyes stood out against his unnaturally pale skin, and he stumbled a little as he took a step backward. He would be dormant in a couple of days and was looking even worse for being at the end of this month's grueling experiment.

"Look at you," Violette stated, wrinkling her nose. "Even

though your impressive display with the marble sword back there seems to have tired you out a bit, you should in actual fact be dead. Only someone with the strength of the Champion could follow the Dark Way for more than a few weeks. Absorbing all that numa energy should have killed you by now. You've had two forces battling within you: good and evil waging war inside your reanimated body.

"Gaspard was stupid to believe me when I told him it would make you stronger. Now you're weak enough for me to take you on myself. You know the prophecy. If I destroy the Champion, his power will be mine."

"You're crazy," I whispered.

Vincent put a slight pressure on my arm and pulled me slowly backward, behind him. "If anyone knows their dark prophecy, it's you, Violette. But even *I* know that if the Champion offers himself freely to his captor, his *full* powers will be transferred. I'll trade myself for the life of the girl, Violette."

Violette hesitated, her grip on Georgia loosening.

She let him take one step toward her, allowing him to come an arm's length away. "It is written that if the Champion offers himself up to death by his own volition, his power will not be diluted by murder," she said, greed flaring in her eyes. "You would be willing to face death for these humans?"

"I would," said Vincent without hesitation.

"No, Vincent!" I cried. "What are you saying?"

Vincent wouldn't look at me. "You're right, Violette. I'm weak enough for you and your men to take. And I'll go with you. Just put the girl down and you have yourself a deal."

Violette stared at him, weighing his offer.

And before I knew what was happening, a figure raced up on Violette's left. Arthur took advantage of Violette's focus on Vincent to wrench my sister's body from her grasp and pull her away to safety.

"Sorry, Vi. Deal's off," Vincent said softly, as if consoling a small child.

She screamed and threw herself on Vincent, using her fingernails to scrape long, red lines down either side of his face.

And it was because I was staring at the crimson blood flowing down Vincent's cheek that I didn't see the numa coming.

As the giant man lunged toward me, Vincent turned from Violette and threw himself forward, grabbing the numa in a crippling embrace as the two of them smashed hard against the guardrail. I screamed as the force of the impact bent the rail backward, and locked in each other's arms, they toppled over the leaning barrier and out of sight.

My heart fell with them. It felt like my entire chest had been ripped out, lungs and all. I couldn't breathe as I ran to the guardrail and peered over, desperate for a miracle. Desperate for something from the movies—a branch sticking out that Vincent could grab on to. A ledge conveniently placed just feet below the rim of the precipice.

But this wasn't a movie. It was real life. And by the time I got to the edge, their bodies had already hit the ground, and neither one was moving. "No!" I shrieked, as a man in a fur coat rushed into the area below, a couple of others following him closely. Turning, I saw that Violette was gone.

"Arthur, stay with Georgia!" I yelled. I arrived at the bottom in time to see the numa leap inside the back of an awaiting van and slam the doors behind them, and the van sped off. Panicking, I doubled back and ran toward the bottom of the cliff but stopped halfway there. There was nothing to see. The bodies were gone.

THIRTY-SEVEN

VINCENT WAS DEAD AND HIS BODY HAD BEEN taken by the numa. The realization of what that meant filled me with an immobilizing horror. Normally, he would simply reanimate in three days. But the numa would never allow that to happen.

If they destroyed his body immediately, he would be gone. Forever. However, Violette could do worse. She could wait a day and destroy him once he was volant. Eternity as a wandering spirit, unable to take physical form again—that seemed like an even more horrific fate to me. I had to do something before the numa and their new leader had a chance to act.

I called Ambrose.

"Katie-Lou? You still at Montmartre? Has Vin gotten there yet?" he asked before I could speak.

"How did you know—" I began.

"Jules was volant at the house when you girls decided to tail

Arthur, so he followed you. Once he saw where you were going, he let Vincent know and then came to get me. You guys okay? Hand Vin the phone, will you?"

"Ambrose, Vincent's gone. Violette and a numa killed him and took his body. They've got him, Ambrose!" My voice was starting to sound hysterical. It was all I could do to get the words out.

"What? Violette?" he yelled. "Where did they go?"

"They drove off from the base of the Sacré-Coeur staircase in a white truck. Like a delivery-van-looking thing."

"How long ago?"

"It's been two minutes, tops."

"Is Arthur still there?"

"Yeah. He's with Georgia. She's hurt."

It took him all of three seconds to come up with a plan. "Okay. Arthur will know if Georgia needs a hospital or not. If she doesn't, the three of you get back to Jean-Baptiste's. I'm calling him now. He'll sound the alert for our Paris kindred to begin searching. You just hang in there, Katie-Lou."

"Thanks, Ambrose." My voice cracked as I hung up. But I couldn't let myself cry. If I did, I wouldn't be able to stop. And I needed to be strong.

Looking back up the staircase, I saw Arthur making his way down with a fully conscious Georgia, who leaned heavily against him. The handkerchief she held to her mouth was stained poppy red with her blood. I sprinted up the stairs toward them.

"I looked down and couldn't see his body," Arthur said as soon as I caught up.

"Violette took him. I called Ambrose, and Jean-Baptiste's sending out a search party." My voice was flat as I tried to rein in my emotion. Just a few more minutes and I could let go, I told myself, and wrapped Georgia's free arm around my shoulders.

"Took who, Katie-Bean?" Georgia slurred as she shifted some of her weight onto me. She had been knocked unconscious before Vincent arrived and had seen none of it. I didn't feel like explaining. Not yet.

"Should Georgia be moving?" I asked Arthur.

"She's injured, but I don't think any bones are broken. Some tourists at the top got a good look at her. I think it's better if we get away before someone calls the police."

We made our way to the bottom of the stairway and onto the street, where we slipped into a cab that had just dropped off a group of black-habited nuns. I glanced up at the basilica. Two policemen were standing at the top of the stairs, looking down at us as people pointed in our direction. I closed my eyes in relief as the taxi pulled away. The last thing we needed was to be stopped for questioning.

Vincent's gone. The thought raced through my mind and turned my body numb. *No. Don't think about it. Hold yourself together, or you won't be of any help.*

I squeezed Georgia's hand as she leaned her head on my shoulder. "Are you okay?" I asked.

"Very sore," she said. "The inside of my mouth's bleeding where that bitch from hell kicked a tooth loose."

I glanced at Arthur. "Ambrose said if she doesn't need a

hospital, get her home to Jean-Baptiste's."

"That's where we're going," he confirmed.

"Um . . . I don't think so! I'm banned from even entering," Georgia exclaimed.

"I'm not giving you a choice," Arthur said firmly. "I'll call a doctor to meet us there. Better to get you private medical care than to take you to a hospital. And we can get some ice on your face right away instead of having to wait in a crowded emergency room."

He reached over and laid his hand against her arm. Georgia immediately relaxed, resting her head against the back of the seat. "Don't think I don't know what you're doing, Mr. Tranquilizing Superpowers."

The edges of Arthur's mouth curled up. It was the first smile I had seen on his face since the time Georgia had called him geriatric in the café. "Would you like me to stop?" he asked.

"Hell, no," she replied. "Feels great. I just didn't want you to think you were pulling one over on me."

His eyes flitted from my sister's face to my own, and the smile left his lips.

"I thought it was you," I said numbly.

"I don't blame you," he replied.

We just stared at each other, unspeaking, until I sank back in the seat, testing my painful shoulder and closing my eyes as the horror of the last half hour settled over me.

"What's wrong?" Georgia asked.

I exhaled deeply. "Oh, Gigi," I said, using my pet name for

my sister from when we were small children. "While you were knocked out, Vincent came. He and Arthur saved you, but the numa . . . they killed him. And then took off with his body."

I was able to control myself for exactly one more second before I burst out crying.

"Oh, Katie-Bean." She pulled away from Arthur and wrapped her arms around me. "Oh, my poor Katie," she said, her voice wavering as her own tears began to fall.

And as the taxi drifted through the quiet Paris streets, my sister and I sat locked in each other's arms and wept.

The doctor was waiting for us when we arrived at Jean-Baptiste's. Arthur helped Georgia into the sitting room and then left, closing the door behind him. The man asked Georgia a lot of questions about what happened and how long she was unconscious, shined a light in her eye, and finally declared her healthy. He suggested she see a dentist for the loose tooth, and then gave her some instant cold compresses to put on her jaw and a box of painkillers.

My painful shoulder turned out to be a cracked collarbone. The doctor wrapped my chest and shoulders in an Ace bandage and told me to put an ice pack on it to reduce swelling. "You should both rest," he told us.

Yeah, right, I thought. As soon as I got Georgia home I was going to look for Vincent.

As I led the doctor to the front door, Arthur reappeared with an envelope. He handed it to the man, shook his hand, then pointed him to the front gate.

Turning to me, he seemed to be struggling as his face began to lose its aristocratic coldness. This minor transformation suddenly made him feel like a real person for once, instead of a statue from a wax museum.

"Kate," he said, "I'm so sorry for what has happened. I should have done more to stop it. But Violette . . . she's gone through these strange phases before, and I thought I would be able to bring her around. I had no idea what she was up to."

"If you even knew she was communicating with the numa, why didn't you say something about it? You put everyone in danger by staying silent," I said, feeling a simmering fury at the pit of my stomach. If he had done something before, none of this would have happened.

"Everyone knew Violette had distant ties with the numa. And they all depended on that to get the information they needed. But no one, including me, knew exactly what she was doing.

"When she began communicating with Nicolas, I thought she was using him to get closer to Paris's numa. So she could taunt them. Flirt with them in a way before we dug in to destroy them. In the past she has enjoyed toying with our enemies before killing them. But when Vincent told me the numa knew how Lucien was slain, I began to suspect she had—unwittingly—given the information away. I never once imagined she was working in conjunction with them."

I stared at him. He and Violette had been together for centuries. How could he have not known what she was up to? But his actions back at Montmartre, as well as the tortured look on his face as he watched me, convinced me that he was telling me the truth.

I looked up to see Jean-Baptiste making his way down the double staircase. His usual rigid-as-a-general posture had crumpled as he strode slowly across the hall toward me. I knew Vincent was his favorite. His second. That he thought of him as a son. He paused in front of me, and then, in a gesture that was so uncharacteristic of him that I did my best not to wince when my shoulder touched his, he solemnly took me in his arms.

"I'm sorry," was all he said.

Those two words put the fear of God in me. This was Jean-Baptiste. And he was offering no long-winded speech about how we would get Vincent back. No encouragement about which options should be considered. Nothing except those two words—which might as well have been "No. Hope." Because that's essentially what he was saying.

THIRTY-EIGHT

I HELPED GEORGIA HOME, THANKING MY LUCKY stars that Papy was at work and Mamie nowhere to be seen. I got her into bed, where the pain medication she had taken a half hour before kicked in. She began falling asleep before I even left the room. As I closed the door, she called after me in a dozy voice, "You'll get him back, Katie-Bean. I just know it."

By the time I got back to La Maison, the troops had been dispatched. Jean-Baptiste informed me that Ambrose had taken a search party to the man-made caves that honeycombed beneath Montmartre. Not only had Violette met the numa at Sacré-Coeur, but several of the Paris revenants reported numa sightings in the area, so it seemed a logical choice.

Jules, volant, had accompanied a group led by Gaspard, following another tip in the south of Paris.

The two remaining revenants sat in the library, trying to draw up some kind of strategy. Arthur eagerly volunteered his knowledge of Violette and her habits. He had already informed JB about the most important fact: that Violette's plan was to capture the Champion and overthrow Paris's revenants. But since he had caught only that end of the conversation between Violette and Vincent, I started at the beginning and told them the whole story. And after that, I recapped everything else I knew. I explained every detail about my contact with Gwenhaël and Bran. I recounted every question that Violette had ever asked me about Vincent, and the information—however intentionally misleading it had been—that she had given me about the Champion and her stories about the numa.

Jean-Baptiste took notes, and when I was finished, he thanked me in a way that meant I was excused to go. I stood, watching him and Arthur for a moment, until the older revenant looked back up at me expectantly. "What else can I do to help?" I asked him. Over the last hour, my despair had transformed into a burning determination, and if I left them, I didn't know where I would go.

"There's nothing we can do now," the older man said gravely, "except hope that our teams come up with something."

"But I want to do something. I *need* to do something."

"You have fulfilled your role, dear Kate. You alerted Ambrose as soon as it happened. You took care of your sister. You gave me some very valuable information. Now the only thing you can do is wait." His tone was sympathetic but practical as he turned back to his notes.

He was just as duped by Violette as the rest of us, I realized, and left the two revenants in the library to work out their own penance for having been so blind.

News came a couple of hours later. A numa had confessed to Gaspard's group that Violette and some others had taken Vincent's body out of the city and were headed south. Upon being informed, Ambrose's group returned—with a huge haul of weapons they had taken from a freshly deserted numa hideout.

I was waiting for them outside, seated on the edge of the angel fountain.

"What do you think she'll do?" I whispered as Ambrose sat next to me, dressed from head to toe in Kevlar and black leather.

"Katie-Lou, regarding Violette, I don't know what to think anymore."

"If she burns his body today . . ."

"He'll be gone. If she waits until he's volant tomorrow or the next day, and destroys him after he leaves his body, his spirit will remain on earth. Or, if she gets in touch with us in time, and we can offer her something she wants badly enough, she might be willing to barter for his body. That's what we will focus on, little sister. Don't even think about the other options."

He leaned over and gave me a tender kiss on the cheek. "That's from Jules. He says to tell you, 'Courage, Kates. We'll find your man.'"

I wiped a tear away and thanked them both, as Ambrose left to report to Jean-Baptiste. I stayed, watching the moon rise in a spectacularly starry sky. In Paris the stars are usually invisible, unsuccessfully competing with the city's lights. But tonight they were luminous, offering a breathtaking display for us mortals below. I was transported back to the months after my parents' death, where at every turn I felt like nature was mocking my despair with its beauty. How could the world go on—how could this twinkling celestial extravaganza take place—when Vincent was helpless in the hands of his enemies? Nothing made sense.

In need of a reality check, I took my phone out of my bag and texted Georgia.

Me: Are you okay?
Georgia: Pain drugs = good. Told Mamie & Papy I got mugged.
Me: OMG!
Georgia: Said you went to a friend's house after school, so you weren't with me.
Me: What did they say?
Georgia: They're freaking and want you home.
Me: I can't. We haven't found him yet.

I had seen two missed calls from Mamie and knew I would have to come up with some explanation for not calling her back, but I couldn't even think about that yet. A life in which I could return to the love and security of my grandparents' home seemed like part of some other girl's story. Finding Vincent was the only thing that mattered.

I shivered in the cold, but resisted the urge to go back into the house and ask if there was any news. Someone would surely come tell me if there was. Or would they? For the hundredth time, I felt an overwhelming sense of not belonging. Anywhere. I had been training with the revenants. I knew their secrets and held their symbol around my neck. I was part of their world now, and they were a major part of mine. But I was not one of them.

Neither was I comfortable in the skin of the human teenage girl I had been a year ago. I had gone too far now—out of the world of believing only what you can see and into one where the mystical was mundane.

Vincent had been my link with the revenants. But—if I was honest with myself—without him I would be drifting between the two worlds with no anchor to ground me and no oars to navigate. I pushed that thought out of my head. *We'll get him back*, I promised myself.

THIRTY-NINE

THE MOOD AT LA MAISON WAS FUNEREAL. GAS-
pard had pressed his captive numa for further information, but it
seemed that Violette didn't trust her minions with the details of
her plans. A couple of other numa had been found in the meantime, and none knew where Vincent had been taken—only that
their leader had left Paris with her prize.

I found Ambrose in the armory, sharpening a battle-ax with
an old-fashioned grinding wheel. He looked as antsy for action
as me.

"What's all this mean? Where do we look next?" I asked him,
unwilling to accept that we were all just . . . giving up.

"We have no other leads, and no clue of where the numa have
taken Vincent. JB, Gaspard, Arthur, and some others are working on a longer-term plan." His eyes met mine as he turned the
wheel, his frustration materialized in the sparks flying from the
edges of the ax blade. "Because in the short term, Katie-Lou,

there's nothing else we can do but wait to hear from them."

I sat with him for a while, and then made my way back upstairs. Dozens of Paris's revenants moved from room to room like ghosts, speaking in hushed voices and waiting for a phone call that might never happen. The hours passed and there was no news. Yet nobody left. The revenants were quiet, but on the alert. Ready.

Jeanne had insisted on staying. She wandered around, placing trays of finger food on every available surface and cleaning up after everyone.

"Do you want me to make you something special, my little cabbage?" she asked, hugging me for the millionth time since we had returned. I had cried the first time she held me, but my tears seemed to have dried up, leaving numbness in their place.

"I can't eat, Jeanne."

"I know," she said, patting my shoulder. "But I had to offer. It's the only thing I know to do for you."

Finally, around midnight, I told Ambrose I was leaving. I couldn't stand the grave faces and hushed conversations another moment. "I'll come back. I'm just going to take a walk."

"Then I'm going with you."

Shaking my head, I asked, "Ambrose, after the numa hunts that you and Gaspard staged today, do you really think any of them will be hanging around the center of Paris?"

"No, but some of the humans around here can be just as bad."

I tried to smile. "I'll be fine. But if you guys hear anything—" I began.

He cut me off. "I will call you. I swear."

"Thanks, Ambrose."

I slipped out the front gate and headed toward the river. And when I reached its edge, it was if something possessed my arms and legs and I started running. My hurt shoulder ached with every step, but I ignored it, running from my heart's pain and my mind's fear. And even when those emotions were exhausted and the ghosts chasing me were overthrown by a second wind of determination and denial, I continued to run.

I finally came to a stop, leaning over and panting to catch my breath. Beside me, the Pont des Arts stretched dark over the Seine. Without thinking, I moved toward it, climbed the steps, and stepped out onto the wooden walkway. When I got to the center of the bridge, I stopped and, leaning against the guardrail, stared down into the dark, churning water. A gust of winter wind blew my hair around my face, and I pushed it back and inhaled the marine smell of the river. And let myself remember.

This was where Vincent and I had kissed for the first time, just five months ago. It seemed like a lifetime already. It was the day I had told him I wasn't sure I wanted to see him anymore. That I would commit only to the next date and no further. And he brought me here and kissed me anyway. Now that I knew him better, I was sure he had planned it. He figured if he could steal my heart, I might abandon my reason, too. I couldn't prevent the nostalgic grin that forced itself onto my lips.

I wondered if I would see him again, and defiantly choked back the tears welling in my eyes. I couldn't think like that. Because if

I did, it would mean that Violette had destroyed him and he was gone. Forever. I spoke to the water rippling beneath me: "I refuse to believe it."

"You refuse to believe what?" came a low voice from behind me.

I spun to see a man dressed in a long fur coat standing a few feet from me. And though I knew instantly who—and what—he was, I wasn't afraid. Instead an incendiary hatred rose inside me. "You!" I snarled, and threw myself at him, fists raised and arms flailing. He dropped something he was holding and, moving quickly, grabbed my wrists before I could strike him.

"Now, now. Is that any kind of way to greet a messenger?" Nicolas said, glancing at the objects at his feet.

My eyes flew downward, and when I saw what was lying there, something broke inside me. "No," I whispered. He let go of my arms, and I bent to pick up the white lilies scattered at my feet.

"Violette said that if you didn't have your book handy, I should tell you what they mean."

"White lilies are for funerals. I don't need a flower manual to tell me that." I wanted to strangle him, but instead I took the flowers in both hands and crushed them, ripped the heads off the stems, and hurled them over the side of the bridge into the water. "What have you done with him?" I demanded.

"Our dauntless leader has taken your lover's body to her castle in the Loire, where she will dispose of it when she sees fit. I was instructed to pass that message on."

"And what else were you instructed to do?" I felt my knees

350

bend slightly and my fists clench as my body took on the defensive stance Gaspard had taught me.

Nicolas smirked. "Charming. As if you could fight me. Actually, I am under strict orders not to touch you. Violette is of the opinion that letting you suffer would be more fun."

I finally voiced what I had been wondering since our battle at Sacré-Coeur. "What did I ever do to her?"

Nicolas chuckled. "I wouldn't think it's anything personal. She merely wanted the Champion, and you helped her verify that it was indeed your Vincent. Now that she has him, she doesn't need you anymore."

"Then why make me suffer?"

"Oh, that. Probably because you're human. She's not very fond of mortals, you know. Five hundred years of saving you miserable beings in order to maintain her existence seems to have left her a tad bitter."

I shook my head in disbelief. If centuries of being obliged to rescue humans had warped Violette's perception of the value of life, it didn't seem to have done the same for Arthur. What could turn a young, hopeful human into a centuries-old bitter immortal? I just couldn't understand.

Something else had occurred to me. "Why would she go through the trouble of taking Vincent's body hours away if she's just going to destroy it?"

"Well, now," he replied pedantically, "she didn't tell me that, and I didn't ask. But in her negotiations with Lucien, she assured him that she held the secret to some sort of mystical transfer of the Champion's power to the one who destroys him. Whether that means destroying him today to ensure his permanent riddance, or finishing him off tomorrow and keeping his ghost as a pet, I couldn't really say. She's the expert on all things Champion. Which, of course, is why we welcomed her with open arms.

"And now that my commission is complete, I will leave you. I'm sure you will want to go back and inform the others. Oh, and please tell them that a rescue attempt would be useless. If Vincent's not gone now, he will be before they can get to him." He wrapped his coat snugly about him and strode off into the night.

Stifling the desire to run after him and attack him from behind (he was right—I couldn't take him), I slid down to sit with my back against the guardrail. Nestling my head against my bent knees, I closed my eyes. A church bell chimed twelve. My thoughts were battling over hope that Violette was lying . . . and utter hopelessness that she wasn't. Over despair that I would never see Vincent again . . . and determination that I would do anything it took to keep that from happening. I knew I should call Ambrose immediately to pass along Nicolas's message, but the thought of taking my phone out of my pocket seemed too monumental of a task.

I felt the *signum* cold against my skin and, raising my head, traced the outline of the pendant through my shirt. My attention was caught by something white floating beneath me on the surface of the water. The crushed lilies had floated under the bridge and were making their way toward the spotlit Eiffel Tower.

And suddenly I knew. She had done it. Violette had destroyed

Vincent. After more than eighty years of walking the earth, his spirit had now left it. If we'd lived in separate worlds before, now we were in separate universes. The finality struck me like an anvil.

The smile that lit his face whenever he first caught a glimpse of me. His hand clutching mine as we walked the city streets. The look in his eyes before we kissed. Those experiences were now trapped in the past. And the future that I had imagined with him now drifted into oblivion like those mangled flowers.

I had lost him.

And as the weight of that realization snapped the last remaining threads of hope in my heart, I heard it.

Two words spoken clearly inside my head: *Mon ange.*

ACKNOWLEDGMENTS

THIS BOOK WOULD NOT BE HERE, RESTING IN your hands or playing on your audio book or appearing on your e-reader if it weren't for the following people. I owe them all my deepest gratitude.

My super-agent Stacey Glick of Dystel & Goderich, whose continued advice and hand-holding have provided me with a much-needed stabilizing force. Thank you, Stacey.

My editor, Tara Weikum, and assistant editor, Melissa Miller, who helped me tame all of my wild ideas into ones that actually worked. The patience you've shown and insight you've given have shaped this book into something exponentially better than it would have been. I am eternally grateful.

Copyeditors Valerie Shea and Melinda Weigel worked with both this book and *Die for Me*, polishing the rough edges, pointing out my mistakes, and patiently correcting my embarrassingly bad punctuation, especially the dreaded commas and em dashes. *Merci!*

My crack team of beta readers were of invaluable assistance, including the indefatigable Claudia, my beloved Kimberly Kay, book-smart Olivia, and *Buffy*-quoting Katia and Kylie Mac. And my friend Josie Angelini lent a hand, both as reader and tireless cheerleader. *Mes remerciements sincères à vous tous!*

Mark Ecob and Johanna Basford made the covers of *Die for Me* and *Until I Die* the works of breathtaking beauty that they are. My publicist Caroline Sun has energetically promoted the books, along with the marketing team of Christina Colangelo and Megan Sugrue. And I am in awe of the enthusiasm and support given me by my UK Little, Brown/Atom book family, including editor Sam Smith, editorial assistant Kate Agar, and publicist Rose Tremlett.

Several friends lent me and my manuscript their homes during the times I needed to run away. Much thanks to Lisa in New York, Laila and Terry in Paris, Nicolas and Paul in Saintes, and Jean-Pierre and Christiane just down the road.

I could not write without the support of my family and loved ones, especially: Laurent (my anchor, without whom I'd be drifting up among the clouds somewhere); my children, Max and Lucia; my sister, Gretchen; my darling Grammy; my resourceful cousin Melissa; my whole eccentric and devotedly loving H. clan; and my French family: Jeannine, Jean-Pierre and Christiane, Alex and Romain.

And lastly, but not any less importantly, I thank my readers. I was astounded by the enthusiasm with which you rallied behind me and my first book—you are the most supportive fans a writer could ever hope for. Thank you all from the bottom of my heart. This book is for you.

UNTIL I DIE

Songs to Die For: The Official *Until I Die* Playlist

Kate's Favorite Things

Who's Your Bardia Boyfriend?

Immortal Inquiries: An *Until I Die* discussion guide

"When I Died": Relive the final moments of *Until I Die*
from Vincent's point of view

Sneak Peek: An excerpt from *If I Should Die,*
the sequel to *Until I Die*

Songs to Die For: The Official *Until I Die* Playlist
(Chosen with the help of fans)

"Brand—New—Life" by Young Marble Giants
"Rolling in the Deep" by Adele
"And the Boys" by Angus & Julia Stone
"My Immortal" by Evanescence
"The Only Exception" by Paramore
"Enchanted" by Taylor Swift
"Your Guardian Angel" by The Red Jumpsuit Apparatus
"All I Need" by Within Temptation
"Born to Die" by Lana Del Rey
"I Will Follow You into the Dark" by Death Cab for Cutie
"A Thousand Years" by Christina Perri

Kate's Favorite Things
My Favorite Books (and Why I Chose Them)

The Princess Bride by William Goldman—A point of contention between Vincent and me. You'll find out why in *If I Should Die*.
Winter's Tale by Mark Helprin—Shows how magical New York City truly is.
Edward Gorey's books—I love his morbid sense of humor and bizarre illustrations.
Ooh-la-la (Max in Love) by Maira Kalman—A children's book about a dog poet from New York City who falls in love with Paris.
A Tree Grows in Brooklyn by Betty Smith AND *The Chosen* by Chaim Potok—Both books are about teenagers growing up in Brooklyn, near where I did, who faced hardships in becoming their true selves.
The Age of Innocence AND *The House of Mirth* by Edith Wharton—Old New York love stories. Are you sensing a theme here?
Like Water for Chocolate by Laura Esquivel—So romantic and heart-wrenchingly tragic it made me weep.
The Harry Potter series by J. K. Rowling—Are you kidding me? Epic!
To Kill a Mockingbird by Harper Lee—Scout is one of my all-time favorite protagonists.

My Favorite Movies (and Why I Watch Them)

Films that make me want to wander Paris hand-in-hand with
Vincent:
When the Cat's Away
Gigi
Amélie

Dark films to watch while your boyfriend's out saving lives (to
remind you that some people are having a worse time than
you):
Harold and Maude
The Virgin Suicides
Edward Scissorhands (and pretty much every other Tim Burton
film)
Donnie Darko
La Femme Nikita

Chick flicks to watch alone when your boyfriend's dormant:
Breakfast at Tiffany's
The Princess Bride
Bridget Jones's Diary
Romeo + Juliet

Who's Your Bardia Boyfriend?

1. Your boyfriend has invited you for a musical night out. Would you rather go to:

    a. a jazz club for a night of swing dancing
    b. a punk or metal concert
    c. *Don Giovanni* at the Paris opera
    d. a performance art "concert" (all of the instruments are made from power tools)
    e. a chamber music concert in one of Paris's Gothic chapels

2. For Valentine's Day your boyfriend has given you:

    a. kickboxing lessons for two
    b. an All-Saints T-shirt with skulls and roses
    c. a collection of your top ten favorite books and movies and a box of chocolates
    d. a Pre-Raphaelite-style portrait of you
    e. a first edition of *Pride and Prejudice*

3. You're going on vacation with your boyfriend. Would you rather go:

    a. to the Alps for helicopter-skiing and mountain climbing
    b. to the Glastonbury music festival for a week of camping and music
    c. to the carnival in Venice for costume balls and gondola rides

d. to a Greek island for a week of sunbathing by day and dancing by night

e. to a medieval festival in the Loire Valley while staying in a converted castle

4. You are having an argument. Would your boyfriend:

a. say that you're right, even if you're not, and laugh the whole thing off

b. stalk away, but come back with a present after cooling down and thinking things over

c. talk it through and figure out why you're seeing things differently and then finish up with makeup kissing

d. argue heatedly and then make out passionately (perhaps leaving the problem unsolved)

e. avoid the argument, hesitantly talk things through, and then bring you flowers the next day

5. You told your boyfriend a secret that is so juicy he can't help but share it. Would you rather he:

a. blurt it out at the dinner table

b. tell his sibling, but urge him or her not to tell anyone else

c. write it in his journal, which can easily be found by anyone snooping

d. depict it in a painting that people can subsequently see in an art exhibition

e. put it in his next novel, changing all of the people and places but leaving the forbidden story intact

6. Your boyfriend is taking you to the cinema, and you tell him to pick the movie. He chooses:

   a. *Rambo* (testosterone and big guns)
   b. *Shaun of the Dead* (zombie humor)
   c. *Titanic* (high romance)
   d. *Un Chien Andalou* (surrealist art film)
   e. *Dangerous Liaisons* (eighteenth-century court intrigue)

7. Your boyfriend offers to cook dinner for you. What does he make?

   a. hamburgers with a wide choice of toppings and oven-baked French fries
   b. a vegan meal with tofu ice cream for dessert
   c. a creative and tasty appetizer, main dish, and dessert: all recipes he got from one of Paris's top chefs
   d. homemade sushi with miso soup and seaweed salad
   e. a seven-course meal of tiny but beautifully decorated French dishes

Key:
A = 1 point, B = 2 points, C = 3 points, D = 4 points, E = 5 points

5–10: You like a boy who loves his sports but who doesn't play games of the emotional sort. You'll get a good workout and a minimum of drama dating Ambrose.
11–15: You like a boy with a rebellious side. A deep thinker, Charles will be passionate not only in his philosophical arguments but in his affection for you.

16–20: Sensitive and romantic, Vincent is the one for you. He'll second-guess your deepest desires and, once he earns your trust, will prove faithful to the end.

21–25: Artsy flirts are more your style. Jules will sweep you off your feet and keep you guessing: His unpredictability and love of fun are a good match for your creative ways.

26–30: You like brainy boys who are big into chivalry. Arthur will woo you in the good old-fashioned manner and will always be ready to discuss your latest reads.

Immortal Inquiries:
An *Until I Die* discussion guide

1. Kate was paralyzed by fear at the onset of her first fight with a numa, but once the adrenaline kicked in, she began fighting instinctively. Have you ever been in a situation where you felt overwhelmed until you found your confidence and pace?

2. Was Charles selfish to get involved with the numa, even though he didn't mean to put the others in danger? Was it fair of Jean-Baptiste to send him away?

3. Throughout the book, Kate felt as if she was an outsider, not belonging anywhere. Has there ever been a time when you felt that you truly didn't belong?

4. What were your suspicions when it was discovered that a fellow revenant was leaking information to the numa? Like Kate, did you think that Arthur was behind it?

5. Kate couldn't believe it when she discovered that her friend Violette was the true enemy. Has there ever been a time when you placed your trust in someone who ended up betraying it?

6. What are your views on Georgia and Arthur? Is it just Georgia's flirtatious personality, or do you think she actually liked Arthur? Do you think they will get together in *If I Should Die*, or will she have already moved on to another guy?

7. How did you feel about Papy's reaction when he discovered that Vincent is a revenant? When he ordered Kate to never see Vincent again, do you think he was being unfair? Or do you think he was just trying to protect her?

8. Kate and her family are in constant danger due to her relationship with Vincent. Do you think this is selfish and unwise of Kate, or does her love for Vincent justify her actions? Have you ever had to choose between love and family?

9. What did you think of Vincent taking the "Dark Way"? Although Violette confessed that it hurt Vincent more than it helped him, did you initially think it was a good idea to pursue? Why or why not?

10. After Vincent gives Kate a *signum bardia* at the wedding, she says, "I wish there was only today, just right now, and no forever." Have you ever experienced a moment when you wish time could have frozen?

11. Kate can't handle seeing Vincent die over and over again, but she doesn't want to make him suffer by resisting the urge to die. Do you think Kate and Vincent will ever find a way to stay together? How do you think Geneviève and her human husband managed it?

12. What do you think Violette will do with Vincent's body? Will he be rescued, will his soul be left to wander, or will he be gone forever?

"When I Died": Relive the final moments of *Until I Die* from Vincent's point of view

My mind awakes.

As usual I have a moment of fogginess. Of wondering where exactly I am, while my spirit lingers inside its dead shell.

As my awareness grows, I feel a stab of alarm. Something is very wrong. *Wake up!* I urge my sluggish thoughts, and force myself to focus. My eyelids remain firmly closed—my muscles have been dead for hours—but I don't need them to see. Not when I'm volant.

Normally it's the white gauze of my bed curtains I notice first. Not an enormous fireplace with white-hot flames sending dark billowing smoke up the chimney and spilling out into the room. Where am I?

"Ah, I can sense you now. You're awake, my dear Vincent." The voice of a young girl echoes around the empty room, the clipped monotone sending a preternatural chill through my being.

Impelled by terror, I jolt up and out of my body and hover high above the room. But the speaker has left, slamming the door behind her. Her voice . . . it's one I know well, but in the haze of awakening I can't quite place it.

I scan the area around me. There is no one else here. My dead body lies on the stone floor of a cavernous room decorated only by a large wrought-iron chandelier fitted with burning wax candles.

I move closer to my body to assess the damage, as I always do. Most awakenings—the months I manage not to die—I find nothing. Maybe a few minor injuries accumulated during the past weeks, which will heal rapidly over the following two days of dormancy. Possibly a broken bone caused by throwing myself in harm's way for some hapless human.

But occasionally I see my body like this and know that I didn't even finish out the month. I died . . . pretty violently this time, from the look of things. My body is twisted. Shattered. Many bones broken, some so brutally that they have pierced the skin and stick out of me like twigs off a tree. My clothes have been stripped off, and I am so bloody and skinned up that I look more like a flayed animal than a man: like a beast gutted and skinned after the hunt.

My face is battered and swollen, and though the skin is intact, there are four red slashes down each cheek. The stripped flesh looks like war paint. I wonder for a split second if I was attacked while saving someone from an animal.

And then I remember. Those aren't claw marks. They were made by fingernails. By Violette.

It all comes back at once: the struggle with the numa at the top of the precipice beside Sacré-Coeur. The crunch of metal as we smashed against the guardrail, bent it backwards, and toppled over the side. Kate's scream—one of the most gut-wrenching, heartrending sounds I've heard in eighty years.

I swore to her I wouldn't die, I remember with a rush of guilt. With her parents' recent deaths, she can't bear that kind of trauma. But I broke that promise, however unintentionally. And even worse, Kate saw it happen.

The door opens and a figure in a long, flowing dress enters the room flanked by two hulking numa. The flickering light from the candles catches her face. "Are you awake yet, my Champion?" Violette says with a mocking musical lilt. "You young ones take so long to wake up."

Then, dropping the faux-sweetness, she barks, "Move it, you brainless thugs. We don't want this fire to cool just when we need it at its hottest." Something she carries drags against the floor with a metallic scrape. It is a cage, and inside it a living thing moves.

She sets it on a table that I hadn't noticed before, back in the shadows, outside the firelight. I move closer to see what it holds, and catch the glint of a knife reflected off the cage, and lined up beside it a series of surgical instruments, flasks, and bottles. The creature in the cage flinches as I near: It is a small brown rabbit.

"Don't let its cuteness deceive you, Vincent," Violette says as she takes a box of powder from the table, and crosses the room to my body. "This animal will play a role in an ancient ritual that will bind your spirit to me once your body is burned. I'll need your spirit close by in order to perform the power transfer. You and I will be extremely close from now on," she says, pouring the powder onto the ground in a black stream as she moves in a circle around my battered body.

In one of those ghost-limb moments—when I experience physical sensations while unconnected to my body—I feel my flesh crawl. Something abhorrent is going to happen. Something I can do nothing about. But if I want to see Kate again, I have to act fast.

As my spirit flashes out of the room at top speed, I hear Violette call, "Go ahead, fly away, Vincent. I'll bring you back in a few minutes."

I speed through the castle's thick stone walls and soar over the rooftops of the tiny town, across vineyards, and up rivers toward Paris. It is only minutes before I feel myself homing in on Kate's presence. Since I've known her, she has been like a beacon to my spirit. When I'm volant, I always know where she is.

Kate. Her name is a panacea to my soul. That one syllable brings warmth . . . stability . . . the certainty that there is more to my existence than mere survival. She is my home. My anchor.

I am close now, her presence guiding me directly to her.

Just let me get to her, I pray. Just give me the time to say good-bye before that evil traitor pulls me back to her with whatever dark ceremony she is preparing. Just give me the time for a couple of words.

I see her now, standing on the bridge—dark hair whipped around her face by the wind and a look of desolation on her face. She thinks I'm gone. . . . I can read it on those features I know as well as my own.

Now I'm close enough to touch her and ache to hold her in my arms. What can I say to reassure her that I still exist, at least for the moment?

I speak the words into her thoughts: *Mon ange.*

**A special sneak peek at
If I Should Die,
the sequel to *Until I Die***

IN THE DEAD OF NIGHT I SAT ON A BRIDGE SPAN-
ning the Seine, watching a bouquet of crushed white lilies float
toward the spotlit Eiffel Tower. I strained to listen for the
words I thought I'd just heard. The words of a dead boy—of
my boyfriend's ghost. I could have sworn he spoke to me a second ago. Which was impossible.

But there they were again—his words appearing once more in
my mind, the two syllables cutting me as sharply as a whip crack.

Mon ange.

My heart hammered. "Vincent? Is that really you?" I asked
with a trembling voice.

Kate, can you hear me?

"Vincent, you're volant. Violette hasn't destroyed you!" I leapt to my feet and spun around, searching anxiously for a glimpse of him, though I knew there would be nothing to see. I stood alone on the Pont des Arts. The surface of the water rippled and moved beneath me like the back of a great, dark serpent—the twinkling lights on the riverbanks reflected in its writhing smoothness. I shivered and pulled my coat tighter around myself.

No. She hasn't destroyed my corpse . . . yet.

"Oh my God, Vincent, I was sure she had done it." I wiped a tear from my cheek before a flood of others followed. Just moments earlier, I had given up all hope of ever hearing from him again. I had been positive that he was gone forever, his body burned by his enemy. But here he was. I didn't understand. I choked back tears.

Kate. Breathe, Vincent insisted.

I exhaled slowly. "I can't believe you're here, talking to me. Where are you? Where did she take your body?"

I'm lying dormant in Violette's castle in the Loire Valley. I only became conscious a few minutes ago. As soon as I figured out what she was doing I came to you. Vincent's words sounded bleak. Hopeless.

My hands shook as I whipped my phone out of my pocket. "Tell me exactly where you are. I'm calling Ambrose—he'll get a group together and we'll be right there."

It's too late for a rescue, Kate. Violette has been waiting for my mind to awake, and now that I'm volant she will burn my body. When I left, some of her henchmen were stoking a fire while she performed some kind of ancient ritual she claimed would bind my spirit to her once I'm reduced to ashes. I only have a few minutes, and I want to spend them with you.

"It's never too late," I insisted. "We could try to stop whatever it is that Violette's doing. I'm sure your kindred could come up with some kind of distraction. We have to try." Why was Vincent giving up so easily?

Kate. Stop, he pleaded. *Please don't waste the little time I have trying to call Ambrose when there is no way that you can reach me in time. There is* no way, *believe me.*

The force in his voice made me hesitate, but I kept staring at my phone as a lump formed in my throat. If I couldn't do anything, it meant that all was lost. My initial shock was being overtaken by an icy shawl of realization: the boy I loved was minutes away from being burned on a pyre. "No!" I cried, willing the horror to go away.

Vincent was silent, allowing the truth to sink in. I was losing my love—forever. If Vincent's body was destroyed, I would never touch him again. Never feel his mouth against mine. Never hold him in my arms.

But he won't be completely gone. Will he? I had to make sure. My voice came out in a strangled croak. "At least you're volant, right? If Violette had burned you before your mind awoke, you would be gone forever—body *and* spirit."

I wish she had. Vincent's words were bitter. *She said she needed my spirit present in order to perform the power transfer.* A few seconds passed before I heard his voice again. *I think I'd rather be nonexistent than help Violette become powerful enough to destroy my kindred.*